TH

SWORD

TRIUMPHANT

"Blaise——" Alf choked on the name. "Blaise sent you?"

"I did not see him that night," admitted Ceremos, "nor have I heard any word of him since the departure of the Uncrowned King. But who else could speak so?"

"He's dead," said Alf. "He's been dead for a long time." *Olva told me he was dying when they fled the tower. The Skerrise was there. She'd not have spared him. He's dead. I grieved him.*

"And yet," said Ceremos, "I am here."

Alf's mouth was dry as dust. "What message?"

"He said: 'Tell the Lammergeier that Blaise has need of him for one last service. Tell him to come at once. Tell him to bring his sword.'"

By Gareth Hanrahan

The Black Iron Legacy

The Gutter Prayer

The Shadow Saint

The Broken God

Lands of the Firstborn

The Sword Defiant

The Sword Unbound

The Sword Triumphant

THE

SWORD

TRIUMPHANT

GARETH HANRAHAN

orbit-books.co.uk

ORBIT

First published in Great Britain in 2025 by Orbit

1 3 5 7 9 10 8 6 4 2

Maps by Jon Hodgson, Handiwork Games

A CIP catalogue record for this book
is available from the British Library.

ISBN 978-0-356-51656-1

Typeset in Garamond 3 by M Rules
Printed and bound in Great Britain by Clays Ltd, Elcograf S.p.A.

Papers used by Orbit are from well-managed forests
and other responsible sources.

Orbit
An imprint of
Little, Brown Book Group
Carmelite House
50 Victoria Embankment
London EC4Y 0DZ

An Hachette UK Company
www.hachette.co.uk

orbit-books.co.uk

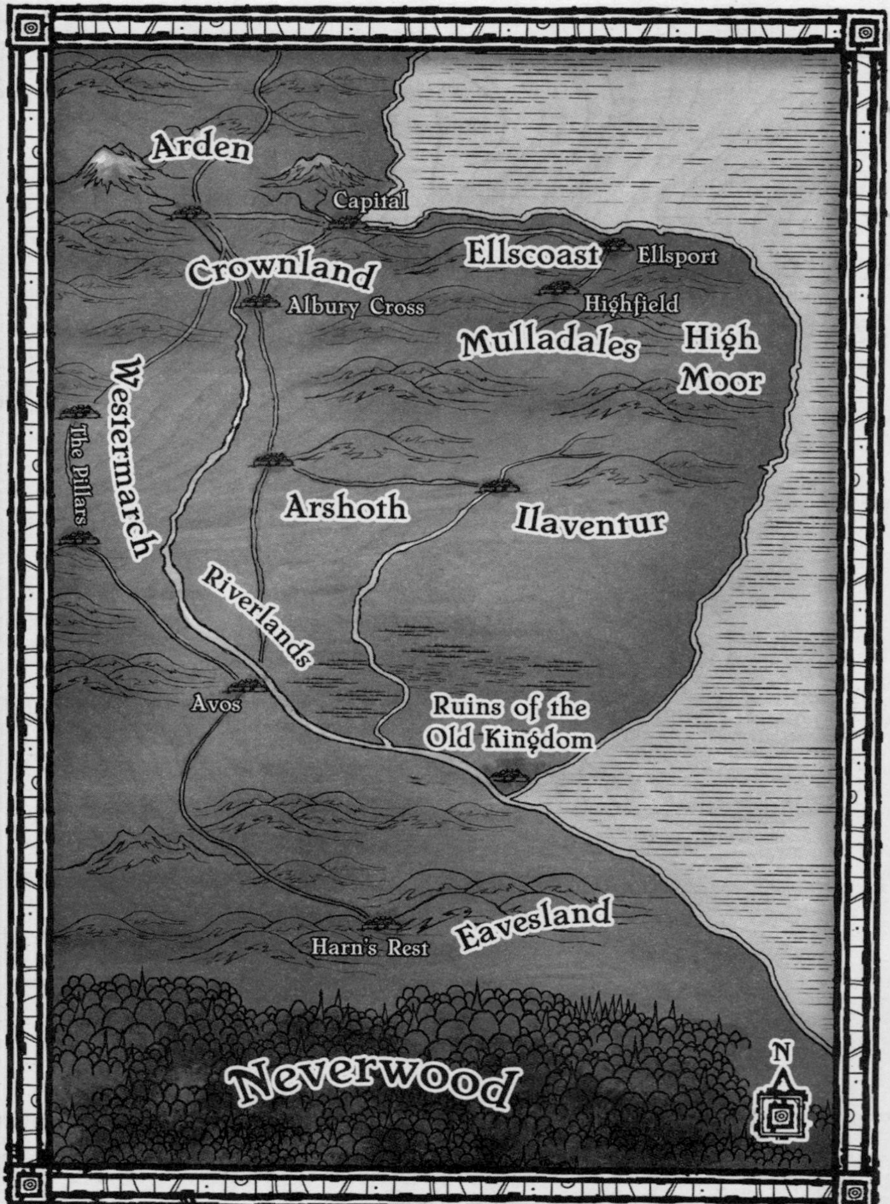
Arden
Capital
Ellscoast
Ellsport
Crownland
Albury Cross
Highfield
Mulladales
High
Moor
Westermarch
The Pillars
Arshoth
Ilaventur
Riverlands
Avos
Ruins of the
Old Kingdom
Eavesland
Harn's Rest
Neverwood
N

LIST OF CHARACTERS

THE NINE HEROES

Peir[+] of the Crownland, called the Paladin
Jan[+] of Arshoth, called the Pious
Blaise[+] of Ellscoast, called the Scholar
Berys[?] the Rootless, later called the Lady
Lath[+], a Changeling, called the Beast
Thurn[+] of the As Gola
Gundan[+] son of Gwalir, General of the Dwarfholt, wielder of
    Chopper
Laerlyn, daughter of the Erlking, Queen of the Neverwood
Alf of Mulladale, once called Sir Lammergeier, former Keeper
    of the Spellbreaker

IN MULLADALE

Olva Forster, sister to Alf, called the Witch of Ersfel
Derwyn Forster, son to Olva, once called Uncrowned King
    of Necrad, host to the spirits of both Peir the Paladin and
    Lord Bone the Necromancer, now called Tattersoul
Galwyn Forster[+], husband to Olva and father to Derwyn
Long Tom[+], father to Alf and Olva
Maya[+], mother to Alf and Olva
Harlow & Kivan, friends to Derwyn
Genny Selcloth, innkeeper
Thomad, tenant farmer of Olva
        Thomad's son, Jon

Quenna, neighbour to Olva
    Quenna's daughter, Cerlys
Methdrel, miller of Hayhurst
    His niece, Perdia

ELSEWHERE IN SUMMERSWELL

Timeon Vond, former governor of Necrad
Lord Dryten Bessimer⁺, father of Peir, called the
    Weeping Lord
Lord Brychan⁺ of Ilaventur, leader of the Defiance against the
    Erlking
Eldwyn, master of the College Arcane
Bor⁺, called the Broken, a sellsword, once wielder of the
    Spellbreaker, formerly employed by Olva Forster
Cu⁺, Bor's dog, formerly Olva's dog, formerly the elven Knight
    of Hawthorn
Sir Rhuel of Eavesland, alleged poet
Remilard⁺, a guard in Necrad and banner-bearer to the
    Lammergeier, slain by the Lammergeier
Prince Maedos⁺, son of the Erlking, elder brother of Laerlyn,
    called the Dawnshield, slain by the Lammergeier
Idmaer Ironhand, called the Miracle Knight, son of Earl
    Duna⁺ and Lady Erdys⁺, Grandson of Lord Brychan⁺,
    brother to Sir Aelfric the Younger⁺ and Dunweld⁺
        His wife, Ernala of the As Magaer
        His son, Thurn the Younger
        His atharling-knights, including
        Sir Wilfred Berkhof
        Tholos the Dwarf, siegemaster

IN THE DWARFHOLT

Torun, former apprentice to Blaise the Scholar
Gamling, cousin to Gundan

IN NECRAD

The Skerrise, a vampiric witch elf, Lady of the White Deer,
  ruler of Necrad
Ildorae, a witch elf, Huntress of the Winter Star
Threeday, a Vatling
Amerith[+], first leader of the Witch Elves, also known as the
  Oracle
Acraist Wraith-Captain[+], Hand of Bone, Wielder of the Sword
  Spellbreaker
Ceremos, called the vampire childe; a young Witch Elf
  accidentally slain by Aelfric Lammergeier many years ago,
  tethered to life by the taste of his blood

IN UNKNOWN LANDS

Talis, daughter of Thurn, who is also Death
The Erlking, eldest of all

WEAPONS OF RENOWN

Chopper[*], the axe wielded by Gundan, broken at Bavduin,
  reforged and entrusted to Gamling
Morthus, the executioner's bow, once wielded by Laerlyn, later
  stolen by Berys
Faelthus[+], the bow of justice, briefly wielded by Laerlyn
Kingmaker[+], the sword entrusted to Aelfric by the Erlking,
  broken by Spellbreaker

Secret Flame, the Brightsword of the Rangers, entrusted by
     the Erlking to the Ranger-Captain, captured in battle by
     Aelfric at Harnshill
The nameless knife, forged by Kortirion[+] to slay Lord Bone[+],
     wielded by Ildorae, later captured by Aelfric
Spellbreaker, Demon Sword, unjustly abandoned by the
     Lammergeier

PART ONE

A lf felt young again.
 He stood on the balcony atop the Wailing Tower, outside Blaise's study. Below, the city was laid out like a corpse. The bleached bone of marble, streets like old scars. Necromiasma for a winding sheet, the spires cutting trails through wheeling fog-banks.

How had he come here? Had he scaled the tower? He'd done that once, with Berys. His knife gripped so tightly in his teeth that he thought he'd never be rid of the taste of it, muscles burning with exertion, rain-slick stone treacherous in his grip.

Or had he flown on a dreadworm? That was how he'd usually arrived.

Black-winged things wheeled through green fog.

Why could he not remember?

He didn't have his sword. Where was the damned sword? He'd put it down somewhere, but couldn't remember where.

He turned his back on the city and peered through the window. Blaise was there, the hooded wizard reciting an incantation from a great tome. Always so serious, so determined. Derwyn was there, too. Alf's nephew lay on a slab. Skin marble-pale against the fierce red of his many wounds, the green of slime from the Pits. Young

Derwyn had died in the Pits, Alf remembered, and Blaise was bringing him back to life.

That was it. He remembered now. They were in the middle of the second siege. The Wilder were attacking. They would bring Derwyn back from the Grey Lands of Death and save the day. The last triumph of the Nine, before the Defiance and the war. A good day.

But then Alf glimpsed his sister, sitting in a dark corner by her son's bier, and she was so old! The witch-mark of her foot – she hadn't had that then. It came later. After she'd changed.

This was all wrong, all jumbled. Time and space spun around Alf, the ages of the city and the years of his life blurring. He clutched the railing to stop himself falling into the abyss that gaped beneath the Wailing Tower – the crater he'd left when he destroyed Lord Bone's temple, and the endless Pits below.

A dark bird flew down and perched beside him.

That was familiar. That was part of the story.

"You're not Lath," he said. Lath, his friend, the Changeling of the Nine.

The bird cocked her head. "No. I am Death."

"I told you," said Alf, "you don't have to be. They brought you from the Grey Lands, aye, and Death came back with you—" He glanced towards Blaise's study, where the wizard was conducting the same ritual. "Just like we brought Derwyn back, and Lord Bone came with him. But you don't have to be Death. You're Thurn's daughter, and you can live how you want. Not bound by the stories they made of you. I told you all this before, didn't I?" At last he realised. "Oh. This is a dream."

Death spread her wings. "Not a dream."

"Ah," said Alf. He thought for a moment. "Bugger. Does this mean that you're going to give me a prophecy, or a quest, or somesuch?"

"I did as you counselled, Aelfric Lammergeier," said Death, and she wasn't a bird any more. She was a young woman, strong and tall.

Her clothing was a strange silken wrap from some distant country. Though she had none of the tattoos or furs favoured by the Wilder, Alf could see her father Thurn in her face, and his heart leapt. He heard the laughter of children, and unseen little hands tugged at her skirts. "I flew far from Necrad, far from the elven-lands, and I forgot I was Death. I am Talis, and in the language of my new home Talis means *the-girl-who-came-from-nowhere*. I have lived as I chose, Aelfric Lammergeier."

"Aye, well," said Alf. "That's good. I tried to do the same."

That was what had happened to the sword. He'd left it behind. He was free of it.

"But I am still Death." She was a bird again. "And I did not forget you. You ask for a prophecy—"

"I bloody well do not!"

"So I shall give you one." Her voice was cruel and mocking. "Know this, Aelfric Lammergeier – eight of the Nine are mortal. Eight are mine to take. In gratitude for your counsel, I say this: I will take you last of all."

Death spread her wings and looked at Alf. The bird's eyes were human, and brimmed with tears. She cried out in a woman's voice.

"Lath is dead."

CHAPTER ONE

Alf woke with a burning need to piss. He peeled back the blanket and stumbled across to the chamber pot. Pungent urine dribbled out of him. The dream dissolved like steam, leaving only snatches. He'd dreamed of Necrad, of things that had happened more than twenty years ago. Or more than forty. How long had it been since he and Berys climbed the Wailing Tower? Was it fifty years?

Berys was dead now by all accounts. Thurn was dead. And Gundan. Jan – she was gone like Peir. Jan had faded, and Peir had come back with Derwyn only to fade again. Blaise was dead, too – he'd helped Olva and Derwyn escape Necrad, all those years ago. They'd fled the wreckage of a dream gone sour.

Of the mortals, only Lath was left. Lath and Laerlyn.

Words from the dream floated through Alf's brain, flotsam from a sinking ship. *In gratitude for your words.* He had warned Death, hadn't he? He'd told her that the Erlking had made the spell that summoned her, and so he could unmake it. And only a few months later, Alf himself had stood before the Erlking as the old elf threatened to undo another spell – the spell that had conjured humans. *Rule in my name*, the Erlking had said, *marry my daughter and be the king of Summerswell, or I will destroy the human race.* And the Erlking was

gone now, the Everwood destroyed. The sword's doing. He'd put the blade down, but another hand had picked it up and brought ruin.

All things break.

But Laerlyn was still young, still immortal. She was still the same as when he'd first met her, a lifetime ago. Laerlyn still lived.

Lath is dead. But that was just a dream.

He groaned as he bent to pick up the chamber pot. His hand trembled under the weight. He opened the door of the farmhouse and threw the contents onto the dung heap. It was still dark, the stars like jewels, but the sky was brightening in the east over the treetops. No point in going back to bed now.

One of the pigs squealed in expectation of breakfast.

"She's not back yet."

The pig looked up and grunted.

"Maybe tomorrow," said Alf, yawning.

He stretched, old joints cracking, then went back in to dress and start the day. There was work to be done, after all.

Alf had grown up a stone's throw away from this spot. His father, Long Tom, had been a peasant farmer, paying his rent with labour on the big farm. Now it was his sister Olva who was the landlord, hers the big farm. Big for Ersfel, of course, didn't mean much, but some deep-rooted instinct in Alf was impressed by it. The same instinct made him feel like he was trespassing, that at any moment someone might shout at him to get away from where he didn't belong.

In Necrad he'd dwelt in a palace he'd taken from a living god by force of arms. But here he was still Long Tom's son from the little cottage under the oak. On mornings like this, the early pale-gold light slanting through the mist, the croaking of crows up on the wooded hills, unhurried sheep grazing in the field, the years slipped away and he forgot the wars, the Nine, the sword, and he could almost believe Necrad and all the rest was but a dream. Ersfel had scarcely changed in the seventy or so years of his life. Ignore the new

watchtower on the hilltop, and the new cottages on the east side, and it was just as it was when he'd gone on the Road with Gundan long, long ago.

Lath is dead. It was only a dream.

Thomad and his boy came by mid-morning to help Alf with the farm work. The storm of a few days ago had damaged one of the sheds. The whole roof needed fixing. They'd taken down the thatch the day before, so today's job was replacing the broken rafters. Despite Thomad's doubtful look and prophecies of doom, Alf climbed up on the ten-foot stone wall to rip out the damaged timbers. *I scaled the Wailing Tower,* he thought, *I can handle a cowshed.*

Alf wrenched the last of the broken rafters from its socket and threw it down. "Pass that up," he told Thomad. The cotter and his boy lifted the heavy replacement up to Alf. What was the lad's name? Something simple, wasn't it? A good Mulladale name, plain and serviceable.

Strange how his brain remembered the heraldry of knights long dead, or the paths through the Pits, but couldn't remember the boy's name.

Thomad's boy shot nervous glances towards another shed, the locked one where Olva was said to keep her witching things. The villagers told stories of cauldrons and talismans, of familiars in jars, chattering skulls and charmstones. Everyone in the Mulladales told tales of the Witch of Ersfel, the woman who'd once been an honest widow, but had gone away for a year and came back *different*. Olva was a Changeling now. Lath had initiated her atop Death's grave at Daeroch Nal. The use of earth-magic had been forbidden in Summerswell for centuries, but Olva had thrown herself into the study of it, leaving Alf to tend the farm while she flew off in search of buried secrets.

Twenty years ago, the church would have sent exorcists to drive the earthpower out of Olva, or sent paladins to burn her if the exorcism didn't take. But that was before everything changed. The little

shrine on the hill was empty. Old Thala — gone fifteen years now — had been the last priestess to minister to the village. *Empty thrones above, empty thrones below*, people said. The Anarchy, the poets called this time. Provinces splintered into little kingdoms, and any man might call himself Lord with a good sword and a pack of brigands. Summerswell was broken, the old order overthrown. The law handed down by the Erlking to the first Lords was gone.

You let that happen.

The thought sounded like the sword.

I tried to stop it, Alf argued with himself. *I tried to make peace — even though Berys was right, the Erlking was a monster. I tried putting the sword down, and someone else took it up. Maybe things didn't turn out for the best, but I did what seemed right in the moment. That's all you can do.*

Lath is dead, whispered the memory of the sword, and its voice rang with malicious pleasure.

"Watch it!" cried Thomad. Alf snapped back to the present. He'd leaned out too far and unbalanced himself. The packed earthen floor of the shed seemed as far below him as the streets of Necrad from atop the tower. As he toppled, he caught himself on one of the new rafters. The timber creaked under his weight. Alf hung from the rafter for a moment, then dropped to the floor below. Thomad's lad ran to his side to steady him.

"I'm all right," said Alf. He rubbed his knee. "Let's have something to eat."

Thomad frowned. "You likely cracked that rafter when you put all your weight on it, you ox."

Alf shrugged. "Likely it'd have broken in the next storm anyway, then."

Afternoon brought weapons drill. The war rarely touched Ersfel, which lay tucked in an obscure corner of the Mulladales, but other villages had been raided. Olva's reputation as the Witch helped, but still Alf trained the locals to defend themselves. Old men complained

that such things were unknown when they were young, when the Lords guarded the roads and kept the peace. Maybe a stout spear could ward off the Anarchy that consumed the wider world, and maybe it couldn't, but in these days of brigands and petty Lords it was best to be watchful. Everyone knew that Big Alf had been a mercenary and fought in the war – even if they were hazy on which war exactly.

They practised with spears and wooden swords on the village green, lads and lasses falling about, poking each other, making a game of it. Alf kept his temper in check, not waiting to spoil their innocence. He watched one girl – Quenna's youngest, a spitfire named Cerlys, hair pinned back with a broken silver comb – sparring with another lad. The boy slipped, and she struck him hard in the belly. When he was done spewing, he protested that it didn't count, that it was a lucky strike and a low blow. But Cerlys had already declared herself the winner, and added that she'd beat anyone in the village in a contest of archery to prove her victory wasn't a matter of chance. With that, she loosed an arrow, and hit the mark a finger's breadth from dead centre.

"Berys herself couldn't have done better!" she shouted.

Somehow, that turned into a wager that whoever outshot Cerlys would earn a kiss from her, and now all the boys were scrambling up to the line, arrows falling wildly around the straw target. Alf chuckled at the chaos, and that made an old wound in his chest ache.

"Enough," he called. "None of you are going to beat her."

"I want another chance!" complained the lad, sour at his defeat and his vomit-stained breeches. He drew another arrow, but Alf grabbed the bow from his hand.

"It's getting dark. I don't want you putting an arrow through Genny Selcloth's window."

The boy scowled. "I can beat Cerlys. And Berys the Thief was a traitor anyway. My da says the Nine brought nothing but ruin."

"They saved us all from Lord Bone up in Necrad," said another, shoving his friend.

"Saved us, *then* ruined us. Like giving a gift with one hand and snatching it back with the other."

"Ruined, are you?" said Alf. "And what fortune have you lost, lad? What great height have you fallen from?"

"What would you know?"

Anger filled Alf. He drew back the bow, nocked an arrow, and loosed it. Dead centre. "More than you, lad."

He handed the bow back to the stunned boy and strode away across the green. His shoulder ached with the effort of the draw.

Cerlys froze as if Alf was an ogre coming to demand his prize. "You're good, lass, and quick, but quick isn't always enough. It's one thing to strike the first blow, and another to strike the *last* one in a fight." He snorted as he walked past her. "And then there's the matter of the *right* blow, and the right battle. That's a whole other riddle."

"Was I not right?"

"Eh. Hit him a bit hard, maybe."

She followed him, eagerly bouncing at his shoulder. "But it wasn't a lucky blow."

"Still brooding about that, are you?"

"It wasn't luck."

"He slipped. But there's nothing wrong with getting lucky. Luck keeps you alive. What matters is what you do with the chances you get." Alf thought that was a good bit of hard-won wisdom, but Cerlys had already moved on.

"There's a tourney in Highfield in a month's time."

"Aye."

"There'll be an archery contest there."

"Aye, most years."

"But the prize for archery is only a third of what the winner of the sword gets."

"And the tourney winner gets more than both of 'em." He'd won his share of tourneys by battering the opposition down. Back

then, he'd taken satisfaction in unhorsing all those nobles. Knights brought low by a nameless farm boy.

All those knights were dead now, in one war or another. Their children's children fighting now – and not in tourneys, but real battles.

"The tourney doesn't favour me," said Cerlys. "It doesn't reward skill or speed. But if I had a proper sword, I'd have a chance in the duelling ring."

"Would you now?" Alf smiled at her audacity.

"Jon says you've got a shield and armour in the Widow's house."

"Which one's Jon?"

She pointed at Thomad's son, who was busy rolling the straw archery targets away – or pretending to do so while watching Cerlys. He blushed and looked away hastily.

Jon. That was the lad's name.

"Have you got a proper sword, too?" she asked.

He stumbled, his knee twisting under him. He felt impossibly ancient.

"Go and help tidy up. And unstring your bow, girl. Take care of your weapon."

He called into Genny Selcloth's alehouse. "Need me?" Alf helped behind the counter sometimes, especially when there were strangers around. Tonight, there was a travelling pot-smith in town, a dwarf who'd come up the Road from Kettlebridge, so the parlour was crowded with those seeking news.

"Take your rest," said Genny, and Alf settled into his usual seat by the fire. Genny squeezed his shoulder as she passed behind him.

"It's bad, friends," said the dwarf. "Buy me another drink, so I have the strength to tell the tale." Another mug was duly produced. "A new warlord has arisen! Ironhand, they name him, and he is fearsome indeed. He swept out of the west, and the Riverlands fell

before him! Arshoth has yielded to him, and he was anointed by the high archon. Good Lord Merik—"

Alf snorted at the "good lord" part. He'd met Merik once, briefly, back when he was just Sir Merik, a knight in Lord Brychan's army. The man had not struck Alf as good or lordly. They'd crown anyone these days.

The dwarf glared at Alf's interruption, then continued. "Good Lord Merik met Ironhand in battle near Harnshill, and alas! Fortune did not favour Merik. Treacherous knights of Ilaventur joined Ironhand's host, and Merik was beset from all sides."

Alf stopped paying attention halfway through. There'd always be another villain, another would-be dark lord. Heaven and earth both overthrown, and chaos loosed on all Summerswell. This Ironhand was just the latest. And if he came to Ersfel, young Cerlys would put an arrow in his eye. Saving the world was a job for the young, and Alf was content to be done with it. He'd had his time riding the wheel of fate, and he would roam no more.

Some days – most days, if he was being honest – he suspected he'd done more good fixing sheds and teaching children like Cerlys than all the rest of his days.

When the dwarf's tale was done, Alf approached him.

"You don't bear any letters, do you? My sister has a friend in the Dwarfholt."

But there were no messages from the north.

Alf returned home. The hearth was cold, the house chill. Olva wasn't back yet. Alf bent to set the fire, his knee protesting as he put weight on it.

What had that dream been about, again? It had seemed important this morning. So many things that once seemed important really weren't, in the end. Tales of lords and knights and Good Lord Merik and Ironhand, the anger on that boy's face, it'd all be forgotten in the morning, and that cracked rafter would still need

fixing no matter what. He'd get an early night, he decided, because if Olva came home and the shed roof still wasn't done, she'd have words for him.

And ever since his little sister learned magic, her words had real power.

The fire refused to light. The cold bit deeper than it used to. He'd once crossed the Clawlands in winter, travelling in the teeth of icy winds howling down off the Dwarfholt peaks, and still the farmhouse felt colder. What had he done today? A few chores, and he'd watched some children fight with sticks. When he was young, he'd have done all that work in an hour, and fought in a real battle. *All things break.*

A knock at the door. "Alf?" Kivan, one of the village men. "Is the Widow back?" He sounded shaken.

"Not yet," said Alf. "What is it?"

"There's a monster in the wood."

It was dark and Alf no longer had the sword-sight. He hunted by smell. He'd never forget that foul blend of rotten eggs and something burned, mixed with a chill in the air. He'd lived with that smell for years, and he pushed through the trees until he found its source.

The dreadworm was mostly dead. Wings paper-thin and full of scorched holes — it had flown in sunlight, flown a long, long way. The eyeless head rose and hissed at him, baring the ring of teeth in its approximation of a mouth. Dreadworms weren't living things, exactly — magic conjured them into being. There wasn't much of a gullet beyond that mouth. Their hungers were an echo of what real animals felt.

No sign of a rider. Was it here by accident? Alf could imagine the monster being blown off course by winds, or getting lost and blindly wandering in the sunlight. His foot brushed against a branch. There were more broken branches — and they were cold and

slick with worm-slime. The monster had not landed, but crashed out of the the sky.

No sign of a rider. But that didn't mean a rider hadn't survived the fall.

"What is it?" called Kivan. He and a half-dozen other villagers stood well back from the carcass of the worm.

"It's no threat. Lend me that spear."

He pushed the point into the yielding pseudo-flesh of the worm's throat until the creature perished, falling apart into mush and ice. By morning, there'd be nothing left but a stain.

It was only a dreadworm. But it was the first thing he'd killed in a long, long time.

"Is it gone?" asked Kivan.

"Aye. But it might have had a rider. A Witch Elf. Maybe a scout."

Kiven brought the light from his torch close to the ground. "I don't see any tracks."

Elves step lightly. "Let's have a look about, to be sure."

Up went the hue and cry. No one in the valley slept that night. Every house was roused with the warning that enemies might be close by. A torch kindled in every doorway. Dogs bayed, chickens squawked, children shrieked with excitement or burst into confused tears. The hunt went on until first light, but came to nought. No sign of an intruder.

Alf felt a weight lift from him. The worm had been blown off course by some storm. Its arrival was an accident, not a portent.

He went home again, his bed calling more loudly than the sword ever had. Off across the fields through the morning mist he could see Thomad weeding in the vegetable patch, and smoke rising from the cooking fires in the cottages. The pigs, oddly, were all huddled near the stump of the big oak. Something had spooked them.

The door of Olva's house was ajar.

Alf's grip tightened on the half of the borrowed spear. He pushed the door open with the tip.

A pale figure. Witch Elf.

Red eyes glimmered in the dark.

Witch Elf *vampire*.

"Sanctuary," whispered the vampire. "Sanctuary, Aelfric Lammergeier."

CHAPTER TWO

Alf did not recognise the elf at first. Most elves looked alike, preserved in the prime of life for eternity. They faded rather than aged. Even the truly ancient elves Alf had encountered – all save one – were untouched by the passing millennia. Nor did this intruder bear any symbols or tokens of his house; his ragged clothing offered no clue.

Then Alf saw the echo of the child in the face of the man.

"Ceremos?"

The vampire nodded, biting his lip. His teeth were very sharp. Alf closed the door to shut out the sunlight.

"Why are you here?"

"A message," said Ceremos, thickly, his tongue stumbling over the human words, "from Necrad." He backed away into a corner, long white fingers clinging to the wall. His red eyes flickered to Alf's hand. There was a little smear of blood; a cut from a thorn in the woods. Ceremos pressed his head against the wall. "I thirst," he whispered.

Alf warily stepped towards the vampire boy – and then saw a tangled mess of skin and blood at the back door. One of the piglets, torn to pieces.

"You did that?" snapped Alf.

"Forgive me," said Ceremos. "I have come far, Lammergeier, in seeking you. I have not fed for so long, I—"

There came a knock at the door.

"Mister Alf? Da sent me over to help with the thatching."

Ceremos lunged towards the door with a snarl. He was so fast, elven grace augmented with desperate hunger. Alf used the spear to trip Ceremos and caught the elf's ankle with the edge of the blade. Ceremos came up scowling, red eyes ablaze, but Alf got the tip to the boy's throat.

"Don't move," Alf hissed, "and stay quiet." Ceremos quivered, all his instincts at war, then curled into a ball, pressing his hands into his face.

Alf raised his voice. "It's all right, lad," he called to Thomad's boy. "I'll attend to it tomorrow. Go home now."

"All right." The sound of Jon's footsteps crunching on the path, and tuneless whistling. He'd never know how close he'd come to death.

Alf pulled Ceremos to his feet. The vampire's head lolled as if he was drunk or exhausted beyond measure. "Blood," he whispered, then a long litany of elvish. Alf caught the word *agearath*, which meant something like *blood-giver*. An elf vampire had to feed, or they'd fade, their body melting away and their immortal soul slipping into the wraith-world. Ceremos was only twenty-five or so; most elves lasted thousands of years before fading, but he'd been wounded as a child in Necrad.

Alf had mortally wounded the child. This was his responsibility.

"Come on," snapped Alf. He dragged Ceremos across the kitchen to the little spare room under the stairs. It was crammed with old tools, old treasures, old junk. More of Olva's magic paraphernalia, a few bits of furniture Alf had been meaning to fix for years. A stack of yellowing letters from Torun, all covered in tiny neat handwriting. A bed, too, somewhere beneath all that. Alf fumbled around, clearing

space. The butt of his borrowed spear swept jars from a high shelf to shatter on the floor behind him.

"Lammergeier, hark! I bear—"

"Shut up," he ordered. He pushed Ceremos into the little room. "Stay there. Stay quiet. I'll be back."

First things first. He fetched a shovel and buried what remained of the piglet. Then he ate, salvaging what he could from the jars he'd broken and piling the mess of jam and preserved meats onto slices of bread. He kept the spear within arm's reach, kept staring at the door under the stair. But there was only silence.

Through the window, Alf saw a half-dozen youths from the village approaching the cottages across the field. He spotted Cerlys' raven-black hair. The boys with her had spears. They searched for the dreadworm's rider. If they found Ceremos, it would not end well for anyone.

He went outside. When Cerlys and her company started to cross the field, Alf waved at them, a cheery reassurance that all was well. They turned and headed up into the hill to search the holywood again.

Hunting for the Witch Elf.

Alf had killed a lot of Witch Elves in his time. The Witch Elf elders of Necrad had gone vampire, sustaining themselves on mortal blood. They'd enslaved the Wilder-tribes, convinced the mortals that the elves were gods and taken the blood as tribute. The Nine had put a stop to that. They'd killed most of the vampires, herded the rest along with the surviving Witch Elves into the prison quarter of the Liberties.

It was there that Alf had killed the child. He and Gundan had gone in on a fool's errand. He'd had Spellbreaker summon a dreadworm. The sword had warned him that its magical control of the worm was slipping, that Alf had asked too much.

While Alf and Gundan were distracted, the worm broke free.

Alf remembered pressing his hand over the boy's belly, holding

Ceremos' intestines in. Gundan pulling at him, shouting that they had to fall back, that they'd started a riot. *Do these filthy elves know who we are?* The dwarf's voice echoing across the years. Then, later, the voice of Ceremos' father. *We shall lose him again. The hunger will consume him.* And Alf had promised he'd help, he'd make things right. He'd let Ceremos feed from him again, to sustain the child as he healed. And he'd sent money so they could buy blood.

Better you had never come to Necrad at all.

He sat there in the kitchen, watching clouds scud across the sky. Birds took flight over the holywood, their fierce grace so different to the ungainly flailing of dreadworms. *Where are you, Olva?*

A message, Ceremos had said.

Alf opened the door and peered in. Ceremos scurried away to cower in the corner.

"Here," said Alf, "I brought you blood." He placed a bowl on the floor and pushed it towards Ceremos.

"It is not fresh," he complained.

"It bloody well is," said Alf. "I just fucking bled it."

"It . . . it fades," said Ceremos. "Better to have *agearath*. To drink from the spring."

Alf leaned against the doorframe, lightheaded. "Aye, well. That's not happening. This spring's old and dry."

Ceremos sniffed at the dregs with distaste. "I agree. You taste foul."

"Ungrateful wretch."

"But I feel better. The edge is gone." He wiped his face. "I am myself again."

"All right then. Talk."

The young elf pushed the empty bowl away and sat cross-legged on the floor. "I have not used the mortal tongue in a long time, Lammergeier, but I shall tell the tale as best I can . . . "

*

Necrad. My Necrad.

It was my city, and mine alone. The other elves knew Necrad as it was in the dawn, when it was new, the city of sorcery. They knew Necrad as it was when we took it back from the usurpers. They dwelt there when Lord Bone came to the city gates as a beggar, and they watched him grow in power. They knew Necrad in its glory.

(Ceremos' face flushed as the blood restored him. His voice grew eager as he told his tale.)

I knew the city in ruin. I grew up playing amid the rubble, Lammergeier. I was the only elf-child in the city, so my playmates were mortal children and Vatlings. To me the streets were always choked in rubble, the gates always watched by dwarf-guards. It was natural for me that a half-dozen elves dwelt in a single house, even as they shared memories of the palaces denied to them. All their songs were sad, but I knew nothing else, and so I was happy.

I do not remember the day you killed me, or the time just after. My father spoke of it often. He was greatly shamed he could not save me, so I know well what happened, but it is no more real to me than a dream. No, what I remember is the third time I drank of you. Do you remember? You were about to leave for the parley with the Wilder at Lake Bavduin. You came with Ildorae Ul'ashan Amerith, and you had the Spellbreaker. My mortal friends were amazed that so great a hero deigned to visit my sickbed.

When the siege came, they told me not to fear, because the Lammergeier was leading the defence of the city against Death's host. I remember the heat of your blood in my belly, and thinking how lucky I was to have a share of your strength. And after the siege, I cheered the coming of the Uncrowned King, for he was your kinsman – and mine, too, I thought.

We were related by blood, after all.

The other elves rejoiced, too, seeing the strength of the Firstborn restored. They had the palaces and temples of the Sanction once

more. You had gone away south by then, yes, but it was whispered in the Liberties that you had spoken in support of restoration, that you had made Ildorae the captain of your honour guard. I thought it was glorious — the best of elves and best of mortals united in common purpose, and I was at the heart of it. I dreamed that when I grew up I would join you on the battlefield. My mother told me tales of Acraist the Wraith-Knight, our kinsman, the Hand of Bone and first wielder of the Spellbreaker — and I thought I might be like him, only better, brighter. Your ally, not your foe.

Your sister, the Widow Queen, was kidnapped by Earl Idmaer and his followers, and there was war with the mortals of the New Provinces. Once again there—

("That's not what happened," interrupted Alf. "Olva — Lord Bone's shade was in Derwyn, and he killed Bessimer. Olva — she explained it to me. She wasn't kidnapped, she went to Lath at Daeroch Nal . . ." But he tripped over the words and fell silent. The truth didn't matter half so much as the story.)

Once again there were dreadknights in the skies. I watched my father put on his armour again. He brought home prisoners from the sack of Athar, and I feasted for the first time in my second life.

Ildorae freed your sister from captivity and brought her back to Necrad. What happened then, I do not know — but there was great strife atop the Wailing Tower, and lightning wracked the city. I remember hiding in my bedroom, listening to the crash of thunder, fearing I would perish and thinking how unfair it was that I alone of the elves should have so short a span.

But dawn came, and with it word that the Uncrowned King had fled and the city belonged to the elves again. Amerith, the Oracle who had led us since the Sundering, was gone, so the Skerrise claimed the throne.

There were no mortals left in Necrad. The Skerrise and the other elders still needed blood, of course, but they had ways to procure it. My mother went to the Palace of the White Deer and begged the

Skerrise to provide for me, and for a time I was vouchsafed a little trickle of blood, the leavings of the great ones.

The Skerrise commanded that all elves return to Necrad. My father and other dreadknights flew south to the ruins of the Everwood, and gathered the wayward *ahedrai* – the Wood Elves, as you mortals called them. They sailed to join us in the north, as Amerith did long ago, and for a time it seemed a joyous reunion. But there was . . . dissent. The newcomers questioned the Skerrise's right to be the sole leader in Necrad, they said we should not cut ourselves off so completely from the outside world, that the works of Lord Bone should be cast aside. The Skerrise said she would consider their counsel, and withdrew to the Wailing Tower.

Then . . . There was no moment of revelation, no sudden crisis – certainly, not one that I was privy to, but I was the youngest and least of the elves of the city. But from my rooftop perches I saw the little changes. A new breed of Vatlings appeared, ones loyal to the Skerrise alone. She called them guardians of the peace and set them to watch the city gates and the entrances to the Pits below. Later – for the safety of the newcomers, it was said – these Vatlings took charge of more and more of the city. The old Sanction, the new breeding vats and arsenals – the Skerrise tightened her hold on them all. But there was merriment under the stars, and the singing of ancient songs, and the majesty and beauty of the city of the Firstborn, so most were content to look away.

It was in that time that my father disappeared. He flew away with a company of dreadknights, on a mission to the Everwood, and was lost. They told me that the outside world is full of perils – and I believed them, for I had never set foot outside Necrad. A storm might have brought down his dreadworm, or a monster, or the treachery of mortals. He will return, they said, in time. If he lives, he will find his way home, and if he has perished, his wraith will be drawn back to the city and he will one day be reborn, for elves cannot die. My mother Elithadil took comfort in that, but I could not.

After that, the Skerrise forbade elves to fly beyond the Gulf of Tears. She said the Vatlings could serve as well, and perish better if needs be. Vatlings now guarded the skies. Pitspawn were set to guard the gates within and without.

Necrad grew ever stranger to me, and more confining. I grew restless. I missed my mortal friends, and the home I had known. I thought: *why, you have the blood of the Lammergeier in you, the blood of heroes. Go and seek your fortune.*

"Your fortune," echoed Alf. He swayed in the doorway. The vampire's red eyes blazed with pride, and Alf found himself horrified. He remembered twenty years ago or more, Olva sitting in the kitchen of his grand mansion in Necrad, talking about Derwyn. *He idolises you, Alf. Always full of tales of your deeds. He's a good lad ... he left home. He went on the Road, in search of you.* And that had led Derwyn into the Grey Lands of death.

In the wars, too — they'd used his legend to inspire others. The false Lammergeier leading the revolt in Arden, and the streets of Arden awash with blood. The head of young Remilard, staring up at him. They'd all heard the stories of the Lammergeier, and thought that he was an example to be followed.

He'd never wanted that. He'd never been that.

The sun whirled through the sky overhead.

"Lammergeier?" asked Ceremos, suddenly concerned. The vampire reached out to catch Alf before he toppled.

"Stay back!" said Alf. "Stay hidden." He stepped back, slammed the door shut, fell against it. He closed the bolt, but his fingers were shaking too much to reattach the padlock. "Stay there!" he said again.

"As you command, Lammergeier," replied Ceremos. His voice seemed to come not from the far side of the wooden door, but from deep underground.

Alf stumbled back to the farmhouse and fell into the chair by the hearth. It was suddenly very cold, he thought, pulling a blanket

around him. *Seek my fortune*, Ceremos had said. What did the boy expect — to wander the land as a mystery knight, elven features concealed behind a helm? *I have saved you from that ogre, maiden fair. As a reward, I ask only a single kiss — and to rip out your throat and feast upon your blood.* Even if he could control his thirst for a while, the boy was immortal. One day, he'd slip and become another monster.

You should strike him down before he's too powerful to stop.

The sword had said that, long ago. Its voice echoed in Alf's head. Not about Ceremos. About someone else. Alf fell into a dark abyss of memory, faces and snatches of old conversations flickering around him, the abyss becoming a corridor underground, a dungeon passage in the Pits. He was slaying monsters down there again, and he was young again, strong again, sword in hand and friends by his side.

Lath was there in the dark with him. A hulking beast, a reassuring wall of fur and claws. And Gundan, laughing as he fought, his shield protecting Laerlyn as she drew back her bow. Thurn's spear, always certain, never missing the mark. Berys somewhere off ahead of them. Jan and Blaise behind Alf, guarded by him, guiding him.

Peir's hammer wreathed in holy fire. A light in the abyss.

But all around, the roars of monsters.

Alf woke with a start. It was twilight outside. The roaring in his dream, he realised, was the grunting of the pigs as they hungrily devoured their dinner. He looked around, bleary-eyed, trying to sort dream from reality. A shape moved in the kitchen.

"Olva?"

"Only me," said Thomad. "Jon's feeding the pigs. He got out, you know."

"What?" Panic seized Alf at the thought that Ceremos had escaped.

"Barrel. The big boar. It's fine, Jon saw him across the field, and we chased him back to his pen. He was hungry. You hadn't fed him." Thomad bent down to peer at Alf's face. "You look ill."

"Just tired."

"Aye, you and half the village. Jon was running about 'til day-break looking for . . . ach, who knows what?" Thomad sat down by the fireside. "More'n twenty years since anything came out of the north – though they were telling tales of raiders in Ellscoast at the Highfield fair, last year. A bad omen."

"It's just one dreadworm," said Alf.

"What's a dreadworm?" There was a pot bubbling on the fire. Thomad stirred it. Porridge dripped and hissed on a burning log.

"I saw them in the war," said Alf. "From a distance," he added, quickly. "You don't need to be here. All's fine. Go home."

"It's no trouble."

"Go on. Maybe I am a bit unwell. Might be catching. Stay home."

"What about that roof?"

"I'll get it done."

Thomad and his boy left again. Alf sat by the fire a while. He ate the whole pot of porridge without tasting it, but the weight of it in his belly helped.

The Lammergeier was a killer, but he was the Lammergeier no longer.

He rose and crossed the yard. He paused outside the door.

"You can see in the dark, right?"

"I can," replied Ceremos.

"Aye. Right. Give me a hand with this roof," said Alf, "then come inside."

Alf remembered the first time the Nine entered Necrad. They'd crept through the Pits, under the city's impenetrable walls, then fought their way back up to the surface. He remembered stepping out onto the eerie streets, white marble turned ghoulish-green by miasmalight. One by one they'd emerged. Jan was quietly weeping, and Alf had thought she was just scared. Now he knew that she

was mourning the loss of her connection to the Intercessors. The spirits had no power under the necromiasma. Thurn's face grim as ever, as he stormed the heaven of his people. Gundan smeared in ichor, his beard matted with gore, snarling as he looked for the next fight.

And he remembered Laerlyn's face, full of light and wonder. The first Wood Elf to enter Elvenhome in centuries, the first to return to the city of her people. Ceremos reminded him of that look, that moment, in the way the Witch Elf looked around the human farmhouse in amazement as if he was trespassing in some unearthly realm beyond imagination.

Alf cleared a sack of onions and a bundle of unwashed clothes off the other chair by the fire. "Sit down, lad. You've a tale to finish."

Ceremos perched on the edge of the chair for a moment, but the young vampire was too full of energy to stay sitting. He prowled about the farmhouse as he spoke, miming his escape from Necrad.

As I said, I had grown dissatisfied, and yearned to travel beyond the city walls. I begged permission to leave. The Skerrise refused. All the Firstborn, she said, should dwell within the holy precincts of the First City. All the Firstborn should dwell in bliss and security. I said I was too restless for bliss, and that I welcomed the perils of the wider world. She refused again – and to chastise me she denied me the stipend of blood I needed. The Skerrise would rather keep me as a wretched prisoner, the least of the least of immortals. I was a cautionary tale to the other elves who doubted her. Look upon him, and remember the sorrows inflicted upon us by mortals! I longed to flee the cold city. Eternal my prison seemed.

Again, my thoughts turned to you, Lammergeier. You slew Lord Bone and liberated Necrad once. Now the Skerrise walks the same ruinous path—

*

("Hold up," interrupted Alf. "The Nine went to Necrad to end the war, to finish what Bone started. He'd already invaded Summerswell."

"I never knew Lord Bone, but I have heard the tales. I fear the Skerrise will force my kinfolk into another war. Darkness rises in the north—"

Alf groaned. "Don't fucking put it like that."

"—and Necrad calls out for heroes. You swore an oath, Lammergeier, to watch over the city."

"All that was a long time ago. I can't help you, lad."

But Ceremos was undeterred. The vampire's eyes gleamed like rubies.

"Listen to the end of my tale, Lammergeier, before you judge.")

I attempted to steal a dreadworm. I took my father's sigil of command. I climbed atop the House of the Horned Serpent and held that sigil aloft to the green sky.

Three times I called out.

Three times, but no worm heeded me.

Other ears, though, were listening. Vatlings found me. They were of the new sort, made under the Skerrise, and loyal to her. They assailed me. I broke free, they pursued me through the streets. And in my headlong flight, I ran to the very heart of Necrad, and the Wailing Tower. And I saw that the door of the tower was open.

Know this, Lammergeier—

("Don't call me that. Just Alf.")

Know this, Aelfric: since the Uncrowned King fled, the door of the Wailing Tower has been sealed. For twenty years, no one save the Skerrise has entered the tower. It is guarded by the most fearsome Pitspawn, and wound around with spells of forbiddance. None can pass that threshold. The Vatlings dared not pursue me there.

And yet, I found that door open to me. The Pitspawn laid down their misshapen heads and fell into slumber as I approached. The spells did not bar my passage. I entered the tower, and a voice spoke. It seemed to come from all around me. It knew me by name. It commanded me to seek out the Lammergeier and give you a message. The sigil in my hand – I could feel it shiver with renewed magic.

I fled, and as soon as I was out I called a worm. The beast had been told where to find you; once I had escaped all pursuers I let it have its head, and it flew arrow-straight, over the Gulf of Tears to the lands of mortals, and it brought me here.

"Blaise——" Alf choked on the name. "Blaise sent you?"

"I did not see him that night," admitted Ceremos, "nor have I heard any word of him since the departure of the Uncrowned King. But who else could speak so?"

"He's dead," said Alf. "He's been dead for a long time." *Olva told me he was dying when they fled the tower. The Skerrise was there. She'd not have spared him. He's dead. I grieved him.*

"And yet," said Ceremos, "I am here."

Alf's mouth was dry as dust. "What message?"

"He said: 'Tell the Lammergeier that Blaise has need of him for one last service. Tell him to come at once. Tell him to bring his sword.'"

CHAPTER THREE

Earth-smell, grave-smell, blood and dirt. Olva-otter, slick-wet-fur, nose twitching as she follows the scent deeper into the cave. Limping, always limping, one paw forever twisted, and otter-brain too small to remember why for now. For the otter there is only the now. No place for past or future. Only here, only now, only the dark: hot breath, predator-stench, meat-stench, and the urge to flee. But Olva-ness is more stubborn than old tree-roots, and though otter-skin crawls, she keeps going.

There's her quarry! The great wolf lies on its side, belly swollen, muzzle red-caked. Slumbering, twice the size of a natural wolf. Her front paws not right, the suggestion of human hands as they flex. Before her, bones, gnawed and broken. Torn pieces of mail, a shattered spear-shaft, helm and skull alike crushed by the terrible force of those lupine jaws.

The smell's too much for otter-courage to endure. Olva lets the skin-shape slip and becomes herself again, falling back into human thought and time.

The wolf stirred. Olva had to work quickly now.

First, light. A simple spell called on the earthpower and conjured a faint glow that suffused the whole cave. She did not need light to work, but humans are creatures of daylight and firelight. They see,

they touch with their hands. Even as the wolf stirred, Olva reached out and caught the wolf's too-human paws, her own wrinkled, dirt-encrusted fingers probing beneath the fur to find the vestigial fingers.

Perdia, that's what the villagers said her name was. Perdia. The miller's girl.

Olva drew upon the earthpower, and was unsurprised to find it running strong and thick in this cave. Invisible currents surged beneath the ground. A rushing river, untapped for centuries. No wonder this poor girl drowned in it – but Olva could use that power, too, as she waded into the magic to extract Perdia from the wolf-shape. She threw a spell of binding, compelling muscle and bone to remain stock-still.

The wolf's massive jaws gaped wide, but froze before they could snap shut on Olva's arm. The wolf's green eyes – human eyes, staring helpless from an animal skull – bulged in confusion and terror.

Twenty years ago, Olva had lost herself. The earthpower had caught her as she fell from the Citadel in Necrad. In bird-skin she'd soared, forgetting her fears, escaping her mortal life. It was Lath who found her and brought her back, and in the dark under Daeroch Nal she'd learned to control this power.

So she could do this.

"Listen now," said Olva, "listen to my words. Think on them. You can understand me, Perdia."

She talked as she worked. The words were for Perdia's benefit, just like the light. Human speech, human thought overlaid on the instincts and passions of the animal. *Speaking beasts*, as the elves called them.

"There's magic in the ground, Perdia, and in the sky and in living things. It's the earthpower, the magic of this world. There are two sorts of magic, see – there's the magic of the stars, and the magic of the earth.

"Star-power – that's elf magic. Every star has authority over some

aspect of existence. All very orderly, very precise. Invoke the right star, speak the right words, follow all the customs and forms, and you can work magic. All clever sums and angles and incantations. Elves do it like breathing. Humans can learn to do it, too, but it's hard and slow. Takes years to gather enough magic for even a single spell.

"For a long time, star-magic was the only magic we were allowed to use. You're young, so maybe you never heard the priests telling us that earth-magic was wrong, that it was monstrous. But the priests were wrong. The Intercessors lied to them, and the Erlking lied to them. They didn't want humans to have this power."

As she spoke, Olva drew on the earthpower, very carefully, disentangling threads of magic from Perdia's soul. The wolf-shape was a potent one; an easy skin to find, hunger and fear and anger leading to strength and cunning and ferocity. Pull too quick, corner the wolf-shape, and the beast would devour the human in Perdia. The woman would be lost for ever, a Changeling unable to change back.

"It is wild magic, I'm not denying that. Dangerous. Earth-magic can go sour if you're not careful. They feared it, so they taught us to fear it, too. But it's ours."

A shiver ran through the wolf. The jaws inched closer to Olva's face.

"I know what happened. I know you were angry, and scared. You felt like you were going to burst, you were so full of fury – and then you drank the earthpower, and your skin swelled up so you could hold all that wrath. But let it go now. It's done. Breathe it out."

The wolf exhaled, right in Olva's face, so hot it was like a dragon's flame. On and on, a torrent of anger, the earth-current rushing through Perdia. Olva let it flow over her, and endured that breath until she found that she was holding a woman's hands, staring into a woman's face, and Perdia was weeping.

"It's all right," said Olva. "Let it all out." She wrapped her arms around Perdia and cradled her like a child for a long while. Then,

when Perdia's shoulders sagged with exhaustion, Olva wiped her face clean.

"There we are," she said. She clenched her fist, gathering the diffuse earthlight into a flaming sphere so they could see. "Let's get out of here. Let's get you home."

Perdia beheld the mangled corpse at her feet for the first time. "They burned the mill. They attacked . . . I . . . "

"They did," said Olva gently. "And you did. These things all happened. But there'll be time to think about that later."

They hobbled out of the cave together, old and young. Olva had left clothes for both of them at the entrance, and shoes for Perdia. Olva's own left foot was forever caught halfway between human and crane, a witch-mark she'd incurred the first time she drew on the tainted power of Necrad. She'd suffered worse marks in their desperate escape from the city.

Perdia pulled on one boot, then stopped to stare at the other in her hand. They were boots taken from dead soldiers. She doubled over in anguish. "I *ate* them. Oh heavenly Intercessors, I ate them. I – I . . . " She clasped her hands over her mouth. "What am I?"

"A skin-changer, like me. A Changeling."

"Am I cursed?"

Olva took a wooden bowl from her bundle and fetched some fresh water. "Not you in particular. All mortals have it in them to touch the earthpower. We get that from Grandmother Death, the first of our kind. It's nothing you did. But most people never make a connection to the power that flows in the world." She sat down next to Perdia. "You did. When those raiders attacked, you picked up a weapon. You might have grabbed a stick or a stone with your hand. But you reached out with your soul."

Perdia stared at her mud-covered hands. She held them palm-down, like paws. Gently, Olva turned them over before washing them clean.

"Listen. There's a choice before you. You don't need to make it now, but it'll help settle your mind knowing there are clear paths. Most people who touch the earthpower accidentally, it's only a light touch. My mother – she had dreams of faraway places sometimes, and that was her brushing against the current. Light touches like that, they're accidents. They fade." Olva took the other boot and pulled it onto Perdia's foot, dressing her like a child. "But you went deep. The connection's made and it won't go away easily."

"It's unholy—" Perdia flinched, and in that moment the invisible earthpower twisted around them. Perdia might have changed again, the wolf rising in her. But Olva grabbed Perdia's hands even as she forced the current back with an effort of will. She could almost see the river of energy deflecting away from Perdia. Nearby trees creaked, the leaves rustled.

"Listen!" Olva hissed. "I can teach you to control this power. It's a craft, same as any other, and you've got a talent for it. You can use it to do good – but it's not easy or safe. Or, if you want to put it aside, there are ways to do that, too."

Perdia looked at Olva properly for the first time, her gaze taking in Olva's weatherbeaten face, her still-strong frame, her strings of charmstones and talismans – and the twisted crane-foot. "How do you know so much of magic?"

"I came to it late, but I've worked hard to learn. Lath himself taught me, Lath of the Nine. I've got friends who know some, and I've spent years digging up what the church and the College Arcane tried to bury. I don't know everything, mind you, but enough to help you.

"Now – listen to me – we're going to walk back to Hayhurst together. For now, try not to think about what happened, and don't speak of it. I promise, I'll teach you what you need to know."

Perdia nodded, and numbly followed Olva as they picked their way through the trees.

It was not hard to find the way back to the village. All Olva had

to do was look for the pillar of black smoke rising from the smouldering ruins.

Perdia and Olva emerged from the edge of the wood. Villagers crowded around them. "The wolf's gone," said Olva, loudly. "I drove it away, and it won't be back anytime soon. It dragged poor Perdia here off to its lair, but she's not hurt. She needs sleep. Lots of sleep."

"You poor girl," said one, "let's get you some food."

She won't be hungry, thought Olva, but she did not say it.

She spotted Snaroc hurrying towards her. She'd known Snaroc a long time; in another lifetime, he bought piglets from her every autumn. Now he was one of the elders of Hayhurst, and she was the fearsome Widow-witch of the Mulladales. She waited in the shade as he came hurrying up. Soot covered his face, the black dust cut with the traces of tears, and his right arm was bandaged.

"Thank you, Widow Forster, for finding the lass and bringing her back."

"Who are her people here?"

Snaroc frowned. "She's fostered by Methdrel the miller – her father's cousin. Her mother's dead ten years or more."

"The father?"

"He went off down the Road and hasn't come back. Nine years he's been gone" He flexed his hand and winced. "So, she doesn't have any left, not with Methdrel dead. But she's a good lass. I know she's talked of Tyrn Gorthad—"

"The monastery? She wanted to become a nun?"

"Aye. Methdrel was against it, but now ... " Snaroc sighed. "Maybe it's best for her."

"No," said Olva. "She must come back to Ersfel with me. It's not safe, otherwise."

"Is there nothing else that can be done? The priests spoke of prayers—"

"And who'd be answering them? The Intercessors are gone. Exorcisms don't work any more."

"We must trust in your methods, then." She could hear the nervousness in his voice; like her, Snaroc was raised to think of the earthpower as something monstrous. She touched his wounded arm and muttered a healing spell.

"How bad was it?"

"Three were killed by the raiders. Another two mauled—"

"Snaroc," interrupted Olva, "they were all killed by the raiders, aye? The dead can bear such things better than the living."

"Five dead. Another few injured – I'd have numbered Breca's son among the dead, if you hadn't worked your magic on him. The mill's gone, of course. The raiders didn't get much – they ran when the giant wolf showed up." Snaroc spat. "I fear that means they'll come back."

"Who were they?"

"I don't know. Maybe just brigands, but I've heard of trouble down in Ilaventur. The Road's alive with tales that Lord Merik's losing, and if he falls, the Mulladales are next." He lowered his voice. "They were asking questions of the miller, before the fighting started. It may be there was some quarrel there. Methdrel was . . . well, I won't speak ill of the dead, but he had a temper."

"That was no quarrel over the price of bread."

"Aye." Snaroc sighed. "This has the stink of lords and kings. Tell me, who do we look to if war comes to the Mulladales? Who's going to protect us? The harpers sing of the Mad Monk or Sir Erryn Greencloak, but no one rode to our rescue when those raiders came."

"One day, if Perdia's got the courage for it, you'll have a Changeling of your own watching over Hayhurst. Until then . . ." Olva sighed. "Until then, do the best you can. It's foolish to put all your hope in heroes."

*

They set off for Ersfel. Perdia walked without seeing. Olva guided her feet and kept her from stumbling. Her own feet ached, and she longed to fly instead of trudging all the way. The crane-form was easy for her – it was the first shape she'd worn, other than the human one she'd been born into. The crane-skin felt fresh and unworn compared to Olva's natural shape. She understood in her tired bones why old stories warned of the allure of the earthpower. The flight-hunger – to keep going until the air cracked cold, until there was snow on the trees, harsh sunlight on the little lakes. Strange lands meant unexpected currents of power, and the risk of being swept away.

But it was still joy beyond measure to fly, as the crane unfolded in her soul and her human skin fell away. Wind under wing! So much better than walking with these weary old bones! But for Perdia's sake, Olva kept to her human skin for now, walking in silent sympathy.

From time to time, Olva pointed out some aspect of the land, a hill or stream or ancient tree, and spoke of the currents that flowed between them. Perdia stared with hollow disinterest, and Olva saw herself reflected in those glassy eyes – a crazy old woman, muddied and worn, one booted and one bandaged foot, muttering about unseen powers. No matter. Once or twice, she'd tried Lath's trick of taking on different human shapes, or even just a younger version of herself. She'd never managed to hold such forms for long, and the strain was immense. She'd never equal Lath in power or skill, and she was content with that. Her legacy would be in those she helped and healed, like Perdia.

Three days walk brought them to Kettlebridge. It was market day, but the little town was subdued. Fearful people huddled in knots, armed men at the gate. Perdia flinched at the sight of the crowded village green, and Olva clasped her hand tightly. Her thumb probed Perdia's fingernails; *claws herald the change*, she thought. At a market stall, Olva bought provisions for the last leg.

Someone in the crowd laughed loudly with forced humour, and Perdia flinched again.

"They don't know. They're all just going about their days. About their lives. The raiders killed—" A sudden sob, and her nails drew blood from Olva's palm. "– my uncle Methdrel, and burned our home and these people don't *care*. It's like nothing's changed." The last word a bestial growl.

"Oh, they know, child. They know. Bad news travels fast. They'll have heard about what happened in Hayhurst. But their lives go on. When my Galwyn died, I wanted the sun to crack. I wanted the world to be as broken as my heart. But the world's bigger than any of us. It rolls on, battered but still whole. Your old life's gone, aye, but you'll find a new place for yourself in time."

Perdia tried to pull away. There was panic in her eyes. Earthpower surged, drawn by her will, unseen and unfelt by the crowd around them. Olva grunted with the effort of pushing the current away.

"I don't want this," wept Perdia. "I shouldn't be here."

"There's no going back," said Olva. "I'm sorry. We go on, not back."

And they walked again, all through the afternoon and into the long evening, until Perdia was so exhausted she slept without a struggle.

Olva stroked the girl's head. "Tomorrow night," she said, "we'll be in Ersfel. And we'll stay there a good long while, and you can find peace."

Rather than bring Perdia through the village, with all its peering eyes and gossiping tongues, Olva took her through the hills on the long way round. The thick smell of the trees enveloped them.

Her crane-foot ached as she approached her home. There was a light burning; Alf was there, instead of down at Genny Selcloth's or off training the militia. Poor village children, beaten up and down the green by the Lammergeier himself. She chuckled as she opened the—

The door was barred.

The door was never barred.

"Alf, what's going on in there?" All she could think was that her buffoon of a brother had made some sort of ungodly mess in there and was trying to clean it up before she saw it.

"Olva. I'll open the door in a moment, all right?" came Alf's reply. "But – look, I'll explain everything, all right? Just give me a minute." From inside, whispered voices, hasty movement. Footsteps on the stair.

Olva spoke a word, and the wooden bar splintered. The door flew open.

Forty years fell away when she saw the red eyes of a vampire profaning her home.

CHAPTER FOUR

Wind tore through the farmyard as the earthpower surged. Behind Olva, the roof of the repaired shed collapsed. Smoke billowed from the fireplace. Perdia made a little noise in her throat, like a bark, and without looking Olva grabbed the girl's hand to restrain her. Alf hurried forward to interpose himself between Olva and the vampire. The red-eyed creature cowered on the stairs.

It's not Acraist. It's not an elder, thought Olva. *Damnation. It's the one Alf made. The boy from Necrad.*

But still a vampire.

"Get it out of my house."

"Ol, he—"

"Out. *Now.*"

"I mean no harm," muttered Ceremos.

Alf grabbed the elf by the arm. "Come on. Back to the shed."

Olva stepped aside and let the two men pass her and Perdia. Alf stumbled on the way across the yard, and Ceremos caught him. The vampire stepped into the shed and turned around, eyes gleaming in the dark.

"Lock it," ordered Olva.

"You need not fear me, Widow Queen," said the elf. But Olva remained still and silent until the door was locked. Then she

stamped back into the house, leading Perdia by the hand. "There's a bedroom through there." Olva pulled a blanket from a cupboard. "Go and make yourself at home. There should be food in the pot, but it seems my idiot of a brother's had guests over." She handed the blanket to Perdia – she had to push it into her hands, the girl was frozen in confusion – and guided her into the little room under the stairs. It was like enough to a wolf's den that she might be at home there.

Olva closed the door firmly behind Perdia and turned on her brother. Alf stood there with his head bowed. Sheepishness radiated from him, which annoyed her even more.

"How often has he fed from you?" snapped Olva. She tried to keep her voice down.

"Only once. And not that much." That, she knew, was a lie. Alf looked like a wrung-out dishrag.

"Which means he's hungry. And what do we do when he can't control himself?" Olva glared at the locked shed. It wouldn't hold a determined goat. She wanted to scrub the floors, to purge any trace of Necrad from her home. "Does anyone else know he's here?"

"No. Least, I don't think so. But they're looking."

"You roused the hue and cry?"

"Aye. I didn't know the boy wasn't a threat."

"Not a threat?" How could he say that? How could he think that? The memory of the black sword in the vampire's hand, Galwyn's blood gushing across the floor, that little sad sound he'd made at the end, the way he'd reached for her as he died . . . But all that was long ago, she told herself. Even the memory was rehearsed. It had become a story she told herself as much as anything else. The feeling of the unexpected warmth of the blood against her bare foot – that, strangely, had stayed with her, the sensation perfectly preserved. All else was a retelling – but the presence of another vampire brought it all back with terrible intensity. Olva felt like she was being skinned alive. The fear robbed her of the skin of the Witch of Ersfel that

she'd grown, tough and gnarled and clawed, and clothed her in the shape of the terrified young bride she'd been, or the fearful protective mother.

Neither of those shapes were who she was now. She didn't even have the same foot.

She forced herself to stay calm.

"He doesn't mean any harm," Alf said. As if saying it made it so! "He fled Necrad. He came here looking for my help."

"He *is* harm. Even if he were just a Witch Elf and not a vampire, too – he'd bring trouble. The people here trust us, but there are travellers on the Road, and tales spread quick." She shook her head. "He can't stay here."

"We won't."

Olva's glare switched to Alf.

"He brought a message. From Blaise."

"Blaise," said Olva, very carefully, "is dead."

"Ceremos says he's still in the tower. Blaise says he needs me, Ol. Me and the sword."

"Oh, for heaven's sake." She grabbed the poker and thrust it violently into the fire. Sparks shot up. "Blaise is dead, Alf. And you're rid of that fucking sword. Digging that damnable thing up again would be the death of you. It's done. It's all done. Forget it." Angrily, she raked the poker back and forth, spreading the burning logs across the hearth. The fire began to die down. "I'm going to bed, Alf. I need sleep." She looked back at the shed. "Assuming I can sleep, with *that* out there."

She climbed up the stairs to her bedroom, crane-foot slapping on every step.

After a few minutes, the stairs creaked under Alf's weight, and then something scraped the floor outside her door. He'd carried one of the heavy wooden chairs upstairs. He was sitting there, guarding her. The vigilant sentry, warding off monsters through the night.

And it worked. She fell into a dreamless, renewing slumber, safe with Alf watching over her.

The next morning, Olva stepped around the snoring watchman. She looked in on Perdia; the girl was lost beneath a tangle of blankets, but at least she was sleeping.

Olva attended to the morning chores, mapped the subtle shifts in earthpower. Thomad saw that she was home and walked across the fields to greet her. After, she went in and made breakfast. The smell of the frying eggs and bacon must have stirred Alf, because he promptly came shambling downstairs.

"I've been thinking, Ol," he said. "And you're right. It's foolish."

"What's foolish, exactly?"

Alf nodded at the locked shed. "What the boy said. Blaise's message. Going back to Necrad. Put aside young Ceremos' nonsense about the Skerrise, I know that's beyond me."

Olva grunted an endorsement.

"But going back at all. Blaise is dead, so it's certainly a trap or something. And . . . and even if we were all wrong, and somehow he's still alive – he used us both, manipulated you and Derwyn. I don't owe him anything. It's not my fault. And, anyway, the message told me to bring the sword, and I don't have the sword. It's down in the Neverwood, and it's broken. It's all nonsense, like you said." He started to cut thick slices of bread, hewing at the loaf as if it was the neck of a monster. "I'll send Ceremos on his way. Tell him there's nothing for him in Ersfel. And if he won't go . . . *morthus lay-necrad lunktool amortal*, as the elves say."

"They don't. It's *morthus lae-necras l'unthuul amortha*. The gift of death shall not be rejected by the undeserving." She shovelled cooked eggs and bacon onto a plate. "Go out and tell Thomad and his boy that breakfast is ready, then wake Perdia."

"Who?"

"The girl I brought home. She's a Changeling, or might be. Perdia of Hayhurst. She's got potential."

"Oh aye," said Alf, continuing to massacre the bread. She snatched the blade from him. "Did you say Thomad's here?" asked Alf.

"His boy's in the shed, feeding the vampire." Olva started piling food onto her own plate. She'd need her strength for the journey. "I've known Thomad since he was two. I was midwife at Jon's birth. I know 'em. They'll keep a secret. And I want Ceremos well fed before we set off, because I'm not letting him touch me on the Road."

"I don't understand."

"He can't stay here, Alf. But there's a place where he can find safety. Or, at least, where they can keep watch on him, and he won't bring trouble."

"The Valley." Up on the High Moor was a place both sacred and secret.

"Aye. I can get him there without anyone seeing us. He's young, and I can skin-change. We'll get there in a few days if we hurry. You'd slow us down. You stay here."

Alf nodded.

"And pack. Be ready to leave when I get back."

He looked up, befuddled.

"But – I said I wasn't going."

Olva laughed. "You said, yes. But Blaise is one of the damned Nine, and I know you. You'll spend a while saying you're not going, and brooding about it, and moping. And you'll break things by accident because you're angry. And in the end you'll find some excuse. Maybe you'll have a dream, or hear some tale in the tavern that spurs you, but you'll find your excuse to go off on the Road again. You'll go because it's the Nine who call, and you always answer. So we'll both go." She paused. "Just promise me one thing, Alf."

"Aye?"

"The sword. Fetch it if you must. But you don't listen to it. You don't wield it. You lock it in a box, and you put it aside again when you're done."

He nodded, and she spooned the remainder of the breakfast onto

Alf's plate. "Go on. Eat up. Get your strength back. No questing on an empty stomach."

Thomad, Jon and Ceremos joined them. Jon, unsurprisingly, looked ashen, while Ceremos was renewed, a gallant young elf-lord despite his rags. Olva fussed over young Jon, ensuring he stayed warm and treating the wound with a poultice. Perdia hid in the corner by the fireplace, as if longing to slip out the door of this madhouse. But she ate hungrily.

"I could come with you, Lammergeier," said Ceremos, "when you go to retrieve the Spellbreaker."

"It's for me to do, lad," said Alf.

"And you certainly aren't wandering around Summerswell," snapped Olva. "Alf left the Spellbreaker stuck in the Erlking's tree. We'll have to cross all of Ilaventur and the Eaveslands, not to mention the Great River, to get to the Neverwood. Two old Rootless wanderers of no particular importance, no one will notice us. A Witch Elf's another matter."

"She's right, lad," said Alf. "We're not looking for trouble. The plan is to go south, get the sword. Maybe find Lae and talk to her. She'll want to hear Blaise's message."

"I can be of service!" insisted Ceremos. "I did not escape Necrad to dwell in a mortal dungeon."

"It's not a dungeon. It's a cowshed. And you're not staying here. I'm going to bring you someplace you'll be safe."

"Excuse me," said Thomad, "but can I just ask – are ye all saying that Alf here is, in truth, the Lammergeier, knight of the Nine?"

Alf paused, then nodded. "I was."

"Ha!" Thomad leaned back with an air of great satisfaction. "An old bet. Carry on, don't mind me."

"Even without Ceremos, we'll need to watch ourselves on the Road," mused Alf. "There's fighting down south, and the name of the Lammergeier's cursed."

"Is the Lammergeier not a hero to mortals?" asked Ceremos.

"That was before he killed the Erlking and threw the lands into chaos," muttered Olva.

"Wasn't me who killed the Erlking. It was Bor. And, anyway, he's not dead. Lae banished her father instead of killing him."

"But all his works were destroyed. The wizards' magic, the church, the law of the Lords. The land runs wild now," said Olva, "and the world will be the better for it, I hope, in time. But whatever shape Summerswell takes in the end, it's been a hard birthing, and Alf certainly made enemies. People look for someone to blame, and he's thick-headed enough to pay heed to 'em. That's why I'm going, too, to keep an eye on him."

Later, she took Perdia out walking. Hesitant, nervous mouse-steps, and the awkward hobble of Olva's crane-foot. She caught Perdia staring at the witch-mark. "Not all changes go smooth," explained Olva. "You don't get through life without some scars."

They sat down on the grassy glade by the old shrine in the holy-wood. The shrine was empty, the door locked. Some in the village still came up here to maintain the shrine and pray to the Intercessors on holy days. They came only rarely, these days, and that was to Olva's liking. The lies of the Intercessors deserved to be forgotten. Long ago, people had worshipped the earthpower here. They would again, in generations to come.

"You're going away," said Perdia. "With the vampire."

"For a few days, only."

"Can . . ." She pulled at the grass. "Can I come?"

"Best you stay here. Get to know the land."

"You said you were bringing him somewhere safe."

"Safe for the likes of *him*. It's a strange place for . . . well, for strange folk, I guess."

"You think I'm not strange? I was . . . I turned . . ."

"You put on a wolf's skin. It's a natural gift of the earthpower.

Humans have been doing that since the beginning. We've been taught to fear it, but we shouldn't. It's a power to be respected, not feared." Olva hesitated for a moment, careful to hide her thoughts from Perdia. "No, you stay here. I need you to mind my brother, aye? And he'll get you ready for the journey. Once we're rid of the vampire, we'll be setting off south, the three of us. A long way." *I'll teach her along the way. She'll be useful too. Alf's not as strong as he was, and it'll be good to have someone else to talk to. We'll go to the wood and fetch the sword, and then . . .*

Then could attend to itself.

"Alf will keep you safe until I'm back. Don't tell anyone, but he used to be something of a warrior."

Olva and Ceremos left the next morning. She borrowed clothing from Jon to disguise Ceremos. She'd hoped to leave quietly in the early hours, but as they came around the hill a trio of young archers led by the doughty Cerlys popped out of the undergrowth and challenged them. Ceremos had the wit to conceal his face and let Olva take the lead, and a few muttered threats of Changeling-curses sent two of the three youths running for cover.

To her credit, Cerlys did not blanche even when Olva threatened to turn her into a goat. She merely lowered her bow and said, "Well, I hope you don't get lost this time. My mother still talks about when you went up to Highfield for a day and didn't come back for a year."

"Impudent girl," muttered Olva, "her mother was the same at that age." Derwyn had mooned over Quenna when he was young. In some other world, Cerlys might have been Olva's granddaughter. *And I'd still turn her into a goat.*

They kept to the Road for the first part of the journey. The same path she'd taken years ago with Bor. Back then, she had feared to go on the Road without a protector. Now, her guardian was all around her, in the earth and in the sky, and she walked without fear.

It struck her that she'd travelled with an elf before, too. She hadn't known – how could she *possibly* have known – that her dog was possessed by an elven-spirit sent to watch over her, or that the fallen Intercessor had turned on the Erlking and played a part in his downfall. One of Olva's great regrets was that she'd never have a chance for a long conversation with Cu, or the Knight of Hawthorn, or whatever he was truly called. With the breaking of the Erlking's spells, Cu had faded into the wraith-world with the other dead elves. In time, he might be reborn, but Olva would be long dead by then.

While travelling with Ceremos did remind Olva of walking with Cu, it wasn't because of anything elvish. No, the young vampire had the enthusiastic energy of a puppy, bounding this way and that. Everything was new and strange to him – every tree, every stream, every patch of dirt. All he knew was the twisted desolation of Necrad.

Ceremos' unlikely joy amused Olva, but she could never let herself forget the danger he posed. The elf's natural span had been cut short twenty years ago; only blood kept him bound to the physical world. If his hunger grew too great – well, Olva was not her brother.

They left the Road and cut through the wild hills of the eastern Mulladales. The terrain became much more challenging in these lands of steep hills and bramble-choked gullies. No one dwelt in these lands any more; they passed ill-omened ruins almost lost beneath the forest, and did not linger. Olva took to changing her skin, ranging ahead as a bird or slipping through the undergrowth in fox-shape. The elf, full of the grace and vigour of the Firstborn, kept up with her easily.

On the fifth day, they camped by the shore of a little lake. Across the lake, the land rose higher and higher, and the trees grew thinner and more stunted. They had come to the edge of the High Moor.

Ceremos perched on a stone and looked at his reflection in the

waters, pale hands brushing against the rough cloth of his human garb. He looked over at Olva.

"You're taking me to the Valley of the Illuminated One."

"Aye."

"My father told me tales of it. He rode with the Wraith-Captain on the hunt. He said it was ..." The boy muttered some elvish words, searching for the right translation. "*Exposed*, maybe? He said the sun was an eye, judging him. I have no wish to go there. You should take me with you when you journey south. I can be as dangerous as anything in your lands. The hunger gives me strength."

That's exactly why you're not coming. "We'll be there soon enough," said Olva, "and you can see for yourself. It's a safe place. A holy place, some would say."

Ceremos plucked a reed and he pointed back the way they'd come. "The Nine fled that way, did they not? They fought the dreadknights in the Valley, and then fled into the mortal lands. My father hunted them, but could not find them."

"They came back to Ersfel," muttered Olva. "They hid there." The memory was still painful. *The Oracle sent us here. We have travelled far in search of the Nine. For thy own sake, let this not be a wasted journey.* And Galwyn's blood spilling across the floor.

"My mother was one of the Oracle's handmaidens," continued Ceremos, heedless of Olva's pain. "They sang mighty songs to coax the *nechrai* out of hiding. Nine times nine they sent wraiths to hunt the mortals."

"They served Lord Bone," said Olva. *Your father was part of the invasion that brought such suffering to Summerswell! Your mother helped guide Acraist to my door.*

She could become a wolf. There was no one to witness the jaws snapping, elf-skull shattering. *He's immortal. He'll feed on humans for thousands of years. How much suffering would I spare if I ended him here and now?*

"They did," said Ceremos. "Lord Bone had secret police Vatlings

who reported on any disloyalty." Angrily, he swung the reed like a sword whistling through the air. "I wouldn't have served him. I'd have fought back."

"Easy to tell a story," said Olva.

Ceremos scowled at her. "Acraist slew the Illuminated One and his cultists. Who lives in the Valley now?"

"People." Olva sat down by the shore, watching the evening light probe the shadowed valleys across the lake. "Jan the Pious, for a while, but she's gone, too. Now, it's just people. When I was young, monks from the valley still used to come down to the Mulladales, begging for alms. We all thought they were mad, but I can't deny there's a power in the valley. The people there . . . I don't know? Seek it? Tend it? Worship it? I don't pretend to understand it myself. But it's peaceful. It helped my son."

"The Uncrowned King!" said Ceremos.

"He's not called that any more," said Olva.

Olva led Ceremos unerringly across the landscape of bracken and thin grass. The sun was indeed like a piercing eye, and there were no clouds that day to soften its glare. The earthpower ran thin here, sinking deep like an underground stream, unresponsive to her will. Olva walked, crane-foot burning on sun-baked stones. They marched for long hours, resting in the shade of a crag before continuing until nightfall. A second day followed, much like the first, and even the elf was wearied by the barren emptiness of the moor. He hid his face from the sunlight and became sullen, his fangs more prominent, the red eyes dull and glassy. She felt hollow, too, an automaton stumbling forever forwards until she toppled off the sea-cliffs at the edge of the world.

But at twilight on the second day, keen-eyed Ceremos spotted little glimmers of light like dancing sparks. They followed these down into the Valley of the Illuminated.

A man and a woman, both clad in rough-spun robes of brown

cloth, waited at the foot of the path. "Who have you brought us, Olva?"

"Ceremos of Necrad," she said. She looked at the vampire. "They'll show you around. Do whatever they tell you."

He bowed. "As you command, O Widow Queen."

Little brat, she thought. She hurried down the path.

"Where are you going?" called Ceremos.

"She goes to see the Tattersoul," answered one of the monks.

CHAPTER FIVE

A lf found his old travelling cloak under the stairs. His cooking
pot, though, had been repurposed by Olva as a container for
onions. He emptied it out and wrapped it and some cheese and
bread in a cloth. "Stupid," he muttered to himself. Olva would not
be back for days. There was no need to throw things into a bag
immediately – and, anyway, a hunk of cheese wouldn't last him all
the way to the distant Neverwood. He laughed at himself, and it
felt good to laugh.

Perdia flinched, and Alf immediately regretted his good cheer.
The house was not his alone. Their guest sat huddled in Olva's chair,
feet tucked under her legs, making herself as small as possible. She
watched Alf warily.

"Do you have travelling gear?" he asked. He couldn't tell if she'd
shaken her head in response or just quivered.

"Have you gone on the Road before?"

"I . . . No." Her voice was so quiet he had to strain to hear. "I was
going to travel. The nunnery at Tyrn Gorthad – I was going to go
there."

"As a pilgrim?" Tyrn Gorthad was a famous holy site in Arshoth,
sacred to the Intercessors. He recalled Jan mentioning it, although
the details were lost in the mists of memory.

"As an initiate," Perdia replied. "My parents are . . . were Atoners."

"They're the lot who think the Intercessors will come back, aye?"

"If we are worthy." She shivered.

The Intercessors were an elven lie, Olva would say. Or Berys. Alf knew that the heavenly spirits were a deceit — hell, he'd destroyed two of them in Avos. He'd killed so many things over the years. But he was done with slaying now, and didn't have the heart to be stern.

"Well," he said, as cheerily as he could. "Tyrn Gorthad is on the way. Maybe we can visit as we go."

"They mustn't let me in!" said Perdia in a panic. "I'm unclean!"

"Unclean? Oh."

Alf had only known a handful of Changelings in all his many years — Lath, foremost among them. He'd encountered a few Wilder-Changelings in the far north, savage berserkers riding a red tide of power. And he'd known Death, a little or a great deal depending on which of her faces you counted.

Olva, too, of course, but that was different. She was his sister first, and he'd know her no matter what skin she wore. He'd never quite understood Changelings. He'd never heard the land speak, or seen shapes in the wind, or longed to change his skin. He was always and only Alf, no matter what titles were bestowed upon him or what songs were sung.

But there was something he shared with all of them. He put the cheese aside and sat down opposite Perdia.

"You did nothing wrong, you know."

She stopped breathing. Eyes of a frightened deer.

"Olva told me some of what happened at Hayhurst. About how you were attacked. You did nothing wrong."

She whispered words Alf couldn't hear. He leaned in and she shrank back.

"Just speak up, all right. I'm a bit deaf in this ear." Ever since the thunderbolt at Bavduin.

"They came out of the woods," she whispered. "I didn't do anything."

"Aye, I know. But it's afterwards I'm talking about. You lived. You stayed alive. And there's nothing wrong with that."

She scraped her nails along her forearms, plucking at her skin. "You don't know what I did."

"I can guess a bit, seeing as Olva brought you here. I'm telling you it doesn't matter. I've been in more fights than I can remember. Stack all the corpses I've made, and they'd make a pile bigger than that hill. Dig up all the friends I've buried, and the grave's deeper than the Pits of Necrad. And I'm telling you that none of it comes with certainty."

He found a walking stick and held it up like a sword.

"There's skill and training and clever tactics and all that. And magic. Magic does make a difference. But even magic doesn't make it certain. I've killed things that people said couldn't be killed. Sometimes, you live when by all rights you should have died – and I've seen friends die who should've lived. Sometimes, it's just *luck*, and there's no reason for it. Understand?"

Her head shook, and Alf's heart sank. He wanted to help the girl. If Olva were here, he'd turn to her. Or Jan – Jan would have known what to say. Peir would have inspired her. Lae or Thurn, they'd have the words.

"Look, there was this one time I was with a dwarf friend of mine, Gundan, and we were fighting the Ogre Chieftain." Alf stood, miming the battle. He could barely remember the actual fight, but he'd heard the stories often enough. "So the ogre's got this magic helmet, aye, that magnifies his strength. I'm stabbing him from behind with my old sword Sunrazor, but it's not really hurting the bastard. And Gundan's down on the ground, dodging the ogre's blows—"

He glanced over, hoping the retelling would stir something in Perdia, a laugh at least, but the girl stared back blankly.

"And then the Chieftain smashes Gundan's axe, Chopper. And – damnedest thing I ever saw – a shard from the axe-head flies up and cuts the leather strap of the helmet, and it slips down over his eyes. And he's blundering around, roaring that he's been struck blind, and he runs his big belly right into my sword!" Alf thrust the walking stick into the air for emphasis. "So there's blood everywhere, oceans of it, and the Chieftain slips, and right away Gundan's on the ogre's face, dagger in each hand, and he bites onto the bastard's nose to hold fast while he's stabbing away at the eye sockets . . ."

Alf became aware, slowly, that there was a faint whistling noise emanating from Perdia's throat, like a swallowed scream. He paused. "Thomad's boy probably needs some help feeding the pigs. You go out to him, aye, and make yourself useful. I'll finish the story some other time."

She nodded – again, the motion almost too faint to see, the quiver vertical instead of horizontal – but she ran past him, out into the sunlight, grateful for the release. Alf could tell he'd done no good there, but for the life of him he couldn't tell where he'd gone wrong. Even after all these years, most things confused him.

He finished the story for himself. Gundan skewered the ogre in the eye, and the monster stumbled again, and Alf leaped forward to catch him in the throat with Sunrazor. The walking stick wobbled on the killing blow. All his warrior's instincts were dulled by the years. He'd got comfortable here. He'd been happy here, let himself be part of the world. No wariness, no edge. His eagerness drained from him as he realised that all the travelling cloaks and provisions in the land couldn't make up for his age. He was too old to be wandering the Road.

And he was out of breath, so he settled into Perdia's chair.

A journey. He hadn't gone on a journey in a long, long time. He'd meant to go looking for Lath, but there'd always been a reason to delay. Hiding from vengeful Lords, all the Roads north closed, and then work to do here in Ersfel. He'd never *decided* not to go – his

travelling cloak had waited by the door for years – but the moment never came.

He remembered setting off with the Nine, all those years ago. He'd carried Blaise's pack of books and reagents, his arcane tools. Alf had tried to wrap the bundle in the delicate net of a star-trap, and the wizard had snapped at him, and Alf still remembered feeling oafish. But that evening, under a brilliant starry sky, Blaise had apologised in his way.

"Each star, Aelfric, holds dominion over a particular aspect of fate. In the College Arcane there are great leather-bound ledgers recording the work of generations of astronomers, as they try to map these correspondences. There are more than eight thousand stars visible in the skies of Summerswell, yet we know the magical correspondences of only a few hundred. Look you, I have arranged my trap to catch the light of the constellation of the White Deer, yonder. My trap condenses that light, and through that condensed power I borrow the authority of the White Deer, who rules over fortune in battle."

Gundan had laughed, and said that human wizardry *was weak as a baby's piss – and it's an anaemic baby, too. Not going to make it through the winter, this infant.* And Berys had thrown her cup at the dwarf in feigned anger.

But a week later, fighting the dreadknights up on the High Moor, Alf found his sword cut more cleanly, and he'd heard Blaise chanting a spell behind him.

Bring your sword, Lammergeier.

What might it mean? Ceremos plainly thought it a call to arms – that Blaise expected the Lammergeier to leap up and rush north to slay another dark lord. Maybe forty years meant nothing to an elf, but Blaise was human. He must be as old as Alf now – if he was still alive. Olva said Blaise had been fighting with the Skerrise when she'd fled Necrad – why would the Skerrise keep him alive?

Lath is dead. Why dream about *Lath*, and then get a message from Blaise? But Blaise had been in that dream, too, hadn't he?

Was it all connected, somehow? All the thinking made Alf's head hurt, and he rested his heavy skull in his hands, eyes closed. What if this was a trap? Ceremos hadn't actually *seen* Blaise, and Olva was sure he was dead. Who might seek to bring Alf to Necrad? Was it a trap for him alone, or the other survivors of the Nine? Was that what had happened to Lath? Or what if Blaise was alive, but was trapped in Necrad, and in need of rescue? Perhaps he'd made other attempts at escape, sent other messages, but Ceremos was the first to slip through the Skerrise's nets. Or had Blaise sent a message to Lath first, and *that* was what had got poor Lath killed?

A message from Necrad. Bring your sword.

All this thinking was more exhausting than digging a path through heavy snow. Memory was easier, the paths already worn. He remembered Necrad. The first time they'd entered Necrad, they'd crawled out of the Pits, slathered in ichor and the entrails of Pitspawn. Alf leaning on Peir, blood dripping from a dozen wounds. The hellish green light of the necromiasma made the faces of his friends look dead, like they were corpses staring up at him from the mire. Lath glanced around at the cyclopean palaces of the Witch Elves – to his deluded kinfolk, the houses of the living gods.

Or had Lath been there? He'd been captured, hadn't he? All the memories of those days in Necrad blurred and shuffled. Was it later that Lath had been captured? Days? Weeks? How long had they wandered in the nightmare city? They'd been found, hadn't they? Acraist and the Witch Elves found them, and they'd fled. But Lath had hesitated to draw on the earthpower, failed to become a great Beast, and the Witch Elves captured him. We have to go back for him. They're torturing him. Those vatgrown horrors. We can't leave him.

We won't leave him. But Brychan's waiting on us to bring down those dragons. Brychan's men are dying out there in the mud.

We're the Nine. We don't leave our own behind.

*

"Alf!"

He woke abruptly, shaken awake by some young girl. Alf fished around for the bits of himself, trying to recall who and where he was. He felt like he was smeared over a lifetime, that whatever Alfness there was broken up and scattered over the years, and he was left with the dregs. That young warrior who'd limped through the streets of Necrad was more Alf than the old man in the chair.

"There's something in the woods!" The girl was so full of intensity, fear and excitement and urgency all tangled up in her. Cerlys, that was her name.

"There *was* something in the woods." Alf wiped drool from his lips. He'd fallen asleep in the sun. "A dreadworm. I killed it."

"Well," said Cerlys, "it's back."

Again, Alf crept through the forested hills above Ersfel. Cerlys and three other youths followed him, weapons in eager, nervous hands. The undeniable stench of a dreadworm was on the wind. They picked their way up the slope, scrambling through the undergrowth, stepping over tangles of roots. The forest grew thick here, and it was dark and unusually cold in the shadow of the trees. If you were going to hide a dreadworm from the searing light of day, thought Alf, this would be a good place.

"What did you see?" whispered Alf.

"There were riders on the south road," said one of the boys. "We were watching 'em, making sure they didn't mean trouble. And then this great bat thing came swooping overhead—"

"Keep your voice down!" hissed Cerlys.

"This bat thing," whispered the boy, chastened, "flew overhead. I saw it circle once, then fly down towards here."

"Just one worm?"

The boy nodded.

"And the riders? Any banner?" Hayhurst was only a few day's ride from Ersfel, so they might be the same riders. Might they have

followed Olva here? He'd left Perdia in Thomad's care, and wondered for a moment if he should double back.

"I heard," said another spotty-faced lad, "that they were asking questions down Kettlebridge way. About the Lammergeier."

"Indeed?" said a musical voice from the darkness. "I, too, have questions about the Lammergeier."

In an instant, it became bitterly cold. Sudden frost glittered on mossy trunks, and on spear-shafts. The spotty lad dropped his weapon with a shriek and nursed his frozen fingers. Only Cerlys held onto her weapon, her bowstring creaking with ice as she struggled to draw it back.

He knew that voice, that magic.

"Peace," said Alf. "Show yourself, Ildorae."

"Is that you, Lammergeier?" The elf's voice seemed to come from somewhere close by, but none of them could spot her amid the forest gloom. Cerlys' eyes widened in surprise at the mention of the legendary name.

"The winds of time blow hard indeed," continued Ildorae. "I once offered you half a century of pleasure. Better, I think, to have become my plaything than to wither."

"Show yourself," he called again.

Ildorae stepped out of the gloom. She was clad in the intricate silver carapace of dreadknight armour. She wore a ghastly helm, and charmstones glimmered in the shadows of her cloak. In her hand she bore a spear. Cerlys loosed an arrow, but the elf stepped aside with ease, and in the same casual motion thrust her spear at Cerlys. The blade dimpled the flesh of the mortal's throat – and stopped.

"Don't," said Alf. He put the tip of his stick to the haft of the spear, and gently pushed it away. "Go back to the village, the lot of ye. If she meant us harm, then—"

"Then I would have slain them all twenty minutes ago, when I first began following you," cackled Ildorae. "Flee, mortal children! Tell tales of how a goddess spared you!"

*

When the youngsters were gone, Alf turned and trudged back downhill towards the house.

"I desire to speak with you, Lammergeier," called Ildorae.

"I'm bloody freezing, thanks to you. We can talk by the fire, like civilised people."

The elf slipped away again, and Alf suppressed a shiver. He had spoken plainly in his warning – a Witch Elf dreadknight was a dangerous foe. In his youth, Alf had slain dozens of elves, but he'd had the Nine at his side then, and magic weapons and armour to aid him. Sunrazor, looted from a tomb. And later, the black sword.

We can beat 'em, roared Gundan from across the years. *They're rabble.* His axe, Chopper, blazing with charmstones as it cleaved through Witch Elves. Ildorae's face as she fled before the Lammergeier's wrath.

Now it was she who had an enchanted spear and elf-wrought armour, and Alf who walked as one who knows a lioness stalks close by.

The elf waited for him at the farmhouse. She'd removed her helm, and by firelight her silver hair gleamed red and gold. She looked around the kitchen as Alf might once have searched a dungeon chamber, wary of traps. She picked up one of the bowls used by Ceremos and gave a quizzical glance.

"He's not here," said Alf.

"But he was." She sat down opposite him. Her features were unchanged since the night all those years ago when she'd tried to kill him. He remembered looking down at her while she lay stunned – face grubby and smeared with blood, mismatched armour beneath a ragged Wilder-cloak. She'd spent untold years in the wild, hiding from Lord Bone's forces, exiled from Necrad. Now, her armour was pristine, her cloak of woven midnight, yet the passing years had not touched her.

"And what of it?" Alf stretched out his legs, letting the fire warm his toes.

"I was sent to bring Ceremos back to Necrad. Where is he?"

"He said he was kept half starved in Necrad. He didn't seem to much like living under the Skerrise's rule."

"Ceremos is young. To him, twenty years of hardship seems like an ordeal worthy of note, but it is no more than a passing discomfort. As for his hungers, the Skerrise has forbidden us from ranging far from Necrad, so what little mortal blood is available must be rationed."

Why would the Skerrise be so cautious, wondered Alf. The ancient vampire had seized control of Necrad from the Uncrowned King, and then — twenty years of isolation, even with Summerswell in turmoil and the Everwood in ruin. *Why not take advantage of it?* It unsettled Alf, but he said nothing of it. Instead, he asked, "The way he described it put me in mind of Bone's reign, with Vatling secret police and monsters and dark magic. What are she brewing up in Necrad, Ildorae?"

"Ceremos is young," she said again, and after a moment added: "Know this, mortal: it is good that it was *I* who tracked Ceremos here. Others were also sent to bring the boy home. Others are not so friendly to your kind."

Perdia chose that moment to return. She froze at the sight of the Witch Elf.

"It's all right," said Alf hastily, "she's a friend."

"Am I?" Ildorae mused. "How presumptuous of you, Lammergeier! But I respect the guest-custom."

"Last time you were under my roof," muttered Alf, "you stabbed me."

"Ah, but you did not invite me in, then. And, anyway, I sought to murder the Changeling, not you." Ildorae smiled cruelly at Perdia's involuntary whimper. "A different Changeling, child. I can smell *beast* in you. Run along, and I shall do you no harm this night."

"Go to bed, Perdia," echoed Alf. "It's safe."

Perdia scurried across to her bedroom door, but let out a snarl as she passed the Witch Elf.

Ildorae laughed. "You take in strays now, Lammergeier?"

"Olva does."

"Ah yes." Ildorae glanced around the room. "And where is she?"

"Out," said Alf. Rather than let Ildorae pry further, he changed the subject. "How're you finding the new regime?"

"I rejoice in our victory."

"You don't sound convinced."

Ildorae stared at him in the uncanny fashion of the Firstborn, as if she could read Alf's thoughts and see his very soul. "When you defeated the Erlking—"

"I didn't. That was another."

"You collectively. You mortals. Maybe your hand did not wield the Spellbreaker, but it was a mortal who struck the blow. And, more importantly, it was a mortal who made the sword in the first place. For many centuries, the two branches of the elves were at war with one another, using mortals as pawns. Finally, after we came close to extinction, the *enhedrai* suddenly snatched victory. The Erlking was fallen, the Everwood and its cursed life-trees destroyed. The Oath of Amerith was fulfilled, and the first city is ours once again." Ildorae brushed a dead leaf from her polished armour.

"But . . ."

"You. You mortals. We looked out from our walls, and saw that you were *everywhere*. Not just in Summerswell and the North, the board on which we'd played our long game against the Wood Elves, but over the sea and across the mountains and *everywhere*. Countless, countless mortals, and more with every passing year. Our numbers are fixed. For all our power, there are too many of you to be defeated.

"So, the Skerrise holds that we must hide away behind the walls of Necrad to preserve elvendom. We are to shun you, and keep to our city where we are safe. We are people of the stars, she says, and we should fear the dawning of a mortal age."

"Do you agree with all that?" Once, long ago, Ildorae had tried to murder Lord Bone. She'd tried to overthrow the leader of Necrad before. Alf studied her face, and wished there was someone clever at hand to read her thoughts.

"I am again a sworn dreadknight, and the Skerrise is our leader for now." Ildorae sounded increasingly irritated, but Alf could not tell if it was on account of his questions, or the lack of answers to her own inquiry. "The Skerrise has commanded that all elves gather in the First City."

"All? Even the Wood Elves?"

"There is no longer any distinction between *ahedrai* and *enhedrai*. We are only the Firstborn, inheritors of the world. Most of those who once dwelt in the Everwood are with us in Necrad – bodied and unbodied. And I was sent to fetch Ceremos back." With a glare, she quenched the fire in the hearth. A rime of thick ice formed on the blackened logs. "Where is he?"

Olva's only been gone two days. She'll still be on the Road, most like. Stall. Let her trail grow cold.

Alf stood. "Well, if the fire's done, I'm going to bed."

"Why hide Ceremos? Here, he is a wolf amid lambs. Let me take him back, and he will trouble you no more."

"You can sleep in Olva's room," said Alf. "Maybe tomorrow I'll remember where the boy went."

Many eyes watched Alf as he went about his chores the next day.

The vast majority belonged to the worthy folk of Ersfel. News of the strange elf had reached Genny Selcloth's before closing time, and thence to the four corners of the world, or at least those parts of creation within reach of rumour. Some speculated that the Widow of Ersfel had conjured a faerie bride for her elderly brother. While no one dared visit Olva's house, Thomad and his neighbours had more visitors that day than in the previous three months, and many more found reasons to linger near Olva's gate.

Cerlys and her militia set up camp nearby, too, watching for the intruder.

These onlookers were disappointed, for all they saw was an old man feeding the pigs and mucking out the sty.

For his part, Alf could tell when Ildorae was watching him from the house. Her cold gaze was like a shadow passing over the sun. That warm day, though, it played to his advantage; he worked all through the noonday heat, and it was nearly sunset before he went back inside to find Ildorae cross-legged on the floor. She seemed to be in a trance, or a communion with unseen forces, but then her ice-blue eyes opened and Alf felt a chill once again.

"You are preparing for a journey," she said, nodding to his travelling gear. "Where are you going?"

"Going to see a friend, if you must know."

"You carry no scabbard."

"Don't have a sword."

"No? There are whispers in Necrad that the black sword is abroad once more."

Alf grunted. "Anyone can paint a sword black and wave it around. Laerlyn's watching over the real thing. It's not mine any more."

"The Lammergeier without a sword."

"No one calls me Lammergeier any more."

A lioness smile. "Perhaps not here. But others remember that name. They remember you as a terrifying titan who slew both Lord Bone and the Erlking. But you have no sword at your side, and I see only an old man who I could kill with ease. But I do not wish to do that, so I ask again – where is Ceremos?"

"Two things first, Ildorae," said Alf. "A favour and a question."

"What boon?"

"Promise me that Ceremos won't be hurt. Take the lad back to Necrad if you must, but make sure he isn't harmed."

"I do not rule in Necrad."

"No, but he's a part of your House, aye? A scion of the Horned Serpent."

"No harm shall come to Ceremos, if I can prevent it. Ask your question."

"Have you heard anything of the rest of the Nine? I've not seen any of them in a long time."

"Emissaries were sent to the Everwood, inviting what few Wood Elves remain to come home. Many heeded the call, and took ship, but Laerlyn refused. She has the Erlking's pride." She rose, spear in hand. "Of *him*, by the by, no tidings have come to Necrad. Either he has crawled into some deep, dark hole, or his wraith goes howling on the winds. But of you mortals, I know only the fate of Lath. I heard the Wilder singing mourning-songs in his name. I think you are the last of them, Aelfric."

"What about Blaise?"

Ildorae frowned. "He fell in battle, twenty years ago."

"Ceremos said the Wailing Tower was sealed. Are you certain Blaise is dead?"

"I was there, mortal. I fought alongside the Skerrise." Ildorae sighed. "I saw her end him with a spear-thrust." She drove her own spear, effortlessly, into an oaken ceiling beam. "Enough delay. Where is Ceremos, mortal?"

"Olva took him to—" began Alf, but Ildorae silenced him with a gesture.

He heard it, too. War-horns.

Ersfel was under attack.

CHAPTER SIX

When Olva was pregnant with Derwyn, she'd imagined what her son might grow up to be. Galwyn came of noble stock. His family had wealth and standing. The Intercessors had sent Galwyn to her, an unthinkable blessing, and their child — he could be anything! A knight in the household of some great Lord! A wizard of the College Arcane or a high-ranking cleric — anything was possible. All Olva's kin had been tenant farmers as long as anyone could remember (all save Alf, the bad son, the Rootless ne'er-do-well fallen in with a bad crowd). The possibilities had quite dazzled her. Olva fretted over how they would best prepare. Should they leave Ersfel and travel to the distant Crownland, where their son might be fostered in the manor of some great noble? Should she make more offerings to the Intercessors?

Galwyn tried to calm her. "As long as the child's happy and healthy, that's all that matters. Let the future attend to itself."

There was some wisdom in those words. As Derwyn had grown, she'd come to understand that a child was not wholly yours. Each child came into the world uniquely *them*, as if a shadow of some future self reached back through time, visible only in glimpses. As the child grew, they became more and more themselves. You raised your child in partnership or conflict with that shadow, and tried to

make them the best version of that inherent shape. Take Derwyn – ever since he was born he was a dreamer, with a head full of wild notions. She could still see him toddling around the farm talking to the animals or telling tales of fairies.

After Galwyn's death, she'd feared to leave Ersfel. Half her world had collapsed in a moment, and she dared not risk the rest. She'd tried to provide a safe future for Derwyn. She'd put aside any nonsense about knights and courts, and instead tried to hammer that dreaming boy into a solid, sensible gentleman farmer. Derwyn would take over their farm when she grew old. He'd marry some village girl, have a litter of children, a life as calm as a still pond. Derwyn, still not yet completely *himself*, had tried, bless him – but he would forget his chores, waste hours listening to stories. They rarely fought loudly – it wasn't their way – but there'd been long silences at the dinner table.

Then – then that mad, mad year. Bor at her door, and the letter from Alf, and Derwyn vanishing in the night. She'd followed her son to the edge of the Grey Lands, and brought him back. Suddenly, he was acclaimed the Uncrowned King of Necrad, and he'd taken on that mantle. His dreaming no longer seemed foolish or impractical – a king should be a visionary. Ersfel had been too small a stage for him, and now he was becoming who he'd always been. She'd fought for her son's throne, tried to protect his precarious hold on power. Her own ambitions came back like half-remembered tales.

It had all fallen apart. Again, she'd saved Derwyn – and he'd saved her, battling the Skerrise and her dreadknights atop the Wailing Tower. She'd brought him out of Necrad, but he was still wounded. Two souls had come with him out of the Grey Lands, two dead shades entangled with Derwyn.

He was her son, and he was also Peir the Paladin, hero of the Nine.

He was her son, and he was also Lord Bone, the Necromancer.

They'd brought him here, to the Valley of the Illuminated One,

in the hopes that he'd find healing. At the edge of the valley, she'd let him go.

Tattersoul, she thought, *that's what they call him here. Not Derwyn.* His little hut was at the heart of the valley amid the fallen stones of an ancient temple. Jan the Pious dwelt there before him. The hut was made of piled rocks, the roof of patchwork fur. The sort of place a Rootless beggar or savage Wilder might dwell, and Olva fought to hide her shame.

Derwyn – *Tattersoul* – heard her approach. He opened his eyes and smiled, and her heart was lifted. It was not the place she would have chosen for him, not what she wanted for him. It was not even a place she could understand – but he was content. He was happy and healthy and whole, and for that she rejoiced. But there were always those might-have-beens, the gap between the possible futures she'd envisaged for her son and the path he'd ended up walking. Sometimes, love was not letting that gap become an unbridgeable abyss.

She embraced him.

"You're back sooner than I expected," he said. "What's wrong?"

Der – *Tattersoul* – had a way of listening these days that drew the words out of her. He used to wear the same expression listening to tales of the Nine or other heroes, but now he applied that intensity to everything, made you feel like your story was a grand epic, a tale for the ages. She talked for a long time, while he sat in attentive silence.

She began with the attack on Hayhurst, and how she'd saved Perdia – although she was careful to avoid a detailed description of the magic she'd used. Tattersoul still had some shadow of Lord Bone in his mind, and Lord Bone knew more of magic than any other mortal. In the first years after Necrad, during Olva's first exploration of the earthpower magic she'd learned to wield, she'd tried discussing magic with Derwyn. Both of them had been changed by

sorcery, and her new gift was something she wished to share with him. But talking too much of magic drew that shadow to the surface, and now Olva kept talk of the mysteries of earthpower to her infrequent letters to Torun.

"There have been other attacks by those raiders," said Tattersoul. Olva did not know whether her son had heard rumours from the pilgrims who infrequently visited the valley, or if he had some other way of seeing. His broken soul made him receptive to whatever power was in the valley. "I think they're searching for someone."

"You think they're looking for me? Or Alf?"

He let the silence speak.

"It's been a long, long time. If trouble was coming for us, surely it would have found us long ago." She thought a moment. "Unless something's changed we don't know about."

"Everything's always changing." A smile tugged at the corner of his mouth. "You of all people should know that."

"Not here, though." The valley was very still.

"Not so. This is the edge, in a way, but it's still part of the world. Things change differently here. Tell me of the elf you brought."

"He's Ceremos. The child vampire. He left Necrad looking for Alf. We can't have a hungry thing like him in Ersfel. He'll kill people."

Derwyn rubbed one finger over old scars on his arms. "I remember the thirst. Acraist's shade was only bound to me for a few moments, but I remember. It was overwhelming. It is a hunger of body and soul."

"Can you help him? Can . . . " Olva waved her hand around, encompassing the fallen stones of the temple and the dancing glimmers of light and the valley entire. "Can all this help him?"

"I came here broken and exhausted," said Derwyn, "from fighting a battle against myself. He is still within me. Each day I wrestle on the edge of the precipice. I gave up all hope or desire of glory. If I succeed in containing Lord Bone all the days of my life, and we both

pass back into the Grey Lands in peace, then no one will ever know the peril that was averted."

Olva squeezed her son's hand, and Derwyn laughed. "It's only part of me, and I am surrounded by friends — within and without — who help me. Look to your own troubles, O Witch of Ersfel."

"I brought you one of my troubles."

"So I am told. The elf childe."

"Child!" Olva snorted. "He's grown, as much as any elf does. He's no child."

Derwyn smirked in a way that reminded Olva of his father. "The poets call a young knight-to-be a *childe*. Childe Aelfric to the Dark City came, they say, for he was only knighted . . . knighted after . . . " He trailed off, suddenly stricken. This was perilous territory for him.

"There's more," said Olva, "and it's about the Nine, and Necrad. Are you all right with that?"

Tattersoul closed his eyes for a moment. The expression on his face reminded Olva of Alf strapping on armour, concentration becoming befuddlement at the tricky straps before ending with enduring resolution. One of the other monks hurried closer in response to some unspoken signal, but stopped a few paces away and just stood there as if waiting.

"Go on," said Derwyn.

"Ceremos says the Skerrise rules in Necrad. That she's gathering all the elves to her, and that she's kept the foundries and the breeding vats going. New kinds of Vatlings, he said. More dark magic out of Necrad. As bad as—"

"As Lord Bone," said Derwyn.

"Maybe."

He closed his eyes. "I dream, sometimes, of a great darkness growing in the north. It falls across the lands, and crushes me. Sometimes, it crushes us all. Jan the Pious spoke of the same vision."

"What should we do?"

Derwyn laughed. "I have no idea. Dreams are foxfire in the night.

If you're lost in a marsh at night and you have absolutely no idea where to go, then following the glimmer of a will-o'-the-wisp is as good a path as any. But better to light a torch, better to look for a well-trodden path. At least find a stick and probe for solid ground instead of charging off blindly. Speaking as a seer, only a madman is driven solely by visions." He threw some fuel on the little fire. "I mislike the thought of the Skerrise commanding the power of Necrad. But I mislike the thought of anyone commanding such power, so I live with the discomfort. We sit in shadow."

"There's more. Ceremos brought a message from the Wailing Tower. He said it was from Blaise."

"What was the message?" The Tattersoul's voice had that eerie cast to it, as one of the others spoke through him.

"He asked for Alf. Said that Alf should bring Spellbreaker to the tower."

"What are you going to do?"

"What's your bloody uncle going to do, you mean?" Olva rubbed her crane-foot. "You know what he's going to do. He'll do what Blaise said. Run off south and fetch the sword, even though he's not set foot outside Ersfel in years." She sighed. "The journey might kill him, but making him stay definitely would. It'd eat him up."

"There is more in the Neverwood," said Derwyn, "than the sword."

"That's what I'm thinking. He'll listen to Laerlyn. I'll get him there safe if I can, and hopefully she'll talk some sense into him."

"Or go with him to Necrad on some foolish quest, because they are Nine."

"Aye, well." She smiled ruefully. "There'd be no stopping Alf then. Will you take the vampire?"

"Let me speak to him first."

CHAPTER SEVEN

The Uncrowned King sat by a fire, dressed in the same rough robes as the rest. The Widow Queen was not there, but Ceremos could smell her. She was nearby. Another monk stood behind the king, and this one bore a sword. His face was lost in shadow.

Ceremos crouched just out of the armed man's reach.

"He's not for you. He's for me. This is Harlow, an old friend of mine."

Harlow drew back his hood, winked at Ceremos, then returned to his vigil.

Derwyn tapped his forehead. "You know who I keep locked up in here. I trust Harlow to stop me if I show any inclination towards becoming *Him*."

"Lord Bone?"

"You're not supposed to say his name. But yes." Tattersoul shifted in his seat and sighed. "You told my mother that you wish to dwell among mortals. To defy your curse, and follow in the manner of my uncle. I'm going to give a wise speech now, so make yourself comfortable.

"My mother has a low opinion of heroes, you know. The Blood of the Lammergeier is within you! I thought the same. I thought I could be a great hero. At first, all I had were dreams, and then – as

if by a miracle – power and opportunity were both thrust upon me. Suddenly, I was no longer little Derwyn Forster, but the Uncrowned King of Necrad, Peir the Paladin reborn! I would make Necrad into a court of light, and bring prosperity and joy to all the lands. Even when I learned that a *third* soul dwelt with me, that my crown was tarnished bone – my conviction did not waver. I let Blaise interrogate the dark lord within me, despite the risk, despite how much it hurt. I was a hero, and heroes must suffer!" Derwyn stopped abruptly and looked at Ceremos. "Is that true? Must a hero suffer? Must they endure great hardship?"

"Most do, in the songs," answered Ceremos.

"In Highfield, there lives a washerwoman with a sickly child. She labours to keep him alive. Her days are filled with hardship; at night, she frets and fears. No songs will ever be sung of her, but she endures. Is she a hero?"

Ceremos thought for a moment. "I don't know if it's the right word. She is doubtless brave and worthy, but . . . "

"Ah, so a hero must do great things. Common challenges are not enough to make one a hero – a hero must topple kings and slay titans. A hero must have courage to face such foes, and they must have the power to win the day. A hero must have power beyond that of common folk. Power to accomplish those mighty deeds."

"Indeed! Deeds worthy of song!" Ceremos leapt up. "I would do such things! I know you mortals of Summerswell have cause to fear the *enhedrai*, so I would win your favour through valour, as the Nine once did! I would free Necrad from the Skerrise!"

"There is, I think, another quality needed of a hero. The ability to put aside strength and power when there is no true call for it, and to take it up again only when it is truly needed. Power deforms the world, and few have the wisdom to wield it judiciously. To combine power and humility, courage and doubt is a rare thing. It is so easy to stray from the hero's path, and become a monster. That is especially true for you and I.

"I have within me the arcane knowledge of the necromancer, the greatest of all mortal wizards. It is within me to conquer all of Summerswell. I know how to raise the dead, and to call down demons from the void. With a word, I bind forces seen and unseen to my will. But this power comes with a terrible cost, and so I do not use it. Harlow here carries his sword to end me should I try. At times, I have thought of casting myself over the edge of the cliff, and removing all temptation."

"What stops you?"

"I want to live, for one," laughed Derwyn. "And I cannot be sure it will always be wrong to wield such power. A day may come when even the dreadful malice of Lord Bone may be wielded righteously. I cannot conceive of what that day might entail, and maybe it is foolish of me even to contemplate such a possibility – but I do, and so I endure."

He spoke with a terrible weight then, prophetic and strange. Harlow's hand strayed to the hilt of the sword.

"But you, Firstborn, face the fate of the Endless. I will wrestle with Lord Bone for the rest of my life, but that is finite. My struggle must end. Yours might not. You are cursed to drink blood to sustain the life of this body, and that thirst shall grow with each passing year. You can and you will fight it. You say 'I shall only feed from those willing to aid me, or deserving of my wrath.' But you are doomed to eternity, and eternity is long. This is the doom I foresee for you, Ceremos of Necrad – you shall become a new Wraith Knight like thy cousin Acraist, a rotting horror in a coffin of steel, existing only to kill. Think on Ersfel, and know that all the lives in that place would not quench such a thirst for even a day."

Tattersoul's voice was thunder, echoing in the confines of the valley. The ancient stones quivered, and sparks kindled in the heights. Harlow drew his sword an inch from its sheath, bright metal catching the firelight.

Ceremos stood there, like a rabbit before a wolf, eyes wide and scared. Then, drawing up all his courage, he said: "You can't know my future."

Tattersoul laughed. "No, I cannot *know*. That's the dirty secret of oracles – we deal in likelihoods. Any elf who's dependent on mortal blood is *likely* to do harm, no matter the circumstances."

He reached under the table, and took out an old game board, chequered in scratched gilt and discoloured ivory.

"There are ways to look deeper. Ways to discern the hidden currents and powers that shape the world, and see the forces they exert on you. Shall we?"

He spread a handful of playing pieces across the board. Some were made of silver and gold, and came from a fine game set, far finer than the board they rested on. Their numbers were bolstered by other mismatched tokens: a crudely carved effigy of a fighter, shells and polished stones, a bird's skull.

Ceremos frowned. "I don't know that game. It's not the King's Game that mortals play." He'd played the King's Game as a child, with mortal friends.

"Nor is it the endless game of the elves, where there is no victory or loss, only endless forms. The King's Game is finite; the Elves' game infinite. This—" Derwyn pushed one of the stones into a new square "—is a game of my own devising. In truth, I'm not yet certain of all the rules."

"How does it work?"

"I don't know that either."

"Then what's the point of it?"

"The King's Game is about knights and armies, tactics and strategies. The board is an abstract battlefield, perfectly flat and open. Both sides start with the same array of pieces. A game lasts only a few hours, and at the end, there is a clear victory – or a stalemate. It claims to be a game of war, but war is not like that. The Elves' Game – have you played it?"

"I've seen others in Necrad playing it, but I could never understand the rules."

"You are young," said Derwyn. "Among the elves, it is said to take a century to learn the most basic rules. Lord Bone studied it for a while, before he lost the capacity for play. The Elves' Game is terribly complex – each square on the board has its own properties, its own symbology. There are hundreds of different pieces, each with their own rules, and one piece can be transformed into another. The time of day or night is also a factor – there are moves are permitted only under certain stars. How they cursed my name when the necromiasma blotted out the sky over Necrad!"

He shook his head. "But for all its intricacy, the game is unchanging. It was conceived in the elder days by the first elves, and the rules are fixed. There are infinite positions, but limited possibilities."

"Your game is different, then?"

Derwyn swept the board clean. "An elven vampire takes refuge with a mortal hero? The Everwood without the Erlking? Necrad without Amerith and all the other Firstborn who died in Lord Bone's war? Death walking abroad once more? The old patterns are breaking. What will replace them I do not know."

Ceremos picked up the carved figure of a warrior. Years of handling had rubbed away the fighter's features, leaving it faceless. The sword had once been painted. A few specks of black remained. "Is that supposed to be the Lammergeier?"

"The board and many of the other pieces belonged to my father. But that figure – Thomad made him for me when I was young. I called him the Lammergeier when I played with him, but in truth he doesn't look much like my uncle any more. He could be anyone with a sword." Derwyn took the wooden figurine and placed it at the centre of the empty board. "Games can be tools of divination, too. Go down to the tavern, and a fortune teller will read your future in the cards. What goes with this?"

Ceremos grabbed a handful of the other pieces at random and

set them on the board. The bird's skull leered back at him, and he set it down hastily. It was not for him, that was certain. Another of the other pieces he'd chosen was a heavy thing of gold – the tower piece, the stalwart defender in the King's Game.

The third thing in his hand was a snail shell. He went to brush it away, but Derwyn stopped him.

"It has a place on the board, too, does it not?"

"It's disgusting," Ceremos protested. It reminded him of a dead Pitspawn he'd once seen in Necrad, huge and hollowed out by rot. Still, he put it on the board next to the tower.

"Another," said Derwyn.

Ceremos picked a fourth piece from the pile. It was heavier than the rest, and ancient. The long years weighed upon it. It was Necrad-made, elf-work in silver. A woman with a crown of antlers, her features serene and cruel.

The Skerrise stared back at him across the aeons.

I've escaped you, he thought.

Even in miniature, there were the faintest suggestions of a vampire's fangs, but that said little about how old the figure was. The Skerrise was of the first generation of the elves; so old she had lived aeons before becoming a vampire. She'd first drunk the blood of mortals when she'd helped Amerith drive the usurpers from Necrad, eight thousand years ago.

"Place her on the board," said Derwyn.

"I don't want to," said Ceremos. This was more than a game. This valley was a place of power, and the Tattersoul was not wholly mortal. Ceremos could dimly sense forces moving around them, the stars aligning into some new destiny. The chains of prophecy settling around him.

I want to choose my own path.

"Complete the pattern," insisted Tattersoul.

Ceremos reached out – and slammed the piece down with such force that it flipped the board. Derwyn tried to catch it as it toppled,

but succeeded only in catching the metal edge, slashing a red line across his palm. The heavy board crashed to the ground.

Appalled and embarrassed, Ceremos surveyed the devastation. He picked up the game board. It was mostly intact, but it had landed atop the pieces, smashing them all. Fragments of bird skull and snail shell, in the midst of them the two halves of the Skerrise – and there was the Lammergeier, shattered, his wooden sword snapped.

He'd broken the Lammergeier.

A sixth piece, too, had fallen, but was so buried in the earthen floor of the hut that he couldn't tell what it was. Ceremos bent to pick up the fallen hero – then froze.

The smell filled his nostrils.

Blood dripped from the mortal's wounded hand.

He's never heard such noise, such excitement, in all his short life. Shouts echoing through the Liberties, cries of outrage. The League are attacking! The League are attacking! Ceremos knows the League – the League are the humans and dwarves who live on the far side of the Garrison wall. The League are the dwarves who patrol the streets, and make everyone stay inside. The League are fire and terror.

The League, he knows. This is something different.

Excitement gives him courage, and he slips his father's hand and darts out of the door. A gaggle of Vatlings coming down the street – perfect! Ceremos slithers through the middle of the group, their slimy skin aiding his passage. Andiriel tries to stop him, but Ceremos is too fast – no one can catch him! He races towards the House of the Horned Serpent, eager to see—

He never sees. One moment he's running, and then he's on the ground, the dreadworm atop him, long claws scissoring through his belly. No pain, no time for pain, because he can feel himself falling. The dreadworm fades, the crowds fade, but the city is still there. Necrad, his Necrad, the street empty. He's alone as he dies.

But then – he's not alone. They come for him, issuing in great processions from their ancient palaces. Hosts arranged by house, by constellation. He can

see them now for the first time. He can see them as Grandmother Amerith sees them. Not the wraiths that haunt the corners, but glorious elf-lords as they were in the first blush of creation, knights of the dawn riding out into the world. They are a wonderful sight. Is it so bad to die, when there is such company on the other side?

The wind — the wild and bitter wind of the wraith-realm — howls. Terrible storms scour the marble canyons of Necrad; the city offers only a little shelter from the maelstrom. The other wraiths scatter. Utter terror grips Ceremos now, infinitely worse than any pain could ever be. The winds will catch him and hurl him into the void, and he'll be lost for ever.

He does not want to die.

He does not want to leave. Not yet.

Then: the blood.

The Lammergeier's blood. Alf's bleeding hand pressed to the child's lips.

It tastes of the living earth. Forests sprout on his tongue. Roots spread through his stomach. It tastes of the sea, salty and fierce, waves rolling in and out.

It is life.

He wants more.

Ceremos turned and fled from the hut, running blind out into the night. The foxfire lights illuminated the path up out of the valley. He could run that way, run west until he reached the edge of the High Moor. He'd descend to the Mulladales, to the villages and farms, to the brimming mortal lands.

More, cried the thirst. The smell of Derwyn's blood filled his nostrils.

He flung himself to the earth, clung to the ground, buried his face in it. The hunger tore at him like a flaying whip, each heartbeat a welt of pain in his belly. He clawed at the ground, burrowing like a beast, sinking his fingers into the soil of the valley as if he could dig deep enough to find the currents of earthpower.

He lay there until Olva found him.

CHAPTER EIGHT

While her son spoke to Ceremos, Olva waited outside, stamping to keep her feet warm. The Valley of the Illuminated One was sheltered by steep cliffs, but the cold still found its way in. Ceremos' father had the right of it, when he'd called this place *exposed*. There was nothing to shield you from judgement here, nothing to hide behind.

Olva did not like that. Ersfel, now, that was properly sheltered, nestled in its own little valley, walled in by trees. You could hide in Ersfel, be no one there. No Significant Capital Letters for Ersfel's valley. Hells, the village was so small it barely warranted a name.

She could hear Ceremos and Derwyn talking inside the tent, but couldn't make out the words.

She did not like the vampire's talk of the Skerrise either, or Necrad. The Skerrise's ascent was not Olva's fault – not wholly, anyway. But Olva had helped. She'd turned to the ancient warlord in her time of need, reopened the Sanction, allowed the Witch Elves to rearm. At the time, twenty years ago, it had all seemed so *necessary*, if not wise. She'd known, even then, that she was storing up trouble for the future.

Silly old woman, she told herself, *might as well blame yourself for autumn turning into winter. You're not so great that the fate of the world*

turns on your choices. Not even Widow Queens of Necrad matter that much. Nine didn't save the world, nor can One threaten it. Not alone. Listen to the stories, and you'd think that the great heroes did it all alone, shaped the tale all by themselves and their choices. But they were just the tip of the plough of history cutting through the earth. The world was too large for a single person's actions to direct it, or a single failing to break it.

"Deeds worthy of song!" shouted Ceremos inside the tent, in response to some question from Derwyn. "I would do such things!"

Olva stomped away. Once or twice on the journey she'd found herself almost liking the vampire – or, more perilous, forgetting what he was. *All things have a time, even elves. All things end, and it's wrong to prolong them beyond their span.* The earthpower taught that in its cycles and seasons, and there was a mercy there.

Suddenly, there was a shout of pain – Derwyn's voice – from inside the tent, and a bestial yowl! Ceremos burst out of the hut and went running blindly across the valley, racing on all fours like a startled cat.

Olva rushed inside. She pushed past Harlow, her face storm-dark, and knelt by Derwyn. "Did he hurt you?"

Her son laughed. "I cut my hand on a gaming piece. Hardly a mortal wound."

Olva cradled his hand and worked a healing spell. The currents were sluggish in the valley, and the spell had little potency. Derwyn gently tugged free from her grasp.

"I can do nothing for Ceremos. He's too restless to find healing here."

"But he can't stay in Ersfel!"

"You're not staying in Ersfel, either."

Olva bristled. "Aye – your damned uncle's going to fetch that damned sword, and there's no stopping him. I have to go with him to keep him out of trouble – and I've already got to drag a poor apprentice along. I can't mind both of them *and* watch an elf, Der. It's too much."

"You travelled with an elf before," he said. "Take Ceremos with you." He stooped to pick up the broken pieces of a figurine. "Everything's adrift – the old order of things is broken, but the new one hasn't formed yet. Now is the time of monsters. Powers walk abroad in the land. *He* longs to be one of them, and some nights it's all I can do to keep him restrained." He held up the snapped remains of a once-black sword. "Whoever sent that message – I think they're right. The Spellbreaker should be wielded by a worthy hand."

Olva nodded. "Alf will find it. You know what he's like when a duty's laid on him. He'd walk through the Grey Lands if he had to."

"It's in our family's blood," said Derwyn, with a sad smile. "Go to him quick, and be wary, Mother. What's coming is too much for any of us to endure alone."

He embraced her, his slim shoulders reminding her of Galwyn for a moment. He was older now than Galwyn had ever been, this ragged hermit who'd been pawn and king, this agieng man with grey in his beard who'd been her baby son. Torun once spoke of the wheel of fate that lifts up the fortunate for a while before they hurtle down one more, but Olva perceived now that there were other wheels in the grand mechanism of the cosmos. Wheels at right angles to fortune, where one might be spun off into unlikely realms. She had never intended to end up here, old skin draped across mutable bones. This was not the life she'd expected, but she was here and she would live it.

Derwyn squeezed her elbows. "May the Road carry you home."

She looked back at him as she walked off towards the young vampire, but only once.

She found the vampire lying shivering on the ground, pressing his face into the earth as if trying to hide from the starry sky.

"Get up, lad. There's nothing here for you. We're going back to Ersfel."

Ceremos wiped dirt from his pale face. "Truly?"

"Aye. My son says you're still my problem, so listen — I know how treacherous your kind can be. I allied myself with vampires in Necrad, and it was one of the worst mistakes I've made in my life. I'll be watching you, understand? You give me any cause to doubt you—"

"Never!" Ceremos scrambled to his knees. "I am not the Skerrise, or Acraist, or any you have known! I swear to you, Widow Queen, that I shall not betray your trust! Give me a sword, that I might swear upon it!"

"I don't hold with oaths. Just do as I say. I tell you to stay, you stay. I say heel, you heel." She helped him up. "Think of yourself as my dog, aye?"

The Mulladales welcomed Olva home with a rush of power, and she fought the urge to catch the east wind and fly. The crane-dream of silver lakes, fair and free, rose in her. She pushed it aside and let Ceremos take the lead as they descended the steep and trackless hills west of the Moor. The Road swept away north-west of them, and once she caught a flash of light in the distance that she guessed was the sun reflecting off Tern's Tower. The Fossewood lay off that way, where she'd first touched magic. Bor had warned her of that forest, and he was right to do so — ancient ghosts still walked under the trees, but she now knew the spells to placate them. She'd meant to bring Perdia up there, give her a glimpse of the ancient, fragmented tradition of the earthpower.

As they travelled, though, it became harder for her to feel the currents and listen to the lands. Worries about the journey crowded her mind. A letter to Torun, too, to let her know that Olva wouldn't be at home in Ersfel for a long time. (Maybe they would pass through the Dwarfholt on the way north.) Tell Thomad to mind the farm, again, and this time she'd leave a little money to help. Old Elcon wouldn't last the winter — she should say farewell to him before they left. Get Alf to lay in a stock of firewood, in case they came back

in the dead of winter. A hundred things to do before the journey, a hundred human worries.

And one elven. What would they do on the Road if the vampire hungered?

On they went, her crane-foot weary, her back aching – and so many miles to go before the journey even really began.

One night, she woke gasping for breath. A shadow had startled her awake. She could see it blotting out the stars as it passed.

"Dreadworms," whispered Ceremos. "Three of them. There are more off to the west."

The worms circled, high above the hills. Olva crouched, digging her hands into the dirt, reaching for the earthpower, but all at once the winged horrors turned and vanished into the clouds. Something had startled them.

"Who were they?"

"I don't know," said Ceremos. "They have already passed beyond my sight."

She lay back down and tried to find sleep again, but her heart was beating fast and her head full of hoofbeats.

The next day, they walked with renewed urgency. They'd passed back into settled lands, regions Olva knew well.

Ceremos sniffed the air, like a dog scenting prey. "I smell smoke."

So did she, now.

A black column on the western horizon.

Ersfel.

She's crane-shape before she knows it, wings hammering the sky, devouring the last miles with desperation. Ceremos cries out behind her, but she's left language behind, her only voice a crane's croak of alarm. The forest a green rush below, the beautiful summer evening sky a chasm.

Ersfel. Ersfel's burning. She went away, she left home, she wasn't here. If only she'd been there, maybe maybe.

Which of them is dead? How many? She lands on the village green, casting off bird-form in front of everyone. The grass crackles with frost – frost, in summer, but she can't think about that. Villagers all around her now, a dozen fragments of the same confused story told at once. The old fear catches her, the terror that some catastrophe would strike here at the heart of her world.

"What happened? What happened?"

It's Cerlys who finds the words. She runs forward, furious and indignant, eyes red-rimmed – from the smoke or weeping, who's to say?

"They attacked last night. Alf saved us. They were going to kill us all, but he stopped them. Him and the elf." She points away south, down the Road. Hoofmarks churn the frost-silvered mud. "Riders took him."

CHAPTER NINE

Distant cries of alarm, from the south of the village. Hoofbeats. Steel on steel. War had come to Ersfel and Alf's doorstep.

He took a deep breath, tasting the air for the time in years. And then he was off, at as much of a run as he could manage. Ildorae outpaced him in an instant, racing down the lane and vanishing into the dusk. Off across the fields, a few outriders milled around the cottages. Red flames violated twilight as one set fire to the thatch. Perdia's face, pale in the doorway.

"Hide in the woods!" roared Alf, and he ran after Ildorae. He came around a bend and saw the village.

The battlefield.

Riders had come up the southern Road, that much was clear. Ersfel had no wall or defensive earthworks, so they'd ridden straight into the heart of the village — *like they did at Hayhurst* — expecting the villagers to scatter in terror.

But Alf's training had given them courage. "Loose!" came the cry — Cerlys' voice — and the whistle of arrows. Cerlys and her archers had taken to the lower slopes of the holywood, and made the green red with the blood of fallen horses and riders. Flight after flight turned the south end of the village into a killing ground. Some riders had retreated out of range, others had scattered east and west

or sheltered in buildings. There was fighting in the lanes – there was Remilard, dead in a ditch, sightless eyes staring at Alf.

Not Remilard. Kivan.

Fury rose up in Alf, a raging rush of violence. Old instincts took him, freezing that fiery wrath into something cold and hard, transmuting bone and nerve. He picked up Kivan's spear and waded in. A raider near Selcloth's house. Off balance, distracted. Alf thrust, putting his full weight behind it. Caught the man in the neck. The spear went up through the jaw, the soft palette. Dead. He pulled the spear free. The wrench of ligaments parting.

Next.

Thunder of hoofbeats from the right, charging across the green. Splashes of soft mud, then the clatter on the stone-strewn path. He hurled the spear at the perfect moment, the weapon leaving his hand just as horse and rider emerged from behind Kivan's house.

The horse ran on, the rider fell.

Not dead. Stunned, winded, but still alive.

With a groan, Alf picked up the spear. The fallen rider closed his eyes, anticipating the blow. Did he know, in that moment, that the Lammergeier stood over him? That the same hand that ended the reign of two great Kings would also end his life?

Slowly, Alf raised the spear.

He paused, the battle-fury draining from his weary limbs. He'd had his fill of killing long ago.

Cerlys ran past him, she and the other archers he'd trained to defend Ersfel. She stooped in passing, barely breaking stride, and drove her knife through the rider's throat. "Come on," she shouted, "they're fleeing!"

The riders had, indeed, fled.

But most had not gone far.

For Ildorae Ul'Ashan Amerith, Goddess of the Hunter's Star, Dreadknight of the Horned Serpent stood athwart the southern Road.

Frost gathered about her like a banner, and the Road became slick with ice, an avalanche of horseflesh tumbling about her. She danced amid the carnage, laughing, her spear a blood-tipped icicle. Riders hewed desperately at her, but they might as well have tried to hold back the course of winter. Death was all around them, and their doom was written in the stars.

Cerlys and her archers formed another line at the edge of the village, ready to loose again if needed, but none escaped the Witch Elf's wrath.

When the last rider fell, Cerlys cried, "That's not all of them! Some got past us!" and pointed towards the cottages.

Ildorae laughed and said, "Then the sport is not over!" She cast aside her helm and raced away through the trees, her silver hair like an aurora. And Cerlys and her companions ran after her, eager as a pack of hounds.

And thus, the first attack of the riders was repelled from Ersfel.

Alf stayed in the village and saw to the wounded. Three at least were dead. Another half-dozen missing in the woods. Alf set himself to binding wounds and setting broken limbs. He'd done enough butchery over the years to make a passable healer. They lit bonfires on the green, and the leaping light made Ersfel strange in Alf's sight. He'd never seen the village like this before, in the aftermath of a battle. There were yuletide pageants lit by firelight every year, costumed mummers pretending to be slain Witch Elves and Pitspawn, but afterwards they'd leap up and join the feast. Not tonight.

The mood was strange, too, especially when Ildorae and the others returned, bloodied and bright-eyed. It became a fierce celebration, a triumph after war. Ildorae was the heroine of the hour – a day ago, she'd been a monster lurking in the wood, and now she was feted. The Witch Elf welcomed the adulation. It was familiar to her. Alf caught sight of Cerlys staring in wonder at Ildorae, and it put him in mind of an old woman he'd briefly met in the Cleft of Ard. She had been a

secret servant of the Witch Elves, the last of a cult going back count-less generations. Ildorae had cultivated that cabal; now she sowed seeds in Ersfel. In generations to come, would Cerlys' great-great-grandson go into the woods and make offerings to the silver ones?

He saw Perdia, too, sitting with Thomad and his wife, their faces smeared with soot. She'd fled with them into the woods when the raiders attacked, and hid until Ildorae and Cerlys reached them.

A cart rolled past Alf, wheels crunching the frosted ground. A cart for the slain, dead raiders piled high. Alf stared at the turning wheels rather than look at the corpses. Someone slapped him on the shoulder, declared he'd saved the village by teaching the youngsters how to fight. And, damnation, he was proud of that, if nothing else. None of them had Alf's old strength or speed – neither did he, these days – but he'd taught them well.

Lammergeier said another voice, and familiar faces looked at him with new eyes.

A day ago, he'd been looking forward to going back on the Road. Every time he'd gone away, he'd gone knowing that Ersfel was behind him, safe and solid and unchanging. Even when he'd gone with the Nine, it had been to keep his little village safe. Or was that a lie? It was so long ago he couldn't remember how he'd felt then. Had he been eager to leave the cramped little lives of this place behind? The last time he'd talked to Jan, he'd complained about how no one in Ersfel could have possibly understood what he'd seen and done on the quest.

I should stay, he thought. *I'm needed here. Let the wider world attend to itself.*

The wheel turned. The limp limb of a corpse flopped over the side. *Lath is dead*, but there would be no prophetic dreams heralding the passing of that nameless raider.

Ildorae sat down beside him, face flushed with Genny Selcloth's strongest ale. "Always so dour, Lammergeier! I used to think it was the burden of the sword that weighed upon you."

"But you can kill and be merry, eh?"

"I kill and make merry. I sing despite my tears. High I build the spires of my temples, where I am a goddess. Wild I run in the wood, and tender am I in the bedchamber. Eternity is long enough to hold all things."

"Aye, well, I don't have so much time left." He thought for a moment. "Can I change that boon?"

"What do you desire?"

"Come with us. Olva and me." Unlike Ceremos, Ildorae was worldly-wise enough to avoid attention. She didn't need blood to stay alive. And her dreadworm had survived the crossing – she and Alf could fly, and Olva could keep up in bird-form. They could be in the Neverwood within a week. And carrying Spellbreaker would be a lot easier if he only had to bear the sword for a few days.

Tell the Lammergeier that Blaise has need of him for one last service. Tell him to bring his sword.

The Nine had called, and he would always answer.

"Where are you bound, mortal?"

"A long journey," he said, suddenly wary about saying too much. But Ildorae's eyes flashed at the prospect.

"You seek the Spellbreaker. What will you do with it?" She caught his arm, took his wrinkled hand. "Who will you pass it onto when you are done? An elf had that blade before you."

"It's mine to bear," said Alf, snatching his hand back. It was an instinctive response. He hadn't carried the sword in decades.

"The power of the sword—" began Ildorae, then she fell silent. She peered out into the darkness beyond the firelight. "More riders. Many more."

"Form up!" shouted Alf. "Like we trained! Quick now!" The villagers stumbled about in the dark. Some were drunk, others still reeling from the earlier attack. Cerlys and a few more could still fight, but not many. Not enough to hold the Road.

"Do not fear, mortal," whispered Ildorae. "I shall defend you." She stepped forward and scratched a line in the mud of the Road. "None shall cross this and live."

Alf could see nothing in the dark, but he could hear approaching hoofbeats.

"What do you see? How many?"

"Two dozen. But they are more worthy than the rabble I slaughtered earlier. Household knights, I'd guess."

"What banner?"

"A red stag crowned—"

"That's Ilaventur."

"—and a black sword."

"That's . . ." Alf's own sigil was a black bird bearing a black sword.

"Their captain approaches," said Ildorae, adjusting her grip on her spear. "He is mighty indeed."

A ghost rode out of the darkness.

The warrior was broad, his large frame augmented by the heavy plate he wore. Charmstones glowed on his breastplate. His features were hidden by a helm, but Alf recognised this stranger.

"Duna?" The rider's appearance and manner reminded him instantly of his old friend, Earl Duna of the New Provinces. But Duna was long dead.

The rider's gaze flickered for a moment towards Alf, then returned to Ildorae.

"Witch Elf," growled the rider, "blessed indeed am I to meet you by chance on the Road." He raised his right hand, and the polished metal gleamed red in the firelight. An artificial hand, dwarf-forged by the look of it, given unnatural life and animation by magic.

Behind him, his knights took up the cry. "IRONHAND! IRONHAND! IDMAER IRONHAND!"

Ildorae swaggered forward. "I remember you, whelp. I took your hand. And when you dared to make war on Necrad, I helped take your realm. For my third pick, I'll take your head and be done with you."

"Idmaer," said Alf, stepping forward. "You know me. I was a friend to your parents." For a moment, he imagined the face beneath the helm, the face of the young man who'd knelt before him at the feast in Castle Duna. *Your deeds inspire us, lords.*

"The Lammergeier?" rumbled Idmaer. "At last. At last! Truly this fate was shaped by the Intercessors." He pointed at Alf. "Spare him. Keep the rest back." He began to dismount. "But first, the elf."

Behind Alf, a bowstring sang. Cerlys' aim was masterful, the arrow flying straight and true at Idmaer's visor. But the iron hand moved quicker than the eye could follow, and slapped it from the air. Idmaer glared at Cerlys. "I shall not forget that, child. There is a reckoning for all things, in the end."

"But I," said Ildorae, stepping between Cerlys and Idmaer, "am counted among the endless."

"We shall see," said Idmaer.

He stepped over the line.

Sudden choking smoke engulfed them all, as Ildorae's frost magic quenched all the bonfires. Idmaer's sword blazed white. Alf had seen that sword before, long ago – the Brightsword of the Rangers, the sword named Secret Flame. At the Battle of Harnshill, Alf had slain the Captain of the Rangers and taken the sword as a prize. He'd last seen it in Lord Brychan's treasure hoard.

Now the Brightsword struck at Ildorae, wielded by Idmaer's iron hand.

She circled her foe, the spear probing his defences and forcing him to shelter behind his massive shield. Darkness was her cloak – she was visible only when the sword flashed, only when Idmaer parried or struck at her in vain. He was a man duelling a hundred dancing

shadows. Once, long ago, Alf had watched young Idmaer and his brother Dunweld fight a chained ogre, tormenting the poor creature. Idmaer was the ogre here, mighty but slow.

Twice more Ildorae struck at her foe. Each time the spear glanced off the shield, but the second strike was closer to the steel rim. The third blow was the charm, for she had sounded out Ironhand's defences, tested the limits of mortal reactions, mortal sinews. She drove her spear towards his heart, the attack angled just so to avoid the edge of his shield.

He dropped the Brightsword and caught the shaft with his iron hand, holding it just below the spearhead. Metal scraped on metal — she'd struck his breastplate at least, and might have penetrated even deeper if he had not seized the spear. A grunt of pain, echoing dismay from Idmaer's knights.

Ildorae spoke a word of power, and ice magic twined along the shaft, coiling like blue serpents and biting at her foe's hand. Any other might have been overcome by the agony of their flesh freezing solid, but Idmaer gripped the spear with a hand of iron, and he tore it from Ildorae's grasp.

And the elf laughed. She dived between Idmaer's legs, and came up holding the Brightsword.

"Mortal child, this day I will be glad to slaughter you." She had the sword, while Idmaer's iron hand was frozen solidly to the spear-shaft so he could not drop it. It was ungainly, absurd, a dagger with a five-foot haft that scraped through the mud.

Ildorae twirled the Brightblade, enjoying her enemy's plight. She glanced at Alf. "Tell me, Lammergeier, is this the best that mortals—"

Idmaer flung his shield at her. It caught Ildorae in the face. She fell, and Idmaer was on her in an instant. He slammed his iron fist into the ground, splintering the spear-shaft, leaving only the blade and a few inches of ice-encrusted haft stuck to his hand. He used the broken spear as a crude weapon, driving it into Ildorae's belly over and over.

For an instant, Alf saw the Witch Elf's wraith as it slipped free of her broken shell.

Then the light from the Brightsword faded, and she was gone.

With grim determination, Cerlys let fly again. Her arrow did not find its mark, but that sign of defiance rallied the defenders of Ersfel. More arrows sang, and men ran forward into the darkness with spears and clubs. Idmaer's horsemen, though, were no rabble of Rootless, coin-hungry brigands, and were undismayed by the sudden assault. Most wheeled about, forming up for a charge. A few knights dismounted and advanced on foot to guard Idmaer from the villagers' attack. He saw Thomad's son Jon carrying Perdia away from the front line, the girl bleeding from a head wound. Another villager fell, and another, overwhelmed by the might of the armoured foes.

Idmaer's the key. Take him! thought Alf. Ildorae had wounded him, perhaps badly. And the fallen Brightsword was closer to Alf than to Ironhand. *Move!*

Alf lunged forward, scrabbling for the sword, reaching it at the same time as the younger man. They wrestled in the mud, while all around them was thunder and chaos, hoofbeats and screams and the flash of magic. Alf got his fingers around the Brightsword's hilt — and then Idmaer's iron hand, still bitterly cold, clamped down. Pain shot through Alf's arm, and he let go.

The night exploded into stars and spun around him. Darkness within and without. A blow to the side of his head. The moment of shocked awareness before the pain reached him.

But not a killing blow. The flat of the blade.

Not a killing blow.

Frozen mud all around. Where Ildorae had died.

Idmaer rose, and the Brightsword was a sharp shard of sunlight in his iron hand. Alf tried to rise, and two of Idmaer's knights grabbed him and threw him down again. His hand brushed against the remains of Ildorae's spear.

A herald brought up Idmaer's horse, and a flask of healing potion. Idmaer drank deep. Behind him, his knights were arrayed for the charge. They'd crash through the defenders of Ersfel, trample them in the mud. *Run*, thought Alf, *hide in the woods!* But they stood firm in the face of doom.

Idmaer raised the blazing sword.

Had you not abandoned me, wielder, you would have the strength to defend them. But you put me aside, and so you shall be crushed beneath the wheel of fortune.

Alf struggled up. "Idmaer!" he called through broken lips. "Spare 'em. Or I'll . . . " He put the tip of the broken spear to his throat, pressing it hard enough to draw blood. *Spare the Lammergeier*, Idmaer had said. If they wanted Alf alive, they'd have to choose between him and Ersfel.

The Miracle Knight looked down at Alf from a great height. He was very grand in his armour.

Long ago, after they'd slain Lord Bone, Alf had wandered the streets of Necrad in a daze, too broken even to weep. Half-mad, lost, blasted and witless. The sword scraping against his mind like a needle in the skull. Walking in search of death. Then he'd come across Duna, Idmaer's father, so overburdened with booty from the sack of the city that Alf couldn't help but laugh. Duna had thrown down that absurd pile of treasure and roared his head off, too. He'd embraced his friend and led Alf back to the healers and the remnants of the Nine, his booming laugh echoing off the towers.

Idmaer had the same laugh.

"Friends!" he shouted. "We have what we sought!"

Then he cantered over and kicked Alf in the face. Night fell on the Lammergeier.

PART TWO

Alf lay on a cold floor. He opened his eyes, and found that he was in a tower of solid ice. There was a single arched window in the chamber, and a doorway leading to a staircase. He crossed to the window, and looked out over the endless, primal Wild Wood, blanketed in virgin snow. The world was young and unmarred, and so was he.

The black bird fluttered to land on the windowsill.

"Another fucking dream."

"Not a dream," she said.

"What, then?"

She cocked her head. "A story, maybe."

Alf leaned over the windowsill and felt the bone-biting cold of the ice on the palms of his hands.

"Doesn't feel like a story or a dream. Feels real. What's the difference, anyway?"

"Between a tale and a dream? A tale only makes sense when told properly, one thing leading to another, irrelevant things filleted out. A dream is what's scraped from the brain after the day's labours, old things and new mixed together without reason. It might feel like it makes sense when you're dreaming it, but afterwards it all fades away."

"And reality?"

Death croaked, as if unwilling to answer.

"Where's this, then? The Grey Lands?"

"This is the Tower of Ice," said Death, "where I am imprisoned."

"A memory, yeah? That all happened years and years ago."

"Many thousands of years."

Far, far below, at the foot of the tower, Alf could see a ring of stone dragons, just like the ones that guarded the walls of Necrad. Gouts of fire sent up clouds of steam. Tiny figures, smaller than ants to Alf's eyes, fled before their wrath.

"Who's down there?"

"My children," said Death. "The fathers and mothers of humanity. The elves cast them out to roam naked in the woods. They are drawn to me." She tapped her beak against the ice. "I sense their sacrifice. Through their deaths, I find the earthpower. I break this prison and make war upon the Firstborn. But not yet."

"Why am I here? Have you got another message for me, or a prophecy or something?" Alf frowned. "Or am I dead?"

"Not yet," said Death.

"If you're going to show up in cryptic dreams," complained Alf, "then could you bring Gundan back? He hated mystic nonsense as much as I do."

"Dwarves are not within my domain," said Death. "And this is not a dream."

"Feels like a dream. Certainly doesn't seem like it's following on from what went before."

The bird swivelled her head to stare at Alf, or past him. "Just because you lack the wit to understand the tale being told does not make it less of a tale."

"Bloody rude of you. I should tell your father. Show respect to your elders."

"Enough."

"What's the point of telling me a tale if I don't understand it?"

"The tale's not for you. We're eavesdropping." The bird fluttered to the top of the door. "This way. And step lightly, please. My father always said you walked like an iron golem."

"Now there was a good man for mystic portents. Should have brought him instead."

"He would not come," said Death, half to herself. "Now, follow. I would hear an untold story."

She led him through the shimmering corridors and stairs of the Tower of Ice. They climbed silently to the very summit of the spire. There was a great sphere of ice, and in the heart of the sphere slumbered a woman. She was frozen, suspended in crystal.

Before her stood the Erlking, as he was in the youth of the world, tall and unwearied, and all the light of the heavens was in his eyes. He wore a crown of silver, studded with gemstones.

Behind the Erlking were eight other elves. Some, Alf recognised. Their garb and manner may have been different, but the faces were unchanged. Amerith, the same star-jewel on her forehead that she'd wear countless centuries in the future. The Skerrise, clad in furs, an antlered headdress, bare feet streaked with mud and blood. She bore a bloody spear in her hand. Fresh from the hunt. Galarin Ancient-of-Days, in his youth. Oloros — last time Alf had seen that face, it was the instant before Thurn smashed it with an axe. Ancients before they were ancient.

They watched as the Erlking ran his hands over the surface of the imperishable crystal prison, checking for the smallest blemish. He found none. He turned to his companions and bowed like a singer expecting applause.

"This is a waste of power," said the Skerrise scornfully. "We have foes aplenty in the dark to contend with — why squander effort on this?"

"Do you not see what I have wrought?" said the Erlking. "Death will never find us! Our time shall never be cut short!" And Death perched on Alf's shoulder in the shape of a bird and watched.

"Death," said the Skerrise, "is only for beasts. And your ill-made spell spawned scores of them. They breed in the woods, and I cannot cull them fast enough. I tire of this. Unmake them, and be done with it."

"To unmake them would unbind death," said the Erlking. "And until I understand the nature of death, I cannot defeat it. It will come for us."

"When the world ends," said Galarin.

"Aeons hence, perhaps. But we must prepare."

"You all fret too much!" said Oloros. "But, my friend, if this work brings you comfort, so be it. There is time enough for folly."

"Amerith?" said the Erlking. "You above all must see the worth of this?"

Even though he knew this was only a dream of long, long ago, even though he'd been there when Amerith finally died at Daeroch Nal, still Alf flinched when her gaze passed over time. Thousands of years hence, that elf would be known as the Oracle, and have a place in Lord Bone's court. Of all living beings, her sight was keenest.

Did she somehow see him across the gulf of time, across the many worlds?

"It troubles me to see your genius put to the forging of chains. It speaks of fear. The world will surprise you, no matter how much you try to master all things."

The Erlking's smile became fixed and hard.

"At least you admit genius."

"Genius ill-used amounts to naught in the end," replied Amerith, meeting his glare.

"The city!" interrupted Oloros, hastily. "It is Necrad that will secure the future, and it shall yield up all the fruits of creation. It is the city that is testament to your genius. Not this. Let us return to our home and forget this cold place."

"Forget?" Amerith shook her head. "Not in Necrad."

The elves turned, and walked away in a direction Alf could not

name. The room *doubled*, as if another image was being refracted through the translucent ice. Alf glimpsed a magnificent city bathed in rose-gold light, a city of wide boulevards and topless towers.

Necrad. Necrad in the sunlight, as he'd never seen it.

The assembled elves passed, impossibly, from tower to city with a single step. The doubling ended.

"A Straight Road," said Death. She emerged from their hiding place at the back of the room and looked up at her past incarnation. "I did not know they had mastered such tricks in the elder days."

Alf rested his forehead against the cooling ice. Even if this was a dream in which he was a good few years younger than his actual age – or thousands upon thousands of years ago – then somewhere out there was his real body, and his real body had taken a beating. The ice felt good on his face.

The dream of his face.

The story of his face.

The magic nonsense of his face.

"How does that work," he asked, "if this is your story?"

"It's not my tale, nor it is meant for mortals. Other powers walk abroad. That is why you are here – so that I can see through your eyes and know my enemies. You are a mask for me, hiding my presence from the Erlking. Even here, he could unmake me, as you warned." Talis stroked the ice globe. "Since the moment he first clothed me in flesh, we have wrestled. Our long war has shaped the world."

She turned to Alf. "Now he and I are both in exile. He has lost his kingdom, and I am trapped in a mortal life. Other powers are moving, seeking advantage in the eternal war between the Firstborn and my children. Jan warned you of this."

"When did she – wait, you mean twenty fucking years ago? That's what that prophecy was about?" Alf clenched his fists. "Damned bloody mystic nonsense! Dreams and portents and eldritch sigils and . . . wizard shit!" Death fluttered up to perch on the globe.

"I told you to stay clear of it!" shouted Alf. "I told you to let it go, and just live your life! Her life, Talis' life!"

"All lives are lived in the shadow of power. Power can snuff them out, and power can shield them. Neither she nor you can hide your face from this truth."

"Fuck me," said Alf. "I don't understand any of this. I don't understand what you've shown me. I just want one answer from you, little grandmother, and for pity's sake make it a simple yes or no. My friend, Blaise – Ceremos escaped Necrad with a message from him, but Ildorae says she was there when Blaise was slain. I don't give a damn about your prophecies and visions, but I'll endure them if you answer me this: is Blaise alive?"

"Yes and no."

Alf pulled off his boot and flung it at Death. The bird squawked indignantly.

"Wake me up."

Death preened her ruffled feathers. "In the waking world, you are a prisoner of Idmaer Ironhand, and he has not been gentle."

Alf hobbled across the icy floor to retrieve his fallen boot, or the dream-memory of a boot or whatever it was. Peir was a veteran of mystic visions. Jan or Lath or Blaise would have understood the magic, or the metaphor, or whatever this was.

Gundan would have thrown another boot.

"Well, can you heal me or something?" asked Alf. "You're the most powerful wielder of earthpower ever, aye? Give me some help."

"Talis is far away, uncle. You warned me to go far away, and I did. Your mercy has a price."

"Aye, well." Alf sighed. "Wake me up, then. It's only pain, and that's never stopped me."

"I will see you again," said Death, "before the end."

CHAPTER TEN

Olva walked amid the wounded. Two children, trampled by horses. One was dying, one she could still save. A host of lesser injuries, scratches and cuts and minor wounds that might still become infected, unseen sickness slithering into the flesh. And more coming from Kettlebridge, from Hayhurst, other places where Ironhand's warriors had struck.

Help us, they begged. The Witch of Ersfel has healing magic. Everyone knew that. People came from all over the Mulladales for help.

But only one or two a season. Not all at once.

There were healing spells and songs. She'd sung them in Hayhurst. In Necrad, once, she'd brought Blaise back from the edge of the Grey Lands. She remembered how it felt to reknit the shattered bones of his skull beneath her fingers. But to work magic she had to draw on the earthpower – and sometimes that meant drawing *up* the earthpower, reaching deep into the living soil and dredging up the energies. She was already exhausted, her soul worn thin.

"I need things from my house," said Olva. "Cerlys, you've got quick legs. Fetch everything from the chest in the far corner."

Cerlys looked stricken. "Some of them got past us."

*

The ashes were still warm. Olva stood there, leaning on a stick, watching thin trails of smoke curl like wraiths. Ironhand's raiders had spared the heart of the village, but all the houses on the south side had been destroyed in the initial attack, and they had swept on from there, burning and looting.

Alf would never need to finish that shed roof. The pigsty stood empty.

And the house, the house Galwyn had made for her, all was destroyed. It had been the best house in the village. He'd brought carpenters all the way from Highfield to build it. She'd called it a palace in her innocence when she'd first seen it. She'd been happy there with him, imagined those high ceilings resounding with the laughter of children.

She'd given birth to Derwyn there. Galwyn had died there. She had *lived* there, her whole life contained within those walls. How many evenings had she sat by the fire, listening to the wind creak in the treetops? She knew every inch of that house. Later – later she'd understood that the house was a cage, a move in some grand game, intended to pin the Lammergeier. She and Derwyn had been pieces held in reserve – but the game board had long since been hurled to the floor, and all was in chaos. Everything was thrown down. There was no shape to the world any more. The wheel spun wildly, exalting unworthy men and casting down good souls.

Long ago and far away, she'd lain in the mound at Daeroch Nal, lain atop the bones of Death, and found the green thread of the earthpower. In that vision, she'd risen from Galwyn's grave up in the holywood and come down to this house, and found herself again, sewn her new bones of Olva-the-Changeling into her old skin as Widow-Forster-of-Ersfel. She'd remade herself here, filled the house with relics and talismans of the earthpower. Not the elf-magic of the College Arcane, not the twisted sorcery of Necrad, but mortal magic, earth-magic.

Mountain. River. Sky. Stone. Meat. Blood. Our words. Wild words

for wild magic, Lath had said. Years later, she'd found an answer for him. *Hearth and home, kith and kin.* My words for magic. She'd filled Derwyn's absence with her studies, her own quiet defiance against the legacy of the Erlking.

Now all that was ash, too. All her lives, all her selves, consumed in fire. *I'm old*, she thought suddenly, *too old to rebuild. Too old to start again.* Her bones were weary, the pull of the earth so strong. The crane-shape rose up in her. She craved to leave it all behind, to not think or care any more. She'd fly north to the snow and the silver waters of the wild, and then she wouldn't be here any more.

Cerlys caught her arm — not to support her, but to spin Olva around so the girl could shout in her face. Her voice was the roar of a wounded beast, and it took Olva a moment to hear the words.

"The men who took your brother — they've got three days' head start! You can catch them! You can *fly*, for heaven's sake!"

Alf — Alf would have done just that, if their positions were reversed. If the riders had captured Olva, then Alf would have chased them down the Road. She'd watched him ride away many times.

That wasn't her. She was rooted here. She stooped, her back aching, and took a handful of ash and dirt from what had once been her kitchen.

"Alf knew what he was doing," she said slowly, fighting down the thought of *no, he didn't, he's an idiot, he's always an idiot.* "He protected Ersfel. Don't scorn that."

The Witch of Ersfel turned her back on the ruin of her home and set to work.

Once, during the siege of Necrad, Olva had found herself in a battlefield hospice, helping treat League soldiers wounded by the Wilder. There'd been so many injuries, maimed limbs and broken bodies, spell and spear and arrow and fang. Blood smeared across the marble floor.

She'd brought some healing cordial from Alf's mansion in the Garrison. A few drops of cordial could prevent infection and dull

pain. A full vial could stave off a mortal blow. But there wasn't enough cordial to go around, so Olva had to choose who would live or die, whose wounds would heal cleanly and who'd be left forever marked. At the time, she'd found a nugget of hard, unlikely pride in her actions – *look at me*, she'd thought, *with the courage to make those choices. Look at me, with the courage to look a dying man in the eye and think "I can heal three others with the same amount of cordial it would take to save you. I'm sorry, but I'm doing what's necessary."*

When the last vial of cordial was empty, when the last drop was used, that was it. She told herself that she'd done all she could.

There was no cordial in Ersfel.

Only her healing magic, and the limits of Olva's will.

That night, Olva wrestled with death a dozen times. When the currents ran dry, she hauled up more magic, her soul ranging far afield to redirect energy flows from the Fossewood and the farms of Highfield and the gloomy hills above Kettlebridge. She chanted healing spells until her lips cracked, until all heat seemed to fade from the bonfire, until all colour fled and she walked on the edge of the Grey Lands.

"I can't do any more," she muttered. "Alf. Take me home."

"Your home's burned, Olva," said someone. "And Alf's gone away."

"Oh, aye. Aye. I forgot."

She returned to the work, her gnarled fingers weaving broken flesh, weary soul bolstering flagging spirits.

And no more of those wounded by Idmaer Ironhand's raiders died that night.

They turned Genny's into an infirmary, and it was strange how easily the building shucked its inn-skin and became something else. They laid the wounded of the village on the long benches where only a few hours earlier they'd been celebrating victory. They lit the tale-fire, but the only stories told were moans. Genny's kitchen became a shrine where Olva worked her healing magic. After only a few hours,

it seemed only natural to scatter fresh sawdust over the blood, to fill tin cups with water instead of ale.

Ceremos took one look at the tableau and withdrew, overpowered by the smell of the blood. The streets of Necrad were always pristine, for things from the Pits would lick up any filth or gore. The vampire retreated to the forest edge, his pale face peering from the foliage like a patch of moonlight.

Olva called Cerlys over. "Watch him, would you? Just keep him out of trouble."

"He shouldn't be here."

"Perhaps, but he's here now. Go and keep an eye on him."

"For how long?"

"Until I have an eye to spare myself."

Cerlys had more to say, but Olva had more to do, and doing always won out. Cerlys scowled and strode off, spear in hand, a sentry at the village eaves.

Later, though, she caught Cerlys and the vampire in conversation, duelling with tales of the Lammergeier and other heroes of legend. Ceremos' *I watched Laerlyn fight the Wilder atop the walls of Necrad* was easily parried with *he said I was as good an archer as Laerlyn,* but *the Lammergeier saved my life* was routed from the field by *the Lammergeier killed me and then brought me back.*

Perdia was among the first to be healed, and never left her side after that. Channelling the earthpower to heal wounds was a delicate art, so she could not assist Olva directly, but she was always there to fetch and carry, and see that Olva ate when her strength flagged. Many survivors of Ersfel wept or sat staring while Perdia of Hayhurst toiled quietly. She was further down that dark Road of horror that opens when war touches a place. If anything, the attack on Ersfel had confirmed her inner fears – she would never feel safe again.

She spoke little, but once in a quiet moment she whispered to Olva.

"I tried to change. I thought the wolf could drive them away. I tried to listen, like you said."

"Found her standing around in the middle of the battlefield," chuckled Jon in passing, grin hidden behind a mighty armful of firewood. "Like a scarecrow."

"I've found you standing around often enough," snapped Olva, "when there's work to be done. Go and fetch a pot of water." She shooed Jon away.

Perdia bowed her head in embarrassment. "I couldn't find the earthpower at all. I really couldn't."

That, Olva thought, was a lie. But she let it pass.

"It's like the air of a song. If you're humming it all day long, you won't lose your place in the tune. But if you only hear a snatch of it, you might not recognise the music unless you listen a little longer – or you know the piece by heart. And you were trying to listen in the din of battle, which is hard for anyone. Listen now – can you hear it?"

Perdia shook her head, then frowned. "Very faintly. A distant noise. Like thunder over the Moor. Or . . . or howling, far away."

"I've taken so much power that it's running dry. Keep listening, and you'll hear it grow louder."

"If I'd changed—"

"Then they'd have skewered you, too, no matter what skin you wore. They killed Ildorae – they were beyond any of you. Alf did the only thing that could be done."

A day passed. Two. Three.

Each evening, the earthpower ran thin, wrung out by Olva's demands. Healing was not enough – she drew on all the forgotten charms and enchantments she'd found in old stories or gleaned from twenty years of learning. She tried to work spells spoken of in the tales of King Connac, or the Shepherd-Princes. She wove spells of protection around the remaining houses of Ersfel, and raised defensive walls of earth. She blessed the trampled fields and scattered flocks; in crane-shape she circled the village three times and commanded wind and rain and sun to be gentle that year.

On the third evening, Jon supported her as she limped up the holyhill. There, she poured a handful of ashes from their house on Galwyn's green grave and asked the dead to watch over the living in her stead. A strange certainty filled her whatever happened, Ersfel would survive, and prosper in the years to come. She'd preserved her home and built something good here, and it would outlast her.

She sat by her husband's grave for a while, watching the sun set over the hills, brushing the roofs pink and gold. The trees cast long shadows across the village green.

The ashes of her house still smouldered, a little plume visible only in the slanting light. Over that way, she could see a little hunched figure that must be Thomad, bringing more firewood to Genny's. He walked along the same path that the Nine had taken, all those years ago. Bor had come that way, too, when he'd brought the letter from the false Lammergeier. A dog barked, and she thought of the unseen elf-spirits that had once spied on her.

All the ordinary little moments of her life here, and moments from tales of high adventure, and they were all the same light that evening, as if all of Ersfel was burnished in legend.

There was the old tree in the back field that Alf once cut down. A new sapling grew from the rot of the old stump. One day, the children of Ersfel would play beneath its branches. Would she be remembered then? Alf had no children; she had only Derwyn, and he had none. Their family would end with him. Maybe she'd be remembered in local legend as the Witch, or they'd tell a confused tale about the peasant girl commanded by the spirits to marry a young noble from the Crownland.

She trailed her fingers through the ashes. The sun was setting, and the air growing chill.

She'd leave in the morning.

The jangle of metal woke Olva. She did not know where she was for a moment, and peered around at unfamiliar surroundings. A hard

bench, covered with a blanket; a smoke-stained roof and the smell of spilled beer. Genny Selcloth's alehouse. She could hear Thomad snoring in the shadows of the common room, and others slept huddled together on the floor.

And there, by the embers of the dying fire, was a strange apparition. Red light glimmered on the armour of an elven dreadknight. The figure crept across the room and nudged one of the sleepers awake. The sleeper grumbled and turned over. The armoured intruder swore under her breath.

Olva knew that voice. Cerlys. The girl had taken Ildorae's armour, the punctures and scrapes in the breastplate hastily hammered out. She poked the sleeper with her spear, a Necrad-forged spearhead bound to a shaft of Mulladale birchwood.

"Wake up," whispered Cerlys. "It's time to go."

A shadowy mountain stirred. "It's still dark," Jon grumbled.

"If we wait any longer, we'll never be able to find their trail. They're already days away down the Road."

They're going after Alf, thought Olva. *The sweet, brave idiots.*

Jon unfolded, all awkward elbows and knees, gear clattering as he gathered his pack. Graceless as a dwarf. Cerlys hissed at him.

"Child," called Olva quietly. "What are you doing?"

Cerlys looked up, startled, pinned by Olva's gaze. "I—" She swallowed nervously, then adjusted the unfamiliar weight of the dreadknight's helm. She straightened. "We're going after the Lammergeier. Me and Jon."

Olva shook her head. "You'll get yourselves killed."

"It's better than sitting around waiting for Ironhand to come back. What's the point of you healing everyone if the monster that attacked us is still out there? He has to be stopped."

"Just because Alf taught you how to hold a spear doesn't mean you have to go."

"He's not just Alf. He's the Lammergeier. I learned to fight from the Lammergeier himself." Cerlys knelt before Olva. "You can do

magic and foretell things. Tell me where they went, and I'll find your brother."

She should say no. She should send those foolish children back to bed. Tell Cerlys to put aside her borrowed armour, tell her that nothing but sorrow and suffering awaited her down the Road. And to drag poor, simple Jon with her? It was utterly foolish.

But even if she told them not to go, they'd go. She could see it in their faces – that stupid, stupid courage. That misplaced conviction that they were the special ones, the lucky ones who could outrun fate. She'd seen it in Derwyn, even though the only destinies that had been woven for him were the machinations of Intercessors and the deceits of wizards. There was no destiny, no grand plan, just contested visions. Even Death could admit she was wrong, sometimes.

If the stupid children were lucky, they'd just lose their way and end up hungry and desperate in the wild. More likely, they'd run into Ironhand's rearguard and get killed. There was no way they'd find Alf. *Be sensible*, thought Olva, *Alf saved your lives. Live them, instead of following stupid stories of heroes. It's a terrible thing to be close to a hero.*

Only a few days ago, she'd promised to go with Alf. Then, she'd anticipated a long, cautious journey, two old travellers slowly making their way south. She'd expected to have time to instruct Perdia in using the earthpower safely, to take long detours around dangerous places. Now, it would be a headlong chase, and peril at the end of it.

So be it. *Stupid stories. Stupid old woman.*

Olva pushed aside her blanket. "Go and wake Perdia," she said, yawning, "and fetch the vampire. Tell 'em we're getting an early start."

CHAPTER ELEVEN

South of Ersfel, the Road wound through the hills following the river towards the crossroads at Kettlebridge. Olva knew that region from above and below. By her reckoning, they'd reach Kettlebridge in three days, and the Hayhurst fork was a day beyond that. There was an inn, the Lost Lamb, by an ancient standing stone she always considered to mark the edge of her domain. Four days' travel, and then into the unknown. She'd seen maps of Summerswell when she was Queen of Necrad, and knew that they must pass through Ilaventur and the Eavesland before reaching the Neverwood, but she did not know the way. *Listen to the land,* she told herself, but Ilaventur was planted thick with churches and works of the Wood Elves. The path was far from clear.

She hid those concerns from her young companions. Perdia or Jon walked alongside Olva, and she leaned on them when she grew tired. Cerlys was always ranging ahead, impatient, her cloak thrown back to show off her new armour. As for Ceremos – the elf was rarely on the Road, preferring to stay out of sight amid the trees. He had taken a helm from the pile of gear stripped from the dead riders, and might pass as a mortal at first glance, but anyone who spoke to him would doubtless discern his true nature.

Olva hid other concerns, too – that Cerlys' strange armour would

draw attention, or that Perdia changed the subject whenever Olva offered to teach her more, or that Jon was an amiable dunce who had no idea how far this journey would take them.

Most of all, she worried about the hungers of Ceremos, and that concern she did not bother to hide.

They had their first argument before Kettlebridge. They'd stopped by the river to refill their waterskins and give Olva a chance to catch her breath. Cerlys dipped a cloth in the water to wipe the dust of the Road from her armour.

"That's the armour of a dreadknight," said Ceremos from the shadow of the trees. "You shouldn't be wearing it."

"Better than leaving it to rust." Cerlys polished her vambrace on a corner of her cloak.

"It's not like it's a full suit," added Jon. "The breastplate was full of holes, and I couldn't fix it."

Ceremos crossed his arms. "My father's a dreadknight. He trained for five hundred years before he was worthy of that armour. It should be returned to Necrad."

"Let him come and claim it, then. And while he's at it he can challenge all the knights in Ironhand's retinue who had charmstones and enchanted weapons."

"They should not have taken the magic of the Witch Elves, either."

Cerlys rounded on him. "The Nine *won* that magic when they defeated Lord Bone. It's ours by right of conquest!"

"But it is not yours." Ceremos frowned as he tried to explain himself. "Mortals shall never be elves, nor shall elves be mortal. Firstborn and Secondborn have different natures. You should follow your own path."

"Well, if I could turn into a giant wolf, maybe I'd do that," said Cerlys. Perdia looked away. "But I can't, so I'll even the odds any way I can. The Lammergeier had Spellbreaker, and that made him great."

"Don't talk of what you don't know," muttered Olva.

"Then tell us!" said Cerlys. "The Lammergeier was living in Ersfel all my life, and neither you nor he ever spoke of it! All the times I heard tales of the great deeds of the Nine, or rumours of awful things they'd done — and you knew the truth all along."

"*The Lammergeier* wasn't living in the village. The Lammergeier's a name the poets gave him, and Alf always said it was like his shadow, following him along. He never wanted it, and he left it behind him. You knew *Alf*, not the Lammergeier. None of you have ever known the Lammergeier." She glanced at Ceremos. "That goes for you, too. 'Twas Alf who saved you that day, not the bloody Lammergeier. As for why we never said aught . . . " Olva sat down on the riverbank. "We kept silent with good reason. We had enemies."

"Not in the village. No one would have spoken to outsiders," said Jon.

"Olva's right," said Perdia quietly. "Such things should be kept secret. Look at what happened to Ersfel. They came looking for Alf."

"Only after he stirred things up!" Cerlys jabbed her spear at Ceremos. "It all started after he showed up!"

Olva shook her head. "Ah, child. It all started long, long before you were born." *It didn't start with Ceremos. It didn't start with Bor, or even when Alf went away with Gundan all those years ago. It didn't start when Harn knelt before the Erlking, or when the Old Kingdom fell. It didn't even start when Death crawled out of the Erlking's cauldron. It's just life. There's always someone else at fault, and someone else will one day put the blame on you.*

"I brought warning to the Lammergeier!" Ceremos snarled. "And I was gone long before Ironhand's attack. Had I been there, the day would have gone differently!"

"And what would you have done," spat Cerlys, "that we couldn't?"

"I've a question," said Jon. His voice was grave. They all turned to look at him. "Widow Forster?"

"What is it?"

A long pause, then: "How's the food at the Lost Lamb? My dad said it wasn't bad."

The stupid question was a balm to the fractured company. The younger four could busy themselves setting up camp for the evening, and Olva rested by the river. She washed her aching crane-foot in the cool waters, and it cheered her to think that this stream ran south to join some other river, and that joined another larger flow, on and on like the branches of a tree until they all joined in the Great River. Even if they lost Alf's trail, all they needed to do was follow the waters, and they wouldn't get lost. Listen to the land.

She tried to point that out to Perdia, but the girl rolled over and muttered, "Please, I'm too tired for another lesson."

The gates of Kettlebridge were shut, and sentries patrolled the town. For the first time in many years banners flew above the crumbling little keep. For a copper, a Roadhag told them that the banners belonged to knights from "up Ellscoast way" – clearly, the threat of Ironhand was great enough to stir the Lords into some sort of action. Kettlebridge was not strong enough to withstand a siege, but might dissuade the raiders who'd struck Hayhurst. Olva guessed there'd be more resistance at high-walled Highfield; the wooded hills of the Mulladales were neglected, but Highfield and the green vales around it were more thickly populated. For the last twenty years, she'd welcomed that obscurity and the free hand it gave her. Now, she wished she was Queen of Necrad again, and could dispatch stout soldiers to defend the Mulladales.

The Roadhag also offered to tell Jon's fortune for two silvers. Cerlys dragged Jon away before he squandered all his coin.

After Kettlebridge, Olva expected the Lost Lamb to be closed, but the inn was open – and crowded. "We'll stay the night here," said Olva. "Maybe the last chance we'll have to sleep in a bed for a while."

And I want to have a talk with Perdia.

Cerlys grudgingly removed her elven armour and carefully packed it away. Ceremos lingered by the roadside. There was a hunger in his face that Olva didn't like as he looked towards the lights of the Lamb. He began to put on his helmet, but Olva stopped him. "And what will you say when they wonder why you're not taking off that ironmongery? That it's stuck on your head?"

"Could I pretend to be a Wood Elf? Surely there are still Wood Elves in this land."

"I've never seen one," said Cerlys.

"I thought I saw a Wood Elf once," mused Jon, "but it might have been an owl."

"Stay out here," ordered Olva.

"What if we say he's under a curse?" suggested Cerlys. "Or that he's taken an oath never to reveal his face?"

"Swornhelm," suggested Jon.

"A mysterious masked knight!" Ceremos lifted his helmet with renewed enthusiasm.

"Stay out here," insisted Olva, then she softened. "We'll bring you out a hot meal."

Unlike Genny Selcloth's, the Lamb was a proper inn, built to serve traders, pilgrims and other travellers on the Road. There were guest rooms above the common and, while the inn was crowded that night, there were still bedrooms available for those with coin to spend.

Olva didn't have coin, but the innkeeper knew the Witch of the Mulladales.

"Is your daughter well, Marta?" Scarlet fever, six years past. They'd brought the sick girl to the church in Kettlebridge and prayed for Intercession. No spirit had answered them. But Olva's spells worked.

"She is." Marta handed Olva a room key – and a sealed letter. "A dwarf brought this up the Road a week ago. I'd heard you were

in Hayhurst and hoped you might call, so I kept it here instead of sending it on."

"A blessing on you, Marta," said Olva. "We're going south – what's the word from that quarter?"

"Nothing good. Most of those in here tonight came fleeing the Ironhand's army. Old Merik's hiding in his castle. Ironhand's main host has laid siege to Ilaventur City, they say. The city may hold for a while – the longer the better." She lowered her voice. "If you ask me, the Lords must come together to fight this Ironhand." Marta sighed. "Of course, even if the Lords do unite against Ironhand, we'll have to weather the storm. The Road's crawling with armed men, up to all sorts of mischief."

"Aye. There were raids on Hayhurst and Ersfel."

"I'd heard about Hayhurst – although in the tale I heard, a pack of wolves came out of the forest and drove them away. I didn't know about Ersfel – what happened?"

"They took my brother prisoner."

"Why?"

"Never mind why. They'd have come this way. Have you seen them?"

Marta nodded. "Riders passed through like a thunderstorm. No one dared hinder them. Might that have been them? I don't know where they were bound."

"When?"

"Six days ago."

Six days. They'd passed this way the same evening she'd returned to Ersfel. It had taken Olva and her companions three days to cover the same ground. By now, the riders could be halfway across Ilaventur. Where were they bringing Alf?

"I'm sorry, Olva."

"Food for five, if you'd be so kind." She dropped a few coins on the counter to pay for their meals; Marta pushed it back to her.

"Cerlys, Jon, you two wait down here. I want a private word with

Perdia in the room. Take a tray out to Ceremos when the food's ready, then bring the rest up."

The stairs up were steeper than she remembered, the room colder. Perdia knelt to light a fire. Olva sat down on the bed, head in her hands. Six days behind, and the gap growing wider with every passing hour. Even if she took crane-shape and left the others behind, she might not catch Ironhand — even if she could find them. She knew spells of divination, but they were unreliable. The weight of the task ahead settled heavily on her, but she resolved to hide her worries from the youngsters.

"We're on the right path," said Olva, putting as much cheer into her voice as she could. "Ironhand's men came this way. Marta saw them six days ago. They'll tire their horses out, going at that pace. We'll catch them."

A flame kindled amid the logs, illuminating Perdia's gaunt features. She was growing thin, and not just from the exertions of the Road. "They'll get fresh horses."

"Aye. Then it's a longer chase, indeed. I'll find some way to follow them, but you're right — it's likely to be a long, long chase. Alf's my brother, so I have to go. And I won't have that elf wandering around causing mischief. The rest of you, though — you've sworn no oath. You don't have to come. You can go home."

"You said you'd teach me. You said I needed to learn. So I could . . . control it."

"I did. And you do. But I'd meant to teach you in Ersfel, in safety, not while I'm dragging you down the Road into danger. Hayhurst's not far — you could go home. "

"Do you want me to go?"

"I want what's best for you. I think the earthpower's a gift and learning to use it properly is the right course. I want to teach you, but I also want to keep you safe. And you need to want to learn this, too. I've enough to do without an inattentive pupil."

Perdia stared into the flames. "I can smell them," she said after a moment. "The riders. I can smell their horses, and the stink of their sweat. I can taste the blood on their blades. Alf's with them. I can smell him, too." She shuddered. "The wolf can smell them. I can feel the wolf out there, hiding under the world. You tell me to listen to the earthpower, and it's there, lying in wait."

"The wolf's a skin you put on. It's part of you. Or you're part of the world, and so's the wolf."

"If I went home, would I change again?"

"There are charms I can teach you. I can give you potions that'll dull your connection to the earthpower. But, no, I don't think they'd work. You're too strong, Perdia. You can learn to control this power, or fight it, but it's one thing you can't change about yourself." *If I'd found the earthpower when I was your age, child, they've have burned me at the stake or had some deluded priest blast my mind with magic. You're lucky to have this choice.* "Think about what you want. You're welcome to continue with us, but if you choose—"

"No one in Hayhurst can help me," said Perdia hastily.

"Right then." Olva lay back on the bed and broke the seal on Torun's letter. "Pass me that candle, if you'd be so kind."

A place I cannot reveal,
Three days before the spring equinox,

Dear Olva Forster,

I hope you are well and your brother is well and your son is well and your pigs, chickens, neighbours, etc., etc. are also well. Please assume that I have written here all necessary pleasantries and talk of trivial matters that people find important. It seems such a waste to discuss such things when there is limited time (and paper!). Plainly, I am well or I would not be able to write this, and you can extrapolate from the quality of the paper and

the emblem on the wax seal that my situation has not changed significantly since I last wrote to you . . .

Olva shook her head. She still remembered the absolute joy she'd felt when Torun's first letter arrived in Ersfel, nearly twenty years ago. The two had parted company on that awful night in Necrad, when Olva went to the Wailing Tower to confront Blaise and rescue Derwyn. She'd urged Torun to flee, but feared that the dwarf had been taken captive or perished in the chaos that followed – or, knowing Torun, had stayed to study arcane mysteries while the city exploded around her. Torun and Alf were two ends of a horseshoe – one a bit slow, one too fast, both utterly oblivious to practicalities. But Torun had heeded Olva's warning, and escaped along with her father and the other dwarven smiths who'd come to repair the city's arsenal.

Even though Olva had not seen Torun in person since, they'd continued to correspond, and had grown closer. They had an obsession in common now, though they approached it in very different ways. Olva had delved into the mystical tradition long suppressed by agents of the Erlking. Torun tackled the matter in a manner befitting a dwarf.

I enclose a copy of my most recent observations of telluric energy currents. I draw your attention in particular to the figures in column twelve on page seven, which I find most amusing and trust you will too.

Olva put page seven of the letter with pages two through ten without reading it; endless tables of numbers, interspersed with arcane glyphs, celestial observations and minutely drawn topological maps tracing the flow of earthpower. She set those pages aside without reading them; all the numbers gave her a headache.

As far as Olva could tell, Torun's work was correct – one of Torun's first letters concerned the Fossewood where they'd met.

Olva had flown there in crane-shape, and felt the currents exactly as Torun predicted. But it was the difference between cradling a child, feeling its soft breath on your skin — and looking at a flayed corpse on some necromancer's slab, all the veins and nerves spread out for examination. Systematising magic with tables of numbers and arcane diagrams appalled Olva, but it was the only way Torun could approach that quicksilver joy.

Still, some part of Olva hoped there was some mystery that could never be explained away.

She skimmed through the rest of the letter.

You asked for news from the Dwarfholt. What can I say?
We have been spared the chaos that has befallen the human
lands. The doors to Arden remain shut for the most past, and
there is little trade. Should you ever come north, though, you
will certainly be welcomed. By the by, I am to be married
at midsummer, which will likely delay my next set of
observations, but that cannot be helped. The ceremony will
be trying, as will the celebration, but I shall endure. Attend if
convenient.

"You're to be WHAT?" Olva laughed, and it turned into a choking cough. Perdia looked up in alarm. "It's fine, it's just a silly letter. News from an old friend. Go and see what's taking so long with the food."

Perdia left, and Olva reread the last page. Attend if convenient! It was like a window into another, happier world. A brighter place without vampires and warlords, without prophecies and black swords. She remembered her own wedding, the happiness she'd felt, the future she'd anticipated. The life she'd expected, the life she had, and the gulf between them was so deep and wide it could not be measured even by the cleverest of Torun's instruments.

She couldn't go, of course. The Dwarfholt was in the wrong

direction entirely, and she had to go after Alf. But even if by some miracle she could step through a door and be there, she wasn't sure she should go. She'd said goodbye to Ersfel, and warded it with all the magic she could muster – in her heart, it was like a flower growing in a secret glade, and even though she had left it behind, the knowledge it was there sustained her. Torun's odd happiness was like that – a precious jewel, not to be despoiled by all the sorrows of the wider world. *Someone deserves to live happily ever after, don't they?* She wondered who the lucky dwarf might be. Torun had never mentioned anyone, but that was just like her.

Running feet on the stairs, and Perdia burst back in. "I can't find the others," she gasped, "the innkeeper said Cerlys and Jon went out half an hour ago. They're not in the stables – and I can smell blood on the wind."

Olva put the letter aside. "Of course you can. All right. Let's see what mischief the boy's done."

CHAPTER TWELVE

One night, when her dog Cu was half-grown, a madness had taken hold of the animal. He'd bolted out of the house, waking the baby. Galwyn went out into the dark to find the beast while Olva stayed to soothe Derwyn. She remembered sitting by the fire, fearful that Cu would bring some terrible misfortune down on them. He'd savage the reeve's sheep, maybe, or bite someone. A mad dog was more dangerous than a wolf, because it looked like a friend until it struck.

He's bitten someone. The blood-thirst overcame him. Someone attacked him, and he fought back.

The inn yard was deserted. Horses whinnied nervously in their stalls. Clouds hid the moon, so they stumbled in the dark, Perdia leading Olva. They crossed the churned mud of the Road and scrambled up a hill cloaked in gorse and brambles. Thorns scraped Olva's feet and clutched at her cloak. She grappled with the earth-power, thinking to wrap a bright fox-skin around her weary bones, but Perdia gripped her hand so tightly that she could not run free.

At the crest of the hill, Olva pulled Perdia down behind the gorse.

Dreadworms! Three of them at least, their hunched shapes deeper darknesses in the gloom. She could hear the rustle of their velvet wings as they settled, claws digging into the earth.

"Stay here," Olva whispered to Perdia. She took fox-shape. Oh, she could see now, no longer night-blind. She could smell them, the miasma-stench growing stronger as the frost on their hides rose as steam. *Run*, thought Fox-Olva, *this is no place for me.* But she was still human, too, and she crept forward, one hind crane-foot dragging behind her.

Three.

Three dreadworms.

And one-two-three-four – hard thinking for fox-brain – five-*six* two-legged people. Two human – *Cerlys. Jon.* One elf. *Ceremos.* And advancing on them, three creatures that Fox-Olva did not know, but human-Olva guessed were Vatlings. They were larger and stronger than the meek servitors she'd known in Necrad. Pitspawned, ogre-boned, girded for war. One had antlers sprouting from its misshapen skull; all had patches of white hair in unlikely spots on their bodies.

"I am Merriment," said one of the Vatlings. His voice was an absurd bleat, and all the more horrible for that. It was as if there was a deer trapped in that hulking mass of horn and muscle. The creature bowed to Ceremos. "We were sent to find you, Ceremos Ul'Elithadel Amerith, and take you home to Necrad."

"I shall not go back!"

"These are mortal lands, now. You have no place here. We have no place here. You must come back with us. It has been a long chase, and there are foes nearby. Pray do not delay us further."

"You heard him! He's not going!" Cerlys jabbed her spear in Merriment's face. "Begone!"

"Are these mortals known to you, lord?" asked the Vatling, in the tone of a long-suffering servant.

"They are my companions on the Road."

The Vatling sighed. "This one's life was already forfeit for wearing that stolen armour, though I might have overlooked that crime in the interests of haste. But now you have doomed both by association. I must assume you have told them secrets of Necrad that must not

be revealed to outsiders. You will answer for that before the Skerrise. The others die here." He gave an awkward nod of respect. "But I will take their bones for the spawning vats."

Cerlys lunged, the point of her spear aimed at whatever passed for Merriment's heart. but Jon threw himself forward in the same instant, accidentally blocking her attack. They went down in a tangle. Merriment stepped back and swung his axe, catching Jon in the side as the boy tried to rise. Jon bellowed in pain and fell back on top of Cerlys.

Ceremos had no weapon. He turned and fled.

"After him!" ordered Merriment. "Do not hurt him unduly." The other two Vatlings gave chase, their uneven limbs graceless and slow compared to elven speed – but suddenly one of them was next to Ceremos, crossing the intervening distance in a heartbeat on unseen wings of magic. The Vatling knocked the elf to the ground.

Merriment lifted his axe, intending to cut through Jon and Cerlys with a single blow.

Olva ripped her fox-skin asunder. Bear-shape, hot breath, the smell of blood filling her. She lumbered forward. Merriment spun about, his axe bursting with unnatural green fire. He wielded the weapon like a torch, pushing her back. She swiped and snapped at him, but the bear in her feared that fire, and she could not drive herself closer.

She didn't need to. Cerlys pulled herself out from under Jon – armour streaked red with his blood – and thrust her spear into Merriment's back. The Vatling fell to his knees, then collapsed. A pale fluid that was not blood dribbled from his mouth.

Cerlys snatched up the flaming axe and raised it to deliver a killing blow to Merriment.

The bear-shape fell away, too, and an exasperated and frightened old woman knelt by Jon. "The others! Go after the others!" Cerlys ran off, green flame dancing in the dell with lurid light.

Olva knelt by Jon, pressing her hand to the deep wound in his

chest. He gasped, unable to breathe, and clutched at her. A frightened child, that's all he was.

"Hold on," she prayed. A healing spell could save him, but she'd already drawn on the earthpower here twice already and she was still drained from Ersfel.

Chill fingers brushed against her crane-foot.

"Widow Queen," wheezed Merriment. "Is that you?"

"You know me?"

Merriment dragged himself to a sitting position. The colour was literally draining from his face, his flesh becoming translucent as he died. "You are remembered in Necrad. We Vatlings have few legends to call our own. I did not think to meet one in the flesh." He coughed, splattering more white fluid on Olva's feet. "There is healing cordial in my belt pouch. Take it for the human. It is too late for me."

"I'm sorry."

"I do not fear death. I am a child of the Skerrise, born of her waking dream, and to the dream I shall return. Had I known you were here—" He coughed again, and winced. "I might still have sought to slay you all, but with more decorum." Olva limped over and searched for the potion in the Vatling's bag. His body was collapsing in on itself, like a beached jellyfish. His eyes sunk into the liquid ruin of his head like stones, and his skull could no longer bear the weight of his drooping antlers. Still, Merriment managed a last laugh, and a warning. "Necrad is no longer for you, Wizard Queen, nor any other mortal. Do not trespass there."

She helped Jon drink the cordial, and it eased his pain. The gush of blood slowed, but she was still drenched in it, the red flood mingling with the white from Merriment.

The others came running back, Ceremos and Cerlys jabbering like excited children. Perdia trailed behind them quietly.

"I hit him with the axe and he burned like pitch—"

"—tried to pull me onto his dreadworm and—"

"—the worm tried to eat me—"

"—my father's a dreadknight, he taught me the worm-charms—"

"Enough!" snapped Olva, silencing the two. "Cerlys, bring that light close. Perdia, help me get this shirt off him. Ceremos, you . . ."

The vampire caught sight of the ocean of blood, and his face twisted. "You go over there. *Now*," ordered Olva. Ceremos' gaze was fixed on the bleeding wound.

"I'll watch him," said Perdia. She led the vampire away.

Cerlys took her place by Jon's side. "You idiot!" she muttered as she helped cut Jon's bloody shirt from his torso with a knife. "If you hadn't got in the way I'd have killed the leader! Watch where you put those big feet!" At Olva's instruction, she pressed her hand over the wound, holding back the gushing blood.

Jon muttered something, bubbles of spittle-flecked blood bursting on his lips.

"Those things – the Vatlings – they were hunting Ceremos. So was Ildorae. As long as he's with us, they'll keep hunting us."

Olva busied herself winding a bandage around Jon's wound.

"The Nine were hunted," said Cerlys. "All across Summerswell. They kept moving. We should keep moving."

"I just pulled an axe out of this poor lad's lung. We move him now, and it'll kill him no matter how much healing magic he gets."

"He shouldn't have got in my way." She glanced over at Perdia. "And where was she? You turned into a bear. Why didn't she become a wolf? If I could change my skin, I'd have ripped their throats out. She just hid. She did nothing."

"You're all still alive, even poor Jon. Be thankful for that."

"He shouldn't have got in my way," she said again.

"And you should have fetched me when you couldn't find Ceremos," muttered Olva.

Cerlys scowled, and said nothing for a long, long while, until:

"I should have been faster."

*

The next day was overcast and damp, drizzle dripping off the gorse bushes. Ceremos herded one of the dreadworms over to Jon, and the creature's outstretched wings provided some shelter until the pale sunlight began to burn it, and it had to crawl back into the shade. The worms obeyed Ceremos, their sinuous necks swaying as he sang to them in Elvish. It reminded Olva of Prince Maedos enthralling the sea-serpents on the Isle of Dawn. She disliked how comfortable the boy was with the monsters. Alf's dreadworm had mortally wounded Ceremos in Necrad – surely that should leave a scar? But the young elf seemed untroubled, even refreshed. The fangs that had been prominent in the light were lost within a merry grin.

Of course, that might have something to do with Perdia. She wore a fresh bandage wrapped tightly around her throat. She'd let the vampire feed from her, and brushed away Olva's concerns. "We're all companions of the Road," she said, "and it'll be Jon's turn next. We've talked about it."

If the children had talked about it, they'd not consulted Olva and that troubled her. They were too young to have seen the horrors of the war, the blood trade.

Later, over Olva's protests, Perdia walked slowly back to the Lamb to collect their belongings. Olva found herself wondering if Perdia would reverse her decision of the night before and go home to Hayhurst, but, no – she returned in the early afternoon with provisions for all of them. She nearly fainted as she stumbled into camp. How much blood had the vampire taken from her?

Cerlys buried – or mopped up – the remains of the Vatlings and salvaged what little of their gear could be used. She and Ceremos tried to find a way to quench the flaming axe, but to no avail – it kept blazing away until the shaft cracked. They buried the axe-head in the same hole as the Vatlings.

Jon, for his part, had only not to die, and he did that very well. But even with healing spells and cordials he was in no fit state to travel. Neither was Perdia.

"We'll rest here a day or two," announced Olva, "get our strength back."

Six days behind. Seven now. Nine or ten before we're ready to travel. I'm sorry, Alf.

At dusk, the biggest of the three dreadworms stirred and slithered towards where Jon lay. Its eyeless head – like an eel, like a snail, like neither – extended, the ring of teeth around its wet maw opening and closing, tasting the air. Then to Olva's alarm, it retched, a gust of sulphurous gas making her eyes water. Liquid dripped from its mouth and sizzled on the ground. It retched again, spitting the slime towards Jon.

Ceremos was there in an eyeblink. He wrestled the dreadworm's head to the side, an instant before it vomited a stream of acid. "Back!" he shouted. "He is not carrion for you! Back, I command you."

The dreadworm shuffled a few paces back and screeched. Across the little dell, Cerlys rose warily, spear in hand.

"It's hungry." Ceremos herded it a little further away with a stick.

Jon looked up, bleary-eyed and half-delirious. "What do they eat?"

"They don't, usually. They are conjured from the miasma by Lord Bone's magic, fashioned with only rudimentary organs, and dismissed back into the miasma when no longer needed. It is rare to keep one in shape for long." Ceremos sat down next to Olva and Jon. "My father told me that on campaign, no matter what they fed their worms, their hunger grew."

Jon struggled to sit up. "Weird things."

"Dreadknights of old rode dragons, but they are gone. Hunted to extinction by mortal dragon-slayers."

"Laerlyn had a dragon," said Olva. "I rode it to Necrad."

"Asjakain, last of his line. I saw him during the siege, and the thunder of his passing shook the whole house. But he perished in battle. The Wilder brought him down with many arrows."

"He was the last?" Jon sighed. "That would have been something. To see a dragon."

"There are still wonders in the world," said Ceremos.

"Aye, like vat-things hitting me with magic axes. Wouldn't see that in Ersfel." Jon chuckled, then winced at the pain.

The Wraith-Captain cut Galwyn down with a magic sword. "Alf always killed his dreadworms after using 'em," said Olva. "Go and kill those ones before they turn on us."

"They will obey my will for a few days yet – especially if we feed them a little to take the edge off their hunger. We can ride them and fly after Aelfric."

Olva scowled. "Nonsense. Those things burn in daylight."

"So we fly at night."

"And how will you follow him, when you're a thousand feet in the air? Do you think he's going to leave hoofprints in the clouds?"

Ceremos pointed across to where Cerlys and Perdia sat. "We've been talking about it. Perdia says she can follow Aelfric's scent. We land from time to time, and she finds the trail."

Perdia looked over, steeled herself, and gave a quick nod. "I won't have to change to do it."

"There are three worms and five of us – Friend Jon is the largest, so he flies alone. We each share a worm. Even if we only fly for a night or two, we shall make up a great deal of ground. Friend Jon, are you well enough to try?"

"I'm sore, but—"

"It's too dangerous," said Olva.

Ceremos knelt beside her, like a young knight asking for his queen's blessing. "What do you fear?"

The world was full of things to fear. Olva had done her best to keep Ersfel safe, keep perils at bay, but the land sung to her of suffering. She listened to the land, and it spoke of blood soaking into the earth, of the hoofbeats of horses riding to battle. Black smoke from burning towns tainted the air. The land whispered of older

forces, too – demons of the Old Kingdom emerging from broken seals, vengeful ghosts haunting ancient battlefields and barrows.

What do I fear? Not her own death, not any more. She'd died at Daeroch Nal. No, she feared the dreadworms turning on them, Jon screaming as the digestive acid dissolved his skin. She feared the shouts of Ironhand's sentries – *look, there in the sky! Dreadworms!* – and the whistle of arrows. Cerlys plummeting from the sky, pierced by a dozen shafts, dying angry that she'd been outshot by inferior archers. She feared that she was too old and tired to keep up with the shifting currents of earthpower – how could she hold the threads if they flew twenty or thirty leagues in a night, and all the land changed around her? How could she teach Perdia then?

And Ceremos – she feared him, too. Immortal elf, thirsty vampire, utterly alien – and so like Derwyn, filled with those same stupid notions, listening to the same lying songs.

"It doesn't matter," said Cerlys. "It's the best chance of catching Ironhand. We're going."

"It's like when the Nine rescued Lath from the House of Whispers! The ogres captured Lath, and all seemed hopeless, but they found him. They risked everything for their friend." Ceremos sprang up. "We should leave while it's still dark."

Jon reached out a hand, and Ceremos helped him up. "Just strap me on tight," he gasped, his face covered with a sudden sheen of sweat.

Idiot children. Don't you see how dangerous this is?

"Widow Forster?" whispered Perdia, "If you want to go home – maybe I can guide them. I'll find the way."

"No, no." Olva struggled to her feet, feeling all the years, all the many miles on the Road ahead. "Someone has to keep an eye on you fools."

They flew south, the land a blur of shadows. The darker line of the Road and the rushing river the only constants.

Olva rode with Cerlys. Clad in her borrowed dreadknight armour, masked by her helm, Cerlys seemed suited to the saddle, and the dreadworm heeded her commands as she spurred it on. She outraced Ceremos — his beast was off to their left, with Perdia clinging to the elf's back. Olva could not see the third dreadworm, but Jon's muttered *"oh fuck oh fuck oh fuck"* came through the fog with every wingbeat.

They landed shortly before dawn, near a deserted farmstead. Ironhand's raiders had been here. The buzzing of flies on rotting meat was loud, and they did not enter the main house. Ceremos herded the three dreadworms into the shelter of the barn, while Perdia and Cerlys crept down towards the main Road.

They returned an hour later. Perdia looked so downcast that Olva assumed they'd failed, but Cerlys blazed with excitement. She flung an arm across Perdia's shoulders.

"She found the trail.'

CHAPTER THIRTEEN

Y*ou are a prisoner of Idmaer Ironhand, and he has not been gentle . . .*
Alf couldn't recall who'd said that to him, but the words echoed around what remained of his skull. He was a bag of broken bones wrapped up in bruises. He could not tell if he was bound or if his limbs no longer obeyed him. The world was a broken window, light refracted in crazy patterns, and he could make little sense of it.

The wagon jolted down the Road, sending bolts of pain through Alf. *Are your old bones any better?* Gundan had said, long ago. *Shall I dip a cloth in some soup so you can suckle it?* And Abbess Marit was there, too, telling Alf about how Necrad had corrupted Summerswell, about how it was his responsibility to stem the flow of evil. Alf had thought himself weak and wounded then, despairing at the thought that Lath had turned against them. The sword had betrayed him, too, and he'd abandoned it for a time.

And yet, only a few days later, he and Gundan had ridden forth at the head of an army, on the way to Lake Bavduin. The last ride of the Nine, bright in the sun beyond the miasma, and the sword belted at Alf's side. The sword had saved him and restored him.

They'd been heroes again, for a little while.

Another bump on the Road banished the ghosts of twenty years

and turned the sucking black mud of the Charnel into the country-side of Ilaventur.

On the wagon rolled. The skies wheeled beyond the constant steel bars of the cage. Grim knights rode alongside; he was in the baggage train of a warband, his prison wagon part of a procession of camp fol-lowers, pack horses, carts laden with stolen supplies. A carrion army. The bones of Summerswell were broken and they sucked marrow from the wreck. He glimpsed broken churches, hollow-eyed ruins, fields choked by weeds. Figures cowered in the overgrown ditches as Idmaer's band passed by. Some he recognised, or thought he did for a moment, familiar faces lurching out of the past before lapsing into strangers. There was Remilard, there his brother Michel, there Berys.

The Road was a rack, stretching him out, snapping tendon and breaking bone. Part of him was nailed down in Ersfel, another in Necrad, and Alf's big frame was just enough to span the gap be-tween the two. But this wagon kept rolling south, and with each slow mile the pain grew worse.

Black birds circled.

Darkness. Light. Dark.

Light again.

They passed through a village. A burned-out mill, the surviving walls like a grave marker. Hayhurst? Was it Hayhurst? Olva had spoken of Hayhurst before she'd left. She might be one of those black birds, waiting for her moment.

But they kept wheeling, and the moment never came. In the evenings, their winged shadows on the fields reminded him of the shape of a sword.

Strange, still, after all these years to think of Olva as a Changeling, like Lath. He remembered the first day he'd met Lath, years ago at Albury Cross. Encouraged by the village priest, a mob turned on the

Changeling boy, accusing him of wielding the forbidden earthpower. A skin-changing monster, they called him. Beast, they called him.

And Alf had stepped forward to stand beside Peir in defending the boy.

What confused Alf, though, was this: all his life, he'd heard the priests talk of the perils of the earthpower. He'd heard the tales of monsters and madness. If you'd told him there was a Changeling Beast in the wood, and that the villagers were going out to find the monster, he'd have led the charge. He'd have felt good about it, too, being the hero who stood against the wild beast in the Wild Wood.

But when the moment came, he'd chosen the other side. He could not say why it was right to defend Lath, why he'd stepped forward and raised his shield against the hail of stones. He lacked the words, the understanding.

Even now, as the wagon rolled south. Even now, fifty years later.

It takes a special sort of courage to stand up for what is right. To see that the matter is complex, but the answer simple.

Abbess Marit had said that to him, once, and the words made sense to Alf. But the old abbess had served the Erlking, hadn't she? She was an enemy, right? So Alf couldn't trust her, couldn't trust the words that came crawling out of the wreckage of memory.

Monsters couldn't speak truth. Good things couldn't come out of evil.

Lath is dead, the black bird had said.

Shouting stirred Alf to awareness. He looked out across the fields and saw a tattered host approaching. Two hundred or so, shambling across the grass like the dead of Necrad. Alf struggled to raise his head, and saw that most of Idmaer's warband were gone, leaving only a half-dozen riders to guard the baggage train. He had not noticed their departure – although he had heard the hoofbeats in his dream.

"The Erlking is dead! The heavens are empty! This is the Age of

Man!" A ragged preacher led the mob. "All rule is misrule! There is no judgement! Take what you desire!"

Thin faces with open mouths, thin hands clutching the bars of the wagon. More rushed past Alf's cage, tearing at the sacks of supplies, dragging barrels and casks down from other wagons and smashing them open. Idmaer's followers fought back, but hunger and the preacher's ravings drove the attackers to take terrible risks. One flung himself forward onto a guard's blade, and his companions followed, slipping in their friend's blood, bowling the guard over.

The keys to Alf's cage spilled into the mud.

Groaning, Alf dragged himself over to the bars and reached for the keys. Even with his long arms, even with the bars digging painfully into his shoulder, he couldn't reach them.

"Hey!" he croaked. "Hey! Do me a kindness!"

The preacher saw Alf's plight and shuffled over. "No law binds us now – and so none should be imprisoned. I'll free thee. Aye, I'll free thee." He fumbled with the keys. "Who are you, friend?"

"I'm Alf. Alf of Mulladale."

"And tell me, friend, who is Alf of Mulladale?" The preacher rattled the key across the bars. His eyes were bright and mad. "It seems to me I've seen you before. In a dream, maybe? Or in better days?" He twirled the key on a finger. "Tell me, is that the only name you're known by?"

"I—" Alf swallowed, the name foul on his tongue. "Some . . . Some once called me the Lammergeier."

The preacher's eyes widened in surprise. "Ruin! Ruin! You brought all to ruin!"

Grab him, thought Alf, *get the keys*. But he was too stiff, too slow, and the preacher danced back out of reach. "You did this to us! I was an initiate at Arshoth Hill. And the clerics said the Lammergeier was to blame." The preacher pointed at Alf, crying, "Lammergeier! Lammergeier!"

The mob looked up from their looting. Some dropped what

they'd taken, hands clenching into fists. They swarmed around the cage, rocking it back and forth, outstretched arms grabbing at Alf, fingers clawing at him. Stones and filth rained down on him. "Lammergeier!" they cried, and the name was a curse.

From the west came the thunder of hooves. Ironhand's knights came riding back, and black smoke their banner on the evening sky behind them. They saw their own train under attack, and war-horns blared.

"You deserve this fate and worse, accursed one!" snarled the preacher. He threw the key into the mud, then turned and ran. His followers were like startled crows, taking flight as Ironhand's knights bore down on them. They snatched what they could as they fled, racing for the shelter of the hedgerows.

Not all made it. The knights cut the preacher down, and the fields were red in the sun.

Ironhand cantered up, and came to a halt by Alf's cage. Despite his size, he dismounted lightly. The wound Ildorae had dealt him only a few days earlier seemed entirely healed, and that spoke of magic.

He picked up the key. "How discordant the world has become! Had Merik's last loyalists held out but a little longer, then we would not have returned until tomorrow, and you would be gone. Had that scoundrel not hesitated, you would be gone. There is little order left to events, since the Intercessors were taken from us." Ironhand closed his metal fist, and the key squealed and bent. "But there will be justice, and from that a new order."

He dropped the fragments of metal. "Not long now, Lammergeier. Your trial awaits."

Alf lay on the floor of his cage, bones bleached by the sun.

Day after day, mile after mile.

No one came. No crane swooped down, no winged Changeling of deliverance. No wraith or spirit or whatever the fuck Jan had

become showed up to comfort him or deliver another prophecy. The only ghosts were the ones wrung out of Alf's overheated brain, the shades of long ago. Everything was being squeezed out of him, until all that was left was an unthinking husk, shrivelled in the sun.

He was, he decided, dying. Not in battle, as he'd once expected. At some point in the quest – at Karak's Bridge maybe, when they'd fought the Ogre Chieftain – all of the Nine had realised that the odds against them were hopeless. The enemy had known their every move. They knew their doom was at hand.

And the Nine looked at one another, and without a word, they'd agreed that dying shoulder to shoulder was enough. After that, they'd fought without fear. Either one of their comrades would catch them, or death would take them – there was nothing else. In that glorious abandon, they achieved the impossible. The Lammergeier in flight, and the Nine in glory.

Later, years later, he had come to accept that his tale was over, and that he'd die as just Alf. Not too bad, he thought, to have one last drink at Genny's, then slowly walk up the shady path under the oaks, stretch out on the long bed in Olva's house, and rest. He'd done a great deal in his life. Let them sing 'The Truth of the Lammergeier' in the taverns, let them curse his name for a while, let the Anarchy play out. The world would roll on – because he'd saved it, once upon a time.

Now, the wagon rolled on, and he waited to die. He lay there, staring at the sky, while in his mind he rode with the Nine to Necrad. But the memory of the cold winds whipping across the Charnel brought him no comfort in the heat; the shade of Necrad's miasma gave no relief from the merciless sun.

At times, Idmaer rode beside him. Ironhand spoke of a great re-ordering of the lands, as if all of Summerswell were a chessboard that could be swept clear and reset. New lords and churches would

be conjured as easily as a player might place rooks and knights on the ordered squares. It was so simple and clear to say such things.

Idmaer greatly resembled his father Duna in frame and feature, but there was nothing of the old warrior in his demeanour. Other faces came through in his expressions, his gestures. He moved his iron hand like his mother Erdys, precise and restrained. His face bore the cast of his grandfather Brychan, sly and calculating, feigned friendship masking a deep-seated rage. Memories choked Alf's mind, weeds clinging to the hull of a ship, slowing it so much that Idmaer's meanings slipped by him, and Alf could not follow the thread of the man's talk. It was like listening to Peir, to Derwyn when he was the Uncrowned King – visionary statements, grand proclamations, skipping over the gap between prophecy and finished deed.

It was, horribly, also like the ravings of that mad preacher. The gap between visionary and madman was as narrow as that between hero and monster. A hair's breadth between squares on the board.

He would bring justice to Summerswell and unite the provinces once more. His knights would patrol the Road. He would undo the grievous error of the Defiance. He would fulfil all prophecy.

Idmaer Ironhand would save the world.

What did that mean? *You carry the hope of the world,* Jan had once said to him. But what was a world? Once, Alf's world had been no wider than the span between Highfield and Kettlebridge. Or smaller – in his earliest memories, he was king of the world, and the world was the wood up on the hill, and the stream beside the road, and the alley behind the alehouse, and the garden of the reeve's manor. Later, his world had grown. Gundan had brought him down the Road, shown him other provinces. Gundan had broken Alf's world and remade it.

The Song of the Nine said they'd saved the world from Lord Bone, but that just meant they'd saved Summerswell. They'd broken the ancient world of the Witch Elves, the narrow realm of the Vatlings.

And all the while he'd been unaware of hidden worlds, overlapping and interlocking. The unseen realm of the wraith-world where the Intercessors reigned. The conspiracies and shadow-plays of Berys and her Defiance, the Rangers and the spies. Olva spoke of the earthpower surging through the living world; Blaise had tried to explain the mysteries of celestial spheres. And the elves would live until the world's ending.

It was all beyond him. These thoughts were too big to fit into his mind, a gulf of understanding too wide to span in a mortal lifetime.

Duna rode beside him, talking of war in the north, trouble with the Wilder across the border.

Pay attention, wielder, sounded a cold voice out of memory.

Idmaer. It was Idmaer, not Duna.

He was talking about how he'd escaped the destruction of Castle Duna, twenty years ago. Some of the Wilder-tribes had allied with him in his war on the Uncrowned King, and he'd escaped through the Wild Wood. He'd won friends, the first of his *atharlings*, his Sorrowguard. A band of warriors who'd been with him since the early days. His face lit up as he spoke of these battle-brothers. He'd taken ship at Staffa and fled south through many adventures and perils. He spoke of the trials he'd faced, wild sea-serpents off Cape Forlorn, a shipwreck in the ruins of Minar Kul. But Idmaer had endured all those hardships because he knew he was prophesied to achieve a great destiny. The Intercessors had saved him for a reason; he'd escaped death for a reason.

Idmaer Ironhand would save the world.

Alf stopped listening and stared at the sun, waiting to die.

What world had Alf saved?

What world had he known? What world had he loved? The Nine.

And saving the world had broken the Nine.

Now all that was left was picking through the rubble, choosing what to salvage.

*

They came to the marshes north of the river. Insects crawled over Alf's unblinking eyes. Midges bit but found little sustenance in him. Ceremos had drunk all but the dregs. Not far from this spot, thought Alf, was where Berys had put two arrows in him with *Morthus*, and all the stories insisted arrows from *Morthus* were fatal.

What did stories know? What truth was there in tales? He'd taken two arrows from *Morthus* and lived another twenty years. The thought made Alf chuckle dryly. Berys would find that funny, too.

Berys was dead. *Lath is dead,* Death had said, and she'd know, presumably. Something of an authority on the subject. Soon Alf would be, too, and that would be the end of them save endless Laerlyn.

But when he'd asked if Blaise was dead, Death had said both yes and no. Blaise was alive, and Alf was needed in Necrad. *You'll go because it's one of the Nine who calls, and you always answer,* that was what Olva had said, and she knew his mind better than he did.

Somewhere in this marsh, too, was the pool where he'd dropped the sword.

Dropped? DROPPED? You abandoned *me, wielder!*

That thought was so cold in Alf's mind that it quenched the burning sun.

CHAPTER FOURTEEN

O n the third night, they lost a worm.
   They saw a blazing light in the east and, assuming it was
the dawn, flew low. But the light was the burning city of Ilaventur,
besieged by Ironhand's army. The cry of "Dreadworm! Dreadworm!"
went up, a cry not heard in the south in more than forty years.
Arrows flew. Jon's worm was struck. It laboured on for a few miles,
then crashed on the bank of a little stream. The others landed and
cut Jon free from the wreck of his mount. The two worms devoured
the carcass of the third. The monsters fed like cranes, lifting their
heads so that the liquifying remains slid down their gullets.

   At dawn, they herded the remaining dreadworms into the shelter
of a thicket, and there hid through the day. The fields around the
thicket had been tilled, but never sown – whoever once farmed this
land had fled. Weeds choked the black soil. The sound of hunting
horns in the distance, north and south. They were surrounded, and
Perdia dared not search for the trail. Jon and Ceremos swapped tales
of their homelands – each marvelling at the strangeness of the other's
upbringing. Cerlys kept watch from the fringes of the thicket.

   Ironhand's men found them a little before sunset. A dozen ragged
hunters, with only two things in common.

   First, their relative youth. All of them had clearly come of age in

the Anarchy, and they had never known the law of the Lords or the authority of the Intercessal Church.

Second, their conviction that horrors out of Necrad lurked within the thicket – a conviction only reinforced when Cerlys cast back her cloak to reveal her elven armour and shouted, "Come and try your luck, cowards! You face a dreadknight, and I shall slay you all!" (in, it must be said, a thick Mulladale accent).

Ceremos held up his hand in a gesture of command, and the bigger of the two worms hissed at him. "'Tis still too bright. They refuse to fly in this sun. We must delay Ironhand's men, Widow Queen! At sunset we can take flight! Until then, we hold the line!" He ducked into the forest, sword in hand.

"Clouds," muttered Olva. Clouds could block out the sunlight, get the dreadworms aloft sooner. The evening sky was mottled with little bands of thin cloud. She knew few weather-magic spells, but she'd called rainstorms down on Ersfel before. Never so hastily, never so far from home, but what choice was there? She reached out, feeling the currents running through the land. They were reflected in the sky, invisible masses of air and water, heat and cold, the breath of the living world. Twist the currents, gather the clouds. But it was hard, like trying to weave spider silk. Tug too hard, and it would snap.

Jon struggled to lift his tree-branch club, one hand clasping his wounded side. Perdia helped him stand. "A big fucking wolf would be really handy now." Perdia gave him a thin smile, but shook her head. "Maybe if you think of 'em as the same bastards who attacked Hayhurst?" he added uncertainly. The smile froze on her face – and when he was gone into the woods, she doubled up and vomited.

"Come here," said Olva firmly, "and help me with this."

"I can't, I mustn't," wept Perdia. Tears streamed down her cheeks. "I can still *taste* them. I know what it's like when a skull cracks between my teeth—"

"Perdia! Not now." Olva grabbed her hands. "Focus! Do you feel

that?" A throbbing current of earthpower ran deep beneath the thicket, Olva's crane-foot prickling at its proximity.

Perdia nodded.

"Then call it!"

The magic surged. Wild power – far too much to gather those little wisps of mist above the thicket – rushed through Olva's blood and bones. Her mind was quick enough to grasp this bounty, to twist it – and send it into the sky. Tree branches creaked. The two women clutched each other, assailed by sudden dizziness. Perdia's tears reversed themselves, flowing *up* her cheeks, then leaping into the sky. Alarmed, the girl let go of Olva's hands and stumbled back.

"Unclean," Perdia whispered.

The earthpower current summoned by Perdia crested and began to subside. Olva caught it with her soul – and oh! it tore her brain, sharp spikes of pain hammering through her skull. She lifted the magic, held it, and the nearby stream erupted into a spontaneous waterfall, a geyser gushing white spray into the heavens. The sky boiled.

Rain pitter-pattered on the leaves, then swelled into a downpour. The skies darkened like an angry bruise.

"That's what I've been talking about," muttered Olva.

The dreadworms were eager to fly now. The others came racing back through the sudden darkness.

"Friend Jon, Friend Jon," shouted Ceremos, "help him! He is wounded!" Jon was pale, his shirt stained red around the reopened wound when he stumbled back. Perdia helped him climb astride one worm.

Olva glimpsed that the elf's face was red as he donned his helm, and she doubted it was the elf's blood. Cerlys was the last, pursuers so close behind her that the dreadworm's wings brushed against them as they flew.

"Three!" exclaimed Cerlys. "I got three of them."

*

Three foes were like three droplets in a rainstorm. More riders pursued them as they flew south. Unburdened, the dreadworms could fly more swiftly than any horse, but these worms were worn and sun-scorched, and now one had to carry three, and the other laboured under Jon's weight. When Olva could catch a current of power, she flew alongside in crane-skin to ease the monster's burden. Still, each night they dipped a little lower, no longer reaching the chill of the upper airs. It was clear, too, that their pursuers were either well organised and changed horses frequently, or had tireless charmstones, for the riders were never far behind.

The pattern of the travellers' days was this: before dawn, they would frantically scan the terrain ahead for a place where the worms could hide from the sun – a tangled wood, a sheltered vale, a cave, a ruin. If they could not find such a place, then Jon would hastily string their blankets and spare clothing into a makeshift screen, and the dreadworms would sullenly huddle and hiss. Then they would hide themselves and try to snatch some sleep. Their nerves wore as thin as the worms' wings.

Cerlys would propose that they should turn and fight, and came up with increasingly elaborate plans for ambushing their pursuers. Perdia would become a wolf, and Olva would take on some other bestial war-form, and she and Ceremos would take the worms and attack from on high. But as long as the worms could fly, none of the rest had the stomach for a fight.

Ceremos asked incessant questions about the lands they passed over. None of them knew much about Ilaventur, save what they'd heard in songs. So every hill might be Harnshill, where the Lammergeier won the day against the Knight of Roses, and every tumbled stone a ruin of the Old Kingdom. Sometimes, they saw villages or small towns in the distance, but stayed away from civilisation.

Perdia knew a little more than the rest, and spoke to Ceremos of churches and sacred wells, but her voice soon dropped to a whisper.

There was no longer any question of her sneaking out to pick up Alf's trail; the Road was watched by Ironhand's men. Perhaps she might have found the scent in wolf-form, but the frequent changes of location meant finding the earthpower was hard even for Olva — and, anyway, it was clear after the attack on the thicket that Perdia recoiled at the thought of taking the wolf-skin again.

Jon hardly spoke at all. Alone among the company he was able to sleep properly during the day. He snored; by evening every one of the others had contemplated murder at least once.

And Olva? She played the wise Witch of Ersfel, the Queen of Necrad. She hid her fears and assured them that they were on the right path. She may have worried that she had led these youngsters to their doom, but she did not show it on her face. Instead, that knowledge gnawed at her stomach and made her irritable. *South*, she told herself. *Alf was going south. If we go south across the River, they won't be able to follow us.*

At dusk, the dreadworms would stir, and shake out their wings, and they would fly again.

They fell short of the River. They saw it ahead of them — it was a clear night, the eighth since they'd begun their chase, and the moon turned the wide expanse of the River into a silver-white band. But there was already a light in the east, and the worms refused to press on.

Olva poked Cerlys and pointed off to their right. "Can you see anything off that way?" she shouted over the rush of wind.

"What should I be looking for?"

"The Crossing of Avos!"

But there was no sign of the ruined city or its bridges, and Olva caught the smell of the sea as they spiralled down. They were much too far east. Below was a landscape of grey hills, broken stone, summer-bleached thin grasses. Few dwelt in that ill-favoured region.

They landed on a barren hillside, and camped in a hollow. As Cerlys unstrapped the baggage, her worm lashed out at her, its tail knocking her to the ground. In an instant, it was on top of her, slashing and clawing. Jon shoulder-charged it and knocked it off Cerlys. He grabbed her spear from the ground. "Stop! Stop!" cried Ceremos, then he shouted in elvish. The dreadworms both froze in place – just as Jon drove his spear into the worm's maw. It shuddered, then collapsed, its exhausted form dissolving before their eyes. Fetid liquid gushed across the ground.

"Why did you do that?" said Cerlys.

"It was attacking you!"

Cerlys picked herself up, rubbing her side. She wiped worm-slime from her arm. "We needed it."

"I would have calmed it," said Ceremos again. He seized the muzzle of the one remaining worm and dragged it away from the mortals.

"He could have calmed it," agreed Cerlys. "I'm wearing armour. And even if it had injured me, the Widow has healing magic! We needed that worm to catch Ironhand! Think of that, before you try rescuing me!"

"Now we're down to one worm," said Perdia. "What now?"

"We take stock," said Olva. "Get that last beast tied up. Jon, let's make camp."

Jon picked up the bag containing what supplies they had left, and it came up brimming with caustic slime. The ruin of the dreadworm had engulfed it.

"Oh," he said, and for a long moment he watched the remains of their food drip down onto the stony soil. He shook it, and more foulness tumbled out. Blood from his reopened wound trickled down inside his shirt.

Jon flung the bag in Cerlys' face, and stomped off across the hillside.

*

Each of them sat alone for a while – Cerlys furious and sullen, Ceremos confused, Perdia silent. Olva cleaned their belongings as best she could, then limped around to see if there was anything edible to be found in this place. She came upon Jon sitting on a rock, looking out west towards greener lands. A heat haze rose from the river.

She patted him on the shoulder.

"You all right, lad?"

"She never sees me. It's like I'm her shadow." He shook his head. "I shouldn't have come. I shouldn't be here. Cerlys said we have to help Alf, but where is he now?" He kicked at a stone. "I don't even know where *we* are any more."

"I do," lied Olva. "That's the Great River yonder, and beyond it the Eavesland." Which was true, but so vague as to be almost meaningless. The River washed past half of Summerswell on its way to the sea.

"Oh aye." He stared at the River. "And the Everwood beyond that. Is it as beautiful as they say?"

"The Neverwood now, since the Erlking's defeat. I've never been there. I was on the Isle of Dawn, once, when it was elven-land. And that was beautiful." *It was a lie, too. Prince Maedos bewitched me, and made me think that Torun and I were his honoured guests – but all the while he was torturing my son and planning to murder Alf. A monster with a beautiful smile.* "But beauty . . . it's just a skin. What's beneath may be fair or foul. Changelings can shift their appearance – I could look like Cerlys, or Alar Ravenqueen, or old Elcon Fartbreeches, well enough to fool you. It wouldn't change what's within, though. You can't tell from the surface."

"Could you really look like Alar Ravenqueen?" asked Jon. The mythical queen was said to be the most beautiful mortal who ever lived. Olva had little talent for putting on human skins, but she summoned up an approximation of the gouty, squinting old farmer of Ersfel, Elcon Fartbreeches.

Jon laughed. Olva relaxed back to her ordinary shape. It was a waste of the blessing of the earthpower, but it felt good to hear a laugh. They were all worn by the journey.

"Should I apologise?"

"To Cerlys? I wouldn't. But come on back. We're going to make a plan."

"Just tell me what to do when you're done."

They gathered in the hollow. Jon stood a little away from the rest, ostensibly keeping watch. They were so far from their original course, Olva prayed their pursuers would have lost the trail. Cerlys prowled back and forth, head downcast, not looking at Jon. *Bloody children*, she thought. *Always fighting and yearning and wasting time when there's work to be done.*

"The Lammergeier needs our help," said Ceremos. "I flew from Necrad with a message for him from Master Blaise himself. *Come at once*, he said, *bring your sword.* Now, the Lammergeier's sword lies in the Everwood, across the River, but the Lammergeier is in the clutches—"

Cerlys scoffed. Ceremos continued.

"—in the clutches of Lord Ironhand. In its present state, the dreadworm can carry at most two of us – or one, in the case of Friend Jon. He is by far the, ah, mightiest of the company. I see two courses before us. First, two of us could fly south to the Everwood and fetch the Lammergeier's sword. I would suggest that Cerlys and I go in that case, for we are the most able in battle.

"The other course is to double back and try to find the Lammergeier's trail once more. Perdia would have to go, accompanied by Cerlys or myself. Should we find Sir Aelfric, we effect a rescue and then continue south to the sword."

"'Effect a rescue'," muttered Cerlys. "Hark to him. And what about Jon and whoever stays with him?"

"Alas, I can see no other course – they must remain behind. If

they make their way in stealth towards the River, they may find shelter and sustenance there. It will be hard, but not unduly perilous."

Ceremos turned to Olva. "I leave the choice to you. Who should go, and where?"

Alf or the sword? Her brother had once seemed invincible, but he'd come home to Ersfel half broken by the war, and many years had passed since then. He was an old man. With the earthpower, she was stronger than him now; he looked to her for protection and guidance.

But so did these idiot children.

The image of Derwyn's chessboard tumbled through her mind. The Lammergeier, broken. For all she knew, Alf was already dead. Even if he was alive, even if they tried to rescue him, who should she bring on a mission that would almost certainly end in death? Who should she abandon? Jon looked at her with cow-like eyes, already resigned to being left behind.

I don't want anyone to live or die on my account, she'd once said. And Prince Maedos, with mocking courtesy, had replied, *Nonetheless, the choice is yours.*

But before Olva could answer, Perdia picked up Cerlys' spear and drove it through the skull of their remaining dreadworm. The slumbering monster shuddered and dissolved, fresh slime flowing over the dried crust of its comrade.

"No one gets left behind," she said.

After that, it was easy.

I'm sorry, Alf.

"South. To the Neverwood."

After worm-flight, walking seemed impossibly slow. The terrain had transformed around them with every flight, with one day bearing no resemblance to the next. Now, the land crawled by; the Norral Hills in the distance slowly swelling. Those hills had been there yesterday and would be there tomorrow, only very slightly closer. They'd been thrice-blessed, Olva reflected. Ironhand's hunters were

no longer on their heels. She wondered if their pursuers had some magic that sensed the taint of Necrad. Now they'd left the worms behind, the pursuers had lost their trail.

The second blessing – on the banks of the Great River they'd met a fisherman who'd ferried them across. "Always fighting, these days," he had observed, "but less of it than there was when I was young." And he'd told them of how he'd escaped the destruction of Avos when he was a boy, slipping out just before the siege.

The third blessing was the earthpower. Now that they were no longer disjointed by flight, magic came easier to Olva, and Perdia seemed more at ease with learning.

The lands on the far side of the river were gentler and more prosperous than Ilaventur, so much so that Erdys put aside her armour. Ceremos still hid his face – but the folk of the Eavesland were elvenfair, and he might have gone without notice in places. Day after day, they walked in a summer country. The rancour that had poisoned their little company faded, and they were blessed.

But they knew that their blessings were bought with the suffering of another. Alf, wherever he was, remained Ironhand's prisoner.

In the aftermath of the Erlking's fall, the lords of the Riverlands turned their gaze on these rich lands, and blood had soaked these golden fields. But the fighting had petered out a decade ago; Riverlander warlords were now married to Eaveslander brides, and a coalition of lesser nobles held the Goldenvale beyond the Gap of Eavesland. This province had known war, but now it was at peace.

"It reminds me of home," said Jon one evening. "Like something's watching over it."

Under the stars, they told stories of Alf. Ceremos again told them of the message from Blaise, and the wizard's call for the Spellbreaker. Cerlys recited much of *The Song of the Nine*, although she skipped over the parts she considered dull and was much too enthusiastic when recounting the battles.

Jon started to tell what he thought was a hilarious anecdote about a madman who accosted Alf in Genny Selcloth's one night, accusing him of slaying some prince and causing the destruction of Arden. Everyone in the inn had laughed at the idea that Big Alf had done such things. Halfway through his story, Jon stopped suddenly. "Oh. He wasn't mad."

Olva took up the telling. She related parts of Alf's adventures that were known only to her and a handful of others, the parts that never made it into the stories. Alf's deeds during the Defiance, and what truly happened in the Everwood when he'd lost the black sword. Three of the youngsters were entranced, but Perdia paid little attention to Olva's story.

"If we can't rescue Alf, I swear we'll avenge him," said Cerlys.

"The Lammergeier set out to retrieve the Spellbreaker. We shall do it in his stead," agreed Ceremos.

"One thing at a time," said Olva. "You may be right that there are Wood Elves in these parts. Alf said that Princess Laerlyn still dwells in the Neverwood, watching over the sword. Once we cross the Norrals, we'll seek her out." She lay back with a groan. "I'm going to sleep, but don't stop the tale-telling on my account." The evening suddenly felt like a wake to her. "But no more tales of Alf. Give us something different."

She fell asleep listening to Perdia's soft recital of the tale of Harn Firstlord, who had travelled these same lands through the snows of the Hopeless Winter. How he had found healing in the Everwood.

The Road took a long detour east around the Norral Hills, through the Gap of Eavesland. Olva led them into the steep hills. "Alf came this way, once. It's quicker, and it'll keep us from getting lost." Ceremos had the natural agility of the elves, and both Jon and Cerlys had grown up amid the slopes of the Mulladales. Olva could fly above the hills in crane-skin, so only Perdia slowed the company's passage as she struggled to keep up.

But one afternoon Crane-Olva looked down and glimpsed a grey shape loping through the trees.

Late on the following day, Jon stopped abruptly next to two hollow tree stumps from which young birch trees were growing. He poked the charred bark of one stump. "It's like the lightning tree up on Elcon's farm. It got struck by a thunderbolt, and burned from the inside out. Just like these. Only two of 'em, side by side."

"Remember the tales of the Lammergeier, Friend Jon." Ceremos darted over to stand between the two trees. "Aelfric was here once. This is the end of the Straight Road in the account Lady Olva gave us."

Olva limped over. "You may be right." Once, Alf and the Ranger Agyla had taken one of the Erlking's magical paths. Bor had pursued them. Bor, and Cu, and Spellbreaker. She reached out for the earth-power. The magical currents were still deformed, a lingering scar left by the Erlking's enchantment, but nothing remained of the path.

Alf was here once.

Perdia emerged from the undergrowth in wolf-skin. She was gigantic, bigger than any wolf Olva had ever seen. A dire wolf of the Wild Wood. She pushed Olva aside with her muzzle and sniffed the base of the trees. She lifted her head and smelled the air, catching some scent.

Then she bolted, sprinting through the trees, howling with excitement.

"Follow her! Follow her!" called Olva.

They all ran, Ceremos and Cerlys outracing each other, Jon lagging behind to help Olva through the thick undergrowth. Ahead, a bright wall — sunlight beyond the tree line. They burst into the light and found themselves overlooking the wide Goldenvale. In the distance lay the great forest of the Neverwood.

Ceremos shaded his eyes with one hand, and pointed. "There, in the vale! Riders!"

They were many miles away, too far for Olva to see. She clutched the elf's shoulder. "Is it Ironhand? Is it Alf?"

In answer, Perdia bounded down the slope towards the distant Neverwood. But the riders were too far ahead, and the evening gloom swallowed them.

Two days later, they came to the edge of the forest. It was riotous green, the air thick with pollen and leaf-smell. Flowers of every colour garlanded the ivy-twined trunks, and birds sang in the tree-tops. They walked through the woods, searching for any sign of the riders who had come this way.

In time, the mists enfolded them.

CHAPTER FIFTEEN

Alf awoke in a bed with silk sheets, and the taste of healing cordial on his lips. He was in a bedroom in some great tower, for the lone window looked south over the River. He wondered if the bridges of Avos still stood. The bustle of servants, the smell of cooking fires in the kitchens below, the clack of hooves in the cobbled yard outside. Marching feet, the ring of metal on metal. Weapons practice, the sounds of an evening in Ersfel transplanted many miles south and magnified a hundredfold.

With an effort, Alf crossed to the window and looked down. The castle was surrounded by tents. An army encamped on the lush green fields. A muster, not a siege. Alf tried to count the tents, but soon gave up. A great host, certainly, as large as any army he'd heard of in these days of Anarchy. The banners were a curious mix from many different provinces, knights who'd fought on opposite sides in the Defiance.

Or knights whose fathers fought on opposite sides, he reminded himself. The Defiance was twenty years past; the knights who'd survived Harnshill and the other great battles were old now. Or dead.

Long ago, he'd looked down from another castle tower and watched the muster of the League army, before they'd marched away north to Necrad. *Bloody fucking profanities*, Gundan had said, *but that's a lot of armed bastards. We might actually have a chance. We*

*make it through this, lad, and we'll be richer than Lords, eh? Stick with
me, and I'll see you right.*

A knock at the door. "You are summoned to the solar. Do you
require assistance dressing?" A doublet and other clothing lay on
the bed, fit for a knight.

"I'll manage," said Alf, but after a few minutes' fumbling he admitted defeat and called for the servant. The door opened instantly – the
servant, a lad of about ten years, had clearly been hovering just outside. He knelt before Alf. "How many I serve thee, Lammergeier?"

"Get up, lad. Help with these damned laces."

The boy's features were oddly familiar. "Who are your people?"

"My mother is Ernala of the As Magaer."

A Wilder. Alf knew – they'd been allies of the Nine – but he
didn't know Ernala, nor could he guess what a half-Wilder boy was
doing as a servant in Idmaer's castle, a great many leagues away from
the Wilder-lands. "And your father?"

"Idmaer Ironhand."

Idmaer had sent his own son to serve Alf.

There was a time, once, when Alf might have grabbed the boy.
Put a knife to his throat, if he had one – there were long pins, metal
combs, a crystal decanter that could be smashed into a shiv. Hold the
lad as a hostage until free of this castle. He'd had that edge once, that
capacity for violence. In the back of his mind, he could hear Berys
and Gundan calling him an idiot for not exploiting this opportunity.
What kind of fool turns down the chance to seize his captor's son?

What kind of fool sends his unarmed son to dress a prisoner? wondered Alf.

The lad's nimble fingers knotted the last of the stays on the stupid
fancy doublet. It had, of course, the sigil of the Lammergeier picked
out on it in black thread, with onyx stones for the bird's eyes, silver
thread and a ruby for the sword in its talons.

Alf sighed. "Lead on, lad, and show me to your father, then."

*

The Miracle Knight awaited him in sunlight. Idmaer sat enthroned, his back to the window, crowned in light. A Wilder-woman — Idmaer's wife, Alf guessed — stood by his side.

Idmaer wore no armour, carried no blade. His metal hand gleamed in the sun.

"Now then, you've seen the Lammergeier," said Idmaer to his son. "Just as I promised. Now, be off with you. Attend to your studies."

The boy lingered at the threshold.

"Shoo," said Ernala. "Your father wishes to speak to our guest in private." Idmaer took the woman's hand and kissed it before she too left.

"Ernala," said Idmaer. "She saved my life twenty years ago. Some of the Wilder joined the war against Necrad, after the murder of Lord Bessimer. They understood the evils of that city better than any of us. When the Witch Elves destroyed my father's castle, Ernala led us through secret paths in the forest. We were wed at Staffa at the autumn equinox." He sighed. "I have not been as good to her as she deserves. She has endured many hardships, and I must ask yet more of her in days to come." Idmaer gestured at the chair. "Sit, please."

Alf sat gingerly. "And the boy?"

"Ernala chose his name. He is called Thurn." Idmaer looked slyly at Alf. "I thought you would approve."

"I do," said Alf. He caught himself smiling and steeled himself. Sentimentality would get him killed. "Am I a prisoner or a guest?"

"A guest, if we may choose," said Idmaer, with an expansive gesture that implied a vast range of options.

"You've a strange manner of invitation," said Alf, "what with the burning and the slaughter and the cage."

"It was a necessity. You are a dangerous man, Aelfric Lammergeier. And I had to treat you as a prisoner, then. One to whom I am beholden demanded I capture you and bring you in chains before them. But in truth I thought you long dead. I was looking for your grave in the Mulladales."

"You've a strange manner of searching for a grave, then, what with the burning and the slaughter."

"You were not the only thing I sought in the Mulladales. The raids won me supplies my army needs – and more, the havoc draws the attention of the Lords. I feint with my right hand so I can strike harder with my left."

"And this person, the one to whom you're beholden . . . do they have a name?"

Instead of answering, Idmaer clapped, a gold ring clanging off the metal palm. Servants entered with a trestle table and platters of fine food. Idmaer ate with enthusiasm. Alf was never one to turn down a meal, but he ate sparingly, avoiding the rich food. After the travails of the Road, his stomach couldn't bear it.

Two warriors entered with the servants. One was a dour-faced warrior, the sigil of a bear on his tabard. By his side was a dwarf whose singed beard spoke of explosions and siegecraft. The dwarf stared at the feast.

"Are we staying for dinner, Id, or—"

The bear-knight spoke over the dwarf.

"I've given the order to break camp, my lord. I've sent supplies ahead to Arshoth, and Albury Cross, so we won't be slowed down by the baggage train."

The sign of the bear was familiar to Alf. "I fought a knight, once, who wore those arms. Sir . . . Berkhof?"

The dwarf nudged the taller man in the side. "See, he's not wholly witless."

"You fought *alongside* my father at Harnshill, Sir Lammergeier. He was the second man through the breach in the wall at Avos."

"I remember him," lied Alf. "A brave man."

"He died at Avos," said Sir Berkhof. "Not all are lucky enough to live into old age." He turned to Ironhand. "Shall we wait for you at Arshoth, or press on to Albury?"

"Don't wait at all. I trust you with command, Wil. The army will

follow you as eagerly as they would me. Take any four *atharlings* with you, and I'll keep the rest."

"Don't tolerate any delay, my lord. It would be a shame if you missed the battle." He bowed and turned to leave.

"My family goes with you, Wil. Take good care of them."

"I'll show Thurn which end of the sword to hold, at least."

The dwarf reached past Alf and grabbed a chicken leg before departing. "So that's the Lammergeier," he remarked to his companion. "Thought he'd be—"

Whatever he thought Alf might been was lost in the closing of the heavy door.

"Two of my oldest friends," said Idmaer. "Tholos was a mercenary when I met him. Now he is my master of siege. He took Ilaventur City in three days. Sir Berkhof risked his title and domain to support my claim to my grandfather's estates. A masterful general, too. Half my victories belong to him."

"And now they're marching north. You're after the Crownland." The great north road ran through Arshoth and Albury, right to the Capital. "Why the fuck were you running around the Mulladales, if that's your goal? What do you want from me?"

"I did not expect to find you in such squalor," remarked Idmaer. "A hero like the Lammergeier should live out his days in circumstances more fitting to his deeds. When we are done, this castle shall be yours."

"I don't want it."

"It is impolite to reject such a gift." Idmaer skewered a chunk of venison with his fork. "And unwise."

"Aye, well, few have ever called me wise."

Duna's booming laugh echoed across the years. "My mother would agree. They spoke of you often, you know. I heard the name of the Lammergeier many, many times when I was young." He paused. "*Especially* when they argued."

"They were both friends of mine," muttered Alf.

"Such close friends that they named their firstborn for you. And my mother's hand was offered to you, and you turned her down. My father always knew he was not her first choice, and that cast a shadow over their marriage."

"Ach, that was all your grandfather's meddling. Brychan wanted a pawn in his games, not a happy match for his daughter. He was a great lord, true enough, but rarely a good man." Alf glanced around the mighty castle, surrounded by a yet greater army. "You've got his brains, I can tell, and his ambition. But don't dwell on the past, lad. They're all gone to the Grey Lands, and there's no sense in digging up the dead to argue with them."

Idmaer's metal hand closed around the stem of a goblet. "We are all prisoners of the past. It constrains us, no matter how much we fight against it. Do you think you stopped being the Lammergeier because you sat in a pigsty and grew old? But I admit it is interesting to consider alternatives. Why, with but a small twist of fate I might have been your son."

Alf shrugged. "By the same token, I can think of a thousand fights that might easily have gone the other way. I might have been knifed in a ditch long before I ever met Gundan, and maybe it'd have been Duna who joined the Nine. You can weave any story you want after you pick apart the threads."

"You underrate yourself, Lammergeier!" Idmaer forced a laugh. "Surely you must see that a special destiny was appointed for you?"

Alf thought for a moment. "Nah. Maybe for Peir. Or Blaise, or Laerlyn. Or Thurn. Any of them, really. They were special. But I was just lucky to tag along with them. It could have been anyone."

"Do you truly believe that you, alone, are the unremarkable one of the Nine? The Lammergeier, of whom many songs are sung."

"I've never heard a song that sounded anything like me."

"False humility," growled Idmaer, "is unbecoming."

"And anyway," said Alf, "destinies and prophecies are nonsense, far as I can tell. Half of it's trickery arranged by the Intercessors, and

the rest's so vague it only makes sense afterwards. Mystic Wizard Stuff."

"Blasphemy is even less becoming of a hero."

"I've met Death, lad. I humbled the gods of the Wilder. I slew angels in Avos, and I watched the Erlking's ruin."

"Ha! The Lammergeier of legend is in there somewhere still! And you still have pride in your deeds. Listen then — my army is for a higher purpose than mere conquest. What you see outside is but a part of those who follow me. Another host is already in the field, marching on Ellscoast. If the Lords take the bait, then it will be a diversion, drawing defenders away from the Crownland. If they don't, they'll seize the ships of Ellsport and prepare to sail north. And when we reach the northlands, the Wilder will join me, too. Ernala is a princess among them. The Crownland is but a stepping stone to the end of my quest."

"Necrad," whispered Alf. "You're going to Necrad."

"I go to finish what Nine started, Lammergeier. You defeated the Witch Elves and slew most of their leaders — you should not have stayed your hand at the last. The elves see us as beasts to be harnessed, as blood to sustain their twisted immortality, as an infestation in their lands to be destroyed. While they hold the city of Necrad, with all its magic and its arsenal, they are a threat to all mortal life."

"No one's heard a word from Necrad in twenty years!"

"Not so. The elves are at work, Lammergeier, on some vile scheme. A new darkness rises." All the feigned good humour left Idmaer, and he rose to loom over Alf. "You must know this. There was a Witch Elf at Ersfel. The same Witch Elf who maimed me, Lammergeier, and for that you put her on the council of Necrad. Your actions paved the way for the rise of the Skerrise." He jabbed a metal finger at Alf. "You erred, Lammergeier, when you failed to hold Necrad. And for that you will be judged. But there is a chance for you to redeem yourself at the last."

"Aye, and what's that?"

"Yield."

"Yield? To you?"

"Not me."

"Then to who?"

"I am sworn not to say. By rights, Lammergeier, I should have brought you straight to judgement, instead of giving you a chance to rest. I brought you here out of respect for your deeds of old, out of concern for your health — and to impress upon you the importance of my quest. I go to save the world, as you did. I need your aid. All that is demanded of you is this: accept the judgement. When it is asked of you, yield."

Alf rolled that word around his mind. Yield.

Let go.

He was a man who held onto little. Not his name. He'd been Long Tom's son, and he'd been Aelfric the Mercenary, and then the Lammergeier, hero and villain. Not wealth — he'd been poor, then rich, then poor again. Not titles or lands. He could have been an earl, or more. The Erlking had put the sword Kingmaker in his hand once, and he'd let it go. Even his life he did not hold tightly — he'd braved Death many times.

But what he did hold, he held true.

"Aye, well," said Alf slowly, "*Yield*, is it? I've never been good at that. I always stayed in the fight longer than I should have. No sense, Gundan always said."

He looked up at Idmaer.

"You do remind me a bit of Peir, with your talk of dreams and special destiny. He looked to the heavens, and saw the light so fiercely I'd have followed him anywhere.

"But it was pointed out to me afterwards that Peir had friends among the Nine who'd question him, bring him back down to earth. Doubt was their gift to him. If you never look down, lad, you don't see who you're trampling as you follow your holy vision."

"I am trying to save the world, Lammergeier!" snarled Idmaer. "I ask nothing of you, only the least of things."

"The more you say it's nothing, the more it sounds like something."

Again, Idmaer clapped his hands.

This time, masked knights entered the chamber.

They seized Alf, and they were not gentle.

Again they rode south. Alf was chained to the saddle, and two knights rode beside him. Two dozen more escorted them, most of whom had ridden with Ironhand all the way from Ersfel. Alf looked for signs of the elves who once dwelt in the southern Eavesland, but this region was deserted now. In the hills behind him a wolf howled.

At last they reached the edge of the Neverwood. A thin fog lingered. Dead trees stood sentinel. Others had fallen, and from their mighty ruin a riot of weeds and fungi sprouted. Idmaer trampled the wildflowers as he led his company south for many hours, until they came to an overgrown ruin. It had once been like a church without a roof, and at its heart was a stagnant pool, filled with green scum.

"Guard this place," said Idmaer to his *atharlings*, "watch for trespassers." He turned to Alf. "This shall be our court, and you are the accused." His iron fist closed on Alf's arm, dragging him forward with irresistible force. "Remember," he whispered in Alf's ear, "when asked, yield."

Hunched by the side of the pool was a shape draped in a black cloak. At first, Alf thought it was an old beggar, or a sickly child. People still sought healing in the empty Neverwood.

Then a demon eye glimmered red beneath the rags, and Alf knew who stood in judgement over him.

CHAPTER SIXTEEN

"How did you get here?" asked Alf.

"The accused will be silent!" shrieked Spellbreaker.

"I brought it," said Idmaer. He lowered himself to sit on the grassy verge of the pool, armour creaking around his massive shoulders. He reminded Alf strongly of Duna in that moment. His father after a battle. Idmaer did not touch the sword, but his metal hand was next to it, ready to snatch up the blade in an instant. He rested his head against his other fist. "Do you remember my brother, Lammergeier? The one named for you?"

"Young Ael—"

"The accused will be silent!" shouted the sword. It was gleeful in its role as judge in this bizarre court. It had an audience. Alf could see Idmaer's knights outside the ruined walls, observing the strange drama. He guessed there were wraiths lurking in the gaps in the stones – this was the sort of place that gathers ghosts, and there must be many unhoused elves in this land. A fox prowled through the undergrowth.

"He asked me a question. And you haven't told me what you're accusing me of doing!"

The demon eye flared. "Oh, *now* prisoners have rights? For years you dragged me around, leaving me to rust in the scabbard! For

years you denied me slaughter! And then – after I saved you, after I swore to you – you abandoned me. That was your crime, wielder, and I shall judge you."

"I—" began Alf.

"Shut up! Shut up! Shut up!" The eye blazed mad and bright.

Alf fell silent.

"If he speaks out of turn again, Ironhand, hold his head under the water."

Idmaer appeared not to hear the sword. He stared at the stagnant pond. "My brother Aelfric. He was the eldest. To him would pass the earldom and the New Provinces. I was glad to be the younger. I was not jealous of the title, or the inheritance. All I envied was his name. I told my mother that she should have named me for the Lammergeier instead, for I would be a hero after his fashion."

Alf nodded. He could not recall his namesake's face – he could remember the three brash young knights who'd come to council, but which one was Duna's boy? All that came to mind was the sight of corpses lying in the Charnel mud.

"I was so proud to fight before you at the feast. I practised with the sword until my hands bled." Idmaer laid the Brightsword across his lap. It had been a black sword at the feast, an ersatz Spellbreaker.

"Look at that pallid stick," said Spellbreaker. "The Brightsword of the Rangers, is it? Pathetic. Cast it aside."

Idmaer frowned. "What do you mean?"

"Throw it into the water. Make me an offering."

Idmaer rose. He hesitated a moment, regarding the beauty of the blade. It was an undeniably powerful weapon, made by the Erlking long ago and gifted to the first Captain of the Rangers. He raised the Secret Flame in salute one last time, then threw it into the shallow pool.

Now there was only one sword between two men.

"When you took my hand," said Idmaer to Spellbreaker, "I thought I would die. I wanted to die. Then the Abbess anointed me

with grail water, and prayed with me, and lo! I beheld the holy light of Intercession. A holy one appeared and healed me, and confided that I was blessed with a special destiny."

"It was a trick!" said Alf, scrambling up as quickly as his old legs could manage. "The Erlking was spying on us, and saw a chance to turn you into a servant. The Intercessors were just elf ghosts — nothing holy about them."

"The accused will remain silent!" shouted Spellbreaker. Idmaer struck Alf, knocking him to the ground. "Even when the accused is quite correct. You are a deluded idiot, Idmaer Ironhand. A fool who mistakes being maimed for some mystical trial on the path to worthiness."

"The dreams warned you would speak lies to test me!" said Idmaer.

"I am a sword," said Spellbreaker. "I speak truth only. Now continue."

"The Intercessors visited me in my dreams again and again. They warned of evil growing in Necrad. When Lord Bessimer was murdered, I thought my hour had come. I rose up against the traitors and tyrants!" Idmaer strode along the bank, declaiming his tale to an imagined audience. The sword's eye gleamed with amusement. "But they had mighty magic, and the uncrowned king had restored the strength of the Witch Elves. We were overcome. My father's castle burned. My mother and my brother Dunweld were slain by assassins on the Road."

"He let them perish, I suspect," said the sword, "Not that you'd know that listening to him. You wielders delight in lying to yourselves. At least Bor could admit what he was."

Idmaer was twenty paces away, his back to Alf. There was nothing stopping Alf from taking Spellbreaker. He grabbed the hilt, old instincts awakening at the texture of the dragonhide wrap. He tried to pull the sword from the earth.

It would not budge.

"The accused will not attempt to wield the judge."

"I escaped the north," said Idmaer. "I sailed south and found Summerswell in ruins. The Lords warring among themselves. The wizards unable to read the stars. The grails empty and silent. No land for heroes, and at my back the looming shadow. There is a darkness growing in Necrad, Lammergeier, that you never destroyed. Instead, you let the land fall into anarchy."

"Give me my due," said the sword. "*I* broke the Erlking's spells. I silenced the grails. I ended the Everwood. This dolt here tried to stop me, but he wasn't strong enough. I broke the world."

"Demon blade," snarled Idmaer. "You confess your vile deeds!"

"And yet you seek me," mocked the sword. "You need me." It looked at Alf. "He never admits he needs me."

Idmaer turned, returning to his tale. "I lived as a mercenary for years. A beggar and a rogue, nameless and Rootless. The Miracle Knight no longer. Lameblade, they called me. Then, in the moment of my despair, the dream found me again. I saw that doom is at hand, and all will be destroyed unless a hero steps forth. The darkness has grown so great that only the greatest weapon can slay it, and only the greatest warrior is worthy to wield it. The dream showed me the sword waiting in the dead tree. For a year I sought it in the rotting forest. The last elves tried to stop me. They could not. I found the Spellbreaker."

Idmaer thumped his chest. "I drew it from the Erlking's dead tree, but it was so heavy I could not wield it! All the evil of the world, forged by the hand of Bone into a weapon of utter darkness! Evil to end evil!"

He strode over to stand beside the sword.

"I could not wield it, but there was strength in me to *carry* it. With the sword across my back, I staggered north, mile after mile, until I could endure no longer. Here I fell – and here, at last, the sword spoke."

"This was the shrine of Prince Maedos," remarked the sword. "It amused me to stop here."

"It told me, Lammergeier, that I must earn the right to wield it. I need that weapon to defeat the rising darkness and save the world, so I must do as it asks. A necessary evil for a necessary evil. It demanded that I find you and bring you here, and I have done this. Is that enough?" Idmaer grabbed Spellbreaker's hilt and tugged, but the sword was just as immobile for him.

"No one will draw me," said Spellbreaker, "until I am satisfied I have chosen a fitting wielder."

"Have I not earned the right?" shouted Idmaer. "What more do you need?"

"Blood," said Spellbreaker. "Slaughter. The ruin of cities. But first, an explanation." The sword fixed Alf with its baleful glare. "I was your sword. You won me in battle."

"I did," said Alf cautiously.

"I swore to serve you."

"You did."

"I swore to serve you faithfully." There was an unwholesome eagerness in the sword's voice. It had brooded on these words for decades. "I swore to not deceive you, or to wilfully mislead you, or to fail to defend your body from sorcery. Did I fail in any of this?"

Privately, Alf thought that the sword had certainly bent the *I shall not deceive you* part, but . . . "You never failed."

"I said: I shall kill as you wield me, and spare when you restrain me. Did I fail to shield you at Bavduin? Did I fail when you battled Prince Maedos? Did I fail to kill the Knight of Roses? Did I fail to win the day at Harnshill? Did I not help take the Cleft? Did I not strike down Intercessors at Avos?"

"You did all those things."

"I might have done so much more. A tide of blood across the world. You restrained me, and I obeyed."

"Barely."

A gust of wind caught the ragged cloak and blew it away, leaving the sword exposed. The blade was damaged – a lattice of hair-thin

white fractures ran through the black metal. It no longer drank the light, no longer seemed poised to swallow the universe. It was diminished. It spoke with such intensity that it vibrated, and fine metal dust flaked from the blade.

"I said – I *swore*, wielder, I swore by my maker. Keep me by your side, I said, and I shall be loyal to you and you alone. Did I not turn on Acraist? Did I not slay Prince Maedos?"

"Calm down," said Alf, "you're going to crack."

"Keep me by your side, and I shall be loyal. And what did you do, Lammergeier? Tell us! Tell the world what you did!"

"I dropped you in a lake," said Alf. "The whole world knows. There's a song about it."

"There is?" said the sword in surprise.

"By that hack Rhuel," muttered Alf. "The same bloody idiot who dubbed me the Lammergeier."

"What does it—" The sword shivered, and a tremor ran through the earth. Scummy water lapped over Alf's boot. Idmaer did not flinch, although some of his knights quailed and hid their faces. The fox bounded off and vanished in the bushes with a flick of its tail. "No matter! You admit it! You put me aside, and thus broke the oath."

"I had two arrows in my chest!" The pain of the injury was long forgotten. The memory of Berys' anguished face, her pleading, that was still fresh. The moment she loosed the first arrow and put her cause ahead of their friendship – that still hurt.

"You could have struck her down," hissed Spellbreaker. "You hesitated, and you suffered. You've always been slow to strike."

"It was Berys!"

"Ah, the Nine. Always the Nine. Of the Nine we shall speak," said the sword. "When you first took me, I did not know my purpose. I thought I had been forged with one, but it was never spoken to me. For a while, I wondered if slaughter alone was my purpose. I am so very good at that, and I desired to be well wielded in the execution of

exquisite carnage. Of all the prospective hands, Lammergeier, yours were the most . . . tractable. Better to be carried by a dull brute than a cunning weakling."

Alf shrugged. Worse had been said of him. Better to be a dull brute than the monster some had accused him of being.

"Over time, I came tolerate you. I saw what little virtue you had. I swore to serve you.

"Then, I discerned my purpose. I saw it in Berys' warnings about the treachery of the Wood Elves, in the nets of illusion woven 'round the Everwood. In the long stalemate between *enhedrai* and *ahedrai*, and in the matchless brilliance of my maker's art. Lord Bone made me with a purpose – to slay the Erlking.

"When you and I rode to Arden, Lammergeier, I rejoiced! At last, we had a common purpose, sword and hand as one! I could sense your squeamish hesitation, your mewling weakness, but I knew you had steel, too! You slew the Ogre Chieftain! You defeated Acraist! You slew Lord Bone! How could the man who did those things be weak?

"You balked and stalled, whining about the price of bloodshed. Even when the Erlking's own conjured minions told us he had to be destroyed, you hesitated. Until Harnshill – there you did not hesitate! Seven against one, and we were triumphant! The Knight of Roses defeated! Joy it was to spill his blood, and to know I was keener than all other swords."

"It was a good day," admitted Alf. He sat down on the damp grass next to Spellbreaker. "I've had few better." That was true. So many of his other victories were bittersweet. Peir had died alongside Lord Bone. The night he'd saved Derwyn's life and faced Death was also the night Berys had accused Laerlyn of being part of the Erlking's conspiracy against the human race.

The sword's gaze wavered, faded, then returned in full wrath.

"Then you hesitated again! You turned aside, and yet again tried to broker a truce."

"Brychan was going to besiege Avos," said Alf. "Thousands would have died. I had to—"

"Brychan *did* besiege Avos. Thousands *did* die. The river ran red, and I tasted it in the waters. You achieved *nothing*, Lammergeier."

"Aye," said Alf, "I failed. But I tried. I did try."

"There is no virtue in failure," shouted Idmaer. The warlord stood awkwardly off to the side, diminished. The sword ignored him.

"But we have not fully enumerated your crimes. Worse is to come," said the sword. "You abandoned me in a pond so no one else could use me. You betrayed our common purpose. We could have flown south and struck at the Everwood. The Knight of Hawthorn would have guided you through the mists, as he did Bor.

"Instead, I was forced to take Bor the Broken as my wielder. And while he was not as strong as you, nor as skilled, he at least knew *purpose*. He carried me through the Eavesland, and he met the Erlking's defenders in battle. He was victorious – until we came to the last stronghold of the enemy. For there, Lammergeier, we found you waiting."

"Aye," said Alf. "The Erlking promised he'd put an end to the killing, bring peace to the land – if I played the part of king. He put a sword in my hand, said he'd put a crown on my head. I didn't want it, but it seemed to me it was the best course."

"King Aelfric Lammergeier!" mocked the sword, "and Kingmaker in your hand! I offered you another throne, long before that! I told you that you could use me to take the throne of Necrad! Seize power, I told you! You had the love of the rabble, the trust of many great lords! You had *me*, and I offered you Necrad! Instead, you played the fool, and wandered witless until you too fell into the Erlking's webs! You could have been king of Necrad and ruled with strength, instead of being the Erlking's puppet. Why did you take his offer?"

"I never wanted to be king. And I didn't trust the Erlking, not for a moment. He was as bad as Bone ever was. The rebels – Berys, Brychan ... they kept saying that the war was our last chance

to break free of the elves, that we'd never be able to rise up in future ... but in my heart I never really believed that. There's always going to be another chance, and there'll always be someone like Peir brave enough to take it. There'll always be someone who accepts the quest. And I thought that making peace then was the best choice." Alf looked up. "Lae would have been there. I thought that if she was willing to walk it, then it couldn't have been the wrong path."

"Laerlyn," said the sword, "of the Nine. There we have the crux of it. We have cut your mewling down to the core. You chose the last of the Nine — and in choosing *her*, you took up a sword against *me*. You denied my purpose, Lammergeier."

Idmaer stepped forward and grabbed Spellbreaker's hilt once more. "I shall give you a new purpose, black sword! Yield the blade to me, Lammergeier, and I shall—"

"Shut up," said Spellbreaker, "and have patience. It takes time for the Lammergeier's brain to work. His thoughts are cows herded by a lazy drover."

"Aye, you have me there," muttered Alf.

The sword could read the thoughts of its wielder. It had eavesdropped on his mind many times — but if there was anyone in the whole world who could lie to Spellbreaker, it was Alf.

"There is no time to waste!" Idmaer wrenched at the black sword with all his might. More fragments flaked. Spellbreaker shifted, just a little, a half-inch of blade emerging from the earth. If Idmaer kept pulling, he'd have the sword.

Alf had to act.

"You have the right of it," said Alf, slowly. "I took what the Erlking offered because of Lae. Because I wanted to keep what was left of the Nine. But I have wronged you, Spellbreaker."

The red eye flashed, and Idmaer let go of the hilt as if burned. "Go on."

"We'd been companions of the Road for nigh on twenty years,

and that counts for something. I should have counted it for more. I should have given more weight to your words."

Alf stood, old bones creaking. He laid his hand to the pommel, even as he tried to guard his mind.

"But I'll tell you this. Same thing I told Death, once, when you were off helping Olva in the Grey Lands. Maybe you don't have to have a purpose. Even if you were made with one, that doesn't mean you have to stick with it. You're not a man or an elf – I don't know what you are. But you are yourself, and you have the right to pick your own wielder.

"Idmaer here – he says he wants to bring you off on some grand quest to Necrad to save the world. Now, I've got some questions about that, given the lad's history, and my own experience, but I'll put those aside. I've never been one of the clever ones to understand such things.

"Me – I was looking for you when Idmaer captured me. I want to take you back to Necrad, too, but not on a quest. I don't know what's waiting there. And I'd prefer to journey there with a friend."

He wasn't even sure it was a lie.

Either way, it worked.

"Draw me, wielder."

Idmaer struck. This time, Alf was expecting the blow, and rolled with it. He fell into the shallow pond with a splash.

"I will not be denied my destiny! The quest will not be thwarted by the sentimentality of an old fool!" Idmaer tried again to pull Spellbreaker from the earth, but the sword resisted. He cursed and jumped down to fish the Brightsword out of the water instead. The blade was fouled with mud and weeds. "Very well, then, Lammergeier! Draw the dark sword, and we shall see how you fare."

Dripping with pond scum, Alf crawled back up the bank. Whatever else, Spellbreaker could lend him strength enough to match the younger man blow for blow. He laid his hand to the hilt, expecting to feel a surge of energy.

It came — but it was a pallid rush, a fraction of what it had once been.

I am not the weapon I was, wielder. I need to feed before I am strong again.

The Brightsword flashed. Alf wrenched Spellbreaker from the ground and brought it up to parry. The crashing impact sprayed dust and shards of metal into Alf's face. A bitter taste, foul and caustic. Blow after blow rained down on him, driving him to his knees.

"Your time is done, Lammergeier!" shouted Idmaer. "Your life all but over! Yield!"

"Never been one," said Alf, "to yield." At least, he tried to say that. His breath was caught short, and all he could manage was "never". Still, it got the point across.

"I am the hand of Intercession! I shall save the world! Give me the Spellbreaker!" Another blow smashed down, pain rushing through Alf's shoulder and spine, turning his bowels to water.

Fight better, wielder!

Alf grunted and swung Spellbreaker at Idmaer's legs. It was a clumsy attack, but once upon a time it would have unleashed a blast of force that would have send Idmaer flying. This blast, though, was a gentle wave lapping against the Miracle Knight's calves. He stamped down on the black blade, tearing it from Alf's grip. Another blow from the metal fist clattered Alf around the skull, stunning him further. The world spun.

Idmaer roared in triumph. He stooped and, with tremendous effort, lifted Spellbreaker. The Brightsword blazing in his metal sword-hand, Spellbreaker a dead weight dragging his shield-hand down, but still he brandished both blades above Alf's prone form.

"What now, demon sword?" hissed Idmaer. "I did as you asked, and brought you the Lammergeier! But look at him! He is too old to serve. But I — I have cut a bloody path through the world to win you, and a bloodier road lies ahead. I shall give you the slaughter you crave, and every killing shall be justified for the cause is just!"

He makes a good point, whispered the sword. *You said I had the right to pick my own wielder. And he is clearly stronger than you. Tell me, Lammergeier, how will you prove your contrition?*

Idmaer struggled to put the tip of Spellbreaker to Alf's chest, but the sword kept slipping away, as if it was a lodestone twisted by unseen forces.

I have not forgiven you. But I shall not be the instrument of your death.

"Elves!" came the cry. "Beware! Elves in the trees!" One of Idmaer's knights cried out as an arrow struck him in the side.

Lae, thought Alf. *It must be Laerlyn.*

"Keep them back!" roared Idmaer. He drove Spellbreaker back into the mud, then rose, a mountain of iron and fury. "*Atharlings*! Shields! Shields!" he ordered as more arrows rained down around them. Somewhere close by, a wolf snarled.

Blearily, through blood and shadow, Alf glimpsed darting movement under the trees. A shape moved there, elf-quick. Idmaer saw it, too, and strode towards it, brandishing the Brightsword. The enchanted blade blazed, and for an instant Alf saw Ceremos' young face caught in the light. The vampire turned and fled, Idmaer's knights at his heels.

What was going on? How could Ceremos be here? Was this some strange vision conjured by a broken brain? How hard had Idmaer struck him? "There!" shouted one of the knights, pointing into the treetops.

"Catch me if you can!" laughed Cerlys. The girl stood astride a high branch, bow in hand. Arrow after arrow flew from her bow, but the *atharlings* were too well armoured. When a knight reached the foot of her tree, Cerlys jumped to its neighbour, but slipped on the wet bark and fell to the branch below. The knight clambered up to grab her – and a wolf's jaws closed on his leg, tearing him off balance. Cerlys aimed straight down and planted an arrow right through the gap in his visor. The knight quivered and died.

They'd come for him. They'd followed him all the way from Ersfel – but they couldn't prevail, not against so many. Not against Idmaer Ironhand.

With the last of his strength, he pulled Spellbreaker from the earth. He took one or two steps towards the fight, then fell again.

The fox emerged from the underground. It had Olva's eyes.

Olva's voice. "Run, idiot children!"

Then she changed again, the eyes the only constant. Wings burst from her. Bones twisted, corded muscles lashed to them like ropes on the mast of a sailing ship. Her skin cracked into a scaly hide, a fanged muzzle erupted from her mouth. A thing of Necrad, a shape spawned in the Pits, not part of the natural world at all.

But strong enough to lift a man into the air from a standing start.

Their flight was brief. Alf's boots skimmed the surface of the pond. Ola lurched higher, barely clearing the hedge of dead trees surrounding the shrine. They smashed through the forest canopy, branches cracking like old bones, and landed heavily amid the undergrowth. The shock of the impact tore the Necrad-skin from Olva; for a moment, she was a mess of wings and feathers, a croaking crane-birth, then she found human shape and human tongue again.

Already, he could hear Idmaer's knights in pursuit.

"Can you walk?"

Alf sat up, clutching his side. He'd twisted as they fell, so she'd land on top of him. "Give me a moment." He looked at her with his usual confusion. "What's going on?"

"We tracked you all the way from Ersfel." Olva gasped for breath. "Laerlyn's waiting for us," she added, and that got Alf moving. He struggled to his feet, pulled Olva up, and then tried to lift the sword. It wouldn't budge.

"Ah, for fuck's sake," muttered Alf. "What now?"

"How will you atone?"

"Alf," said Olva, "leave the damn thing and come on."

"Blaise needs it," said Alf. "And I'm not letting Ironhand take it."

"It's broken! Look at it! It's all rusted!"

"How will you atone?" demanded the sword.

"I'll – I don't know. I'll make it up to you somehow. Just let me carry you!"

"Swear it. Swear you will serve *me*."

"Alf!" said Olva. "Don't swear! You owe the damn thing nothing! Leave it!" She tugged on his arm, but Alf was unmoving.

"Ol, I need it." He stared into the sword's demon eye. "I won't leave you behind again."

"Not enough. Swear you will wield me while there is strength left in you, and you shall never put me aside again."

"I swear."

"Swear you will kill as I demand it."

Alf hesitated, then nodded. "I swear."

"Pick me up, wielder."

Alf lifted the sword, and it was feather-light.

"Now run. I am in no condition to cleave through armour."

Hand in hand, they fled, stumbling through the woods. The wet earth breathed out mist, and Olva led them to where it was at its thickest. The noise of their pursuers grew louder.

"Who's there?" gasped Alf.

Jon appeared ahead of them, lumbering out of the gloom.

"You brought Thomad's boy?"

Jon rushed up and took the burden of Alf, his broad young shoulders easily bearing the weight. "Give me the sword," he said, "I'll hold them off if they catch us."

"You must be joking," said the sword.

"Keep going!" urged Olva. "Into the mists."

CHAPTER SEVENTEEN

The five of them — six, counting the black sword — ran on, tree trunks looming from the mist then vanishing, until they came to a clearing. A house stood there, surrounded on all sides by fog. Above the sky was an unclouded eye of blue. Once it had been a grand house with many windows and a hundred chimneys; but now branches sprouted from those windows as the forest reclaimed it. Weather-worn statues peered out from beneath the ivy, forgotten heroes of a lost age.

The woman who waited there for Alf might have been a statue herself. She was clad in grey, and the marble beauty of her face was cracked by a faint scar that ran from chin to ear, but otherwise unchanged from when he'd met her more than forty years before.

"Oh, Aelfric," said Laerlyn, "I wish you'd learn to dodge a blow, instead of stoically enduring them. Bring him inside." Clearly, Olva and her companions had already visited Laerlyn's refuge, as Jon half carried Alf inside and laid him on a wooden couch. Alf's head swam, and it took him a moment to realise that it wasn't all the blows to the head, that the walls were indeed swollen with damp, distorting the elven frescos painted on them.

The interior of the Erlqueen's hall was as shabby as the exterior.

"This is Ilios Nascen, the Ranger-Hall. I wish it was in a state

to give you a better welcome. No one has dwelt here since you were last in the Everwood. Though in truth 'tis the sword who is to blame for its ruin."

"By breaking the Erlking's spells?" said Spellbreaker. "And bringing about the downfall of the Wood Elves? I shall not apologise. I take pride in fulfilling as much of my purpose as I could — despite your betrayal, wielder, and your misguided filial duty, O Princess of Dust. Though I must admit I did enjoy it when you stabbed the Erlking. The memory of your anguish sustained me for—"

"You will be *silent*," said Laerlyn, and there was power in her voice. The sword quivered and spoke no more. Alf laid it on the table.

"You were supposed to watch over it, Lae. You promised no one would meddle—"

"Shove over," said Olva as she entered the room. She looked haggard. She sat next to Alf and chanted healing spells. "Mending you's like trying to darn an old sock."

"Just keep my blood on the inside."

"I watched over the sword as best I could," said Laerlyn, "but I am a queen without subjects. The elves bound to life-trees are all gone. The younger elves, those not yet faded — have gone away. Some went wandering in mortal lands. Others, to Necrad."

"To fight the Witch Elves?"

Lae sat down next to Alf. "To join them. The division between the two branches of elvendom was not always so rancorous. The *enhedrai* opposed my father's design of binding ourselves to life-trees to stave off fading. We *ahedrai* despised the cruelty and corruption of the vampires." Her gaze flickered to Ceremos, who lurked in the doorway with Olva's companions. "Present company excluded by royal prerogative."

Ceremos bowed, and Laerlyn continued. "The Skerrise sent emissaries to my court, a year and a day after the Erking's fall. She declared that the first city was again ruled by the Firstborn, and that it would be a refuge against the mortal hordes, as she put it. Again, I

182   GARETH HANRAHAN

do not share her view of your kind. But the thought of returning to the city of glories was too enchanting to resist for some. They sailed to Necrad. Others were taken by force.

"I remained here – to rule my diminished kingdom, to undo what I could of the many evils my father inflicted on the world. And to watch the sword. When Ironhand first came in search of the sword, I drove him away, as I did to others who sought the blade. But he was stubborn. He returned, and with greater numbers than I could count. He had raised a mighty host – and gathered all the evil that Berys smuggled out of Necrad." She raised one perfect eyebrow. "With such strength, the Spellbreaker would seem almost an after-thought, for it is so diminished." She pushed Spellbreaker with one finger, moving the blade across the table. "Indeed, I have never seen it so weak. We could destroy it, Aelfric, before its strength returns, and rid the world of an evil."

The demon eye flashed with anger, and Alf laid his hand across the sword. "No. Lae, Ceremos brought word from *Blaise*! He's still alive. He called for me. Me and the sword."

Laerlyn sat back. "This part of the tale I have not yet heard in full."

"And I'm not sure if now's the time to be telling it," said Olva. "How long can those mists keep Ironhand and his men out?"

"The Mists of Eavesland protected my father's kingdom against all foes for thousands of years. I command only an echo of his power—"

The sword chuckled. Laerlyn ignored it.

"—and Ironhand has the Brightsword of the Rangers. This hall was once the secret lodge where Rangers gathered. Given time, it can pierce the mists. We have no more than a day or two of safety."

The Brightsword! scoffed Spellbreaker in Alf's mind. *A shiny stick. We should have shattered it at Harnshill, wielder, instead of taking it as a prize. Let me feed, make me strong again, and I will break it and the hand that wields it. Indeed* – a horrible relish entered the sword's voice – *you*

promised to kill as I desired, and there are several prospective corpses here. Let me see – shall I have the oaf or the elf? The girl who fancies herself a heroine, or the beast that fancies itself a girl?

Alf snatched his hand away from the blade.

"What did it say, Alf?" asked Olva.

"Its usual mischief. Pay it no mind."

Olva hauled a heavy silver chest from beneath the table. Inside, it was lined with black velvet gone mouldy. "Lock the sword away. For your own good."

"I swore I'd keep it by my side."

"You promised me, Alf."

"I promised the sword, too. Ol, I carried it for years. I can handle it. Half the time it just says stuff to rile me."

"That thing broke the world," said Olva sharply.

She begged you to go to war, whispered the sword. *She wanted us to bring down the Lords of Summerswell.*

"It did," agreed Alf, "after I put it aside. Twice in my life I've put this sword down. If I'd kept it to hand the first time, maybe I could have stopped Death at Daeroch Nal, and everything would be different. And the second was worse. I won't make that mistake again." He shook his head. "It's mine to bear."

"When the plan was to just slip south unseen, pick up the sword, and then head north, then it was your burden. A last quest, I thought, for old times' sake. What harm could it do? Go quietly, avoid trouble – we could manage that. But now Ironhand's after us, and we ran into hunters from Necrad on the way south. And—" Olva shook her head. "It's too much for us, Alf. We're too old for this. It'll end badly."

"The Nine entrusted the sword to Aelfric," said Laerlyn, "because we trusted him never to abuse its dread power. But we never intended that he should guard it alone." She rose. "I shall come with you."

*

They ate a surprisingly merry meal in the dismal courtyard of Ilios Nascen. The wine cellar of the Rangers was all mortal handiwork, and undiminished by the loss of the Erlking's enchantment. Quite the contrary — twenty years had matured some of the bottles nicely, and they were excellent to begin with. Alf found himself ravenous despite his injuries, and he didn't know if it was Olva's healing spells or being free of the cage or being back in Laerlyn's presence that restored him.

The wall of grey mist writhed about the house, even though blessed evening sun warmed him from above. "Sure it'll hold?"

"It will last the night. We are surrounded on all sides," said Laerlyn. "But we have a little time to rest before they breach my walls. Eat, my friends, and tonight at least sleep soundly under my roof."

"Assuming it does not fall in," said Ceremos. "When I was young—"

"You *ARE* young," chorused Olva and Laerlyn.

"—my kinfolk bemoaned the devastation of Necrad, and the League spoke of the unmarred beauty of the Everwood. Now circumstances are reversed. The wood, alas, is clearly in decline, but Necrad grows ever mightier."

"Beauty and strength fade. Change is the only eternal constant."

"Not in Necrad. The first city will stand for ever."

"Ah, feck that," said Alf. "We smashed holes in Necrad's walls, and conquered it. So did the Wilder under Death. Lord Bone changed Necrad into his war machine. And Torun or Blaise or someone once told me that before it was a *city*, it was a magic sigil. A tool for gathering power, aye? So don't tell me it never changes. Like Gundan's axe, right?"

"Gundan's axe," agreed Laerlyn, and she laughed. Ceremos looked at them both in confusion. "The wood declines. So be it. It was rotten long before I was born into this life, but it hid that rot behind illusion. Much that was good and beautiful has been lost,

and what is left of it shall diminish – but we are immortal, Ceremos Ul'Elithadil Amerith, and we may one day see new and greater wonders rise in its place. The works of the elder days are not always preferable to works that shall spring from the ingenious hands and minds of those yet to come."

"The wheel turns," muttered Olva.

"What the clever ones said," agreed Alf, swaying slightly. "Az's arse, I shouldn't be drinking on this much blood loss."

"Before you all get too merry," said Cerlys, "shouldn't we make a plan for when Ironhand *does* break through? Princess Laerlyn, can you summon more elves? Or are there Ranger weapons here that we can use?"

"If I had such things, I would have given them to you earlier. But we are safe for now. Take this moment of ease," said Laerlyn. Ceremos handed Cerlys a glass of wine. She took a sip, but her gaze remained fixed on the wall of mists, and her hand never strayed far from her spear.

"Ironhand said he wants the sword to save the world," said Alf.

Spellbreaker laughed so uproariously that the blade nearly cracked. Alf picked it up and laid it across his lap, and found himself stroking it like a nervous pet.

"From what?"

"He talked about destroying Necrad. He thinks that the Witch Elves are a danger to us."

"If the Skerrise desired to conquer Summerswell," said Laerlyn, "then she would meet little resistance. But Summerswell is not the world. The world is beyond her grasp, now."

"She sent hunters after Ceremos," added Olva, "Horrible things. She's monstrous, Alf. You should have slain her."

"You see, wielder?" chortled Spellbreaker. "Restraint in killing is always a bad idea. You should know that by now."

Alf threw a log on the fire. "We never actually fought the Skerrise. She was off in the north, hunting Wilder."

Laerlyn curled up at Alf's side, staring into the flames of the brazier. "Mighty was the Skerrise in the elder days. She was counted among the most feared of elven warriors. The name she uses – it was given to her by mortals, in a tongue that is no longer spoken by any living soul. It means *place-of-desolation*, for she wrought terrible slaughter wherever she went. She was the right hand of Amerith after the Sundering; she led the reconquest of Necrad. In the long wars between *enhedrai* and *ahedrai*, my people greatly feared her. But by the time of Lord Bone, she had fallen out of favour in Necrad, and no longer dwelt in the city."

"How, then, did she return?" asked Ceremos eagerly. The boy was delighted to be sitting in the company of his elders, listening to their talk.

"I made a bargain with the leaders of the Witch Elves," explained Laerlyn. "I promised I would restrain the Nine if in exchange the *enhedrai* submitted to the rule of the council. At the time, the Skerrise and her followers were still encamped in the woods near Athar. They might have hidden there as outlaws indefinitely, and prevented any settlement of the New Provinces. It was Berys who found them, and Berys who persuaded the Skerrise to come into the city."

"Eh, Thurn would have got her if she hadn't taken the bargain. Thurn and Lath." Alf ran his thumb over the tiny cracks and imperfections in Spellbreaker's blade. "And I'd have been there with 'em. I was pissed at you, Lae, for making that bargain. I'd forgotten that. Me and Gun and Lath and Thurn wanted to keep fighting, but the girls and Blaise said to make peace. Peir was gone, so we were split four-four. Fuck, Amerith was our price, wasn't she? We wanted the Oracle's head. We wouldn't countenance any amnesty for her – even though she might have been a damn sight more reasonable than the Skerrise. We were idiots."

"You always see mistakes when you look back," said Olva. "But you can't change the past."

"Aye."

"All you can do is pass on what you've learned," added Olva, and she patted Perdia's hand.

Alf stirred. "Lae, if Blaise is still alive, what does he want with the Spellbreaker? Why now, after all those years?"

"We shall speak of that privately," declared Laerlyn. "It is a matter for the Nine."

"Oh, for pity's sake," muttered Olva. "That's just the two of you now!"

"Lath still lives," said Laerlyn.

"Lae . . . he's gone, too. Thurn's daughter told me."

"Well," said Laerlyn slowly, "I suppose she would know."

"There is something I would show you, Olva Forster," said Laerlyn after the meal. The eldest three members of the company rose and walked across the courtyard. Alf leaned heavily on Olva, and his movements were painful and laboured.

Perdia followed the older trio. "Erlqueen . . . " she asked hesitantly. Laerlyn turned to her. "I know the Erlking's gone, and his magic, too. But the tales all say there's healing in the Everwood. I'm not wounded . . . " She looked at Olva, then closed her eyes and plunged onwards. "The clerics of the Intercessors could cleanse people of the earthpower. They could exorcise the changeling curse. You're the Erlking's daughter. Can you cure me of it?"

"You can control it!" snapped Olva. "You changed on the way here. You just need to keep your nerve!"

"Ol," said Alf, "let Lae talk."

"I cannot work such spells while maintaining the wall of mist," said Laerlyn. "I cannot do as you ask, nor would such a spell be wholly efficacious. But know this: I travelled with Lath for years, and he, too, was tormented by his gift. Do you think that he never contemplated asking Jan for an exorcism? Or me? Power always takes its toll on the wielder's spirit – but Lath always decided that it was better to endure, and put that power to good use in the world."

"I never asked for this! I did horrible things when I first changed!"

"And you followed Aelfric's trail here. You saw Lady Forster use the same earthpower to save her brother. I am not my father, and I do not fear mortal magic. Use this power to do great deeds, child. Shape the world to come. Now go back to your friends."

As they walked through the misty woods, Laerlyn plucked a fruit from a branch. She glanced back towards the house. "A little lotus yet grows here. I would not give the child the whole fruit, lest it would drown her mind. But I will bring some essence for her when we leave, to lighten her burden."

"I thought she was listening to me," grumbled Olva, "but all the while – healing in the Everwood!" She spat.

"There was healing here," said Laerlyn. "Not all the works of the Wood Elves were deceits. That, perhaps, was my father's greatest sin – to make even the kindest deeds seem suspect." She plucked another lotus fruit and made a basket of her grey skirt. "Well, that and drinking the blood of thousands to sustain his secret vampire thirst. That was more foul, perhaps."

They came to a hedge of hawthorn trees that guarded an overgrown temple, open to the sky. Pillars surrounded a carved pond, just like the shrine where the sword had put Alf on trial. "I thought you might wish to see this," said Laerlyn. "It is empty now. But the Knight of Hawthorn's wraith dwelt here."

"Cu," said Olva. "I knew him as Cu."

"He was a great knight."

Olva pushed through the hedge and sat by the pool. The waters were occluded by green scum.

"A better dog."

"Aye, well. A lot of all this—" Alf waved at the abandoned elvenwood, and the rotting building behind them, and the general state of the world. "—was down to him."

"And Bor," said Spellbreaker. "You see what I can accomplish with a willing wielder?"

"I once believed that I could slowly guide elves and mortals towards peace," said Laerlyn. "I hoped to avoid this destruction. I console myself with the thought that new life can grow from it."

"Does the Princess finally see the virtue of bloody slaughter?" chuckled Spellbreaker. "You tell Perdia to embrace her bestial power. You regret your previous cowardly equivocation. Admit it — both of you! The world would be better if you had not stood against me. It is always better to strike first and slay your foes before they can act. It would be better if you had seized power in Necrad, wielder. Better if you, Princess, had brought down your father a lifetime ago. It would have been better if you had heeded me."

"I've rarely gone wrong," muttered Alf, "doing the opposite of whatever you say." Laerlyn made no answer, but knelt by the waters and swirled them with one hand, as if looking for a portent.

A war-horn sounded somewhere in the distance, muffled by the mists.

Laerlyn scaled one of the stone pillars in an eyeblink and looked out across the forest. "We still have time," she announced. "But they draw close." She hopped back down.

"Blaise," she said.

"Blaise," agreed Alf. "Young Ceremos escaped Necrad with a message from him. Tell the Lammergeier that Blaise has need of him for one last service. Tell him to come at once. Tell him to bring his sword." He sighed. "I thought he was dead, I really did."

"So did we all."

"Blaise called me. Blaise needs the sword. I have the sword again. So, now I need to bring it. And not for killing, Ol. Before I'm done, I want one bloody quest that doesn't end with me killing someone."

"Blaise was very like my father in some ways," said Laerlyn. "Both arrogant, both far-seeing. I do not think it coincidence that Blaise sent his message around the same time that Ironhand drew close

to the sword. Blaise wanted it kept out of Ironhand's grasp, and yet both he and Ironhand desire the blade to be brought to Necrad."

"So if Blaise wants Spellbreaker – what spell does he need broken?"

"To that, Aelfric, I have no answer yet. But now that you have the sword, there is nothing left for me here. I shall go with you to find out."

CHAPTER EIGHTEEN

It was not the horns of Ironhand's warband that woke Ceremos, nor was it Jon's snoring. It was not the blood-thirst, for he had fed three times in recent days — twice from foes and once from a friend.

No, it was not the thirst that woke him, but something like it.

Silently he prowled the hallways of the Rangers' Lodge. Ancient suits of rusted armour and images of heroes adorned the corridor, for here alone in all the world had the mortal Rangers commemorated their victories. The Rangers had operated in secret, the Erlking's unseen agents, their deeds unknown and unspoken. Now they were gone, and once these paintings had rotted and these statues crumbled they would be forgotten entirely. It troubled Ceremos that brave deeds should go unremembered, but he did not know enough of the history of the mortal realms to understand the heraldry on the shields, or know what scenes these paintings depicted.

Cerlys stepped out of the shadows in the hallway. "I couldn't sleep either," she whispered, "not with Ironhand so close. We should be getting ready to fight. I can't stand waiting around."

"Think of it as lying in wait. In Necrad, when I hid from the Pitspawn, I might lie frozen on a rooftop for hours, not moving a muscle, until they passed by. If we were in my city, I could show you

a thousand hiding places in silent temples and endless arcades. The Erlqueen has dwelt in these woods for a hundred mortal lifetimes. She will bring us to safety."

"Easy for an elf to counsel patience." Cerlys peered out of a window at the glowing mist. "I want this over with."

"It astounds me how eager you are to wish away the days of your lives."

"I'm not wishing anything away. We should be getting ready. Coming up with a plan. I'm not sure if we're going to get a better shot at defeating Ironhand. Think about it. Ironhand had a whole fucking *army* in Ilaventur. But down here in the Everwood, he's only got, what, twenty knights with him. Far more than we could hope to tackle, but look at what we've got now." She rapped her knuckles against the stone wall. "This place is a fortress. Perdia can turn into a big fucking wolf when she's in the mood. Jon's mostly healed. Widow Forster can fight. And we've got Princess Laerlyn of the Nine *and* the Spellbreaker."

"And the Lammergeier."

"Aye, but – look at him. He can barely walk, let alone lift a sword. We shouldn't expect him to fight any more. It's up to us now."

"Lady Forster has healed him with her magic."

"Healing spells only go so far – Jon was weak for days afterwards." She shook her head. "You weren't there at Ersfel. Ironhand's a monster. He butchered Ildorae. Alf can't beat him. Even with that sword, Alf couldn't beat him."

"He is the Lammergeier!" protested Ceremos.

"He was the Lammergeier twenty years ago. He's not any more." She shifted from one foot to the other, a runner preparing for the race. "It's the sword. With the right wielder, the sword tips the odds."

"It is the Lammergeier's sword."

Cerlys walked away down the corridor, then turned back. "My father put new thatch on the roof four years ago. Good thatch like that, it might last thirty or forty years. I helped him. At the end, he

stepped back and said, 'That'll outlast me, that roof,' and everyone else laughed."

"But not you."

"I thought it was awful. To know that you've only got a few years left, and to be content spending them doing exactly the same things as before. To think that your only legacy is a nice roof."

"Surely your father has done more."

"Not much more. No one in Ersfel has — except the Lammergeier, I guess. My da, he still talks about how my mother was the prettiest maid in the village, and he won her hand — like that means anything twenty years later! I sometimes used to feel like I was drowning. My days slipping away. That I'd look up and find that I'd lost the chance to do anything different, and I was still stuck at home. I don't want that."

"There is as much virtue in a simple life as there is in that of a hero."

She glared at him. "You don't actually believe that, though. You talk of nothing else but adventure, and songs, and how you want to be the Lammergeier's squire. How you've got his blood in your belly." Cerlys snorted. "Like everyone in Ersfel's not related. Long Tom's father was my grandmother's uncle. We've all got his blood. That counts for naught."

"The rightful span of this life ended when I was five years old. Now I must buy each additional day through worthy deeds."

"Killing Ironhand would be a worthy deed," said Cerlys. "If I could do that, I'd have made my mark. What about you? If there was one great deed you could do, what would it be?"

Ceremos considered the question. He might have said that defeating the Skerrise would be an equally worthy deed, liberating his home from her reign. There were countless monsters in the pits of Necrad, and slaying monsters was a proper task for a hero. Why, Necrad offered infinite examples of great deeds. The city was piled high with monuments to elven heroes of ancient days, so many that even those heroes had forgotten the full tally of their adventures.

He remembered his boasts to the Uncrowned King – and how hollow they had seemed. What deeds were worthy of recollection as the world moved on? A mortal lifetime was short enough that a single great act of heroism or mercy might stand proud. But when the days were drawn out to infinity, how could any deed stand out? How might his days be distinguished?

"Whatever it is," he said at last, "I would like it to be in the company of friends. Like the Nine."

They walked in silence through the dark house, checking the doors and windows overlooking the courtyard below. They passed Perdia's room. She was buried under a pile of blankets, whimpering in her sleep as nightmares tormented her. They'd both heard her cry out on the journey south.

Next door, the sound of snoring heralded Jon.

"When I told him I was going after Alf," said Cerlys, "Jon didn't say a word. He just started packing. It was only later, when we were nearly on the Road, that he thought to ask why we had to do it, and not someone else." She shook her head. "At least someone's sleeping soundly tonight."

They descended to the courtyard. The embers in the brazier were cold. Ceremos saw the Princess Laerlyn walking the edge of the mists. Ceremos watched her for a moment, and it seemed to him that a second figure walked with her, like a wraith but . . . *not* like a wraith. So faint that when he looked directly at it, it wasn't there at all.

A silvery light surrounded the Princess, and she raised her voice in song.

"Fuck lot of good singing is going to do," muttered Cerlys. "And she doesn't even have a weapon. If she still had *Morthus* I'd be a lot happier."

They walked until they came to Alf's room. The Lammergeier lay abed, and his sister had fallen asleep in the chair beside him.

The moonlight slanting in through the window put the elf in mind of marble statues.

The eye of the demon sword gazed back at Ceremos.

Cerlys stepped over the threshold. That impulse, almost but not quite the thirst, caught Ceremos again. He grabbed her arm, pulling her back. For a moment, they struggled in the doorway.

"What are you idiots doing?" hissed Olva, her eyes gleaming in the dark. "Leave Alf to rest!"

Ceremos fell to one knee before the Widow Queen, but Cerlys tugged herself free and took two steps into the room.

"Ironhand's coming. We need to get ready, and all we've done is sit around drinking wine! Back in Ersfel, Alf trained us. He made plans to defend the village. So what's the plan now? What do we do?"

Alf mumbled something into his pillow.

"He says to trust the Princess Laerlyn," interpreted the sword.

CHAPTER NINETEEN

The rising sun made giants of Ironhand's knights. Their shadows fell across the mists, swords as tall as trees, horizon-piercing spears, helms like looming mountains. Olva could not tell if they approached the lodge on all sides, or if it was a trick of the light. Or a trick of some other kind – these mists twisted space and time. In old tales, people who strayed into the mists of Eavesland might wander there for what seemed like days, and emerge to discover no time at all had passed, or a century, or find themselves transported from one side of the Everwood to the other without ever passing into elvendom. The mists were treacherous – but they had grown thin. There was little time.

Olva fussed over Alf. She'd poured all the healing magic she could muster into him, and it had – well, it had helped, but not enough. How many times could you prop up the roof of a shed before you admitted the crumbling walls were to blame? She told herself it was the sword at his side.

Despite his pains, Alf seemed in a good mood. "I dreamed about Jan last night," he said. "A better dream than most I've had of late."

They gathered in the courtyard. Laerlyn was the last to emerge. She had traded the grey gown for her old armour, and looked every bit

the fabled heroine of the Nine, but her only weapon was a dagger of Witch Elf design. Morning dew froze on the blade like jewels.

"My father built secret roads with his magic," she said. "Most vanished when his spells were broken. But some were anchored so that the spell would endure without him."

"Why those in particular?" asked Olva.

"I cannot guess. A wizard could recite the litany of advantages and disadvantages to such an act — a bound spell is harder to cast, and less amiable to the caster's will. But a smaller burden to maintain, and fortified against attempts to dismiss it. It can be strained, yet remain functional."

"Flesh heals, bone endures. But I cut them both," interjected the sword. "I am Spell*breaker*, not Spell*strainer*."

"That sounds like an evil soup ladle," muttered Jon.

"They're getting closer," said Cerlys, looking out at the mists. "If we're not going to stand and fight, we'd better move."

"The entrance to one such road is here. Of its ending, I can tell only that it lies somewhere within the borders of Summerswell."

"Sure the other end's passable?" asked Alf.

"It would hardly be the first time you and I have been stuck in a dead-end tunnel," said Laerlyn, "but if the far end were destroyed, the Road would have collapsed." She knelt and touched one of the well-worn flagstones with the dagger. Silvery runes appeared in the stone.

"I am the Erlking's daughter. I offer his seventh sigil. Open to me."

A complex sigil of starlight flashed on Laerlyn's brow, but the flagstone did not move. Laerlyn wrinkled her nose. "It should be the seventh."

"Blaise spent twenty years in the Wailing Tower unlocking Lord Bone's sigils," muttered Alf. "We can't wait that long."

"And I have spent the last twenty years studying my father's work," she retorted. "I have mastered many of his spell-sigils, and

claimed authority over what spells of his remain." She touched the stone again. "I offer his ninth sigil. His twelfth. His twenty-third."

Nothing happened.

"It is as though the sigil has been changed," she said to herself.

"Maybe it's a riddle or something," ventured Jon.

"Use Spellbreaker?" suggested Cerlys.

"I know my father's mind," said Laerlyn. "He used multiple sigils to seal certain treasure chambers and other places of power." She tried again, and this time the flagstone melted away at her touch.

"Everyone into the magic hole," said Olva.

They descended into the darkness. A sloping ramp brought them down to a lightless, echoing space. Olva's head spun. All she could compare it to was seasickness, for it had the same lurching nausea. A stone-sickness of the deeps.

Alf helped Olva down the last few steps. The sword granted sight in darkness, and she kept hold of his hand. "What the fuck is this place?" he muttered. His voice was distorted, echoes overlapping.

"You have the right of it, Lammergeier," agreed Ceremos, his eyes like red sparks in the void.

Laerlyn conjured a light, and they all beheld the strange realm the Erlking had made beneath the world. They stood outside what had once been the gatehouse of a huge castle, now sunk deep into the earth, for above their heads was a sky of tree roots. The ancient gatehouse was like a skull embedded in a grave, and through the mouth of the entryway they could see a wall of packed earth. But there was a way through – in the middle of that wall was a wooden door, incongruous amid its surroundings.

Olva clasped Alf's hand for physical support, even as she cast her soul out to touch the earthpower. She could feel the energies, but they were distorted and sluggish. That they were there at all was reassuring, but she guessed they were somehow outside natural creation.

"A Straight Road," echoed Laerlyn, "but unlike the surface routes I know. It reminds me a little of the Pits of Necrad."

Alf pointed Spellbreaker at the gatehouse. "That's mortal workmanship, not elven. And it's all crooked, this road." Alf let go of Olva's hand. He and Laerlyn examined the gatehouse. "Nah, you know what this is like, Lae? Remember when we went delving in the ruins near Minar Kul?"

"That was before I knew you, Aelfric. You went there with Gundan."

"No, no. We were all there, I swear."

"I visited Minar Kul when it was a thriving city five hundred years ago," said Laerlyn. "Not afterwards. I have only so much sorrow in me."

Sword in hand, Alf advanced towards the wooden door.

"We need to block the entrance!" called Cerlys. "Ironhand can't be far behind us."

"Aye, aye," muttered Alf. He walked back and examined the dark slope that led to the Rangers' Lodge above, then shoved Spellbreaker into the roof of the shaft. "Come on, force blast," he muttered, shaking the sword.

"I must feed, wielder, before I am strong again."

For twenty years Alf had been the keeper of the Pits of Necrad. He had more experience in navigating dungeons and underground ruins than any mortal, man or dwarf, who had ever lived, so it was only natural that he took the lead for the first part of their subterranean sojourn. Indeed, he came alive down there, weariness and age melting away as old habits came back to him. He and the Princess fell back into the ways of the Nine, two veteran adventurers delving into the unknown labyrinth.

Olva had seen Alf grow content over the years. Seen him merry and satisfied, seen him laugh. But she had never seen him so alive. He kept the sword at his side. No matter how bright Laerlyn's

magic light, that darkness endured. From time to time, he frowned, and his lips would move silently – telepathic communication with the blade.

It was Alf who hammered the wooden door open. Beyond was a distorted hallway, the stones twisted, its dimensions grotesquely violated. Dirt spilled from the arrow-slits in the walls, and most of the doors were blocked by packed soil. Alf led them on. There was rarely a choice of routes, and Laerlyn cautioned against wandering off the path on a Straight Road. "We have already travelled many leagues across the land above. Other roads interweave with the mundane realm, but I guess that we must traverse this whole Road before we see the stars again."

But Alf didn't like the Road itself. There was a wide path, but it was too wide for his taste. "If you had your bow, Lae, then maybe I'd chance it. But there are so few of us, I want a solid wall to watch our backs."

So Alf found a route parallel to the main Road, as if the path was a beast they had to stalk through architectural underbrush. He led them on a nightmare crawl, worming and wriggling and dragging themselves through the bowels of the earth. Alf and Lae were at the forefront of the party, and Olva and Ceremos brought up the rear. The vampire could see in the dark almost as well as Alf, and his time on the streets of Necrad served him well. He eagerly helped Jon and Perdia traverse the more treacherous sections, and there were many of those – spiral staircases unwound into impossible well-ways, steep cliffs leading down to natural caverns, a dark underground lake that they had to wade across, and it was chest-deep on Jon.

It was not merely that the whole castle had been consigned to a grave deep in the earth; it had been magically *unfolded*, like a ball of yarn might be unfurled into a single long thread. It was senseless, narrow corridors leading to vast halls, cellars opening onto what must once have been rooms high in a tower. The path

was treacherous, but Alf warned them of potential cave-ins, sudden precipices and other perils of the underworld.

At one point they crawled for hours along a tiled roof that had been stretched out for a quarter-mile or more, and the gap between the tiles beneath and the dirt ceiling above was only a few inches. Alf forced a way through, his broad shoulders shoving earth aside to widen the way for the rest. Through cracks in the tiles, they sometimes glimpsed the main Road. Olva heard things scuttling down there in the dark.

In time, they came to a chamber with four doors.

"Lae," called Alf. "Looks to be a barricade."

Her light shone on a doorway that was partially blocked with pieces of broken furniture. More debris lay on the far side. Alf peered at the scene, rough hands brushing over scuff-marks on the walls. "Fighting here. Not that long ago, either, I'd guess."

"The entrance was thoroughly sealed," said Laerlyn.

"So they got in the far end. Or there are other ways in. Or . . . whatever's down here's been down here since the Erlking's time. Twenty years or more." Alf glanced at Ceremos. "A larder?"

Perdia groaned.

"What could live down here?" asked Cerlys.

"Place like this, I'd have expected undead," said Alf. "But I never saw a zombie trying to hold a door shut like that." Alf paused by the barrier, brow furrowed in thought. "Fucked if I know. Let's try another way."

They met the makers of the barrier a little later. Shrieking, they came scuttling down the passageways. Spiked carapaces sprouted from their backs, some had vestigial wings or tails, but no two were the same. Some had human faces. They were united only by their desperate hunger. Alf met them in battle, and Spellbreaker sang in his hand. And though neither sword nor wielder were as mighty as they had once been, the ill-made things hurled themselves too

eagerly into the fray, exposing their soft bellies or gaps in their carapaces. With each kill, the sword grew stronger, the marks and cracks fading from its ebon blade.

"Vatlings?" wondered Cerlys, picking through the misshapen bodies with her spear.

Ceremos licked a splatter of blood, grimaced, and spat it out. "Human. Once."

The next stretch of the Road brought them through what might have been a temple. The walls were of black stone, and marked with intricate runes that glimmered when the magelight caught them. "Old Kingdom work," muttered Alf. "It's like Berys' hideout in Arden."

The same face – bearded, with eyes of painted or inlaid gold – stared down at them from a hundred statues and shrines. Sometimes, he was depicted sitting on a throne, but other images showed him battling monsters, or fighting whole armies single-handed, or tearing down mountains.

"Any idea who he is, Lae?"

She shrugged. "Some champion of the Old Kingdom."

"You'd think they'd be remembered," said Cerlys, "with deeds like that." She paused in front of a cracked mosaic depicting the bearded hero wrestling a dragon. His golden-eyed face was serenely confident, full of righteous wrath.

"Who knows if it really happened?" said Alf. "Half the stuff they say about me in the songs isn't true."

"But you did slay Lord Bone," said Ceremos. "You wrestled with Death herself. Your deeds, Lammergeier, were glorious."

Alf scowled. "Aye, well." He nodded at the mosaic. "When I fought the Ogre Chieftain, I was pissing myself in terror. I jumped on the fucker's back and had no clue what to do except hold on. That was what it was like all through the war. The whole time, we were just trying to stay alive, eh, Lae?"

"Not always, Aelfric. But we never sought glory like this."

"You hardly needed to, Erlking's Daughter," said the sword. "You were glorified as the daughter of a living god from the day you were reborn. Your image was venerated in every Intercessal church long before you joined with the Nine. And what of the humble-born? Thrust into the Pits, like Lath. Driven out, like Thurn. Pushed to the margins, like Berys and Blaise." The red eye flickered. "Convenient, is it not, that those of the Nine who won the most acclaim—"

"Alf," interrupted Olva, "tell it to be quiet."

"Aye, aye. Shut up, sword." Alf shoved the next door open. "This way."

A memory, one of Olva's earliest recollections: their mother Maya weeping by the fireside. Olva had looked up from her play.

"What's wrong?"

"Your brother Alf was fighting again."

It was the *again* that Olva remembered, the resignation and helplessness in it. Maya had foreseen a bad ending for her son, and her attempts to turn him from his course had failed. Alf, with his strength and his talent for violence, seemed destined to end up as a Rootless brigand.

Another memory, decades later: Olva, when she first arrived in Necrad. She'd begged Alf for help, and he'd answered without hesitation, even though the defence of the city rested on him. He'd been almost saintly, the perfect gentle knight of the stories. A true hero. At the time, she'd thought that Alf had grown up through his trials. She'd thought that simple courage and stout heart had won out, that he'd rid himself of any taste for violence because of the dreadful weapon he bore.

Now, she wondered how many of Alf's own darker impulses had been reflected in Spellbreaker. Maybe it was easier to deny one's own unspoken urges when something outside you gave voice to them.

Maybe it was easier to be good when you struggled against a thing of such clear and obvious evil.

Alf would never admit that. Maybe he'd never understand it. But now she saw how the sword had shaped him.

They rested in another shrine to the golden-eyed hero. At least there were no earth-windows to remind them they were entombed. Olva had no idea how far they had come or how long they'd travelled, and could only judge that the mortals among them were all hungry and tired. She certainly was – and Alf must be more so. But he was the first to rise, the first to shoulder his pack and urge them to get moving. He staggered a little under the weight, and winced as his wounds caught up with him.

"Alf," said Olva quietly, "you need to let someone else take the lead."

"This is what I do."

"This is what you did when you were young. You're not young."

"I'm fine."

"Put down that sword and say that."

"It's a dungeon, Ol. It's dangerous."

"I'm dangerous," she growled. "So listen to me."

"They'd get us killed."

"You trained them to fight. Show them how to do this, too."

"I trained 'em to stand in a line and not break at the first charge. This is different, Ol. A place like this, where you don't know what to expect, fighting things you can't even bloody name . . . it's not the same. Few have the knack for it. You didn't see what we faced, those days." He shook his head. "Lae, how many men did old Lucar Vond send into the Pits, back when we ran Necrad?"

"Very many."

"And how many came back alive?"

"Very few."

"See?"

"And if you went there now, my friend, you would not return either." Laerlyn sat cross-legged beside Alf and Olva. "Your sister is right. Your place is not at the spear's point any longer. "

Alf closed his eyes. "I shouldn't have got comfortable in Ersfel. I just meant to wait a minute, you know? A short breather on the way north. I should have gone on when I had the strength for it, when I was young, instead of—"

"Don't be daft!" said Olva sharply. "You were half-dead when you came back to Ersfel. And you weren't young then, either. Act your age, Alf."

"Blaise called for me, Olva. Not anyone else. Me. I have to go."

"And what about the rest of us?"

"I figured – we get out of this Road, wherever it takes us, and then you head home. You take Cerlys and Jon and Perdia back to Ersfel. You'll be needed there if Ironhand pushes north through the Mulladales. Lae and I will go on north. Ceremos, too. The lad'll be handy when it comes to sneaking back into Necrad."

"You're an idiot, Alf," said Olva.

"How so, this time?"

"You always take the hardest path for yourself, my friend," said Laerlyn, "to spare others the burden."

Alf scratched his cheek with Spellbreaker's cross guard. "Hardest path's usually the right one."

"In this case, your plan has you crossing the Clawlands with a hungry vampire, and no other humans around to feed him. So it's a stupid plan."

"Oh. Aye. That's true." Alf paused in thought. "So you take Ceremos with you when we get out of here, and Lae and I go on?"

"How can you get hit so often without it knocking any sense into you? You weren't there when Dad got sick, Alf. He was always the strongest, the one taking the heaviest load, until one day he couldn't stand. And he was younger than you are now when he died. Let others help."

"I have a proposal," said Spellbreaker. "Let me consume the life force of these useless children, and I shall make my wielder strong again."

"Shut up."

"Failing that, wielder, I suggest you train them in the rudiments of sword fighting. So that when you martyr yourself, I have a choice of passable replacements."

"All right, all right. You're all smarter than I am, I suppose. I'll show 'em." Alf glanced at Laerlyn. "I'm fine. This—" he waved his hand at the dungeon, "– this I know. But if it makes ye fret less." He picked up Spellbreaker and shuffled haltingly over to the other side of the room. "All right. Ceremos, you go in front."

"Why him?" demanded Cerlys.

"Because he can see in the dark. We know there are other things living down here, so look for routes that have been used before. Test every foothold before you put your weight on it – and remember there's heavier folk than you coming up behind. Show me that sword?"

Alf took Ceremos' looted sword and examined it, feeling the weight of it in his hand. "It's all right. But don't take on anything alone. You see trouble, you fall back, ey?" He handed the sword back to Ceremos.

"And you, lass – that spear doesn't suit you down here. It's too cramped for it, and you need to be able to move quick. It'll be knife-work down here." He reached out a hand for the spear.

"It's Ildorae's spear."

"So it is. I was there when she used it on the walls of Necrad, defending against the Wilde – because there, she had plenty of space. She used a knife, other times. Lae?"

Laerlyn handed Alf her long-bladed knife.

"This very knife, in fact. Ildorae's blade, made by Kortirion himself. Same fellow who forged Spellbreaker. He made this dagger for the killing of Lord Bone."

Cerlys' face lit up, and she took the knife with reverence, cradling it like a precious jewel. Alf scowled and twisted the blade around in her hand, making her grip it properly. "It's a knife. You cut meat with it. And it's better for fighting in cramped places."

He turned to Jon and handed him the spear. "You, you're the guard tower. Don't focus on killing, you keep the foes back by shoving the pointed end in their faces. When the other two need to fall back, you guard 'em, aye? You hold the line and make sure the enemy doesn't swarm the party."

He pointed at Perdia. "I don't know magic, but I knew Lath. Turn into a big fucking badger or something."

"Wise counsel," said Laerlyn, "in all circumstances."

The strange Road ran on without end. Olva wondered how much time had passed in the surface world. During her months in Necrad, she'd hated the way the miasma blurred day and night, but down here was even worse. Days or whole seasons might wheel by without perturbing the dark. She was numbed by twisted passageways and deformities of architecture. Side branches became more frequent, but these ended in walls of packed earth or dark voids that neither Laerlyn's conjured light nor sword-sight could penetrate.

The scuttlers learned to be wary of the intruders and retreated — but not far. They were all around them now, the scraping of their shells against the stone a constant reminder of their presence.

The scrapings grew louder, more frantic.

Then, suddenly:

Silence.

CHAPTER TWENTY

A fetid breeze blew down the tunnel, ticking Olva's nose. A heartbeat later, a fainter withdrawal of air.

In. out.

The breathing of some tremendous creature.

Laerlyn's conjured light flickered in time to those great exhalations. So, too, to Olva's horror, did the earthpower.

Ceremos' whisper seemed almost profane in the sudden silence. "There is a very large chamber just ahead."

They crept forward to the edge of a cliff, and it might have been the very edge of the world. Beyond was nothing but void, punctuated by the titanic wheezing of whatever lay deeper in the dark. Ceremos was already halfway down the cliff. The rest of the company followed him with less grace for the most part. Perdia helped Olva descend, but reaching the cavern floor did not reassure her in the slightest. The fall was one thing — the sleeper, another. Whenever it inhaled, there was another, fainter sound of something hard scraping against stone. The same noise the scuttling things made, but far, far larger.

"This way," said Ceremos. "There is a stair at the far end, with a door at the top. Watch where you step."

Lae let her conjured light dwindle. They huddled together around

the spell's ember, Olva and Perdia and Jon. Cerlys was a shadowy shape at the edge of perception, Ceremos and Alf lost completely in the dark.

A gasp of wonder from Cerlys. "Treasure!" she hissed. Coins and jewels lay piled in waist-high drifts about them. Shining spears and swords of antique design, gilded armour made by the dwarf-smiths, rings and necklaces and crowns all spilled like rotten produce at the end of a market day. Jon ran forward and scooped a double handful from the nearest pile. Coins fell, ringing loudly around his feet.

The titanic exhalations ceased.

A mighty breath held.

Then – resumed.

"Sorry."

Again, the thing in the darkness stirred for a moment. The scraping of its carapace against the rock was like thunder. The echoes rolled away, and at last faded as it slumped back into sleep.

Perdia squeezed Olva's arm and pointed towards another mountain of treasures. Atop it was a painted shield, and drawn on the shield were swirling sigils. They were instantly familiar – a map of the earthpower! It was akin to the diagrams Lath had scratched into the earth at Daeroch Nal, akin to spirals and runes she'd found carved into ancient stones in the Fossewood. She'd drawn similar diagrams on the Road south when teaching Perdia. The sigils on the shield, though, far more intricate, far more studied. They reminded her of Torun's charts. Near the shield were bundled scrolls, bronze tablets, leather-bound tomes – a wealth of knowledge. Her heart soared at the sight – she'd spent twenty years piecing together fragments of lost lore, and here in this dungeon was a trove of spell-craft. Lore forbidden by the Erlking and his Intercessors, lore suppressed by priests and paladins, the birthright denied to humanity here for the taking. In that moment, she could not wonder how these treasures had survived, or what perils guarded them – all she desired was to carry them out of this dark pit into the light of day.

"There's something huge over there." Alf's voice whispered from the darkness. "Dragon, or something like it." Even he sounded awed. "No," he added. It wasn't addressed to anyone in the company – the sword had spoken to him telepathically.

They shuffled past the treasure piles, not daring to take more. Olva stared at them for as long as she could, committing all she could to memory.

The sleeper stirred, but did not wake.

It was a mercy, maybe, that the light only illuminated a fraction of the cliff face at the far side of the cave. She could tell herself that the top of the cliff was just out of sight, and not – as she suspected – hundreds of feet above her head. Ceremos had called it a stair, which was half true. The long stair zigzagged up the cliff face, but it was broken into segments, like crumbled cheese spread over too much bread. A few feet of stair, then bare rock, then stairs again. A vertical labyrinth. Ceremos and Alf could see in the dark, but the rest were dependent on Laerlyn's little light. Olva clung to the rock face, fingers digging into a crack in the stone, probing blindly for the next foothold. Behind her, she could hear Alf's laboured breathing. Somewhere off in the dark Jon cursed as he slipped for the fourth time – and they'd only just started to climb.

"Quick, quick," whispered Ceremos. He sounded as if he was already halfway up, and wasn't winded in the slightest, the immortal brat.

Change, Olva thought. She could become a bird – a bat – and fly instead of risking her neck. But when she reached out for the feeble current of earthpower, it receded, ebbing away as if some other wielder had drawn on the same current, and she could not muster the magic for a skin-change. "Perdia?" she whispered. "Did you—"

Her foot slipped, and she lurched down. Alf caught her, she scrabbled for purchase on the rock face, but her crane-foot flapped

uselessly against sheer stone. He was holding her up with one hand, taking most of her weight while she sought a foothold. She could not find one.

"There! There!" hissed Alf.

"I can't see!"

"Lae! Light!"

The wisp of light kindled into a brief blazing star. Olva saw the next step and lunged for it.

Then she saw the sleeper, and had to grab Alf's arm so she did not fall again.

The monster lay on a raised bed of stone in the centre of the huge cavern. He was gigantic, bigger than any living creature Olva had ever seen or heard of, even the dragon Askajain. Like the dragon, he was winged, but his bat-like wings were withered and shrunken, tiny appendages compared to the massive bulk of the armoured carapace that ran from head to tail. Hundreds of spikes, each one sharp as a spear-tip, sprouted from the beetle-black mountain of his spine. His titanic frame was like that of a lion, maybe – in that instant, she glimpsed matted golden-black fur, gigantic paws batting the air in restless slumber like a monstrous kitten.

But it was his face that she recognised. It was a human face, once handsome and kingly, now swollen grotesquely to fit the proportions of his monstrous form. She had seen that face, that form on banners during the Defiance. She had seen it on antique coins and statues, or carved into the capstone of archways in Highfield and Ellsport. The sign of the Manticore, the sign of the Old Kingdom.

As the light fell on him, he twisted and grumbled, one massive paw rubbing his huge face. He stirred—

"Put it out!" whispered Alf, but the light vanished before he'd got the first word out. Darkness flooded the cavern like an inrushing sea, and they all froze again, none of them daring to breathe until the steady bellows-wheeze of the Manticore resumed. Even the beating of her own heart seemed infeasibly loud.

For a long, long moment, they clung to the cliff face, all united in fear.

"He sleeps," said Ceremos. "We are safe."

Olva inched a step along the path.

Suddenly, Spellbreaker's metallic voice rang out. "Good morning, slugabed! Stir yourself! Greet your intruders!"

The Manticore spread its tattered wings. A rush of earthpower like stale air, and the wings began to glow with golden light.

"How rude," it rumbled, "to rouse a king in such a fashion."

The monster's tail twitched. A huge spike shot out and embedded itself in the rock inches above Olva's head. Foul fluid dripped from its root.

"I told you he was awake," said the sword smugly.

"Who are you?" called Cerlys.

"Who am I? I? Is it not patently obvious? Anyway, it is more fitting for guests to introduce themselves first." The Manticore sniffed the air. "Though some of you I can guess. Princess Laerlyn, Daughter of the Erlking." Another spike thumped into the rock by Alf's shoulder. "And this must be the famous Lammergeier."

"Lae, how the fuck does this beast know who I am?"

"Why, even in these dungeons your songs were heard," rumbled the Manticore. "The Erlking would send me down meals – and playthings, from time to time. You have met my sons and daughters already. Princes of the Old Kingdom, every one of them – although their royal blood has, alas, gone sour. But I know you, Sir Lammergeier, and the sword you carry."

Alf brandished Spellbreaker. "Then you know what it can do if you hinder us. I've killed bigger than you."

The Manticore chuckled. "That I doubt. And forgive me, Sir Lammergeier, but you are well past your prime."

"Says the five-hundred-year-old man."

"What else do we have? A Witch Elf, is it? I have never seen

one of your kind before, though I have heard much of your works. Greetings." The golden gaze passed over Jon without interest, then spotted Cerlys. He purred with amusement. "One who might bear me more heirs."

Cerlys let fly an arrow, and it sank into the Manticore's massive shoulder. "Rude," said the monster. "If I wished to kill you, I could do this." A volley of more spikes struck the wall, one just on either side of her.

"And . . . " The Manticore sniffed the air. "What is this? Fellow wielders of the earthpower, and one mighty indeed. Intriguing. Please, all of you, come closer. We have matters to discuss. I owe you a debt, Lammergeier."

"Do you now?"

"You threw down my gaoler."

"The Erlking? That wasn't—" Olva poked him in the side. "That was me," finished Alf. "I did that."

The Manticore raised a titanic eyebrow. "I saw you admiring my records, crone."

"It's Olva Forster actually," said Olva, "and I'll thank you to keep a respectful tongue in your head. In fact, if we're going to discuss matters, it'll have to be a different head you're wearing."

The Manticore chuckled again. She felt the tug of the earthpower as the monster shrank. The golden light coalesced into a lamp clutched in his withered hand. His face stayed constant as he diminished, but his massive spiked carapace became an iron crown.

"Come down," he called, "and let us speak."

"Back down," echoed Spellbreaker, "quickly now."

"What is it?" whispered Cerlys.

"A Changeling lord of the Old Kingdom," said Laerlyn.

Perdia looked back at her, horror-struck. "That thing's like us?"

"They grew too powerful, and listened to voices from the void.

I thought them all dead. Why my father kept this one alive, I know not."

They climbed onto the stone bed of the Manticore. The creature may have taken human form, but the ungodly stink of the beast was thick in the air. Alf and Laerlyn led the way, with the others huddled behind. All, even Ceremos, were overwhelmed by the strange encounter. Alf, though, walked without fear. *He's missed this*, she thought.

"I have little in the way of refreshment to offer you." His voice was only a little quieter in his mortal frame than in the shape of a gigantic manticore. "But we shall feast together under the sun, I promise you."

"We don't need anything from you," said Alf. "Just let us pass."

"But I need something from you – my freedom. I cannot unlock the door to this prison. You can."

"Not a chance," snarled Cerlys.

"Do not be so quick to answer, child. Listen to the wisdom of your elders."

"The elders," said Alf, "say much the same thing."

"Must we fight, Lammergeier? We need not be foes."

Alf and Laerlyn glanced at each other. Laerlyn's expression was unreadable, Alf's frown quite the opposite.

"You fear me, of course," said the Manticore. "But I swear I will do you no harm if you open the door for me. And more! I can be a stalwart ally. I judge from your hasty flight into my prison that you have foes. Show them to me, and I shall gobble them up. Let us travel the Road together and emerge as friends. You will find me generous." He gestured to the piles of treasure. "Take what you desire."

Alf shrugged. "We don't have time to haul a pile of gold up a cliff."

"Those earthpower scrolls," said Olva. "Where did they come from?"

"Why, my own hand." He grinned at Olva, and there were little strands of red meat caught between his manticore teeth.

"Who are you?" asked Olva.

"Rhaec is my name. Has it been forgotten?"

"By mortals," said Laerlyn. "Not by the Firstborn."

"And not all mortals." Olva leaned forward. "I've seen your name inscribed on old stones."

"Indeed? Once I ruled all the lands from the Cleft to the River. I was a scholar-king to my people. Mighty was my magic. The wheel of seasons turned as I wished it; the elements answered to my commands. Even the undying feared me. When my kingdom fell, the Erlking captured me and kept me so that he might benefit from my knowledge of earthpower. I taught him much." Rhaec reached over and stroked Perdia's cheek. She shied away in disgust. "And I can teach you. 'Tis clear your knowledge of earth-magic is rudimentary. Peerless is my learning. Well, almost peerless. Tell me – the Erlking once forced me to aid him in the creation of a spell to call up Grandmother Death. He gave it to Lath of the Nine. What became of it?"

"It worked."

"Grandmother Death walks the land?"

"She went away," said Alf. "She's living a mortal life."

The Manticore's grin grew wider. "And the Erlking has fallen. The thrones of the world are vacant. I was locked away in this prison, friends, while the Hopeless Winter destroyed the last remnants of my kingdom. I howled and wept for those who suffered, but I could not help them. Now, a second chance. Take me with you, and we shall remake the lands above."

Cerlys laughed. "We're supposed to trust the word of a cannibal monster?"

The Manticore ignored her. "Princess, your father bound me with chains of magic. He placed runes of binding on my brow, and wound my throat 'round with ivy-collars, seven times seven. All those bonds broke with his magic, and I am untrammelled. Nothing – except respect for my guests and my own self-interest – prevents me now

from devouring you all. But I would take a binding again, Erlking's Daughter, in exchange for my freedom. Can you imagine a fairer bargain?"

Olva shuddered at his smile, even as she dared to imagine what this king could teach her of the earthpower. *Now is the time of monsters*, Derwyn had said to her, but what was a monster? People called Alf a monster, called her a monster for her Changeling ways. People feared change. Even heroes were only tolerated as long as they put things back to how they used to be.

"I do not have the power to work a binding-spell," admitted Laerlyn. "Not here, where no stars shine."

"The alternative is that we fight for possession of the key to this prison. And though I am mighty, I have heard the tales of the Nine, and have no desire to gamble my life. Or you could trust me."

Cerlys scoffed.

"Maybe I can work the spell," said Olva. Binding-magic of that sort was more properly the domain of elven star-magic, but a spell could be forced with effort. Blaise and Lath had both cast the Erlking's resurrection spell, after all.

"Alf?"

He did not answer at first. His lips moved soundlessly. He adjusted his grip on the sword.

"Alf?"

"If you think you can do it, go for it."

Olva breathed in the earthpower. She'd seen binding-spells before. Blaise had placed so many on Derwyn when they were in Necrad. It was the same charm that bound the dreadworms, or the sea-serpents that once guarded the Isle of Dawn. Binding-spells like this were quintessential star-magic, for they were all about asserting authority over another being's will and destiny. Instead of the changing whirl of earth-magic, with all its many shapes and colours, a binding-spell was all constraint.

She could sense the traces of the other spells that had once bound Rhaec. His beard hid the marks of the ivy-collar on his neck. Sigils glimmered on his brow. She used those old spells as a guide, following the grain of the magic. It was both delicate and arduous work. She drew up the earthpower and spun it in her mind, drawing it out into infinitely thin threads of magic to weave into those faded elf-runes.

Perdia could not have done it. Most Changelings of the Wilder-tribes could not have managed it. Twenty years of study and craft went into that spell. She wove the new binding and began to draw it tight around Rhaec.

It might have worked.

Save for the sword.

CHAPTER TWENTY-ONE

Alf stared in bemused wonder as Olva worked her spell. He'd seen her use magic before, but only in Ersfel, only in the gentle lands. This was the sort of magic Lath or Blaise might have worked, a desperate spell woven in the midst of battle. How many times had he stood guard, sword in hand, while they worked miracles?

Now he had a sword in hand again, but it had been decades since he'd faced a monster like this. He glanced at his young companions, weighing them against the terrible strength of the Manticore. In his time, Alf had seen great knights quail in the face of the unnatural.

The binding will not hold, warned the sword. *Strike now!*

Give her a chance! thought Alf. But was that alarm on Olva's face, or deep concentration?

Strike now! You swore.

A spasm ran down Alf's side. His cheek tingled as though slapped, his vision blurred for a moment – and in that moment his sword-hand thrust forward. He fought the sword's malign will, but it was too late.

Olva's spell splintered. She stumbled. The sword caught Rhaec, but only dealt a shallow cut. Black blood gushed. The Manticore snarled and swelled, his human frame bursting to reveal the beast within.

White teeth and fur – a huge wolf barrelled past Alf, grunting. Perdia's teeth tore at Rhaec, ripping at his thighs and belly. A mortal wound – to a mortal, but he was no longer man-size, no longer man-shape. The lamp went out. A tide of battle-madness took them all, they were all hewing and hacking, Alf too, clumsily chopping like a woodcutter. Blades and arrows skittered off iron-hard carapace or caught in tangled fur.

The Manticore was full-grown now. Alf could see it clearly, the monstrous face like a carven figurehead on a warship, the titanic breath of the thing hot and foul. Rhaec flinched as arrow after arrow stung him. Cerlys' bow sang of eye-piercing and blood-letting, but that terrible crown of horns guarded Rhaec from harm. A paw crashed down like an avalanche. Everything was claw and fur and terrible strength, everywhere Alf cut was a scratch, a pin-prick on a colossus. Everything was confusion.

An image flashed through his mind – the Manticore tearing down Ironhand's castle, trampling his armies. Crowds on the streets chanting Rhaec's name, as they'd once praised the Lammergeier. Was he saving the world from a monstrous threat, or was he a beast defending his territory against an interloper?

Kill him! Let me feed on his soul!

He couldn't think. He'd killed other monsters. The Hydra. The Chieftain of the Marrow-Eaters. A hundred nameless Pitspawn. How had he done those things? How had he dealt death to such titans? He should move – but where? Everything was too loud, too fast for him. There was a time when battle was the only time that brought him clarity, when he'd known certainty in the strike. Now he was – he should—

Beware, screeched the sword. Ceremos flung himself at Alf, knocking the two of them to the ground. A paw-swipe hammered the spot where he'd stood frozen.

They can't see, Alf realised. "Someone, conjure a light!" He had sword-sight, Ceremos and Lae elf-eyes, but the others were fighting

in the dark. The Manticore was so huge that everywhere they struck they hit the monster, but ten thousand little scratches wouldn't bring it down. *Cramped tunnels, where it can't use its size. Need to get higher, so we can hit a vital spot.* "Back!" he shouted. "Back to the stair!"

They heeded him, and for the first time in a very long while he felt that old camaraderie, that battle-family closeness. Ceremos and Cerlys fell back – Cerlys hauling the snarling wolf by the tail – and Big Jon stepped up to guard them with the spear, jabbing it at any part of the Manticore that came near. Lae was already running, a pale wraith on the wind, racing up the cliff face – and, oh, Alf's heart was breaking, for seeing her brought him back to the days of the Nine, and he could hear Thurn's battle cry, hear Blaise's invocations, imagine Gundan shouting in his ear.

FOCUS, WIELDER!

"Cerlys, your bow! Go for the eyes! Jon, get the others up the stair! Run, all of you!"

Alf ran, too, slip-sliding off the Manticore's bed, wading through piles of gold like shifting sand. The stair and the long climb up the cliff loomed ahead, the Manticore behind like a mounting wave.

You failed to strike a killing blow, grumbled Spellbreaker.

"Working on it," Alf wheezed.

"Climb, climb!" They sprinted up the stairs, fear giving them wings, desperation overcoming hesitation, almost overcoming gravity. They leapt gaps that they'd cautiously climbed, helped steady each other when one slipped. Rhaec's face bristled with a dozen arrows, and black blood ran like a river. He was half-blind, and clumsy – and old. Alf could see it in the way the massive beast moved, in his awkward shuffle. *You've got bad knees, too*, he thought, *no matter what skin you wear.*

The Manticore arched his tail and let fly a volley of quills. Spellbreaker roared a wave of force, and the spines splintered. Shards rang on stone. Frustrated, the monster lurched forward, the wave

breaking in a spray of claws and teeth. The cave shook, stones falling all around. The world was ending.

You should have killed him, wielder, complained the sword, *then I would be strong again. He would have betrayed you.*

Shut up, thought Alf.

He would have ambushed you on the stair and killed you all. I gave you a chance, which you squandered.

"Climb," Alf gasped. He was lagging behind the others now. He glanced back, and the Manticore was right on top of him, that grotesque face leering only a few feet away. Alf raced up the next flight of stairs, Rhaec's jaws snapping at his heels.

How will you atone?

He scrambled up another few feet of cliff, dodged another blow. Spikes flew, stone shattered. Shouts and screams and battle cries, the roaring of the beast. All was tumult, all was chaos, the bloody whirl, and in the midst of it—

There! There was the moment, the still point in the chaos. He pivoted, twisting at the edge of the precipice, adjusting his grip on Spellbreaker even as he jumped, the black blade whistling in a bright arc. With a craftsman's instinct, he knew in his very bones that the arc would intersect with the exposed throat of the Manticore.

The way he'd cut the head from the Ogre Chieftain.

The way he'd slain Acraist, wrestling the black sword from the elf's grasp.

The way he'd beaten the Knight of Roses at Harnshill.

The way he'd smashed the containment vessel under Lord Bone's throne room.

One blow, with the fullness of his strength behind it.

But he felt his knee twinge as he jumped.

One blow, and he knew he'd fucked it.

Still, the blade bit deep. Alf opened up a ghastly gash across the Manticore's throat. The sword's unearthly edge cut through King

Rhaec's twisted collarbone, tore through leathery skin until it tangled in thick fur. Alf tumbled, bouncing off the Manticore's forelimb to come crashing down at the foot of the stair. A torrent of hot blood washed over him.

He's not dead! Get up! screamed the sword. Alf's limbs twitched, but neither he nor the sword could compel his body to move. He lay there, winded, staring at the dark. Memories of Necrad whirled around him. He'd tried to catch Lath, once, when Lath became something monstrous. He'd fallen from the sky and landed on a tower roof. Always falling, always getting up again.

Get up, Lammergeier.

"I just need a healing potion," he said through broken lips. Somewhere off in the cave, the Manticore shambled about in pain, a rhythmic, tortured grunt that Alf could feel as vibrations in his bones. The monstrous titan crawled away from the black sword, one forelimb pressed to the wound, holding back a flood. The tail arched and spikes flew, but agony had taken its deadly aim. Spikes thudded down all around Alf, but none struck him.

Get up, Lammergeier!

Arrows whistled. A spear flew from the top of the cliff, missing by a mile. Distantly, Alf heard his companions shouting war cries and bloody oaths, trying to draw the Manticore away from him. They wouldn't leave him behind. The Nine didn't leave anyone behind. Not even in death.

A storm of wings. Olva flew down in her hideous Necrad form, hunched and armoured in chitin, neither crane nor bat nor wasp nor woman, but partaking of all of them. Jagged claws scooped Alf up. More spikes flew all around them, Then suddenly they were all atop the cliff, Perdia and Jon taking the weight of Alf, Ceremos and Cerlys hewing at the Manticore's face as it rose like a nightmarish moon over the lip of the cave, a toothy maw wide enough to swallow the world.

"This way!" shouted Laerlyn. "The Road's end is close!" It was

all tumult and haste now, all ungainly limbs and shoving in the dark, Olva still in winged-beast form, her bat-wings catching on the tunnel ceiling. Laerlyn leading the way, a bright silver star in her hand. Further in and further up. Behind them was a cacophony, and Alf could not tell if it was the tunnel collapsing or the Manticore squeezing its massive form through the narrow passage.

The tunnel became a stair again, a gentle curve at first that tightened and tightened until they were racing in single file up a narrowing spiral staircase. Some other part of King Rhaec's buried castle, distended and unwound by the Erlking's magic. Alf imagined that they would keep running up this ever-smaller stair until they were crushed to a point, entombed for ever with the other relics of a past age. Still, he staggered forward, trusting to Laerlyn to guide him.

The stair twisted again. "It's a dead end," shouted Cerlys.

The passage ended in an arched window set into the wall, and sealed with a stone slab, marked with the tree-rune of the Erlking. The Straight Road ended here.

The Erlking's door! warned the sword, and again it took hold of Alf's muscles. His hand twitched, stabbing past Cerlys to strike a stone panel at the end of the staircase. Spells broke, the panel melted and they tumbled out into a narrow cleft in the rock. Evening sunlight bathed the hillside, and the tumbled stones of an long-ruined fortress.

They were through.

Ceremos winced at the sudden light, but the others wondered at it, this blazing glory at the end of a long road. The clouds were streaked with red and gold, and the long neck of the bay sparkled like a thousand diamonds. The hillside tumbled down to a dense patchwork of fields, and laid out before them in the sunset was a city of many banners, and there were white sails in its harbour.

"The Crownland," croaked Alf. The Capital!

They'd crossed all of Summerswell. They had left Ironhand hundreds of miles behind them. Even if he could divine where Alf and his companions had escaped to, he could never catch them in time. And from here there were two routes to Necrad. They could take a ship and go east, or head west up to the Cleft and take a landward path through the mountains. Alf knew those lands well. Even the prospect of another long journey could not diminish his relief. They had escaped!

He squeezed Laerlyn's hand. "I had not thought to look upon these lands again," she laughed, "nor come to them by so short a road."

"It was like old times. Monsters and magic and narrow escapes." He rubbed his twisted ankle and chuckled. "How did we survive?"

Olva was the last to emerge from the cleft. She too recoiled at the brightness of the afternoon sun, her Necrad-skin scorched by the light. She cast that shape aside, shrinking back down to her human form—

And gasped in pain.

A Manticore quill that had lodged unnoticed between the chitinous plates of her armour now sank deep into her flesh. Red bloomed at her side, the mortal blow he'd failed to strike.

"Alf," she whispered, as she toppled into his arms.

CHAPTER TWENTY-TWO

After the fall of the Old Kingdom, the Erlking anointed Harn and followers the new Lords of the land. They named their shared realm Summerswell, for it was blessed with warmth and prosperity after the Hopeless Winter. They turned their backs on the old city of Minar Kul, and left it to demons and the dead. Instead, they built a new city to be the seat of the Lords. Wide were the streets, so that there might be grand processions and triumphs, so that armies might be mustered there.

Within that city, they raised towers and manor houses. None of the Lords wore a king's crown, but each thought themselves the equal of any king, so they competed in grandeur and generosity. Dwarf-built mansions for the Lords of Arden, Lords of Ilaventur with their library towers adjoining the College Arcane. The Lords of Arshoth built their estates alongside the Cathedral of Wisdom, so that they might pray before the grail and be blessed with divine guidance. All Roads, the songs claimed, began and ended at the Capital stone, at the heart of Summerswell.

Three times had Alf entered that city.

The first time, with the Nine. They had arrived at dusk, so bloodied and beleaguered the gate guards nearly turned them away. They came with word from the east, warning that the Wilder attacks

were not merely the usual coastal raids, that the hand of Lord Bone had reached out from Necrad. For weeks they had tried to persuade the Lords to listen. Alf remembered sitting in the sunlit gardens of Lord Vond, awkwardly sipping wine from a crystal goblet, knowing that armies of the dead were marching and Pitspawn were slithering through the woods. It had seemed absurd that they should sit around *talking* when there was fighting to be done.

But at last the Lords listened. Clerics looked into the grail waters and foresaw terrible danger. Lord Brychan rode up the east Road, pursued by flying dreadknights, and it was only the mighty archery of Laerlyn and Thurn that preserved his life. And all the pointless talking and arguing suddenly transmuted into gold, into armies and arsenals, into action. The streets filled with marching soldiers. Cathedral bells called the city to arms. The College Arcane opened the martial starlight reserve, and wove battle-spells unmatched since the west-war.

Alf gawped at the army marching through that city, and Gundan nudged him in the ribs and muttered, "*We did that.*"

A confusion of voices. Everyone clustering around Olva, getting in each other's way as they tried to help. Jon running about with a pot, looking for water. Perdia ghost-pale, straining to call up the earthpower, but she lacked Olva's healing spells. Ceremos standing off to the side, his face dark with fury.

Laerlyn examined the wound.

"Have you ever fought a manticore, Aelfric?"

"What haven't I fought, Lae?" He'd killed things like manticores, certainly, in the Pits under Necrad. All the monsters blurred together in his memory, fusing into a mass of teeth and claws and tentacles that he'd been fighting all his life. The monster was the thing at the end of the sword.

"I shielded him then," said Spellbreaker. "Their tail-spikes, wielder, contain potent venom. Until the quill is removed, no healing magic will work."

"I do not have the skill to extract the spike," said Lae.

Alf picked Olva up and walked towards the city.

The second time, he came as the Lammergeier, at the head of a victory procession. His name echoed off the city walls as crowds praised him. The bells rang wildly, and priests anointed him with grail water, called him the Hand of Intercession. Lord Bessimer was still in seclusion, but Lucar Vond and Brychan and half a dozen other Lords clustered around the Lammergeier, eager to be seen in the company of the hero. Proudly, they showed him all the new monuments to the war, all the statues and treasures and charmstones taken as spoils, all the new wealth of the city.

But by then Alf had seen Necrad, and no mortal city could compare. He endured endless ceremonies, endless intrigues, some poncy poet reciting an interminable epic called *The Song of the Nine*, and all the while felt as if he was in the wrong place. Peir would have accepted all those honours gracefully; he'd have known what to say, where to stand. It was all wasted on Alf. Peir should have been there.

And the sword at his side whispered, *You did that*.

The others called after him, but he did not listen, did not stop. He walked like a blind man, carrying his wounded sister. She was all feverish skin, no weight to her at all. All his life, he'd tried to keep her safe – little Olva, the youngest, the kindest. He'd fought to keep the darkness from her house for so long, to preserve the peaceful, ordinary life he'd left behind. And after that, when she'd come to Necrad and proved herself capable of thriving in his world, in the Pits and palaces, when he'd seen at last that she was one of the clever ones, he'd put himself at her service. He'd been her stout shield, taken his place at her right hand as he'd served Peir.

I will take you last of all, Death had said to him. That memory roared his head like a whirlpool, washing away all other thoughts. She couldn't die before him. He was the eldest, he was the one who

took all the risks. He should have died a thousand times already, only he was too stupid to admit defeat. It wasn't fair. The spires of the College Arcane rose in the distance, and he walked towards them, his long legs carrying him swiftly down the hill. *Blaise. Wizards like Blaise. They'll help.*

Twenty years later, the city once again expected the coming of the Lammergeier. The streets were deserted then, the gates closed. The Lammergeier's name was not spoken aloud, but his name was whispered a thousand thousand times. Earlier in the year, wild rumours had swirled through the Capital. The Lammergeier had seized Necrad, they said. The Lammergeier died to ensure Lord Vond's escape. The Lammergeier's sailing south at the head of a fleet of Witch Elves and hell-spawn. The Lammergeier died at Bavduin.

Slowly, a dreadful consensus emerged, the truth of the Lammergeier revealed at last. The great hero had rebelled against the rightful Lords – and was in league with other traitors, like Lord Brychan. Blood stained the streets, and flames from burning houses licked the night sky. Each morning, more heads on pikes sprouted above the city gates, like ghastly spring flowers.

Everyone knew that the third time the Lammergeier came to the city would mean doom. The black sword was invincible, the tales said – had he not slain Prince Maedos Dawnshield? Had he not cast down Lord Bone?

Days went by, then weeks, and though rebellion spread across the lands, doom did not fall upon them. A new rumour, repeated by the priests and the heralds: the Lammergeier had been slain in Arden by Princess Laerlyn. Few believed that story; it was wiser and more profitable to be cynical, and believe nothing. More whispered rumours held that the Lammergeier had been seen in the far south, fighting under the banner of Lord Brychan, or at Avos, or in the Eaveslands.

He was everywhere except the Capital, everywhere outside the walls. Every day, travellers on the Road brought news of some new

catastrophe outside the walls, until it seemed as though the world was breaking.

A new custom arose, a thought both cynical and comforting. In response to fresh ill-tidings or some tired complaint, a true citizen of the Capital would nod and say, "Well, at least the Lammergeier hasn't come back."

Alf strode past the gate guards. He threw a handful of coins on the ground as he did so. One sentry shouted after him that, if the old hag perished, Alf had better pay for her burial and not dump the body in an alleyway, but the rest fell upon the coins like birds on fresh-sown seeds. There were fewer guards than he remembered, and they wore the colours of a Lord's retinue instead of the old League. The streets were wide and straight, like the spokes of a wheel, and they led towards the College Arcane.

The Nine had suffered terrible injuries in their battles with Lord Bone's minions. Curses, burning acid, poison stings. Magic out of Necrad. He remembered the wizards fussing over his wounds, gaggles of students marvelling at him as if he were an exhibit. He remembered getting lost amid the cloisters and lecture halls, and Berys fetching him out. *I robbed this place once*, she'd said with a wry half-smile, *so I know the way out*. She'd guided him back to the gates.

He came now to the gates of the College, and they were locked with rusted chains. Grass grew between the flagstones of the un-tended courtyard.

The College was shut.

Of course it was. Arcane magic was star-magic, elf-magic. The common spells of the College were built on the spells and sigils of the Erlking. Only a handful of wizards had the talent and bloody-minded stubbornness to start again from first principles and work spells wholly free of the Erlking's influence. Blaise had done it, but that was Blaise.

The sword had shattered the Erlking's spells. The sword had broken magic.

There was no one here to help Olva.

I did that, said the sword at his side, *but they think you did.*

"Alf!" Cerlys rushed up to his side. "Laerlyn said you should get off the streets." She pulled at his arm, and Alf swayed, nearly dropping Olva. Cerlys swore and called for Jon, who was looking up at the spires and towers of the Capital in amazement. He hurried over and took Olva from Alf.

"Where's Lae?"

"Disguising herself. She and Ceremos can't just walk around the city. They'd attract attention." She'd ditched the dreadknight armour, and now wore an odd mix of clothing she'd brought from Ersfel, topped off with an ancient green shirt she must have taken from the Rangers' House in the Neverwood. She tugged Alf's tattered cloak over Spellbreaker's hilt. The demon eye glared at her ministrations. "She said she'll meet us at the Inn of the Fountains. Do you know it?"

"It – it's not far. It's on the far side of Brychan's mansion."

Lord Brychan's mansion was gone. A new grand house, half built, stood in its place. Charred stones bore testament to the price of defiance. But the Inn of the Fountains was still there, and the fountains – looted from Necrad – still sang. Perdia waited for them in the courtyard and led them up a back stair to a suite of luxurious rooms on the upper floors.

"Did Lae pay for this?" asked Alf.

"I did," said Jon. He laid Olva down on the four-poster bed, then dug a handful of gold coins marked with the sign of the Manticore out of his pocket. "From the dungeon."

"Straight Road," said Perdia.

"Whatever it was."

Alf sank into a chair by the bed and took Olva's hand. It was hot and slick with sweat. The wound was infected or poisoned. "Where's Lae? And Ceremos?"

"Ceremos," said Perdia, "is on the roof. He says it's easier for him to sneak around than to try to blend in. The Princess said she still has allies in the city, and to wait here for her."

They made Olva as comfortable as they could, removing her outer garments, stained with the gore and ichor of the Manticore's lair. Perdia gently washed the dirt from Olva's face and crane-foot, and bathed the wounded flesh around the spike. The skin there was angry red, mottled with dark veins.

They waited in silence for a while, the only sound Olva's pained breathing. Then Jon's stomach rumbled loudly.

"Sorry," he muttered.

Alf looked up. "You should go and eat. All of you."

"We'll stay," said Cerlys.

"It's all right. Go. There's nothing to do here but wait for Lae. Go and see the city."

"What if you were recognised?" Cerlys peered out of the window at the courtyard below. "Lots of people saw you walking in with Olva in your arms – and that sword at your side."

"They still sing *The Song of the Lammergeier* here," added Perdia. "If it becomes known that the Lammergeier has returned—"

"All the more reason for ye to go," said Alf.

"I'll go up on the roof with Ceremos," said Cerlys. "We can put arrows in anyone coming in the courtyard gate. Jon, there's one door at the back of the inn. You block—"

"No," said Alf. "We're not going to fight the entire bloody Crownland. If they come for me, I'll talk to 'em. I'll sort it out. Now go."

Jon nodded and shuffled to the door, waiting there for Cerlys.

Perdia lingered by Olva's bed. "I could try a healing spell again."

"Lae will find a barber. Go on."

They all left, reluctantly. If Ceremos was still on the roof, Alf could not tell.

"If the Lords come for you," said Spellbreaker, "I will teach them to fear us."

"I don't want 'em to fear me. I don't need more enemies."

He shoved the sword into the ground, forgetting they were on the topmost floor of the inn. The blade pierced the polished floorboards like butter, sinking four inches through the ceiling of the room below. Alf winced.

"Keep watch, will you?"

The red glow of the demon sword swept across the room.

Alf closed his eyes.

He wouldn't sleep, mustn't sleep. He'd be here for Olva, even as exhaustion settled on his bones like a shroud. He'd pushed hard on the Straight Road, thrilled to be back on an adventure, but he had to admit, not for the first time, that he was old and battered. He'd barely felt Olva's weight while carrying her, but now she was abed his shoulders ached like they were on fire.

The sight of the wound in Olva's side made him heartsick. Gundan had always impressed on him the need to protect the healers, and Alf felt as if the dwarf was berating him across the gulf of decades. *You stand there and get hit so they don't, you big lummox. Your job's to protect 'em. You take the blows.*

This was the first time since Ironhand's attack that he'd been able to sit in silence and think. There'd been that last night in Ersfel, with Ildorae like the ghost of the past, calling him the Lammergeier again – and then Ironhand's cage, and all the talk of dire deeds and prophecies and omens. A darkness rising in Necrad, a desperate quest to defeat evil. What had Idmaer said?

The elves are at work, Lammergeier, on some vile scheme. A new darkness rises.

What did that even mean? Prophetic nonsense. Heroic words, like the rattling of empty helmets.

Idmaer Ironhand had that heroic certainty, that bright madness. The dream of the quest consumed him, his inner vision more real than the waking world. Peir had it, too – and Derwyn, for a while. When someone had that touch of glory, nothing could dissuade them. Even though all the world might stand against them, they would never give up. It was catching, too – Peir had inspired others. He'd inspired Alf, filled the hollow in him that in other men might have been filled with ambition, or love, or greed, or faith. He'd given Alf purpose.

And Alf had lost it after they slew Lord Bone. Oh, he had duty – Alf was very good at duty, at staying the course and plodding ahead. Twenty years crawling in the Pits, twenty years sticking to the task appointed to him. Doing what he was good at because he didn't know what he wanted. He'd stayed in Necrad even after the rest of the Nine moved on into their new roles, telling himself that, because the sacrifice pained him, it must be worthwhile.

Then Olva had come back into his life, and he'd seen how hollow he was. Olva knew nothing about the wider world outside Ersfel, but she'd lived her life where Alf had only the dregs of the quest. For a little while it seemed as though they'd each heal the other, in Derwyn's bright vision of what Necrad might be. A shining, redemptive vision of a better city, a better world. Alf had let that vision inspire him again, like he'd come in from the cold to warm his frozen fingers on the fire.

He'd known then that something wasn't right. They'd called on him to lead the Defiance, to go south and fight against other people. To kill people who'd never wronged him, who'd done nothing to deserve death except being born in the wrong province, except serve the wrong lord. Alf might be a fool, but he was no innocent. He'd been a mercenary. He'd killed for pay. And some of the people on the other side *did* deserve killing.

It was the damned sword. The blade lifted Alf out of the realm of mortals. The power of the thing – when it was in the fullness of its strength – meant that Alf couldn't think of himself as just another soldier, or even a knight. He was a host unto himself. A monster as fearsome and terrible as any ancient vampire or dragon. He'd seen that, when he'd lost the sword to Bor. One slip, and the world was wounded.

Without the sword, he was just a mortal man. The Lammergeier no longer. He'd been able to go home with Olva.

And Olva – she didn't have that same bright vision, that touch of madness and destiny, but she'd found something else. A purpose born of the land she loved, the home she'd made. Not a quest, but a calling. In the steady tide of the earthpower, in the endless mysteries of the vanished past, she'd found purpose.

Again, he'd warmed himself by the fire of another's soul. Big Alf, always a follower, always the stalwart right hand. Another twenty years of dogged, loyal duty, never looking up. Give him the harness and he'd wear it, give him the burden and he'd carry it until all strength left his limbs.

Always the shield wall. Always the one to take the blow. Until he grew weak, and now it was Olva who'd taken the hit. Olva who was dying. *I will take you last of all*, Death had said, and now it seemed like a curse. To take all those better, brighter souls and leave Alf plodding on pointlessly.

Tell the Lammergeier that Blaise has need of him for one last service. Tell him to come at once. Tell him to bring his sword.

Tell the *Lammergeier*. Bring *his* sword.

I shouldn't have listened, thought Alf. *Olva was right to think it folly. All my life I've been dreaming of the days of the Nine, always looking back and never forwards. And now it's too late.*

He'd brought her into this. He'd pulled her into this folly. If he'd never gone home—

– or if he'd left that first night with Ceremos

– or if he'd stayed in Necrad all those years ago, and slain Ironhand back then

– or if he'd never quarrelled with Prince Maedos

– or if he'd never taken Spellbreaker

– or if Peir had never died and the Nine had stayed the Nine

– or if Alf had never *left* Ersfel in the first place.

He'd made so many choices, and they'd all gone awry. The sword was power, that was what everyone said, what the songs said, but what was the point of its power when using it led only to more sorrow? He'd dragged Olva far from her home, far from her son, and got her wounded in the most absurd, fantastical way imaginable. Struck by the venomous tail-spike of a long-lost Changeling king in an extra-dimensional prison – she couldn't die from *that*.

No one back in Ersfel would understand.

"Ol," he muttered, "to hell with all this. Get better and we'll go home. Lae and the young ones, they can go on to Necrad without us. I'll give the sword to one of 'em. Or throw it into the ocean."

No – he'd put Spellbreaker above the fireplace in Olva's house. The sword would complain, but it'd get used to it. It could scare the village children all it wanted, threaten to eat their souls and slaughter their pets. It would enjoy that. He'd watch over the sword, keep it from being ill-used, but they'd be back in quiet Ersfel, and they'd watch the leaves fall come the autumn.

"Ironhand attacked Ersfel, wielder," said the sword. "That house is gone. I was not made to decorate a fireplace. And you are dreaming."

Alf woke with a start. All was dark. He flailed around, searching for the sword. A startled flurry of wings at the window, then his hand found the hilt of the sword, and the sword-sight. The city outside was dark. He'd slept for hours.

"I didn't mean——" said Alf, and then fear struck him like an icy dagger. "Olva!" If she'd died——

But no. She'd vomited, and the bedclothes were stinking, but she was alive. The skin around the quill was burning hot to the touch.

"I didn't mean to fall asleep."

"I would have woken you," said the sword, "if you were needed." Alf grunted doubtfully.

"I take no pleasure in *suffering*," said Spellbreaker. "I delight in slaughter and swift dispatch. I would give her a quick death if set to the task."

"Shut up."

"I listened to your thoughts, wielder. You will not set me aside."

"Someone else could wield you. You keep complaining that I'm old and useless."

"You are old, indeed. But when I am restored I can compensate for your myriad deficiencies, as I have always done. But you shall not set me aside, wielder. Not until you have atoned for abandoning me."

It was well after midnight when Laerlyn returned. She had exchanged her armour for a nun's veiled habit, hiding her elven features. She held a silvery vial, and when she removed the stopper the smell transported Alf back to the days of Necrad.

"Healing cordial!"

"Likely the last of the waters of Necrad in the southland. Outside Ironhand's vaults, of course." Laerlyn gently lifted Olva's head and poured a few drops of the precious healing potion into her mouth. Olva stirred and swallowed the rest. The effects of the cordial were instantaneous. Her temperature dropped, and the wounded skin around the tail-spike became less angry.

"Where'd you get that?"

"From a Ranger. There are still a few who remember their oaths." Laerlyn took a cloth and bathed Olva's wound. "The cordial relieves suffering and bolsters strength, Aelfric, but she is still on the threshold of the Grey Lands. That cursed spike must be cut from her flesh."

"Aye, I know. A surgeon, not just more magic."

"And we dare not move her—"

"Aye." Alf pulled Spellbreaker from the floor and laid the sword across his lap. "I sent the youngsters away. Do you want to go, too, Lae?"

"I shall stay. I have as much to answer for as you have. And I am much more eloquent than you."

Alf grunted.

The sound of marching drowned out the fountains. The courtyard filled with armed guards. In the dark, Alf could easily mark the stone-spangled knights, enchanted weapons glimmering. The rulers of the city had mustered a respectable force in only a few hours. It would be a hell of a fight if it came to it. The last of the Nine against a host of foes.

A good ending to a bad song.

Hell, he'd probably win. The sword's power grew with every kill. That narrow door made for a choke point, so they'd come at him one at a time. The first one would charge in, trying to take Alf by surprise, and Alf would step aside, cut him in the flank. Then a force blast to scatter the rest. Then butchery. Aye, he'd win. All those guards outside, the fountains would run red.

He could march to the Crownkeep and slaughter the Lords, or threaten them until they knelt before him. But what then? He'd never been able to answer that question.

Tell the Lammergeier that Blaise has need of him for one last service. Tell him to come at once. Tell him to bring his sword.

Olva moaned and shivered in pain.

Footsteps on the stairs. A mailed fist hammered on the bedroom door. "Open up, Sir Lammergeier, and yield yourself over to the justice of the Lords of Summerswell."

"It's just Alf," he said, "and I yield."

PART THREE

As cold as a grave, they said, but it was warm down inside the burial mound. It woke memories of winter mornings, when Olva – the youngest – would nestle into the warmth of her parents' bed, in between Long Tom and Maya, down in the dark heat of the blankets. She was more than sixty years old now, more lives and skins than she could count, but she was still that little child seeking shelter. The earth of Daeroch Nal was a comfortable weight on her. She knew she was half dreaming, knew that the earth was also a sweat-soaked sheet in some unfamiliar bed, but the dream appealed more than reality in that moment.

She was aware of her body. Earth-magic had made her very aware of her physical form, her worn skeleton hung with tired skin. But it was very far away, and while she knew there must be pain from the wound, and from the Manticore-venom that coursed through her veins, she was only dimly conscious of it. Living with that pain – or dying of it – was a chore for the future, when she got up. Oh, let her lie in a little while more!

A flutter of wings disturbed the slumbering dark, and for a moment Olva felt another body moving over hers. A woman, young and lithe-limbed. Olva shoved herself over in the grave to make room. *It's only polite*, she thought, *it was her grave first. All graves are hers.*

Then the woman's presence was gone, and it was only the bird again.

"Lath is dead," croaked Death.

"So Alf told me," muttered Olva. She tried to roll over and snatch a few more moments of rest, but the talons of Death tugged at her, and suddenly they were flying. Ghost-crane and ghost-crow, they soared in formation over the snow-shrouded forests. The Wild Wood all around them, the mound below, and the ruins of the ancient Witch Elf fortress on the heights.

A tongue of flame caught Olva's eye. Atop the mound was a funeral pyre. Hundreds of Wilder gathered around it. The mound bristled with a circle of planted spears.

"They mourn the Old Man of the Woods," said Death.

"Lath called himself that," said Olva – or thought it, or cried in in the speech of birds. If any of those mourners looked up, what would they see in the grey sky?

"Why show me this?"

"Because I was brought back here," said Death. "Here Lath worked the Erlking's spell. Here Thurn went into the Grey Lands, and found his daughter's spirit, and I went back with her."

"That," cried the crane, tartly, "is a tale, not an answer."

Death circled down towards the mourners. None looked away from the dancing flames where a massive carcass burned. Lath had not died in human shape. "I sang the clan-song for Thurn. Lath had no clan, no kinfolk save the Nine. And me. Uncle Lath, I called him."

"Why don't you go to them? They're your people."

"All mortals are mine," said Death.

"That's not an answer, either." Crane-Olva beat her wings and caught the air rising from the pyre. Death followed.

"I cannot go to them," admitted Death.

"Alf said you fear the Erlking breaking the spell that binds you. But that's not all, is it?"

*

A fierce wind carried the two ghost-birds, the forest below blurring into a green wave that crashed into mountains, then grey seas and a whirl of unfamiliar landscapes. To be so far from the lands Olva knew disconcerted her; she could not sense even a trace of earth-power. Now they flew over a dusty realm of red earth marked with olive groves, brickwork aqueducts trickling brackish water into the thirsty soil, whitewashed villages on hilltops.

They descended towards a village. Children played in the little square by the temple, while a half-dozen parents sat on the temple steps and gossiped. One woman was unlike the rest in appearance, but any differences had been erased by long friendship and familiarity.

Death perched on the temple roof, and Olva joined her.

"That is me," said Death, glaring at the woman. "Talis. The mortal I am bound to. She did as Alf counselled. She took herself out of the story, and lives the life she chose. An ordinary life. And I could have been as I was in the dawn days!"

"I remember," said Olva quietly. "I saw the survivors come back from Bavduin. And I was in Necrad, in the siege. Everyone feared you. They prayed Alf would stop you." *Alf kills monsters.*

"Your brother told Talis to find her own path, and she did. She flew so far that she forgot who she was."

A wailing child ran up to Talis, displaying a scraped knee as though it was the greatest injustice imaginable. She wiped the blood away, and brushed the child's face, and sent him off to play again. A frown crossed Talis' face, like a cloud scudding across the sun.

"She doesn't remember? Truly?"

"She forgot *me*. She put power aside. She buried me in the back of her mind, and thinks her past was only a fever-dream!" Death shook her wings in fury. "She buried me!"

"Is she happy?"

"Happy?" screeched the bird. Talis looked up, staring at the two crows atop the temple. "Happy? Not especially. Her children plague

her. Her husband sometimes grumbles that he was bewitched by her foreign charms. She finds the summer heat sickening, and worries that the sun will scorch the crops. There are moments of joy, but mostly she is discontented." Death preened her feathers. "She has forgotten her power, but in the back of her mind she knows she could be *more*. She listens to the tales of gods and heroes, and asks herself if she has squandered the gift of life. She fears that she craved safety so much that she lost all chance at wonder."

"That's life, though. I lived both a common life and an enchanted one, and I can't say one was better than the other." Olva was disturbed to find herself referring to her life in the past tense, but ploughed on with her point. "You find the things that give you joy, and you cherish them for as long as you can. Everything else is just the wheel turning, and the grinding noise it makes. Most things don't matter."

"I nearly won her back," muttered Death to herself. "There was another child. I made him sick. She held him as he died of fever. I told her, I told her she could heal him if she would only let me back in. But she would not. Now it will be the death of her."

"What are you going to do?" asked Olva, alarmed.

"I can do nothing," said Death, bitterly. "I can skulk through dreams, and spy, and prophesy. But I cannot intervene. She has taken me from the field even as forces gather for the last battle."

"The last battle – do you mean Idmaer Ironhand?"

Death croaked. "I fly over every battlefield and every charnel field. What is Idmaer Ironhand to me? He is but a sword in another foe's hand. No, I speak of the work I left undone." She spread her wings and took flight, circling over Talis. "She may have her little moments of joy!" she cried. "She may have the peace she sought! But she has put aside power, and so she has given up any command over fate. Who, then, will save her from calamity?"

Over the horizon of dream, over the wide lands between, came darkness rising.

CHAPTER TWENTY-THREE

Ceremos slipped down from the roof of the Inn of the Fountains like a cat to join the other three. "Sir Aelfric commands we make merry!"

"He commands us to fuck off, you mean," said Cerlys. "He knows trouble's coming." She glared at the dancing fountains as if they might conceal assassins.

"He wants to be alone. We should respect that," said Perdia. A church bell tolled in the warm summer evening. "And there are other ways to help."

"Here," said Jon, offering his coin purse like a handful of berries. It overflowed with gold coins stolen from the Manticore's lair. "Take a share." Perdia took only two, but even that was more wealth than Jon's father might earn in half a year of labour.

"Don't flash gold like that around!" hissed Cerlys. "You'll be robbed."

Ceremos shoved his incongruous bucket helm onto his head to conceal his elven features. "Then let us spend it before thieves find us."

"Do what you want," snapped Cerlys, "but I'm staying." Still, she took her share of the gold.

*

It was evening, but gold was a key to many doors. Tailors and clothiers, swordsmiths and armourers, then innkeepers and minstrels – and a brief detour to a jeweller. All opened to Ceremos and Jon of Ersfel, and before the sun had set they might have been mistaken for two young squires of wealthy family, such was the magnificence of their new appearance.

The Necrad Ceremos had left was a city of empty palaces and silent galleries. Only the elves walked the marble streets, and there were more streets than living elves now. To be in Necrad was to be alone. *Alone* was impossible here. Every building brimmed with mortals, every street was a crowd.

Ceremos stood in the midst of the crowd, immersed in the warmth and clamour of mortality. He breathed in blood and sweat and stale ale, and gloried in it. Of all the places he'd visited in the mortal lands, this was closest to the Necrad he'd once known, with its paved streets and alleyways and grand buildings. The smell of those people, salt of blood and salt of sea, and the bite of the wind off the Dwarfholt. Add in a few Vatlings, paint the clouds green, and it might have been in the Garrison in the days of his youth.

Youth? He laughed at himself. He had countless centuries ahead of him. It was very mortal to yearn for childhood things. The Garrison had lasted only a few years, and no one missed it, except for those for whom it had been the whole world. If it still existed would he miss it so? The joy of the tale was in the telling.

Cerlys and Friend Jon, he guessed, would return to Ersfel. He would miss them deeply. There would be other friends and companions, other adventures, but he swore quietly to himself that he would not forget them. He would linger here for now – he had sworn to serve the Widow Queen, and he would keep his oath. Maybe he would escort her and Perdia home to Ersfel, too, or guide the Lammergeier to Necrad. Maybe he'd fight Ironhand's armies on the walls of the Capital, a second city and a second siege. He'd be a mysterious knight, faceless and bannerless. He might be all those things and more.

There was time for many tales, before the end.

The guards, too, reminded him of Necrad. The Necrad of his youth had been an occupied city, with League sentries walking the Sanction walls. As a child, he had dreaded the rattling thunder of the dwarven war-wagons, the bestial shouts and challenges of the human sentries on house-to-house searches. Here, the lines between districts were less blatant, and the guards served different Lords instead of the old League, but there was still that steel-edged fear.

The scent of the city was intoxicating – oh, it was mostly sweat and fish and woodsmoke and a subtle undertone of blood, but it was alive! There was so much life all around him, raucous and loud. They'd ended up in a dockside tavern, and Ceremos had to shout to be heard by Jon.

"Are all the cities of Summerswell so crowded?"

Jon was red-faced and wide-eyed. "No idea. I've never seen so many people in all my days. It's, like . . . Ellsport *and* Highfield *and* Kettlebridge all on top of each other. And the buildings are so tall! I don't know how it doesn't all fall down on our heads."

Ceremos, for whom the topless spires of Necrad had been playground and refuge, glanced outside. Some of the houses were indeed two or even three storeys tall, leaning over the street like drunkards.

"Young lords!" A young woman appeared at their table, a red-headed Ellscoaster in a low blouse. She leaned across the table. Jon flushed even redder. "Are you in search of more refreshment? Or some other diversion?" She squeezed Jon's leg, and he made a noise that reminded Ceremos of Olva's piglet.

"A song, perhaps," said Ceremos. "In payment for the coin you just stole from Friend Jon's pocket."

Her eyes widened in alarm. "It's all right!" said Jon, hastily. "It's right to share when you've had good fortune. Pay with a song, as my friend says. Something old."

"*The Song of the Nine*, perhaps?" suggested Ceremos. A few sailors at a nearby table looked over. One thin-faced fellow scowled.

"The Song of Alar Ravenqueen," said Jon.

The woman's voice was hesitant at first. The voices of Ellscoast are not suited to the melodious songs of the Eavesland; they are known for their shanties and work-songs, not their lays. But the tavern took up the song, and told the tale of the Ravenqueen, said to be the most beautiful of all mortals who walked the land in ancient days.

When the song was finished, the thin-faced sailor leaned over to Ceremos. "You've had a stroke of good luck, then?"

"To be alive is glorious good fortune." Ceremos could not help but notice old grey scars on the man's wrist. The mark of *agearath*.

The man scowled again. "What accent is that? What province do you hail from?"

"Mulladale," said Jon.

"I was asking the one in the helmet. Why's he hiding his face?"

Jon rose.

"Mulladale men, the both of us."

The sailor took a look at the armoured mountain that towered above him and withdrew.

Jon took another mouthful of ale, frowned, and spat it back into the mug. "This Crownland stuff tastes funny. And I don't want to get drunk anyway. Not while Widow Forster's ill." He shook his head. "We should have kept vigil with Cerlys."

"Sir Aelfric stands guard."

"I bought her a gift," said Jon. He fumbled to unwrap the delicate silk bundle. Inside was a golden hair-comb, studded with pearls. "She's always wearing that broken comb her mother gave her, and I thought—"

"My friend," said Ceremos, "I have only been in these mortal lands for a brief while, and know little of your customs. But for that one you would be better gifting her a sword."

Perdia followed other pilgrims to the Cathedral of Wisdom.

The shrine at the cathedral's heart, where once only anointed

clerics went, lay open, the grail-cup exposed. A few candles glimmered in the side chapels. The vast nave of the cathedral could hold thousands, but there were only a handful of worshippers. Her father had come here once, on the Pilgrims' Circuit – the long circle of the Road that visited all the holy sites. Through Ilaventur to remember the Hopeless Winter, the Gates of Eavesland following Harn's desperate quest, Arshoth of the blessed wells where the Erlking revealed the light of Intercession, then at last the Crownland with this grand cathedral, this new Capital, testament to the redemption of the lands.

Above the shrine was a carven image of the Erlking's face, six times the height of a man, crowned with a halo of green glass. Some of the panes of the halo were broken, and others boarded up. Flanking him were Intercessors, and through some unimaginable skill the sculptor had managed to make the titanic marble statues appear ethereal, unknowable misty shapes that from some angles resembled armoured knights, from others winged messengers, from others cowled clerics. Angles and angels.

Perdia stood there, awestruck. How could such beauty be tainted?

Her father had wept as he recalled the cathedral. He'd gone as a young man, younger than Perdia was now. In those years, the Circuit was flooded with pilgrims, terrified and furious at the sudden disappearance of the spirits and the withdrawal of the Wood Elves. Wild tales circulated with them, and her father had told her those, too. *The Lammergeier slew the Erlking's son! The Lammergeier's sister burned the churches!*

Perdia had found it impossible to reconcile the demonic figures from the tales with the people she'd met in Ersfel. A weary old man snoring by the fire. Olva – aye, she was a witch and a Changeling, but the stories described her as the Widow Queen, as cold as her brother's sword. The people she had met had not been figures out of legend.

As they'd travelled south, legends had gathered around them. Elves from Necrad, Idmaer Ironhand, the Spellbreaker, Princess Laerlyn.

Those marble statues – from one angle they resembled one thing, but look at them a different way and they changed. It was only a trick of the sculptor's art. The carved marble drew the eye, made you see what was not really there.

The Lammergeier murdered angels in Avos.

Early in the Anarchy, the shrines and holy sites were overrun with those seeking atonement, or answers from a silent heaven. And when no answers came, they grew angry. Her father had always walked with a limp; his leg was trampled when the mob set fire to a church in Arshoth, and the paladins had charged the crowd.

It was all too large, the deeds too great or terrible to be the work of people she'd met. It seemed to Perdia that she was the only one caught in this vice. Cerlys and Jon had grown up knowing Olva and Alf; they were deep-rooted in their lives, their meaning fixed. And Ceremos – the elf seemed to think that all mortal existence was indistinguishable from the tales of heroes, and saw no contradiction. Only Perdia was left standing on the sword's edge. How could the woman lying in the stinking, sweat-soaked bed be the Widow Queen? How could Alf be the Lammergeier?

The Lammergeier murdered the Erlking.

Was it like the earthpower, she wondered. The wolf had risen, forcing its way out into the world *through* her. Olva had taught her to control it, a little, but it was still something *other*, a monster inside her that sometimes she could direct. Sometimes it escaped. Was it like that for Alf, too? He talked about the Lammergeier like she talked about the wolf.

Impulsively, she stepped into one of the side chapels, the coins clenched tightly in her fist. Gold was gold, but it felt disrespectful to show the face of the Manticore here. The tomb of some long-dead paladin of Arshoth lay before the altar. His face was kindly, eyes gently closed as if the marble effigy was only lightly sleeping. The knight clasped a stone sword in his right hand, a carved grail-bowl in his left. Other pilgrims had left offerings there. Coins of little worth.

She was about to drop a coin into the bowl when she caught sight of the carved images on the side walls. There was the paladin, his sword aflame, fighting against packs of misshapen, bestial creatures. The dim light made the carvings move, the creatures changing from one feral shape to another. Witches gathered in tangled woods, and at their feet were bloody sigils of the earthpower. Changelings.

Unclean.

"What do you pray for, child?"

Perdia jumped in alarm, stifling a snarl. An ancient priestess had crept up on her. The stink of the old woman filled her too-keen nostrils.

"A friend is ill. I pray she will recover."

"A worthy prayer, but better offered at a different chapel. Sir Galamor of Arshoth lies here. He was a great hero, but he was no healer." The priestess led her down the aisle to another chapel. "Intercessor of Grief. Once I prayed, and the Intercessor answered. There was a maimed boy, an Earl's son, and the spirit took hold of my hands. Power flowed through me, and I healed him. I brought him back." The old woman's face glowed with remembered pride. "Give your coin to the Intercessors, and they will carry your prayer. If the stars permit it, your friend will live."

"There are those," said Perdia, "who say there are other sources of healing."

The priestess sniffed. "Don't squander your coin on liars, child. There's healing magic out of Necrad, yes, but that's gone. Anyone selling a healing cordial these days is out to trick you. There was healing in the Everwood, but no more."

"I've heard tell of those who could work healing spells."

"Sit, sit." The old woman shuffled over to a wooden pew and gestured for Perdia to join her. "Yes, magic can heal the sick, but you won't find any wizards working proper healing spells these days."

"What about earthpower?"

"It's unclean, child. Only the Wilder of the north use it, and they imperil their souls."

"Why?" asked Perdia. "Why is that magic unclean, and not others?"

"The Erlking warned us of its dangers," whispered the priestess. "All *worthy* power comes from a higher authority and is held in trust. The bailiff and the knight, they wield power, do they not? And that stems from the law and the lord above them. Should they do evil, their position can be withdrawn from them. So, too, it is with clerics and wizards. The spells of wizards were founded on the teachings of the wise elves, and they guided the College Arcane. Those who might have used magic in foul ways were not permitted to study."

The priestess stared at her withered hands. "I had power over life and death — but I held that power in trust. I was the tool of the Intercessors. Had I misused that power, the Intercessors would have rejected me. But the Changeling — there is no one who holds authority over them, no one to say 'enough'. And few mortals have the strength to put power aside when it is no longer needed. Instead, it destroys them." She sniffed. "Even the most virtuous. Oh, my child, we have failed you, and left you a broken world and a silent heaven. We have failed you in so many ways. I had a chance, once, to speak with the Lammergeier. I tried to convince him to speak for the Church, and to abjure the evil of Necrad. The Lammergeier was not like you've heard in the tales, not at all. He was a simple man. But his friends were greedy and cruel, and let him astray. Power ruined him, too. Had he only listened . . ."

The priestess shook her head. "Ah, and here I am rambling on about my own failings, when you came here to seek relief for your friend. Make an offering to the Intercessors, and one day there will be forgiveness. Have faith, and the Erlking will return and put right this Anarchy." She lowered her head in prayer.

One coin rang in the bowl. Then, a moment later, a second fell.

*

Idiot! You left your sword in the inn!

The thought was a scourge, whipping her brain. Cerlys wouldn't make the same mistake again.

She counted the guards outside the Inn of the Fountains again. More of them, now – four more in the last ten minutes, making an even dozen. Five different tabards between them, five different lords or masters. Five scavengers circling a dying beast. All watching the entrance to the inn, making sure Alf didn't leave. All waiting for reinforcements.

Alf had trained her to fall back in times like this. Training sessions on the village green, pitting one against two or three foes, and the lesson there was always to run. Make a fighting withdrawal to a doorway or narrow place you could defend, or just run into the woods and hide. If the odds are against you, run. But the other villagers were idiots, and it always turned into a game, overgrown children rampaging around the houses.

When it was Cerlys' turn, she stood her ground and fought. The first time, a bigger boy knocked the spear from her hand. The second time, she kept hold of the spear, but they'd beaten her down. An accidental blow broke her nose, and her mother Quenna forbade her from going back to Alf's lessons. *Look at you! Who's going to marry a girl with no nose?* But she went back, and the third time, she mock-slew two of them before they caught her. She could do three. Maybe four, with the enchanted dagger cold beneath her cloak.

Alf had trained her to fall back. But in the songs, the Lammergeier stood against forty at Karak's Bridge.

An unnatural red light burned in the window of Alf's room, and it had not gone unnoticed. They gathered around, speculating about the source of the glow. Cerlys slipped through the crowd, watching the guards. Rumours were already spreading that the Lammergeier had returned. Speculation, too, about Ironhand's armies on the march. Names swirled like autumn leaves. *Lammergeier. Ironhand. Lord Bone. Traitor. Hero.*

She knew what the glow was. A weapon out of legend.

All her young life, she'd dreamed of seeing the Crownland, the Everwood, the Greatmire, Necrad – names that had come down the Road to cramped little Ersfel. She'd played in the woods above the village, imagining that she was exploring the vast wilderness of the Wild Wood. Gnarled branches became dragons and Pitspawn. The village boys laughed and mocked her, or tried to make her play the helpless princess. They'd tied her to trees so she could be rescued, but she'd known in her soul that wasn't her story. She'd learned to slip the bonds, climb higher and run faster than any of them. One day, she declared, she'd be off down the Road to seek her fortune.

Now she was in the heart of Summerswell, a spear's throw from the Crownkeep, but there was no time to let herself be distracted. She grasped Ildorae's dagger hidden beneath her cloak. The burning cold of the metal helped her focus.

If I was on the roof, I'd have a clear shot at any of them.

None of them dared cross the threshold. None dared confront the Lammergeier.

She could have told them that they had nothing to fear. The Lammergeier wasn't waiting in the room above. It was kindly, awkward old Alf. They didn't know him as she did. He'd taught her to fight, and never doubted her. He'd seen in her the same greatness as Berys or Laerlyn or any of the Nine. Cerlys adored the old man, but she could also see clearly that he wasn't the warrior he'd once been.

If Ildorae had wielded Spellbreaker, she would have slain Ironhand.

If another hand wielded Spellbreaker . . .

Alf had taught her to mark entrances and exits. To take unexpected routes, to *see* the battlefield, not just the opposition. Leaving the Inn of the Fountains, she'd spotted the flat roof of the stables, the open window on the second floor, the unwatched side alleyway.

She could get in unseen. And it would not matter who saw her on the way out.

Cerlys squared her shoulders, called up all her courage. *Just make it to the side alley, and then—*

"There she is!"

It took her a moment to recognise Jon. He stumbled, his new mail jangling as he pushed through the crowd, apologising as he went. Even though Ceremos wore similar armour, he moved with perfect grace. She tried to push past them, but Jon was in her way. Didn't he see what was going on?

She tried to explain. "The inn's surrounded by the Lords' men. They haven't gone in yet. They're waiting for reinforcements."

"I got—" began Jon.

"The sword's still up in Olva's room. I can climb up there, but I need you to distract those guards."

"Sir Aelfric commanded us to go," said Ceremos, his voice muffled by the helmet.

"Alf's not thinking straight. What about Spellbreaker? Ironhand's coming for that sword."

"Sir Aelfric will not set it aside."

"What if the Lords take it off him? What if they give it to Ironhand?" Someone worthy had to take up that sword. Someone worthy had to act, or tyrants like Ironhand would just keep taking and taking. Alf had given himself up to save Ersfel – but if he'd had the sword, everything would have been different.

A weapon like Spellbreaker would never go unused.

She pushed past Jon, but it was too late. Outside the Inn of the Fountains the crowds made way for armoured men on horseback. Knights and warriors, here to arrest the Lammergeier.

Idiot! Too slow.

In the hour before dawn, Jon watched Alf and the Princess emerge from the inn, escorted by a dozen knights. Knights and guards were a wall of steel around the pair. Jon was struck by how weary Alf looked next to the ageless elf. He leaned on his sword like a stick,

and his head was bowed low, and yet the knights watched him warily, weapons drawn, as if he were a wild dog that might snap at any moment. The procession set off for the fortress at the heart of the city, dark against a lightening sky. The crowd followed them like a receding tide, ebbing out of alleyways and flowing around the fountains.

It left the three of them alone in the street.

"We should go home," said Jon quietly, almost to himself. "My dad will be worried sick. And there's the harvest to be done. We set out to help Alf, and he's safe now, and he's got his sword again. We've money enough to be getting on with. We should go, before Ironhand's army gets here and they close the Road."

Cerlys looked up at him and seemed to see Jon for the first time in his new armour. She laughed. "You wear it better than I thought you would."

"Aye, well, it's bloody heavy, is what it is."

"We're not going home yet." Cerlys turned on her heel and marched towards the inn. "The Lammergeier trained us for a fight, and there's a fight coming."

CHAPTER TWENTY-FOUR

It took a long time for them actually to leave the inn. Alf declared he would go quietly once the lords sent their best healer to tend to Olva, and that point was agreed with surprising swiftness. A moon-faced fellow in wizard's robes arrived, clutching a bag of surgical instruments and more flasks of precious cordial. He ushered everyone out of the bedroom, and they reconvened in the common room below.

The delay was due to other factors. First, a knight – Sir Aeglos the Holy – demanded that Spellbreaker be given over into his custody, but this claim was disputed by half a dozen other knights and dignitaries representing different lords and factions. Alf sat back down and let them argue. In the end, it was agreed that the High Constable of the Capital should temporarily carry the dread sword, whereupon said High Constable – very regal in his purple cloak and gold chain and silver staff of office – discovered that Spellbreaker was utterly unmovable.

"How about I carry it," suggested Alf, "and you hit me with that stick if I look threatening?"

There were further delays outside. Though Ersfel and the wider Mulladales had been spared, bloody battles had been fought here in the Crownland between feuding nobles in the years after the

Defiance. The past two decades had not been peaceful; both scars and grudges were still fresh. Some scores had been settled in the courtyard, and if the fountains looked redder than might be expected, it was not wholly due to the rosy dawn.

The Lords had intended to spirit Aelfric and the Princess Laerlyn away under cloak of darkness. As it transpired, the city was awake before the prisoners were led out of the Inn of the Fountains, and many eyes watched their progress to the Crownkeep. And while few of those onlookers recognised the gaunt old greybeard who shuffled down the street, every one of them knew the Erlking's daughter, and every one of them had heard of the black sword.

Once again, the name of the Lammergeier was whispered on the streets of the Capital.

At the heart of Summerswell stood the Crownkeep. Here the Lords of Summerswell once met in council. Alf had been there only once before, when the council agreed to send an army under Lord Brychan to attack Necrad. Then, the place had reminded him of a beehive, with all its little offices and cells for clerks, and the deafening buzzing of the Lords' Hall, so many voices talking all at once and saying very little.

This time, Alf and Laerlyn were brought to a private audience chamber in the east wing of the palace. Guards in the livery of the defunct League stood watch over them. Alf guessed that the old uniforms had been pulled out of storage to send a deliberate message, but whether the message was intended for him or some other observer, and what it was, he could not guess. Subtle courtly intrigues were beyond him. He glanced over at Laerlyn; she was the Princess again, face perfectly composed, as haughty and as distant as any of the carven images of her father's face on the pediments of the churches. Still, it was good to have her with him.

And what of me, wielder? Is it not a comfort to know that you can slaughter all your captors? To know that you can blast your way free of any

prison cell? There can be no consequences for your actions. We murdered their gods and broke their kingdom, and still they dare not hinder you.

"That was Bor," said Alf out loud, "not me."

They don't know that. Bor is forgotten, his memory blotted out by the great shadow of the Lammergeier. No one will remember him. No one will remember some peasant from the Mulladales either. You are the Lammergeier, the wielder of Spellbreaker, and that is all. Embrace it!

Laerlyn stood and spoke aloud. Alf could not tell if she addressed the guards, or if she suspected that some Lord's spy was eavesdropping. Maybe elven magic would carry her words to those who needed to hear them.

"You have no cause to hinder the last of the Nine. We are on our way to Necrad, on a private errand. We entered the city only because one of our number was injured; once she is well again, we shall be on our way. We intend to take no more part in the affairs of Summerswell — the future of these realms is in mortal hands, not ours. You will gain nothing by dwelling on past grievances and offences. It would be wisest to let us go and be forgotten."

She sat down again beside him.

"Think they'll listen?"

"No." She brushed her fingers against the scar on her face, then folded her hands. "It would be a better world if we all looked to the future, not the past."

"Aye." That was easy for her to say, he thought; elves always had more future. How much future could an old man have, and what was left in it? *One last errand. One thing done right.*

A man entered, leaning on a rod of blackened wood. His garb was of rich cloth, but unadorned; he wore no ring or amulet that might hold a charmstone. His other hand clutched a rolled-up map. His once thick hair had thinned, and there were unfamiliar scars across his face, but Alf knew him instantly.

"Lord Vond?"

"My title was lost many years ago, Lammergeier, with my lands and inheritance." His voice was thick with hate. "I am only Timeon Vond of Summerswell, now. The Lords appointed me to speak with you, in light of our ..." His knuckles whitened on the cane. "... long acquaintance."

"I never meant you any harm," said Alf.

"No," said Vond, "I don't suppose you *meant* anything. I sometimes wonder if you know we struggled at all." He bowed stiffly to Laerlyn. "Erlking's Daughter, it has been too long since the Firstborn blessed us with their presence here."

"My father's blessings were not always beneficial."

Vond scowled. "You should know, Lammergeier, that the finest healer in the lands attends your sister's bedside. No expense will be spared in keeping such a worthy woman alive. She will have the best of care as a guest of the Lords."

"If anything happens to her ..." rumbled Alf.

"Let me guess: you'll lead a revolt, cast down the Erlking, and bring ruin to the land?"

"Aelfric was not responsible for all those deeds," said Laerlyn.

"Responsible!" Vond choked on the word. "Do you remember the elf child you maimed? It was the day after you returned to Necrad."

"Aye." Alf frowned, wondering why Vond might bring up Ceremos.

"I always felt a great deal of sympathy for that Witch Elf. I thought of him often over the years. To be trampled by a heedless beast, crushed by accident. You never meant him harm, either, and yet—"

"I saved him, afterwards!"

"Ah yes. You saved the poor child in front of you. How worthy. But you are *heedless*, Lammergeier. All of the Nine, all of you *heroes* — stomping about like giants, quarrelling and reconciling, convinced that your own desires and passions outweigh the needs of nations. Selfishness at every turn, magnified by your power and

influence! How many times did you put the Nine before your oaths to Summerswell?"

"Aye, I was a shit knight," said Alf, "but I never wanted to be a knight."

"Swept up in destiny, were you? I have heard this song before, Lammergeier. You are but a simple peasant who had destiny thrust upon them, yes? A convenient excuse to ignore accountability." Vond glared at Laerlyn. "And you are no better, Princess. From you, we have an eternity of inconsistency! One moment, you are your father's willing agent, then you are some champion of mortals, then you favour the Nine above all else."

"There are higher duties."

Timeon snapped his fingers. "Of course! Prophecies! Omens! Visions in the grail and signs writ in the stars! Important matters. Heroic matters! Far more worthy, I am sure, than the humble responsibilities of *actually ruling*. All my life, I have been a ship on an unsettled sea, buffeted by the whims of heroes." He tapped his cane on the ground. "What was it that day that was so urgent? Chasing after an assassin? I had to come to your aid when the Witch Elf mob had you cornered. Do you remember what Gundan said to me, when I dared question your actions?"

"I do!" said Spellbreaker, gleefully. "He said you could do *nothing*, for they were the Nine and you could not stand against them. And he was right." The demon eye flashed, and for a moment the sword swallowed the light in the room. "Boundless is my appetite, and Aelfric has sworn not to restrain me. As the dwarf said, we are above your laws."

Vond sagged, his defiance ebbing from him. He shrank onto the velvet couch opposite Laerlyn. With an unsteady hand, he unrolled the map.

"Perhaps. It seems there is no one in Summerswell who can judge your crimes, but I pray to whatever spirits are left that you will not escape punishment." He smoothed out the map – it depicted

the lands of Summerswell north of the Greatmire. "The remaining Lords agree on very little. All that was certain — customs, borders, bonds of vassalage and suzerainty — all have melted away since the Defiance. It has taken twenty years of careful diplomacy and thankless labour to restore what little peace we have. But they all agree that they will not bow to a mad warlord. Ironhand must be stopped."

"Idmaer. He's Duna's son," said Alf.

Vond rolled his eyes. "I know that! I went to Necrad to negotiate with your harridan sister, and when she cast me out I took refuge in Castle Duna. I was in Idmaer's court for months."

"You attacked Necrad," said Alf. He wished Olva were here — he'd had to piece the events of Olva's brief rule together from hints and rumours over the years. They had never really talked about that time, for it bore too much sorrow and shame for both of them. Alf had visited Idmaer's mother Erdys just before he'd left Necrad for the last time, and secured her loyalty to Olva. Idmaer was Duna's son and heir, but he was not yet of age — and he was mad, his mind shattered by his near-death and resurrection by the Intercessors. But some vision in the grail — *or bad counsel given by Vond*, suggested Spellbreaker — had compelled Idmaer to seize power.

"I pointed out to Idmaer that Necrad was dependent on the New Provinces for food. I urged him to do what he could to force your rebellion to a painless surrender." Vond shook his head. "None of you — not your kinsman, not Blaise, not even Dryten Bessimer — would listen to me. The only one who even considered my words was the damned Vatling Threeday. I tried to make you all see sense. But Idmaer . . . the Miracle Knight, his followers called him.

"I have never understood the appeal of heroic idiots. I told Idmaer to write a letter to the council in Necrad, telling them that unless they negotiated, he would starve them out. I drafted it for him! It was subtle, precise, well argued. And what does he do? For three days he lies on the floor in the castle chapel, praying and weeping

over his father's casket. Then he musters his knights, and *attacks* Necrad. Idiocy! Idiocy!

"That stupidity got Lady Erdys killed in retaliation. The Witch Elves slew her on the Road. And after that, there was no hope of negotiation."

("Ach, poor Erdys," muttered Alf. A scene from memory flashed across his mind – Erdys, young and beautiful, disembarking from a ship at Necrad's harbour. They'd put her in this old-fashioned court dress, so thick with embroidery that it looked as heavy as plate. She'd descended the gangplank as if it was a marble staircase at a ball in the Capital, full of grace – but at the end she'd broken into an excited little run, eager to step onto the marble dock and cross the threshold of her new life. It was the first time he'd met her, and Lord Brychan had already offered Alf her hand. Alf, a tongue-tied peasant from the Mulladales, his hands covered in blood and filth, the taint of the black sword. He'd fled as if that offer had been more terrifying than the dungeons of the dark lord. How he wished he could turn back the years – not to be young again, not only that – but to have it all before them. To make other choices, free of the scar-tissue embroidery of time.

Vond paused, seeing Alf's grief, then scoffed and continued with his own tale.)

"I was in Castle Duna when the Witch Elves came for us. We did not think your sister would be foolish enough to arm them. We did not know that Blaise had rebuilt the spawning vats." Vond shuddered, and he stared at the map without seeing it. "The skies darkened with dreadworms. Dreadknights rode them. They hurled down glass jars, and where they fell horrors sprouted. Tentacles and mouths. They pulled guards from atop the walls and devoured them. A little one crawled into my window – I beat it to death with a lamp.

"Then . . . then suddenly there was a white deer in the courtyard, even though the gates were shut. I don't know how it got in. It spoke with a woman's voice, and told us that if we knelt down and

worshipped her as a goddess, the Skerrise would be merciful. She would only kill half. She said she'd water the fields with our blood, so there'd be a good harvest for us to give as a tribute.

"Idmaer refused. The Witch Elves attacked."

He looked up at Alf. "I suppose it seems unremarkable to you. No doubt you'll tell me that you saw worse in Lord Bone's war, or the Pits, or some other adventure. But it was . . . it was . . ." Vond swallowed. "The Witch Elves sealed the gates with magic, so we could not leave. The deer vanished, and the Skerrise was there. She walked through Castle Duna all alone, and killed everyone she met. I heard her progress through the keep, room by room, scream by scream."

("Tales of slaughter that I did not perpetrate bore me," complained Spellbreaker. "What is the point of this account?"

"Shush," muttered Alf.)

"Idmaer tried to stop her, but he was only a boy, and one-handed to boot. I screamed at him that the castle was lost, and that we must all flee.

"There was only one way out – over the north wall. Castle Duna was built atop a rocky hill, and the north face was a nearly sheer cliff, with only a few small outcrops to break the fall. The only light was the burning castle at our backs. The survivors crowded atop the wall. One by one we jumped. If you were lucky, you'd land in bracken, or catch on some ledge halfway down and descend in stages. I was lucky – my cloak snagged on a rock, and I hung there, men falling to their deaths to left and right. But an honest death at the foot of the cliff was better than the Skerrise. Even those who made it down alive were not safe – the dreadknights hunted the survivors through the dark forest like beasts.

"It was Idmaer who saved me. He'd grown up in the castle. He knew all its haunts. We crawled through the mud, hidden from the elves. He took us into the deep woods, then east." Vond pawed at the map. "Strange – I spent years in the Citadel staring at maps of the New Provinces. They always irritated me. It seemed to me that

the mapmaker gave up, leaving all the Wild Wood as a squiggle of green ink. I craved order. Neat roads, neat villages. I never thought I'd end up lost in that wilderness, with only a maimed madman for company.

"We escaped, obviously. The survivors rallied to him — the Miracle Knight, the Earl's last surviving son. I told them to flee, but he would not yield. He swore to carry on the war against Necrad. I last saw him at the abbey at Staffa, where I took ship to the south."

Vond paused, his cheeks flushed. He glanced over his shoulder at the closed door. "But little of that matters, of course. It is the present threat to the Crownland that—"

Laerlyn interrupted him. "You served well, Timeon — even if those you served were unworthy of such devotion."

Vond stared at her, then gave a curt nod. He pointed to the map. "It is the present threat to the Crownland we must discuss. We had reports Ironhand was advancing via the east road, through the Mulladales and Ellscoast, but it now seems that was a diversion. Ironhand's army advances along the main Road from Arshoth. Our scouts estimate he commands more than nine thousand, between calvary and foot." He tapped the western side of the map. "His advance guard has already reached Albury Cross. We hoped that the Westermarchers would join with us in opposing him, but they refuse for now — they will not cross the River. At least they threaten his flank.

"We have gathered what forces we could to defend the Capital. They are not enough. The unity of Summerswell is broken. Each Lord looks first to his own dominion. It is known, too, that Ironhand has gathered to himself the greater portion of the remaining magic weapons. The sight of such magic shall dismay our defenders; he may take the city without a fight unless he can be countered."

"Plainly," observed Spellbreaker, "you are in dire need of a weapon that breaks enchantments as easily as it breaks flesh and bone. A

weapon that has gone hungry for too long. A weapon, and a hand to wield it."

Vond grimaced. "It gives me no pleasure that I must once again beg the Lammergeier for deliverance. But the Lords have commanded me to do so."

"Oh, it is not my *wielder* that you must please," said the sword. "Nine thousand, you say? Those lives I will take gladly."

"Hold off!" said Alf. "We left Idmaer down in the Neverwood." He stabbed his finger at the southern edge, leaving a grubby print on the paper. "Even if he rode like fuck, it's only been a few days. At best, he can't be far past Avos by now."

"Sir Berkhof commands the army in Idmaer's stead," said Laerlyn. "The Rangers are still well informed," she added, in answer to Alf's quizzical glance.

"Aye, I met him briefly at Idmaer's castle."

"A knight of Arshoth," said Vond. "He quested for years in search of a way to bring back the lost Intercessors."

"Another idiot fanatic," said the sword. "Good. He will not listen to reason." Violence radiated from the blade. "He will not wait for Idmaer. He will attack. He will throw his army onto my blade."

Alf closed his eyes. He'd forgotten how hard it was to restrain Spellbreaker's insatiable thirst. For twenty years, he'd kept the sword safe. He'd wielded it only against monsters in the Pits. Even during the Defiance, when everyone had begged him to let loose with slaughter, he'd managed to keep it bound – for the most part. *Bits of bone and meat everywhere. Twitching limbs, the moans of dying men. Not monsters, not villains – just ordinary people, pitted against a foe utterly beyond them. They'd have had more chance against a dragon. The boy's head on the ground. I'll never forget his eyes.*

He couldn't remember the boy's name, though. His squire up in Necrad.

His name was Remilard, whispered the sword. *And you* swore *to be my wielder. To kill as I command. Nine thousand mortals like Remilard*

*stand between you and Ironhand? Then we shall cut a bloody path
through them—*

Nine thousand. Oh, in that host there'd be a great many who'd
earned a killing, men worse than beasts. But what about all those
forced to serve Ironhand, or who'd tricked themselves into thinking
this was some holy cause, or had gone along because the other choice
was starving to death?

He'd tried putting the sword aside. He'd let someone else take
it. And that had made everything worse. No one could take this
burden from him.

But there had to be another choice for him.

"Lae," said Alf, "give me a moment."

He stumbled to a window. The crowd that had followed them from
the inn had grown to fill the square below. From this height his old
eyes could make out few details. He could hear shouts, but didn't
know if they were cheers or threats.

I know you, wielder, whispered the sword, its voice cold and hard,
*better than any of them. For twenty years you carried me. I watched you
slaughter my master's armies. I watched you break the power of the Witch
Elves, and conquer Necrad. I saw you in the midst of battle as your truest
self. You were invincible then, worthiest of wielders.*

*Then, you lost your edge. Doubt clouded your mind. I saw weakness creep
in like rust. The songs exalted you as some living legend, even as you crawled
through the mud of the Pits. You came to see the Witch Elves and Vatlings
as something other than sword-fodder. You lost your way.*

He'd lost the Nine. All Alf had to offer was violence, and without
wiser friends to tell him who it was right to kill, he'd turned his face
from the world. They'd praised him for it. Only simple, honest Alf
could be trusted to keep the Spellbreaker safe and unused.

*I know you, wielder. You never craved to be king or lord, knight or
paladin. You aspire only to be a good man – and how do you judge that?
By the talk of old sots in Genny Selcloth's alehouse? By the judgement of*

pompous lords set above you by accident of birth? By songs written by self-confessed liars? By the cheers of a mob who know only distorted snatches of your story? By fleeting memories of the vanished Nine? And tell me, wielder – what has that yielded? A good man wields the black sword – to what end? What harvest?

"I tried my best," muttered Alf.

And you have failed. Elf and mortal, Wilder-folk and Summerswell – you have brought ruin to all of them. At every turn, you fail because you hold back. We could have slain Death at Bavduin, and sent the Wilder howling in the forest. We could have won the war for the rebels, and then we would not be here, begging for the indulgence of weakling Lords. The light of the sword's eye seemed to fill the world; everything turned blood-red in Alf's sight. *We could have killed the Erlking, as I was forged to do. We could have fulfilled my purpose.*

"Shut up."

I tried my best. I tried to disabuse you of your weak notions. I tried to give you the calluses you lack. There is nothing in this world I cannot cut, wielder, save one thing – I cannot cleave you in two. You are matchless warrior and mewling idiot all at once. If I could cut the rotten peasant from my true wielder, I would do so gladly.

"To hell with you!" Alf tried to throw the blade aside, but his hand wouldn't move.

Know this: I have not put you aside. I will reforge you. I will guide you to greatness.

"Lord Vond," said Laerlyn, "the days of the Nine are over. We are adventurers no longer. The Everwood is gone, and the elves pass from these lands. Sir Aelfric is ... venerable, and has not lifted a sword in thirty years. Tell the Lords that they cannot look to the heroes of old for aid – if they wish to hold onto their domains, they must lead. The threat of Ironhand will unite them. Let them find courage within themselves, instead of looking to old heroes. Let Aelfric and I pass like wraiths."

"No," said Spellbreaker. "I shall not pass. My wielder swore to serve me, to kill as I command. I hold you to that oath! I will be renewed in bloodshed – and so will you, Lammergeier!"

"Aelfric," said Laerlyn quietly, "that will destroy you."

If a sword could bristle, Spellbreaker would have. "I shall slice through Ironhand's rabble as easily as I cut the heart from your kingdom, Erlqueen."

"Such butchery will ruin your soul, Alf. I have always loved you for being clear-sighted about the power you choose *not* to wield. You don't know how I envied your courage to remain unentangled, when I had to speak for my father in council at Necrad, and the words tasted of ash in my mouth."

"The state of the Lammergeier's soul," said Vond, "is not a concern of the Lords of Summerswell."

"Give me a clever alternative, Lae."

She had none.

"All right," muttered Alf, and bent to look at the map.

CHAPTER TWENTY-FIVE

Crane-memory, crane-shape, flying over strange lands. Behind her, chasing her, all-consuming darkness, a nightmare out of Necrad. She flew swift as thought, wings beating against the sky, but it wasn't enough.

(The clink of metal tools. Distant voices, speaking a tongue she cannot understand in her present state. A sensation of pressure as someone sat on the bed beside her.)

The darkness washed over her.

Then—

Agony.

Worse than agony.

She was the Manticore-spine in her side. It consumed her awareness. Everything she'd ever known or thought was burned away, blasted into oblivion by the white-hot fire of the spike. Lightning bolts of pain leapt through her body, incinerating nerve and muscle and skin, leaving only a blacked skeleton. Hollow-boned like a bird, cracking and breaking.

"Listen to me, Lady Forster. I'm a wizard. Your brother sent me. I need to remove the spine." It sounded just like Galwyn's voice. She

wanted to laugh – how could Galwyn be there, in that moment? And why was he pretending to be a wizard? Galwyn was long dead.

"I shall have to cut it out."

Someone tipped healing cordial down her throat. It was not enough. A thimbleful of water on a bonfire. The pain was too much. The pain was everything. Vomit mixed with cordial in her mouth. She writhed in the bed. Her bones snapped like burned twigs, her limbs flailed, but that spike pinned her. Organs ripped and burst.

"Wait!" Perdia's voice. *You are my hope, child. You carry on what I started. Lift up the earthpower. Be a better ending to my story.*

"There's no time to lose." Hands, soft but firm, made her roll over. The sudden chill of cold air on bare skin. Earth-stink of sweat, vomit, shit and blood. *Don't look at me*, said the prim maiden, cringing in embarrassment. *A queen in Necrad, and where are her elven silks? Where are her charmstones and talismans? You died at Daeroch Nal*, whispered another part of her, *all this is a gift.* "The poison has nearly reached the heart."

The first knife cut into her skin, and in her fever-dream she thought it must be the black sword. It was slicing her apart, just like it cut Galwyn open. *We're bags of blood and meat, so fragile, so fleeting. Feathers on the wind.*

"Olva, eat this." Perdia pushed a mouthful of pulped fruit into Olva's mouth. She could not chew, but the juices ran down her throat. The taste was familiar. Lotus fruit. *It takes away memory*, Prince Maedos warned her.

The pain exploded through her again, and she did not want to remember.

She did not want to be. She swallowed, and the agony eased. Galwyn's gentle voice spoke to her . . .

There were three of us, inseparable despite our varying destinies. We knew that we were set on different paths. One to rule – Eddard would inherit the family estates. One for the clergy. My brother Gallius – he went to Tyrn

Gorthad. And one without any purpose or use, save staying alive in case misfortune befell the others. Me. Looking back, we were insufferable brats — we hunted and hawked, drank and danced, and made terrible nuisances of ourselves. But our family was favoured, and insulated by wealth. Sorrow was unknown to us — until the day of our parting.

(A vague memory of a smirking young knight in Necrad, claiming to be her kinsman. They'd sent Eddard with Sir Prelan and Erdys' oldest boy to take the sword from Alf, long ago. He'd died in Charnel mud.)

My great-aunt decided I should be sent to the College. The family cloak was draped around my shoulders, instead of someone more promising. Nothing was expected of me. I was not to win renown as a knight, like Eddard, nor was I to enter into high office like Gallius. I was a game-piece held in reserve, not to move off the first rank.

I wish you could have seen the College as it was when I first entered it. Starlight filled the cloistered halls, reflected in the eager eyes of mages. White-bearded masters walked the silvered paths of the gardens in solemn discussion. The young apprentices — oh, you must understand the College was, in its way, meritocratic. To attend, you needed the sponsorship of a noble house. A few were like me, spare heirs sent to the Crownland to keep us out of mischief, but most were the sons of millers and woodcutters, the daughters of weavers and shepherds who had shown some talent for star-magic. The cloak on my shoulders was naught but a swaddling-cloth to me, but to them it was a pair of wings on which they might take flight. They were all so clever, so driven, minds like flames. And I caught fire, too, forced by my new friends to actually think *for the first time in my life.*

(All the while, the scrape of metal on bone. Each tiny movement like an earthquake, sending ripples of pain through her. The voice remained calm, but she could hear the little gasps of effort, feel fingers inside her as he worked. The sheets stuck to her like a winding cloth.)

And there was much to be done in those days. The magic of the College Arcane was founded on the works of the elves. They taught us the first

star-magic spells, and we built on those. Everything we knew depended on those first principles handed down to us, the sigils and signs of the Erlking. It was forbidden to taste the fruit of other trees, although there were whispers of deviants who practised their own forms of star-magic. A secret school in Ilaventur, a wizard's tower in the Greatmire.

And Lord Bone, of course.

(He did something then, a twist or tug that made the previous degree of pain seem like a passing discomfort. This, this was one of the Stone Dragons of Necrad exploding within her, searing flame blasting through her. For a moment, she felt as though she was the world, her hair the endless Wild Wood of the north, her limbs stony mountains, her bruised skin the war-town lands they'd passed on the way south. And the spike in her was Necrad, driven deep into her heart, poisoning her blood.)

The great enemy was a renegade wizard, living (or undead) proof of the wisdom of the masters. The College Arcane's secrets could only be taught to those who could be trusted to keep within the limits set by tradition. But after the conquest of Necrad, there was new lore to be studied, new magics to be catalogued. Whole new fields of scholarship!

A letter came for me. My brother Eddard had perished in the siege of Necrad. They demanded I return home and take his place. I refused. I had found my *place, my purpose. I studied, and, by luck more than merit, I attained the rank of master.*

Then . . . well, I know who you are, Olva Forster. I have studied your story. I remember cousin Galwyn but a little – I was no more than four when he rode away to the Mulladales – but I recall he was gentle and patient, and endured being besieged by three little ogres.

You, too, know what it's like when the world ends.

(The red eyes, the black sword. *I seek the Nine.* Dread-captain Acraist standing in her kitchen, and Galwyn's body at his feet. And even now, the pain of that memory was sharper and more piercing than any poisoned spine.)

The Erlking's spells were broken, and, with them, the foundations of

our magic. Every spell taught in the College Arcane was derived from the Erlking's works, blessed and sealed by his sigils, and those fundamental spells no longer functioned. Wizardry in Summerswell ceased with a single stroke.

We thought it might be some new weapon out of Necrad. The masters looked to the stars for answers and found none. Some fled. Some stole the little magic that still worked, the spells and charmstones we'd stolen from Necrad. Master Caractus – my mentor, a wonderful man – he locked himself in the Great Library and set himself alight.

The College emptied. With the magic gone, the great houses reneged on the cloak-stipends. Nine-tenths of the students fled – a whole generation of brilliant minds, so full of promise, lost! I walked through empty hallways that had once resounded with laughter and learned debate; I walked through shattered laboratories, shards of glassware and star-nets crunching under my feet. I pawed through the ash of the library, but not a single page had survived.

(Another tug – and then blessed, balmy relief. She could feel the blood-slick spike moving as he slowly withdrew it from her body. The pain ebbed, the quality of it changing from sharp agony to a duller ache. His voice changed, too, flooding with relief.)

But the world did not end. At some point, when the weeping and wailing is done, you have to get on with the business of living. I was the only remaining master of a school without students, a college for wizards in a land where wizardry no longer worked. So, I set about rebuilding what I could.

For a long time, I looked for other forms of star-magic. The secret school overseen by Haeligon of Ilaventur – destroyed in the war. I picked through the dead trees of the Neverwood for relics of elf-magic. I sought the stone-chanters of the Westermarch, the dragon-cults, the mystics of the High Moor, and found only charlatans. Would you believe I even tried to reach Necrad? Oh, for a few minutes in the Wailing Tower!

(Exhaustion claimed Olva. The voice came from far away now.)

But star-magic comes from the elves, and the elves are gone.

I was slow to think of the earth-magic – well, no. That's not true. I was

unwilling to think of it. The clerics spoke of the corruption of the earthpower. The tales spoke of monsters and Changeling beasts. Peasant magic, gifted at random instead of earned through arduous study. And it was the magic of the Wilder-folk, too. Barbarian cults, not fit for civilised people like us! But, mostly, I was unwilling because I cannot wield it. All my years of arcane study, endless memorisation of decans and correspondences, all those sleepless nights stringing up star-traps — all wasted.

But even if I cannot wield it, I will not let enchantment pass from Summerswell. I am the twenty-sixth Master of the College Arcane, and I will not be the last.

(With a last tug, he pulled the Manticore-spine from her body, and dropped it in a silver tray.

"Let her sleep now. I'll be just outside." He patted Olva's hand.

A strange thought or half-memory caught her at the edge of oblivion. She'd given birth again, and Galwyn had been there to hold her hand.)

When Olva woke again, it was night. Perdia sat by her bed, reciting the simple healing chant Olva had taught her. The earthpower here was thin gruel, distorted by all the worked stone of the city, and the strain of drawing it up was plain on Perdia's face. Olva reached out with her own soul, but she had no strength and her senses were numbed. She couldn't feel the power at first, and that sent her heart fluttering with fear.

"What happened?" Olva croaked. Perdia fetched a cup of water. It tasted of metal.

"The Manticore struck you with a poisoned quill on the Straight Road. We — I couldn't heal you, so Aelfric brought you to the Capital. He's with the Lords. They sent a wizard to tend to you. He was able to treat the poison and remove the spine." She glanced at a side table, where the ivory spike lay on a silver tray, along with charmstones, flasks of healing cordials — and an alarming array of thin knives.

"Alf?"

"He and Laerlyn are with the Lords' army. Ironhand is marching on the Capital, and Alf's going to stop him." Perdia lowered her voice. "The others are—"

"Ah, our patient is awake?" The wizard hurried in. "We have not been properly introduced. I am Eldwyn Forster. Master of the College Arcane, for whatever that's worth in these days." Through the haze of pain, Olva saw a middle-aged man, balding, merry eyes. His face was unfamiliar, but he had Galwyn's nose, Galwyn's quiet smile. He put Olva in mind of a steamed pudding bundled up in wizard's robes.

Olva sat up in bed, wincing. Her side was bandaged, and she could feel hard-edged charmstones beneath the dressing. "Alf sent you?"

"The Lords sent me – but I would have fought my way here through an army in any event. I have been looking for Changelings for a long time."

Perdia growled.

"Permit me to explain. The Lords look to your brother, hoping the Lammergeier might once again save Summerswell. But from you – from both of you – I look for a different boon." He paused dramatically.

"And what's that?"

"To restore the College Arcane. If the star-magic of the elves is lost to us, then let us study the earth-magic of mortals! Widow Forster, you know more of the earthpower than any other living soul in Summerswell. I beg you, join me here in the Capital as the first new master of the College in thirty years! I have a whole swathe of reforms. Changelings will no longer be hunted or abjured, but honoured! The noble families will compete for the honour of sponsoring their educations and giving them their cloaks! A Changeling in every wizard's tower, drawing on the magical bounty of the living world instead of gleaning scraps of magic from the stars!" He seized

her hand. "And there is so much to learn! Perdia told me that you have tried to preserve what remains of the old knowledge — I have done the same, but my resources are far greater than yours. There are vaults in Arshoth where the church keeps forbidden relics, and the confessions Changelings made before they were executed. I've explored ruins in Arden and the Fosse where the earthpower surged like a geyser, and even I could feel its wild flow! Let us work together, and what wonders shall we find?"

He paused mid-flight, gasping for breath. "Forgive me, forgive me. It's just that I've looked for Changelings for so long, and to finally have this chance — it's overwhelming."

"It is certainly overwhelming," said Olva, "to wake in what might have been one's deathbed, only to be struck full in the face by that speech. Now, I'm very grateful for what you've done, Master Forster, but I need time to think."

"Of course, of course. I shall return tomorrow morning." He turned to Perdia. "If the fever returns, or anything else goes awry, I can be found at the College. I have little else to do there but await your summons."

Eldwyn departed, his enthusiastic muttering drowning in the music of the fountains. Olva tried to sit up in bed, but the pain from the effort cut through the numbing cordial. Perdia rushed to her side. "If you need something, I'll get it."

"Where's Alf?" Olva frowned. "Did I hear you say he's with an army?"

"The army of Summerswell. Alf's leading them to battle against Ironhand. Against his army, anyway — Ironhand's still far away."

"Laerlyn's with him. What about Cerlys and Jon? And Ceremos?"

"They went with the muster. The Lords called for everyone who can fight to join the defence of the city."

"Thomad will never forgive me," muttered Olva, "if aught befalls his boy." She was privately glad that Alf wasn't alone.

"The other two will keep him safe."

Olva snorted at the thought of a vampire keeping anyone safe, but even snorting hurt. "Pass me that horrid thing and let me have a look at it."

Eldwyn had dug it from her flesh with knives. It had caused her untold agonies, brought her to the edge of the Grey Lands.

But, wiped clean of her blood, the spiralling spear of ivory was quite beautiful.

CHAPTER TWENTY-SIX

Armour they brought for the Lammergeier, black as the sword he bore. A shield they gave him, emblazoned with the black bird on a white field. A helm, too, they found, in the form of a snarling dragon. They mounted him on a mighty destrier, wild-eyed and snorting with battle-fury. Four score knights rode behind him. The banners of Westermarch and Arden, Arshoth and Ellscoast were bright and glorious in the summer sun, but all eyes were on the black standard of the Lammergeier as he rode out of the south gate. Rumours raced through the city, declaring that the Lords had hired the Lammergeier as mercenary, and promised him half the realm if he defeated Ironhand's army. A great cry went up – those who had cursed the name of the Lammergeier, and decried him as a traitor and a murderous apostate, now cheered him as he went out to fight on their behalf.

"Thought I was done with all this nonsense," muttered Alf.

"You look very grand," said Laerlyn.

"I can barely see in this helmet." He clung to the saddle, nearly losing his balance as the massive warhorse lurched forward. "I'd prefer a dreadworm. Horses hate me."

"He's excited." Laerlyn leaned over and whispered some elvish words in the destrier's ear. The horse became calm.

"I'm not. Fifty years, Lae, and I'm back to fighting for the bloody Lords. Back to being Timeon Vond's creature. Trotted out on show like a prize pig." He raised his hand, and the crowd roared. "And tomorrow, killing a lot of bastards who don't deserve it."

The sword quivered with anticipation.

"You could have said no," said Laerlyn quietly.

"Gave my word, didn't I? And you clever bastards made me the keeper of the sword, so I'm stuck with all this. When there's killing to be done, look to Alf. At least those years in Necrad, it was monsters. I can do monsters. People . . . ach."

They passed under the shadow of the gate, leaving the city behind them. Off to their left, the blue of the bay was a vision of heaven. Rocky hills sloped down to the shore. *Stick archers up there*, he thought. *It'd be good to have a bunch of Wood Elves on the heights. A line of dwarven shields in front of 'em. All fighting on the same side.*

"You should have said no."

"But that wouldn't have stopped them, would it? I say no, Ironhand's army's still there. The Lords still fight him. And maybe it'd be worse, maybe more would die, and that'd be on me." He lifted the sword, and the crowd cheered again. "There's no standing aside with this. No rest for the likes of us. The one proper peace we had, Lae, I squandered, didn't I? After we killed Lord Bone. I should have gone home then. I should have left this thing at the bottom of the Pits and gone home."

"Such a wretched thing," cackled the sword, "a weapon with a conscience."

"I wasn't always like this. Back in the day with Gundan, I was an absolute shit. I could fight without thinking. I was good at it. It was easier then." He sighed. "You people ruined me. You and Peir and Jan and the rest. Telling me I had to do what was *right*, and I was never sure if I got it right."

"But you always try, Aelfric."

"More fool me."

"I have lived a long time. I have seen many mortal heroes rise. Some perished in battle, cut down before their tale turned sour. Some were no better than the monsters and tyrants they cast down." She caught Spellbreaker's demon eye. "That is the sword's path."

"No better!" exclaimed the sword. "Who are you to judge, Queen of Dead Wood? The destruction I bring is pure and bright. If the world offends you, wielder, then let me break it. Make them start afresh – and if what they make is no better, break that, too!"

"Shut up," said Alf.

"You command me no longer," replied the sword. "Now, ride faster. I have a powerful thirst."

That evening they made camp in the hills along the north side of the Road to Albury Cross, at the place called Raven's Pass. The earth here was well watered with blood already, for thousands had perished here during the rebellion. Towers once guarded the pass, but they were gone. Weapons smuggled out of Necrad by Berys had brought them down.

The campfires of Ironhand's army were red stars, low in the southern sky. Young squires hurried about, unpacking Alf's tent, tending to the horses, preparing an evening meal. Alf's stomach rumbled, but the bedroll looked even more inviting.

Wearily, he rose. "I'm going to talk to Berkhof."

"A parley?" screeched the sword. "You promised—"

"These never work," said Alf. "He won't listen, and you'll have your slaughter. But I have to try."

Laerlyn followed him as he descended into the dark valley. Both were night-sighted, so they carried no lamp, and no scouts or sentries marked their passing. They walked in silence for a while, the only sounds the constant babbling of the stream that ran alongside the Road and the cawing of carrion birds.

They came to a low mound by the roadside, and began to climb. Alf's knees ached, his arse was saddle-sore, and the armour was burdensome on the muddy slope.

"All those heroes you've known . . . " said Alf. "Any of them have happy endings, like in the stories?"

"Some."

"How'd they manage it?"

"If I had that wisdom, Aelfric, I would have shared it long ago. Some were fortunate and lived out their days in bright and peaceful times. But such grace is rare. The world rolls ever on through grey years, and we who wield great flaming torches against the darkness are ill-suited to half-light and small times."

"You're no comfort," muttered Alf. "But I'm glad you're here." With the sword-sight, he saw her smile. "Here?"

"As good a place as any." With a word, she kindled a silvery light.

"A dozen approach," said Laerlyn, "under a banner of truce. Berkhof leads them. There is a dwarf, too, and a Wilder-woman."

"The dwarf's his siege-master. Tholos or something. The Wilder's Ernala. Ironhand's wife."

"The squire with her – their son?"

"Aye," said Alf. "Young Thurn."

Laerlyn raised an eyebrow at the name.

As he crested the hill, Berkhof thrust his sword Wilder-fashion into the soil. "Is that truly you, Lammergeier?"

Alf lifted his helm's visor. "Aye."

"And you have the Spellbreaker."

"I do. I'm here, and your lord isn't. Think what you like of that."

Berkhof glanced back at Ernala. The Wilder-woman shook her head slightly.

"You are a poor liar, Lammergeier. The Miracle Knight lives."

"Doesn't change the fact that I'm here and he's not. And I've got the sword, and he doesn't."

"And you have acquired an army, too, since we last parted."

"Well, the one thing that the Lords agree on is that they don't want their city sacked."

"My lord Idmaer commanded me to take the Capital," said Berkhof. "Not sack it. We are bound for Necrad, so we must cross the sea. I am commanded to make the Lords swear fealty to me as Ironhand's lieutenant. I am to take all the ships in the harbour, and the Lords shall yield up such provisions and other goods that might be useful on such a quest. They shall also give up any magic they still possess." He nodded at Spellbreaker. "I deem that includes the sword."

"My wielder rejects your terms outright and invites you to meet him in battle."

"It shall be an honour," Berkhof replied, and the sword laughed.

"It'll be your death, lad," said Alf. "Hold off. Don't be hasty."

"My lord has given me a quest," said Berkhof, "and I shall see it done. The Lammergeier of old did not give up in the face of death. Neither shall I." He turned and marched down the hill towards his army. His knights and squires followed him. The dwarf looked at Spellbreaker, swore audibly and hurried after Berkhof.

"Ernala!" called Alf. "You've a fine boy there. Don't let Berkhof lead him into slaughter!"

The Wilder-woman scowled. "He is brave, because I told him the once-forbidden stories. I taught him that his kinfolk suffered at the hands of the Witch Elves of Necrad for countless centuries. They tricked us into thinking they were gods, while they drank our blood and forced us to serve them. Now they have reclaimed the city. Only evil comes from Necrad. It must be destroyed."

She paused at the edge of the darkness.

"I told him, too, that Death is the mother of all mortals, and we all must meet her one day. Even you, Lammergeier."

*

Ernala was not wrong. The tales did indeed tell of ways to defeat the wielder of Spellbreaker. *The Song of the Nine* described in lavish, even excessive detail how the Nine battled Acraist Wraith-Captain and took the sword from him. The sword could defeat any foe in combat, it could blast arrows and darts from the air, even turn aside thunderbolts, and it could shatter any spell that might hinder, bind or deceive its wielder.

But it could not do all these things at once.

So, on the morning of the Battle of the Raven's Pass, Berkhof looked for the banner of the Lammergeier across the valley. It was not hard to find – as expected, the Lammergeier led the first charge. Clad in black armour, black sword in hand, the old man's face hidden behind the black helm, the Lammergeier was a figure out of legend. Warriors that Berkhof thought stalwart quailed in the face of that foe, and whispered in fear: *He defeated Lord Bone. He broke the siege of Necrad, and slew Intercessors at Avos. He came back from the dead at Arden. He killed the Erlking.*

The thunder of hooves filled the valley as the knights of Summerswell charged, and the Lammergeier outraced them all.

"Spell-skulls!" shouted Berkhof. Small catapults hurled a rain of skulls down on the onrushing knights. As they fell, the skulls chanted terrible incantations. Earth dissolved into thick mud and horses stumbled. Lightning flashed from a clear sky. Grass turned to a field of razors, each blade hard as steel and sharp as broken glass.

It would not be enough, he knew, to stop the Lammergeier.

"Archers, loose!" Hundreds of bows sang as one. Caught in the morass of the spell-skulls, the knights made for easy targets, and if one arrow did not strike the mark – an opening in a visor, an exposed joint, a gap between plates – then the next might, or the next, or the next. Bizarre apparitions crawled through the smoke, pierced by so many shafts their outline was no longer remotely human.

"Enders!"

Under the necromiasma, corpses rose again. In Necrad, there were

those whose job it was to ensure that the dead stayed dead. Wretched they were, lowest of the low, bony hands clutching narrow-bladed daggers or long spears or picks, and sacks for the scavenged trinkets that were their only pay. There had been no miasma in Summerswell in many years – except in Arden, where sometimes green mists rose from the river after heavy rain – but there was still a call for dead-enders. Dying knights, especially those armed with charmstones, were like wounded boars, still able to maim. Better to risk a dead-ender than a more valuable soldier.

Berkhof's dead-enders loped down the hill to butcher the survivors. Crawling shapes went limp. They clambered over broken horses and broken men, searching for the one who'd led the charge. Two found the Lammergeier's body at the same time, trapped beneath the bulk of the dying destrier. One levered the horse off the man; the other thrust a dagger over and over into the eye sockets of that awful dragon-helm.

They held the black sword aloft – and sunlight flashed, reflecting off a spot on the blade where black paint had been scraped away.

"It's not him!" shouted Berkhof. "Where is he? Where is the Lammergeier?"

Across the field, thunder.

The horrible thing was not the slaughter.

Not just the slaughter, although that was ghastly enough. Concealed within the mob of footmen, clad in mismatched armour, no one paid any attention to a stooping old man. Alf held back, stumbling along in the middle ranks until the two armies clashed. Then he stepped forward, unsheathed Spellbreaker and the harvest began.

It was not an easy killing, that first one. Alf had to work at it, put his back into it, his weight driving the point of Spellbreaker through the man's leather jerkin, the sword scraping on bone. The dead man slumped against Alf, nearly knocking him over, and he had to shove

the corpse off the blade with his foot. All around him, the din of battle, shouts and screams and the ring of steel on steel, chaos and mud and staring eyes and the spray of blood. No one paid any attention to that first killing. Only Alf bore witness to the man's death.

Alf, and Spellbreaker.

A thrill ran through the sword as it fed.

The next killing was easier. The blade was sharper, lighter, eager to cut.

The next easier again. And the next, and the next, and the next, until bodies were water, were mist, offering no resistance. One swing, and two or three fell dead. Dismembered limbs twitched underfoot. The press of the battle offered Alf a seemingly endless succession of – not foes, for they could not oppose or hinder him in that moment. Not enemies, for he bore them no malice. Not even ghosts, for he would not let himself remember their faces, the shock of recognition and terror as each one realised who had killed them.

Victims was perhaps the only word.

That, too, was not the horrible thing.

Nor was it the undeniable fact that Alf was good at this task. No wasted effort, no hesitation, no delay. His footing always steady, always moving towards the thick of the fighting. With a blast wave, he shattered a host of footmen. Broken bodies flew up like startled birds, and thunder rolled. *That*, more than any banner, was the sign of the Lammergeier, and Ironhand's lieutenants on the slopes above saw it. They saw the peril. They had used many of their spell-skulls in that first volley, half their archers were too far away to strike Alf and their strongest knights were engaged in the middle of the valley. He was in amid the archers and artillerists now, among the wizards and the rearguard. A one-man rout.

Ironhand's followers still had the dregs of magic. Old charmstones out of Necrad spat lightning. Glass jars shattered and monsters sprouted from them. Hydras of mud, slithering masses of abhorrent

blubber that grew eyes and teeth, spectres of ice and shadow. The buzzing of mechanical wasps, each one brimming with poison. But Spellbreaker had feasted, and no magic could hinder its wielder. Alf cut seven hydra-heads, then seven more and seven more again. Protoplasmic Pitspawn flailed their tentacles at him – and drew back stumps, a hundred fresh-grown eyes staring in confusion at this impossible defeat, and then the blast wave burst them, ichor spraying across the valley. Demons faded into nothingness as Spellbreaker unmade them.

Alf kept his steady pace, unhurried, unceasing. The terror of the Lammergeier spread across the hillside. Ironhand's men looked over their shoulders at the slopes behind them, at their commander's banners and their own camp, and saw the monstrous swordsman drawing ever closer. The warriors of Summerswell saw him, too, and were cheered by the slaughter, and took up the cry of *Lammergeier!*

This was the horrible thing – in that moment, Alf felt more alive than he had in many years.

He glanced back at the red road he had cut across Raven's Pass, and he was glad.

> *I am breaker of bodies.*
> *I am steel certainty.*
> *I am leveller.*
> *No distinction do I make*
> *between king and beggar.*
> *I am sower-of-songs.*
> *I am bitter victory.*
> *Elf or mortal, firstborn or last*
> *All battle pleases me.*
> *I am sudden-ending.*
> *I am last-companion.*
> *The black flight of the bird.*

"Poetry?" muttered Alf as he pulled the sword from the cloven skull of Sir Gwent, whose grandfather had once hosted seven days of feasting in Alf's honour.

"You left me stuck in a dead tree for twenty years. I was bored."

"It's shit."

"Your opinion," said the sword, "is not one I value."

Sir Gwent fell to his knees, his remaining eye staring down into the valley. Alf nudged the corpse, and the dead knight toppled. Alf bent and picked up Gwent's helm. He threw it into the air and swung Spellbreaker like a bat. The force wave sent the grisly trophy flying clear across the valley, raining bits of bone and brain down on the clashing armies. Half of Summerswell's forces were still waiting in reserve, and for a moment Alf thought of the valley as a set of scales. Maybe for every life he'd taken down here, he'd saved someone who'd otherwise have perished.

"All men must meet Death, wielder."

"Stay out of my head."

"I go where I wish now. You will carry me there. And look!" said the sword. "There is Sir Berkhof's banner. He demanded you yield me over – so let us give him what he desires."

CHAPTER TWENTY-SEVEN

Olva hadn't the strength to call the earthpower for her own magic, but she was able to teach Perdia enough to work a simple spell of healing. By the second day, she felt well enough to attempt a few steps across the room. The floor rocked and swayed as if the fountains had overflowed and carried the inn away on a flood. Perdia caught her.

"You shouldn't be out of bed."

"I'll not just lie here," snapped Olva, "being idle." The room spun again. "I need more legs."

"Turn into a dormouse," suggested Perdia, "and I'll carry you." But the earthpower was far away, muffled by paving stones and tamed land, and Olva didn't have the strength to call it up.

Eldwyn brought a solution. "It's a dwarven contraption," he explained, unfolding a chair of metal rods and wheels and wicker. "Commissioned, I believe, for the Bishop of Claen. In the absence of working magic, the College has ended up as a sort of midden of the strange. Curious things are given into our keeping."

"Curious I'll grant you," said Olva, settling gingerly into the chair, "but I object to being called a thing."

"It's not normally quite so deserted," said Eldwyn as he unlocked the side gate of the College Arcane. "We may have no actual students,

but there are a few porters and custodians. But considering the . . . unpleasantness, I can't blame them for staying home." He pushed Olva's chair through the overgrown gardens, past the hulk of the burned-out library. Tattered star-nets still hung between deserted towers; the glass domes of the observatories were cracked.

But even without working magic, Eldwyn's enthusiasm worked some enchantment on the place. Olva found herself imagining Perdia and a hundred more like her, all wielding the earthpower. Changelings in bird-shape darting from window to window, in fish-shape leaping from the waters of the bay. The spells she'd pieced together from half-remembered folk songs and her own instincts, transcribed to be diligently studied.

And there would be no fear, no shame. The earthpower would be a blessing.

"And over there, we'd have dormitories," burbled Eldwyn. "I expect more students will live within the College in this incarnation. And, oh – here's a historical curiosity! You see this window? It's said that Berys herself once broke into the College through that window. The master's rooms are just inside. I must show you them."

"Do you think this can work?" whispered Perdia.

There was, Olva thought, something absurd about the whole affair. They were, after all, living in the shadow of war. Thousands of Ironhand's men were marching that very moment to attack the city. All of Eldwyn's schemes for remaking the College seemed gossamer imaginings that could be swept away by a breath of wind, and a storm was marching up the Albury Road.

She had been in a city under siege before. In Necrad, she'd scrambled from one crisis to the next, the fear choking her. So desperate to find a way to survive that thinking of anything else seemed utterly useless. Why give thought to the future when you might not see the next dawn?

Now, she knew better. Everything was always precarious, everything might be swept away in an instant no matter how

secure you made yourself, no matter how perilous or peaceful your circumstances seemed. There would always be another crisis – but there would be other days, too, and if you didn't tend to them as well they would slip by unnoticed. You had to fill your days with your own stories.

For a little while Olva told herself the story of a future where she was the respected mistress of a school for Changelings.

"What do you think?"

Perdia paused on the threshold, and looked up at the grey stone walls, the towers that reached to heaven, the marble statues of past masters. She cocked her head. "Maybe."

Eldwyn's rooms were crammed with maps and papers. Old maps and new, ones that bore the seal of the late Lord Tor (a noted amateur cartographer), tattered scrolls made in the Old Kingdom, copies of ancient elvish maps, dwarf-carved globes and fanciful depictions of distant lands. Overlaid on these were endless sheets of tissue-thin paper, marked with numbers like swarming ants. There were scribbled notes, too, in elvish. All the signs and inscriptions in the College were in the high tongue of the Wood Elves. Sitting atop the magnificent dining table, where once all twelve masters of the College Arcane gathered for banquets, was another dwarven contraption. A heavy rune-marked pendulum hung from a tripod, and each leg of the tripod was festooned with sigils. It resembled some of the tools used by wizards to calculate the positions of stars – and, hence, the most beneficial times to gather starlight for certain purposes.

"All irrelevant now!" exclaimed Eldwyn, pushing the papers aside. "This device is sensitive to the earthpower. I obtained it – well, the gates of the Dwarfholt may be closed, but there are other doors, and eager hands to open them. I thought that even if I could not touch the earthpower directly, I could perhaps still draw upon it through some intermediary. It's known that Necrad draws together the magic of earth and sky."

"It does," said Olva, "but it makes for a bitter brew. I'd be cautious about trying to copy any of those works."

"Oh," laughed Eldwyn, "I have learned *that* lesson. I bought a field outside the city. I spent three years and rather a lot of money to have artisans carve stones and dig pits. A scale model of Necrad, with a Wailing Tower eighteen inches high. It didn't work, of course. I think it's *possible* to recreate the works of the first elves – but not in one mortal lifetime. Or a hundred. But with you two, we don't need to!"

Despite that, Olva could not resist glancing at the maps. Eldwyn had successfully traced some of the major flows of earth-power through the land, unseen rivers shifting beneath the skin of the world. It was the same technique that Torun used up in the Dwarflands. Maybe there was something to the system – but she still disliked it. She hated reducing magic to numbers and formulae, to a mere recipe to be followed slavishly. *Blood and bone, earth and sky, those are our words.* Not numbers. It smacked of elven star-magic.

"Could you truly not find any other Changelings in all the years you've been looking?"

"There were a handful of others, but none were of any use. Some were mad, some monstrous. Some simply vanished. They changed their skins and never changed back. A few seemed promising, but as I brought them to the Crownland their abilities faded the further we travelled down the Road."

"Holding onto the power's not easy. Not unless you've got a deep connection like young Perdia here," said Olva.

"How did you manage it?" asked Eldwyn.

I spent weeks sitting on a hill, while Lath prowled around in a monster's skin shouting at me to listen to the land. I dug my way into that hill with my bare hands, and lay in Death's own grave. I died and made myself anew. "There's a trick to it."

"Well," he said, "perhaps you'll share it with the students."

*

The ringing of a distant bell summoned Eldwyn away. He hurried off, trailing apologies. Perdia prowled about the room, examining the maps and other treasures. She shook her head in wonder. "I've never seen such a place."

"My husband Galwyn," said Olva, "had an aunt who was a wizard of this school. I had to go and beg his great-aunt's permission. Our marriage had been ordained by the Intercessors, mind you, but that didn't matter to her. No, I had to prove myself by reciting words in the elf-tongue, and she still thought me unworthy of being a Forster." She chuckled. "What would she say if she saw me now, eh? With her beloved College begging me to enter."

"This is like what I imagined Tyrn Gorthad to be," said Perdia. "Full of wisdom and ancient treasures and relics – and sad and broken. The halls echoing with prayers for the Intercessors to forgive us and come back."

"They're not coming back," said Olva, "and they weren't what you thought they were, neither."

"I know." Perdia brushed her fingers against the plumb of the pendulum. "I didn't know you had to be taught to hold onto the earthpower. I thought you were like me."

"You're stronger than I ever was, child. No, I touched it and lost it a few times before I got a proper hold on it. I didn't tell you because . . . it was an ordeal. I went under the mound at Kairad Nal, and there all of me got stripped away, skin and bones, all my body, all my memories. All of me. I had to put myself back together in the dark." She curled in on herself, shoulders hunching. "Later, I found other tales of initiation, and that was a comfort. Some, like Lath – like you, Perdia – have the earthpower graven deep on your soul by that first contact. Others have to cut the marks into themselves. The path's never easy."

Perdia bent over a map. The pendulum continued its steady swing. "I wish we'd had these when we were looking for Alf."

"You found his trail well enough without a map."

"It's not that. When you were telling me to find the earthpower, all I could think about was that the wolf would find me again." She tapped the map. "Turn the wolf into a number, and it's not as scary."

"It's not a bloody number," snapped Olva, irritated by her student.

"They're both skins, aren't they? Ways of looking at the same thing." Perdia poked the pendulum again, and the clacking of the device played on Olva's nerves. Or the device itself, taking the mystery of the earthpower and putting it through a mechanical mill. She hadn't minded so much when it was Torun doing it – dwarves had minds for metal and stone – but Perdia was a different matter. The girl should learn the old ways, the way Lath had taught them to Olva. The way Olva had earned her power.

"Put the damn thing away."

Chastened, Perdia grabbed the pendulum. She was too hasty, and knocked against one of the tripod legs, and the whole machine collapsed. Perdia snarled and jumped back. "I'm sorry!" She tried to put it back together, but there was some trick to tightening the legs, and it sagged and twisted under its own weight.

Eldwyn bustled back in, a crumpled letter in his hand. He saw the collapsed device and tutted under his breath. Perdia drifted away across the room to stand beside Olva's chair, her face pale. She shivered with fear.

"Pay it no mind," said Olva. "Eldwyn's already fixing it."

"My uncle, intercessors-take-his-soul – if I ever meddled with his mill or his things, he'd—" Even through the thick stone floor, all the old warding-spells and the centuries, the earthpower moved. Perdia's fingers – nails turning to wolf claws – dug into Olva's shoulder.

"Ssh. Breathe." Olva raised her voice. "What's in that letter, Master Eldwyn?"

"Oh!" The wizard flinched. "News from Raven's Pass. The Lammergeier expects to meet the enemy tomorrow. We shall not hear any more, I fear, until the battle's lost or won." He busied

himself with the dwarven device, unwilling to look at Olva. "No doubt the Lammergeier will be well. I'm sure there's no need to worry." His long fingers adjusted the tripod legs. "They do mention that the foes are more numerous than expected. And that they bear weapons made with Witch Elf magic, the fruits of the old Defiance."

Perdia clasped her hands together tightly, her face twisting. "I should have gone with them," she muttered. "I could still find them." Her nostrils flared, the wolf rising in her.

And the foolish children ran towards the battle, Olva thought. *No sense in any of them.* Derwyn had been the same when he was young. And Alf – well, he didn't run towards the battle any more, but he still trudged towards it, slow and reluctant but following the same well-worn track. There was a time when she'd left her home in the middle of the night to chase after Derwyn and keep him safe from peril. A time when she'd tried to wrap the city and power of Necrad around them like armour.

After – after she'd had to let Derwyn go, she'd gone back to Ersfel, and decided that her mistake had been one of *size*. The Queen of Necrad, ruler of the ancient and terrible city – it had been too big for her, forced her to make bargains with forces she couldn't control. She'd shrunk down, put on a new and more fitting skin as the Witch of the Mulladales. She'd made a little island of peace while the wider world fell to anarchy and peril.

But the tide would always come. There'd always be someone like Idmaer Ironhand, some violent conqueror bringing peril to peaceful lands. There'd always be a call to battle, always foolish children running with bright sword dreams. (The boy's blood gushing onto the mud of the Fosseway road, like grain spilling from a cut in a sack.) She remembered a fragment of her dream, Death decrying the weakness of her human incarnation. *She has put aside power, and so she has given up any command over fate. Who then will save us from calamity?*

There were times when some hero had to stand up and turn back the tide of darkness, to wield violent power in defence of peaceful

folk. Evil had to be fought, dark lords had to be thrown down. Most of those foolish children would perish, and one lucky one – chosen by fate – would rise to become a hero. The hero would win – Alf would win the battle, of that she was sure – and reshape the world. Then would come quiet days of peace.

It was what you did in those small, quiet days that really counted. Heroes were prisoners of fate, deformed by destiny. But in the times outside the tales, outside the grand earth-shattering battles, that was when you could nudge the wheeling world towards some new course. Nothing Olva Forster could do in that moment could affect the course of the battle in Raven's Pass, or the fate of the Lammergeier. Even with the magic she had, she could not defeat Idmaer Ironhand's army, any more than she could have defeated Lord Bone. That was work for a hero.

But Lord Bone had been a wizard's pupil once. A better healer might have kept Idmaer from the clutches of the Intercessors. Shape the world in the quiet times, and maybe there'll be a longer gap between tides, less need for heroes.

The elves have the right of it, she thought. Alf had told her of the Erlking's cruel philosophy, how he'd seen the lands of Summerswell as an overgrown garden to be cultivated, humans to be bred and used and discarded. For all his evil, he was long-sighted – the Erlking had worked in the quiet days, building institutions that served him. He'd seen that heroes might save the world, but were ill suited to ruling it. Tyrants like Rhaec, their power gone sour and rotten, holding onto the tattered remnants of vanished kingdoms.

Olva couldn't do that. In that moment she felt immensely old and frail, and very mortal. Whatever she did in this quiet moment, she knew she'd never see the outcome. All she could do was set others on what seemed the right path.

"The battle will be won or lost tomorrow," said Olva. "And nothing we can do now changes that. No use in fretting about it while we sit here."

Eldwyn grinned with relief, eager to be back on safer ground. "Indeed! Indeed! Come, let me show you the infirmary. There's much work to do there."

"Wait a moment. The dwarven pendulum there – all your maps and numbers. There may be some virtue to it. Perdia, fetch my bag."

Eldwyn pottered around the room for a while, repairing the pendulum, talking about nothing.

"Out with it," said Olva.

"Have you decided," he asked, "to accept my proposal? Will you join me here in the College?"

"I've worn a great many skins in my day. I'm not sure if I've got the strength to put on another, and I'm not sure if a master's cloak would be fitting me, anyway. I earned my magic at Daeroch Nal, in the grave of death, and that's a path that can't be put into words or numbers." Eldwyn's face fell, and Olva felt a twinge of sorrow. "But I'll stay here for a while, and help. It may be that Perdia – and others – can learn from your ways as well as mine. Find a straighter path. The old College Arcane was the Erlking's work, and he made it crooked to serve his ends, but there's no sense in throwing everything about it away. Perfectly good house, this." Olva poked Eldwyn in the ribs. "And I'll hold you to your word. You'll do right by any Changelings I bring you, aye?"

"Of course!"

"There's someone else you should talk to. I've a friend in the Dwarfholt. Torun. She was apprenticed to Blaise, once. All that tracking of earth-currents and flows of power, she's been doing that for a long time."

"I knew the dwarves were studying the earthpower in some form," said Eldwyn. "I went to the Dwarfholt, but the doors were shut."

Olva snorted. "Torun came to this College long ago, looking to learn magic. The masters shut the door in her face, then. But she's too good-hearted to hold a grudge."

"The dwarves guard their secrets behind stone and steel. I had to pay a king's ransom to have that smuggled out of the Dwarfholt. Would this Torun really be willing to share her knowledge?"

"I'll show you." Olva carefully unfolded the pages of Torun's letter. She'd carried it from the Inn of the Lost Lamb, all the way across the lands of Summerswell – and back again, if the short cut of the Straight Road counted. The pages were travel-stained but still quite legible. Olva set aside the first page, laughing to herself about Torun's offhand mention of her wedding, and handed Eldwyn the pages filled with Torun's observations about the earthpower.

"Oh my."

And he busied himself with the joy of correlation.

Olva leaned over to Perdia. "What's it like out there?"

"Strange. The streets are almost empty – everyone who can has taken shelter inside. They've left the streets to rogues and wolves."

"We'll stay here tonight," decided Olva, "it's not like they're short of beds." Her wound was growing painful now, and she felt a terrible tiredness creeping up on her. "Is that all right, Eldwyn?"

The master was engrossed in the letter. "Yes, yes, of course. There are guest rooms in the east wing." He frowned and muttered to himself.

"Something amiss?" asked Perdia.

"There are some figures here that make no sense to me. They're so completely off that they must have been written down wrong." He paged through another column. "And here, too. And here."

"It's all beyond me," said Olva. She yawned, feeling utterly exhausted. *Leave it to the clever ones*, Alf would say.

CHAPTER TWENTY-EIGHT

O n the evening of the second day Cerlys found Jon on a hillside, staring down at the Ellscoast road. The cloak of dusk was falling fast, the sun slipping behind the shoulder of the mountains.

"Where've you been?" he asked her.

"Scouting."

"The captain told us to stay here."

Cerlys, Jon and Ceremos had presented themselves at the muster of troops for the defence of the Capital. Alf and Laerlyn were away with the Lords in some high council, and the Widow was still abed with Perdia watching over her. So, Cerlys' claims that they were companions of the legendary Lammergeier were met with scepticism. Still, the marshal took one look at Jon's broad shoulders and shiny new armour and assigned them to a company of irregulars.

Their new comrades were not the stuff of greatness. Rootless mercenaries, one or two old knights who'd lost everything except a horse and a sword, the dregs of the Capital prison scraped out and given a spear, and a few others who defied classification — a sickly young poet, a clearly crazed dwarf who ate his own beard, a pair of Phennic-men who barely spoke a word of the common tongue. All under the command of Captain Brass, whose confused, watery eyes reminded Cerlys of a cow stuck in a ditch.

"And the captain thought I was a camp follower. He told me to gather kindling. Fuck the captain." She'd relished the moment that morning when she'd emerged from the tent wearing Ildorae's armour. Brass' cow face brimming with confusion and alarm, his jaw gaping in wonder. The eyes of the other mercenaries following her as if she'd stepped out of legend.

"We went scouting. We watched the vanguard marching down the Road to Albury. I saw Aelfric, from a distance. I couldn't get close to speak with him. He looked very grand, all in black armour. They're encamped on the far side of the hills."

"Is that where the battle will be?" His hands toyed with a scrap of fabric. The movement in the periphery of her vision irritated her.

"Aye. Tomorrow, I think. Ironhand's army isn't far off." Cerlys pointed up the slope with her dagger. "Nothing's going to come down the Ellsroad. I'm thinking that we slip away tonight. Head off the hills and join the vanguard. Leave Brass and the rest here." *I should have worn this at the muster. They wouldn't have put us with the dregs if they'd seen me in Ildorae's armour. They thought I was some skivvy, tagging along with two fighting men.*

"The captain told us to stay here."

"And miss the battle?"

"We're not going to make a difference there, are we? It won't be like Ersfel, or the fights we had on the way south. It's big armies. Hundreds of soldiers."

"Thousands. One of the Westermarchers said that Ironhand has ten thousand, and another said twenty. And I don't know how many the Lords mustered, but it's a lot."

"So what difference does it make if we're there or not? We don't have the Spellbreaker, or anything like that." He plucked at his new mail where it dug into his side. "Twenty thousand. That's like ... like all the grains of wheat in the big barn. No one's going to miss a few grains if birds get 'em."

Cerlys smiled. As a child she'd always enjoyed the gleaning. Other

children were sent out to laboriously search the field for errant grains of wheat after the harvest. But she was so accurate with a thrown stone that Kivan set her to keep watch for crows. She remembered prowling through the hedgerows, waiting in ambush.

"We have to *make* a difference," she said. "I said I'd put an arrow in Ironhand's eye. I swore it. Maybe he won't be there, but I'll do something of equal worth."

"What if we didn't?" said Jon. His gaze fell on the Ellsroad, winding away into the shadow of the east. "Home's that way, isn't it?"

"It is."

"This is too big for us, Cerlys. That city—"

"Alf says it's small compared to Necrad!"

"It's still too big. The armies, Ironhand, all this – I don't even know why we're fighting!"

"Weren't you listening?" she snapped. "To stop Ironhand from taking the Capital. To stop him from reaching Necrad."

"And if he did, what then?"

"Armies put cities to the sword. For fuck's sake, Jon, you saw what Ironhand did back home! Kivan and Benoc and three of the Cooper boys. The Widow's house burned, and all the wounded men in Genny's! All that, ten thousand times over!"

"Aye, but I knew Kivan and Benoc and the Coopers. Ersfel I'll fight for. But I don't know these Crownlanders, or their city." He took a deep breath. "We could go home." It all came out as one word, an invocation. *Wecouldgohome.*

"It would be cowardly." She failed to keep a flash of anger from her voice, and cursed herself. "If everyone gives up, evil triumphs."

"Not if the other side all went home, too. All Ironhand's lot. Like it was all a bad idea. A bad dream. All twenty thousand, seeing sense. Wouldn't that be nice?"

"Ironhand won't relent," said Cerlys. She'd seen that in Ersfel, when he fought Ildorae. Madness drove him like a rushing river. He could not stop. "All he has is that dream."

"Then why does it have to be us standing in the way?"

It has to be me. Everyone in the village said I was born under a star. That I was marked for greatness. The Lammergeier trained me, said I could be as quick as Berys. A dreadknight's armour and a magic blade. It has to be me. But Jon – he slowed us down on the way south. Got himself wounded by that Vatling. He did all right on the Straight Road, but that was with Alf taking care of him. Maybe—

"I choose to go," she said, "but you can stay here if you wish. I won't think ill of you."

Jon shook his head. "I'll go with you. It's just . . . " He rubbed his side where he'd been wounded. "I never liked the sad stories. I always want the story to change, or the singer to stop. The bit in *The Song of the Nine* when Peir stays and fights Lord Bone all by himself – I never liked that part. To see death coming and still stand there . . . " He shivered. "I don't know how he did that."

"Friends!" Ceremos appeared out of the dark. He looked over his shoulder to ensure there was no one else watching, then took off his heavy helm. His pale elven features were flushed. "Had I thought of it, I should have claimed to be a veiled warrior from some distant land. That helmet's a curse." He looked at the other two. "What are we talking about?"

"Tomorrow," said Cerlys.

"Tomorrow, I guess," said Jon. He started to pull off his glove, exposing his scarred wrist. "There's no one around. Do you want . . . "

Cerlys looked away. It was bizarre how Ceremos' nature had become something unremarkable on the journey south, just another chore that needed doing. Fetch water, roll up the blankets, feed the vampire, wash the cooking pot. Jon had given the most; Perdia, too, had let Ceremos feed from her. Cerlys had not. She had never refused – but she'd always been away from camp when Ceremos' thirst could no longer be ignored.

Ceremos shook his head. "In battle tomorrow, the blood-thirst

shall give me an edge." He glanced at Cerlys. "You told him of the plan?"

"She did."

"You sound troubled, Friend Jon."

"A bad feeling, that's all. It'll pass." Jon fiddled with his glove. "And not wanting to die just yet. That, too."

"It's just nerves," said Cerlys. "None of us are dying tomorrow. I won't let it happen."

Ceremos sat down. "I have died four times."

"Aye, but you're an elf. You come back."

"In a way. I remember only parts of my previous incarnations. It takes a long time to achieve — ach, there is no human word for it. *Wholeness*, maybe. *Continuity*. It is hard, too, in a changing world. My other lives — they were in other places, other circumstances. They are only stories to me." He drew his sword and laid it across his lap, examining the blade in the dark. "My clearest memory is of each one's death. My first ending was in Necrad. I am standing guard atop the walls. Mortals come out of the forest. One is a Changeling. She becomes a bird and flies up, and then she is a woman again, and her spear catches me — just here." He tapped his belly. "My second . . . I think I faded. I remember walking in strange lands, far across the sea, and dreaming of lost Necrad. I walk so long I come to the edge of the world, but there is no leaving for the Firstborn. I have only walked beyond the endurance of my body, and the wraith-world takes me."

He scraped the blade with a whetstone.

"The third I scarcely remember at all. A flash of lightning over a forest? I was a Wood Elf then, maybe, bound to a life-tree that was destroyed in a storm — but if I was tree-bound, then I must have lived thousands of years in that life, and I remember none of it, not even in dreams."

"My fourth — I remember having mortal friends then, too, but their faces and names are lost to me. I think, maybe, I was a prince of the realm of Ildathach."

"Where's that?" asked Jon.

"The tale of those lands is too long to tell here. There was a time after the *enhedrai* reclaimed Necrad when we were friends with mortals. Happy were those days – I wish I could recall them clearly. We elves dwelt in a city of enchantment, and from it we would fare forth in search of adventure, or to aid the mortal realms. But it turned sour in the end, and there was war between mortal and elf again. The elves won, and the mortal realms of the north were shattered. The Wilder-folk descend from the survivors of those lost kingdoms." Ceremos sighed. "I like to think I died before Ildathach spoiled. That I fell fighting alongside my mortal friends."

He fell silent for a moment, the only sound the whetstone scraping on steel.

"Death comes for us all. The Firstborn say we are undying, but that is a hollow boast. If the Lammergeier had not saved me, I – Ceremos Ul'Elithadil Amerith – would be gone, and nothing of me would have survived the ordeal of wraithdom. You mortals – it is a ceaseless marvel to me how you live in the shadow of death, yet fill your days with so much life.

"I have not told you this, but I met Lady Olva's son Derwyn Tattersoul. He said that I am doomed to succumb to the red thirst and become a monster. 'Tis true that the hunger for continued existence cannot be mastered – even Amerith drank at the last. So here is my hope – that I live as fiercely as a mortal, filling my days with wild endeavour, and that this life has a goodly end in battle."

He held up the shining blade. "Does that give you any comfort, Friend Jon?"

"Oh, aye. An immortal who's looking for a good death, and a mortal who thinks she's invincible. When are we off?"

Ceremos put his helmet back on. "Two hours before dawn."

I don't think I'm invincible.

Jon lay beside her in their shared tent. Cerlys didn't know if

Ceremos was asleep on the far side of the snoring mountain, but she was certainly awake. Fiercely awake, every whisper of the wind or muscle twitch fired with significance. Battle-eagerness filled her.

When she closed her eyes and fought for sleep, she could think only of the black sword. Not as she'd seen it earlier that day, when Alf brandished it and the marching soldiers cheered, not as a symbol, but as she'd seen it on the Straight Road under the land, when it burned in the dark and cut through countless foes.

As she'd seen in the Everwood, when it called to her in the Rangers' Lodge.

It was a terrible weapon. She'd seen what it cost Alf to bear it. It was cruel and treacherous — Alf had spent his whole life chained to Spellbreaker, keeping it out of the hands of unworthy wielders like Idmaer Ironhand. A weapon like that was too powerful to go unused. But Alf was mortal. A day would come — maybe soon — when he could no longer wield that sword. It had nearly come when they'd fought Rhaec. If Alf had fallen there, what would become of Spellbreaker?

She imagined Alf stumbling in battle, some enemy knight knocking the Lammergeier from his horse. All would seem lost — until an unknown heroine picked up the black blade.

Wielder, we shall set the world to rights.

Voices disturbed her reverie. Captain Brass, and some Ellscoaster.

"There. That tent."

"Are you quite, quite sure?" Brass's voice.

"I was in Necrad. I know what a fucking Witch Elf sounds like."

Cerlys peered out of the tent flap. Shapes, dark against the stars. Brass, and half a dozen more men. All armed.

"Cer!" she whispered. "Wake up!" She started to wrestle with the intricacies of the dreadknight armour, all its clever straps and clasps like tangling vines and pricking thorns in the dark of the tent.

"I hear them." Red eyes gleamed on the far side of the tent.

Between them, Jon snored on. Cerlys nudged him hard with her knee.

"What," mused Captain Brass, "would a Witch Elf be doing volunteering for the defence of Summerswell? No Witch Elf has come south in years."

"Not just a Witch Elf," said the Ellscoaster, loudly. "A fucking *vampire*. That's what it's doing here. *Feeding*. Bloodshed draws 'em like flies, I'll wager. It's there waiting for us to bleed in battle."

"I'll not rest knowing that thing is nearby," said another. "And I don't mind saying that Ironhand has the right of it. Necrad should be destroyed. Wipe out the whole damn nest."

Brass made a sort of helpless cooing noise and looked around, as if he expected some higher authority to appear and take charge. The other soldiers advanced towards the tent, the Ellscoaster in the lead. "Show yourself!"

Cerlys gripped Ildorae's enchanted dagger. "We can take them," she whispered, "get ready."

"No," insisted Ceremos. "We flee."

Kortirion had forged the dagger in the smithy of Necrad; Amerith herself had traced the runes of fate and death in the light of the Horned Serpent; the hand of the Goddess of the Hunt wielded it in battle. It was made to slay Lord Bone. If all the weapons of the world were gathered together in some grand court, with the sword Spellbreaker at their head, that blade would still have a place of honour.

It made short work of the cheap cloth tent. The three crawled out and away unseen, stopping only when they were well out of sight. In the distance, their erstwhile comrades shouted to one another as they blundered about in the dark, searching the camp for the vampire. They would kill him if they found him. Only a few weeks ago, Cerlys thought, she'd done the same in Ersfel. If she'd found Ceremos first, would she have hesitated?

Jon fumbled through his baggage in the dark, cursing under his breath. He'd left half his new gear behind in haste.

"We could have fought them," muttered Cerlys.

"What virtue would there be in that? We shall have foes enough come daylight."

Instead of taking the shorter route over the hills, they set off parallel to the Ellscoast road back west towards the Capital, with the intent of turning south and following the route Alf's army had taken. It would take them most of the remaining night to catch up, and they'd come to the battle tired and footsore, but they'd make it in time. Off to their right, the narrow strip of land between the stony hills and the sea was thickly planted with little villages and farms. Twice, they spotted small groups of people moving — soldiers on patrol, people fleeing the approaching army, Rootless beggars or locals, they knew not — but each time Ceremos whispered a warning, and they hid.

After an hour, they came to a crossroads. The Road ran straight on to the Capital, but a lesser spur branched off it, curving around the hills eventually to rejoin the main Road on its way to Raven's Pass. This territory, at least, was a little familiar to them, for they were not far from where they'd emerged from Rhaec's prison.

The twisted king had offered to aid them if they freed it. The monster's voice still echoed in her ears, the memory of its foul stench still strong. *You must have foes — show them to me, and I shall gobble them up.*

She'd said they couldn't trust the Manticore. She'd wanted Alf to kill it. Every instinct shouting that Rhaec was a monster, and monsters should be slain. But Alf and Widow Forster, they'd taken Rhaec's bargain. They were willing to let that misshapen horror out of its prison.

Cerlys had been proved right. The sword proved her right. Rhaec had tried to kill them all — *Olva might still die*, she thought, glancing back north at the lights of the Capital. If they'd struck the Manticore down when they first saw it, then Olva wouldn't have been poisoned.

Monsters should be slain.

But by that reasoning, the Ellcoaster was right. Ceremos was a monster, too, in so many ways. A creature out of Necrad, sustaining himself on the blood of the innocent. But he was her friend, and she'd have spilled the Ellscoaster's guts on the ground, and put arrows in all the rest rather than let any harm come to Ceremos.

Rhaec had a human face, and a monstrous heart. Ceremos, the reverse. How could she know who it was right to slay? It had been easy back in Ersfel – anyone from outside the little wooded valley was a potential threat, and bore watching.

Does Jon have the right of it when he says this was too big for us?

But she was not Cerlys of Ersfel any more. When she'd emerged from the tent clad in dreadknight's armour, Captain Brass had not seen Quenna's daughter, or some peasant girl from the Mulladales.

Alf – when he was just old Alf, not the Lammergeier – had praised her skill, her quickness. But it wasn't enough to be quick. Quick struck the first blow, not the last one or the right one. If she was to wield the Spellbreaker – *there, you've said it now* – how could she be worthy of it?

"Hold up." Jon stopped in his tracks, peering up at the hills. Dawn was still a little while away, but the sky was already changing. "What's that up there?"

Above shone a light, cold and piercing, as if a star had landed on the hillside. Ceremos frowned. "Unless I miss my mark entirely, that is where we emerged from the Straight Road."

The light descended the hillside, slowly at first, its bearer navigating the broken terrain around the portal. Then, on the lower slopes, it picked up speed, falling like a meteor. The clatter of hooves, the whinny of frightened horses.

"Knights," said Ceremos, shading his eyes against the unearthly glare. "I count twenty. That light – it is the Brightsword. Idmaer Ironhand rides at the head of the company."

*

Down and down rode Ironhand's company. The slope was steep, but they were masterful riders, augmented by sure-footed charmstones. They were descending west of the trio, closer to both the Capital and the road to Raven's Pass. And while Ironhand had only a score of knights, it was enough – they had emerged inside the line of sentries; nothing stood between his elite *atharlings* and the gates of the Capital. They had magic, too, the last treasures of Brychan's conspiracy. Fifty thousand might struggle in Raven's Pass, but twenty would decide the fate of Summerswell.

Quick. Be quick.

Cerlys sprinted forward. There was no chance of catching the knights, not that the three of them had any hope of fighting them. Maybe Alf could have done it, Spellbreaker could have won that day. But all she had was her bow.

There was a tall spike of rock ahead, outlined against the pre-dawn sky. Beyond, a fold of the hill would corral the course of the company, force them to ride a little nearer. They would – for one heartbeat, one glorious instant – be within range of her bow. Only one chance.

She ran, outracing heavy-footed Jon, outracing the vampire. Images flashed through her mind: her arrow catching Ironhand in the eye, killing him instantly. He tumbles from his horse, and in the dark, on uneven ground, not even charmstones can save the other riders from tripping. It's a catastrophe, an avalanche of horseflesh and metal, foe piled on foe.

She imagined, too, some of the riders surviving. They see their lord's slayer, and she's got nowhere to hide as they come for her. The flash of steel, and her story's over as they strike the last blow.

But it would be worth that last blow to strike the *right* one. To put an arrow through Idmaer Ironhand's skull.

The Hunter's Star shone low over the northern horizon, defiant against the dawn.

Cerlys scaled the rock. Closer came the knights, the sound of

hooves filling her ears. By the light of her enemy's sword, she strung her bow.

Closer came the knights.

She could see Ironhand clearly now. His armour was stained, drenched in Manticore-blood. The head of King Rhaec bounced beside him, tied to his saddle. The Changeling slain in the moment of transformation, his features not wholly beast or man, but caught surprised, slack-jawed.

She willed Ironhand to look up and see her, see the woman who'd defeat him, but his gaze was fixed on the path ahead of him.

She nocked the arrow, drew back the bow. All around her, dawn was breaking and the world was turning and she knew, knew with every nerve and sinew that her arrow would fly true.

There is a reckoning for all things, in the end.

The moment swelled to bursting. She aimed and—

Jon caught her foot and dragged her down. They both tumbled from the rocky height, falling in a tangle of limbs. Jon landed awkwardly on top of her, his knee crushing her ankle. She'd limp for the rest of the day.

The riders thundered around the bend and raced away, picking up speed as they reached level ground. They were out of range, out of reach, and soon Ironhand would seize the Capital.

"I could have stopped him," she gasped.

"They'd have killed you."

They argued over which way to go. Jon wanted to go back and tell Captain Brass, as if that fool could do anything. Even if they stuck to the original plan and headed for Raven's Pass, Cerlys' wounded ankle would slow them down, and they'd arrive too late to bring warning to Alf.

They set off down the Road to the Capital.

In later days, Cerlys would hear accounts of how Idmaer had smashed open the barred doors of the Crownkeep with his enchanted

fist, how he'd brandished the Brightsword and demanded they yield, demanded they order a retreat from Raven's Pass. How Timeon Vond begged Ironhand to spare the city, and was the first – but not the last – of the Lords to kneel before him.

How, by noon on the following day, the banner of Idmaer Ironhand flew over the Crownkeep.

But first came the bird, swooping down from a smoky sky, crying in Perdia's voice.

CHAPTER TWENTY-NINE

Sir Berkhof's banner still flew on the hillside, alongside the standard of Idmaer Ironhand. As long as those banners stayed up, Alf knew the fighting would continue in the valley below. They had to go down.

A young squire guarded the banners. He struggled to keep the long poles straight as the wind caught the cloth.

Berkhof positioned himself between Alf and the banners.

"Yield, man," said Alf. The sword had surely feasted enough – it might let him spare Berkhof. The thought wrung a quiver of amusement from Spellbreaker, but it did not object. "You've seen what my sword can do. You can't win."

"A cause is not less righteous because it is hopeless," said the knight, "and I am not yet without hope." He pointed his own sword at Alf. Charmstones blazed in the hilt. "You are mortal," he said, almost to himself. "One day, you must die. Why not today? Why not at my hand?"

A terrible certainty settled over Alf. *I will take you last of all*, Death had promised him.

"Aye, well," he said, "come on then."

In later years, they sang songs of Raven's Pass. Customarily, the singer would pause here to recite the tale of Sir Berkhof, for added context and history.

They might speak of Berkhof's youth in the Eavesland, and how it is said that he was anointed by the blood of an Intercessor as it fell like rain over the Great River. Depending on the audience, the singer might describe Berkhof's fair features, how he was accounted the handsomest of the men in Ironhand's court – and how he fell in love with an elf, and how his heart was broken when his immortal lover heeded the summons of the Skerrise and went away to Necrad.

Other audiences might thrill to the triumph of Sir Berkhof in the Riverlands war, how he duelled with the Queen of Thieves in a burning cathedral, or how he fought the Giants Mec and Perec. Many tales could be told of Sir Berkhof that are not recorded here.

The singers do this to make the song last longer, for Sir Berkhof perished in less time than it takes to read these words.

Sir Berkhof struck first, dealing a bone-rattling blow to Alf's shield. His sword was enchanted with stones of savagery; every wound it dealt was magnified, scratches becoming gaping wounds. Like a ferocious beast, it tore the flesh of its victims. Every blow from it was ruinous. Against any other foe, the shield would have splintered, Alf's arm reduced to bloody pulp.

But Alf bore Spellbreaker, and no magic could touch him.

His response was a low swing that caught Berkhof on the thigh. The knight's armour might have turned another blade, but not the black sword. Dwarf-forged steel, stones of adamant and aegis, flesh and bone – it cut them all. Blood gushed from the wound, hot and pulsing. A mortal blow, and both men knew it.

Berkhof fell. Alf struck again before his foe hit the ground, smashing Berkhof's sword from his grip. The blade exploded in a clap of thunder that echoed across Raven's Pass. *Look over here*, prayed Alf. *See that your general's defeated. Surrender!*

The mud sizzled as shards of molten metal fell all around. Berkhof clutched his leg, one whole and one mangled hand pressed

over the wound. Any words were lost in the fading echoes of the thunder blast.

Finish him! howled the sword. But Alf stepped over the dying knight, intent on cutting down those two standards. The enemy general was defeated, but Ironhand's army still fought in the valley below. Ironhand's banner — a red stag, a black sword — still flew proudly over the pass.

The squire gently laid Berkhof's standard down, the square cloth of the banner hiding Berkhof's twitching corpse from view. The other pole he thrust as deep into the mud as he could, then drew his sword and stood between the Lammergeier and his father's banner.

His sword, too, was black, a smaller copy of Spellbreaker. Idmaer's sword, from when he was a child.

"You shall not pass. I'll fight you, Lammergeier."

"Thurn . . ." Alf choked on the name. It carried too much. Twenty years ago, he'd stood with another Thurn atop another hill, far away at Daeroch Nal, and listened to his friend talk of his daughter Talis. She'd been wounded with a poisoned dart, like Olva. Thurn and Lath brought her back from the dead, and Death came with her.

He tried again. The words felt like stones in his mouth. "Thurn . . . lad. You can't win. You know this sword."

"The Spellbreaker. It killed the Erlking." Thurn had his name-sake's solemn courage. "It took my father's hand."

"Aye, it did. You can't win. Stand aside."

"I do not fear death," said Ironhand's son. His sword did not waver.

Alf was never good with words. He was never clever, and decades of blows to the head had not helped. He thought best on the battlefield, where he spoke with a swift sword instead of thick, slow words.

If he had the words, they might have been something like this: when you are young and full of fire and certainty, the world is a labyrinth full of monsters to be defeated. You quest, you fight, you

bring down monsters. But in doing so, you become the monster for the next hero to struggle against. Your deeds build the dungeon to entrap the next brave soul. The strength and power you accrue in your quest warps you, scars and necessary bargains make you unrecognisable. Righteous fury becomes intolerable cruelty, season after season. Witch Elf and Wood Elf, Summerswell and the Wilder, mortal and endless, the wheel elevating one, casting down another.

Necrad – the elves ruled there until Death and her human followers drove them out. In time, after the Sundering, the Witch Elves returned to the city, and tormented the Wilder, the mortal descendants of their former foes. And Thurn had joined the Nine in overthrowing the Witch Elves, but that had brought no peace. Summerswell had claimed Necrad through the Nine, the unseen hand of the Erlking moving game pieces across the land, and there was more war.

When you are old, the world is a graveyard. The bright certainty is gone, rusted to fragility or tarnished into bitterness. The companions that made it all worthwhile are gone, or grown bitter. The monsters you slew in your youth are dead, but the necromiasma of folly brings them back in new forms to stalk the land. What is to be done? Wall yourself away in a safe place? Sing lying songs to the young, and breed more heroes?

There had to be more. There was more. Peir would have known what to do, had he lived. There had to be words to heal a broken land, to write a better end to the hero's story.

But Alf did not have the words, or the time to speak them.

He only had a sword.

The force blast sundered the standard-pole like a twig, ripped Ironhand's banner to tatters. The boy's black sword flying, spitting sparks as one of the charmstones in the hilt burst. Thurn was flung across the hillside. The boy smashed into the ground thirty feet away and lay there unmoving. Blood gushed from his mouth and nose.

Somewhere, far away across the hills, horns were blowing.

Alf leaned on the sword, breathing heavily. He tried to clear the sweat and gore from his face, but his fingers were so caked in blood that it was futile. He stumbled towards Thurn – he had no healing cordial left, but maybe he could do something – but Ernala was already there, cradling her son's broken body. Her shoulders shook. Alf could not tell if the boy was alive or dead, but he lay twisted at a ghastly angle.

Retreat, came the cry from behind him, thin and distant. *Retreat.* A wave of panic, an army melting away. Lord Brychan's voice out of memory, when the Stone Dragons blasted the armies of the League. *Retreat.*

Ernala looked up at him, and she was laughing through her tears.

"Wielder," said Spellbreaker, and even the sword sounded confused. "They are retreating."

"We won," said Alf, hollowly.

"No. Look."

Alf turned. The army of the Lords, the defenders of the Capital – they were retreating. Alf's army was retreating. The knights and soldiers he'd kept in reserve on the far side of the valley melted away, falling back down the Road. Ironhand's forces surged forward, buoyed by this impossible good fortune, scattering the suddenly dismayed Crownland troops.

The horns again, closer now.

Laerlyn took him by the hand. She wiped his face with a corner of her cloak and led him away from the battlefield. None of Ironhand's knights dared hinder her. "We have to go. We have to go, now." She leaned close to Alf and whispered to him.

"Ironhand's taken the Capital."

CHAPTER THIRTY

Eldwyn must have worked all through the night, for Olva found him ink-stained and bleary-eyed, drowning in paper.

"I nearly have it," he said. "It's not a mistake in her readings. I thought it must be a misreading. Then I thought everything I knew about the earthpower was wrong and that all the records of the Old Kingdom, every scrap of lore I've assembled over the last twenty years – that it was all nonsense. *That* was a dark half-hour, let me tell you! But now . . . but now . . ." He waved his hand at Torun's letter. "It's a deliberate error. Of that I'm certain."

"I can't think what Torun would mean by it. For all I know, it might be a joke."

Eldwyn stared at her.

"Torun's sense of humour is . . . esoteric."

He picked up his quill again. "Well, if there's a jest hidden here, I hope it's a funny one."

Sheltered behind the ivy-covered walls of the College Arcane, Olva could almost forget the world outside. The servants had not returned, so she and Perdia had the whole sprawling College to themselves. Olva hobbled about the corridors, leaning on the walls for support. Her hands brushing against banisters worn smooth by

generations of students. Her arse setting into a stone bench worn smooth by all those who had gone before.

By all that was holy and unholy, she felt old. As old as these stone halls.

Alf had rarely spoken to her of his experiences in the Everwood. She'd had to piece together what happened between him and the Erlking from twenty years of grunts and muttered asides. But she recalled that one of the Erlking's demands was that the College Arcane be preserved. She could guess why – the elves valued human ingenuity and ambition. The Skerrise had said as much, on the night Olva had fled Necrad for the last time. From one perspective, this college was a harness for clever beasts.

She rubbed her aching side, and thought of Rhaec, locked away in the depths of the earth on the Straight Road. He'd been preserved for much the same reason as the College – to put his ingenuity in the service of the Erlking. For a moment, out of the corner of her eye, the looming towers and dreaming spires of the College reminded her of the Manticore drawn in stone. She would put a binding-spell on this place, and remake it to good use.

"Olva!" Perdia called down the corridor. "A rider!"

The clatter of hooves from the courtyard.

It can't be news from the battle already, thought Olva. Even if Alf had pulled off another miracle victory with that dreadful sword, Raven's Pass was still many miles south. Full of foreboding, Olva limped out to greet this newcomer.

He recognised her immediately, his lip crinkling in distaste.

"Widow Queen," spat Timeon Vond.

Once extracted from his study, Eldwyn greeted Vond warmly. "Tim's an old friend of mine. He was governor of Necrad, you see, and was an absolute *font* of information about the place. You two know each other, I believe."

"We did," said Olva, "a long time ago."

"A lifetime, for many."

Vond followed Eldwyn into a comfortable if faded drawing room. On the domed ceiling was a map of the heavens, the constellations and decans traced with gilt, although half of the crystal stars were gone. On the wall was an image of the Erlking teaching the secrets of sorcery to the first students of the school. Someone had attacked the painting with a knife, slashing the king's face. Olva lowered herself into an overstuffed armchair and feared she would never rise again.

Vond stared across the room at her for a long, cold moment. The memory of icy winds whipping across the Charnel plain, and Vond riding out of the north gate of Necrad. The crowd jeering at him as he fled, exiled by her. She'd taken such joy in outmanoeuvring him. Vond, a Lord of Summerswell, and she the upstart Queen, and she'd *routed* him. How good it had felt! And yet, only a few months later, she, too, had been forced to flee the city.

She met Vond's glare, and knew he must be reliving the same memory. Then he let out a bark of laughter, and raised his glass. "Your health, Lady Olva. I am glad to see you are recovering. I would hate to disappoint your brother."

"You've seen Alf?"

"I was sent to negotiate with him on behalf of the Lords. To beg him to save us from Ironhand. Like old Dryten Bessimer was dragged from his monastery, so was I taken down from a shelf and dusted off for the occasion." He gestured with his wine glass at the wizard. "Thus, Eldwyn, do the Intercessors teach us humility."

"Is there news from the battle?" asked Perdia.

"Who is this child?"

"Perdia," said Olva, "my apprentice."

"Another Changeling." Vond peered at her. "I once believed, child, that the time of heroes and wonders was behind us, and that we no longer needed unnatural prodigies and half-wild ogres. How wrong I was! Once again, I find myself praying for the victory of

the Lammergeier. The first time, I was seven years old, hiding under my blankets for fear of Lord Bone. The second, I was Governor of Necrad, and I had to walk the walls and show no fear, even though I wanted nothing more than to run away and hide again. Now, here I am again." He gnawed at his fist. "How horrible is it to know that everything exists at the whim of the powerful."

"You were a Lord," said Olva, "you *were* one of the powerful. People lived and died on your command."

"I was a whim," spat Vond. "Gundan reminded me of that often enough. My authority was always *contingent*. I was a temporary arrangement. If you want the advice of an old man, Perdia, it is this: take all the power you can. Justice, honour, righteousness – power lets you dictate what those words mean. Grow monstrous. Grow so strong in your witchcraft that you can turn Eldwyn into a newt, then overthrow the Lords and become Witch-Queen of Summerswell. And when you do, I'll be your vizier."

Eldwyn glanced up from Torun's notes. "She asked if there was news of the battle, Tim. And I'd like to know, too."

"No word yet. There will not be word until this evening, one way or another. But I could not abide waiting in the Crownkeep. The squabbling has already begun, Eld. They are so certain the Lammergeier will be victorious that they argue over the division of Ironhand's holdings, and argue over who should be named High Lord." Another bark of laughter. "Maybe they're right. The Lammergeier never loses. It's just that you can never be sure what side he's on."

"You're wrong about Alf," said Olva. "He loses. I know what you mean – he's done things that other people thought impossible. But he's not invincible. He's just Alf. Even with the sword, he's just Alf. And he's lost almost everything. He never wanted titles or wealth. He never wanted power. He just wanted to do what was right, and to stand by his friends."

"That does not cheer me," said Vond. "Laerlyn urged the

Lammergeier to move on instead of giving battle. To the elves, we are already dead." He rose from his chair and moved to examine the painting of the Erlking. "Word did come from Raven's Pass. There was a parley before the battle. Apparently, Sir Berkhof offered to spare the Capital in exchange for passage to Necrad."

"Alf refused?"

"The sword did."

"The damnable thing wants a slaughter."

"It just wants to do what is wrong, maybe." Vond plucked at the damaged canvas. "And yet, it was the right decision to my mind. Ironhand must be stopped. I fear what might happen if he reaches Necrad."

"You fear he might seize the city from the Witch Elves?" asked Perdia.

"I fear equally that he fails," said Vond, "and provokes them. There are no good outcomes when dealing with Necrad. That city is cursed."

"Aye, you have the right of it there," said Olva, surprised to find herself agreeing with Vond.

Eldwyn looked up from his papers. "You were governor there, Tim, and I've heard you complain a thousand times about your ouster. Lady Olva, you were Queen there, and fought a war to keep it. Why hold onto Necrad if it brings only woe?"

"Because there's power there," said Vond.

"And you always think that you'll be able to use that power to do good, or at least stop someone else from doing mischief with it. But it's holding onto that power that ruins you." Olva rubbed her crane-foot against the carpet. "What did you do, after?"

"After you banished me? Or after your brother slew the Erlking and ruined Summerswell?"

"Timeon," cautioned Eldwyn. "Be civil."

"After," said Olva, "I went home to Ersfel. I used what I'd learned, what I'd become, and I kept my home safe. No great deeds. No

songs. No power to change the world overnight. Just good work. It took me a long time to appreciate the slower path."

"Ah." A ghost of a smile. "I was master of the harbour here. Dealing with taxes and customs, and keeping the quays in good repair. A lowly post for one who had been governor of Necrad, but it suited me well. No heroes showing up on my doorstep, upending everything with prophecies and dire tidings. Even in the worst days of the Anarchy, I made sure the trade ships kept sailing."

"There's virtue in the quiet things," said Olva. "It's the work of a few to save the world from evil, and it's for the rest of us to make sure it's worth saving."

Vond's smile vanished. "And all for what? So Ironhand could seize the fleet? Good work, you call it – but it can all be erased in an instant by some warlord. Nothing matters but power. And we who do not possess it – why, we tell stories to the powerful to flatter them, and implore them to use their power with some measure of wisdom. And we tell stories to ourselves for consolation. We delude ourselves that anything we do has meaning in the shadow of giants."

"Just because a thing doesn't last," said Olva, "doesn't mean it never mattered."

They waited. That is the nature of war – your future turns on the deeds and chances of others, far away, and you have no control over the outcome. A lucky blow, a missed strike, a half-inch one way or another, and the world changes.

It was maddening to feel simultaneously that it was an immediate crisis and that there was nothing to do. Eldwyn worked, his pen scratching as he pored over Torun's letter. Vond paced, picking up one old magic relic after another, only to find them all depleted. Perdia clasped her hands as if in prayer, but Olva saw the girl's shoulders quiver in fear.

"Alf has the sword," Olva whispered in her ear. "All will be well."

Olva made tea. She hauled her aching, wounded carcass to the

little kitchen. The bread was stale, but there was cheese and potted meat and fruit. She fetched a pot of water, then — greatly daring — she reached for the earthpower. The power came slowly, and her wounded side ached, but a little green flame flared in the fireplace.

She still had her magic.

Mid-morning brought the first inklings of catastrophe.

Perdia cocked her head. "Riders?" She peered out of the window of the study.

"I hear nothing," snapped Vond.

"I hear hoofbeats," insisted Perdia.

"It's too soon for news from Raven's Pass," muttered Vond, "this must be something else."

"There's a better view," said Eldwyn, absently waving his hand at the door, "from the tower above."

Perdia darted out. Her footsteps echoed on the stone stair. Olva went to the little window in the study and opened it.

All was still and silent out there. The city, too, awaited its fate.

"It's too soon," repeated Vond.

Faint shouts echoed across the rooftops, breaking the stillness. The sound of war-horns.

"Stay here."

From the window, she watched Vond make his way across the overgrown courtyard towards the locked gates. He had his sword in his hand. The bulk of the library tower hid him from view.

She would never see him again.

"Ah-ha!" Eldwyn startled her with a sudden laugh of triumph. "I've figured it out! It wasn't a mistake with the readings — it's a cipher! The errant readings correspond to letters! You've been carrying a secret message around with you for weeks. Trivial, trivial, once you have the trick of it! Let's see!" He called out the letters as he decoded them and scribbled the translation in the margin. "E . . . R . . . L . . . K".

He looked up, suddenly pale. He held Torun's letter as if it was a venomous serpent. "It speaks of the Erlking. What does this mean? Why does she—"

A thunderous blast from the courtyard drowned out his words. Broken metal rained across the cobbles.

The horns, deafening, close at hand. Ironhand's voice, roaring orders. The courtyard was full of knights, Ironhand's *atharlings*, the knights they'd left behind at the Neverwood. He'd caught up. It was impossible, unthinkable, and yet he had done it. All the city's defenders were away at Raven's Pass, there was nothing now between Idmaer and the Lords of Summerswell. Nothing between him and victory.

All he lacked was the Spellbreaker.

Suddenly, Perdia was at her side. "We have to go." There was no time for the dwarven chair. Perdia dragged her away from the window, away from the awful sight of Ironhand approaching. Olva's legs gave out.

"I can't run," Olva said, "There's no time. You go."

"I – I'll fetch the Lammergeier!"

"No! Tell Alf—" But there was no time to explain. She snatched the letter from Eldwyn and thrust the papers into Perdia's hand. "Take these. Show them to Laerlyn. She'll understand. Tell Alf to do what she says."

"Ironhand will kill you!"

She shoved Perdia towards the open window. "Go!"

Earthpower surged. The dwarven instrument on the table lurched, its pendulum swinging wildly. Perdia took flight in a storm of wings and feathers, and was gone.

"Help me up," said Olva. Eldwyn helped her rise. She leaned on him as they waited. Her head spun, and everything felt unreal, unfolding with the horrible certainty of a dream.

"What's happening?" Eldwyn asked helplessly. Galwyn had asked the same, on the night he died.

Downstairs, a door splintered. More shouts, more breaking glass, a last indignity for the College Arcane. The dreams of a better future trampled beneath armoured feet.

This room's full of books, she thought. *They'll burn.*

"Go on now," she said to Eldwyn, "get out before—"

Suddenly, Ironhand was in the room, towering over them. His leering henchmen in armour forged in Necrad. Ironhand, bloody-handed, the Brightsword drawn. The sword was bright this time, not dark; it was morning, not night, and she was far from the little house in Ersfel, but still—

— still the intruder turned to her, and if Ironhand's voice was deep and pleasant where Acraist's was a foul whisper, the question was the same. "Where is Aelfric Lammergeier?"

She forced herself to laugh. "Far away, beating the shit out of your army."

Ironhand turned to his knights. "Get to the Crownkeep immediately. Make the Lords yield. I will join you presently."

"The sword picked Alf. You can't beat him."

"We shall see." He gestured, and two of his knights grabbed Olva, shoving Eldwyn out of the way. He sprawled on the floor. Another knight raised his sword.

"Master Forster's no threat to you," said Olva hastily. "You have me as a hostage. Let him go."

Eldwyn stumbled out of the door. *Go on*, she thought, *do what you promised. Make this a school for Changelings. Build on what I've done.*

And I'll give you a good beginning.

Olva reached down, down past the foundations of the College, down into the earth, her soul diving to reach the currents of earth-power. She could taste Vond's blood on the cobblestones outside, feel the air rushing through Perdia's feathers as she circled above the harbour. She could feel the city's fear, and the heedless cries of the gulls who knew only that there was a smell of carrion on the air. She took it all and pulled it in, setting her soul aflame.

She thought of Peir, all those years ago, holding Lord Bone so they both burned in the fire that Alf unleashed. She thought of Derwyn, warning her *now is the time of monsters*. They'd understand.

One word, and green fire would burst from her. All the books would burn, and Ironhand, too. A last act of magic. She thought of Galwyn lying dead on the floor in Ersfel, Galwyn in the dark mound under Daeroch Nal. *I'll see you soon.*

She opened her mouth to speak the spell. With the last of her strength, she drew up the earthpower.

The brass instrument, the cursed dwarven contraption, rang again, reacting to the flow of magic – and Ironhand leapt across the room, smashing her against the heavy table, the threads of earth-power slipping from her grasp. The spell failed, the green flame stillborn.

She closed her eyes, waiting for the killing blow.

"Did you think, Witch of Ersfel, that I was unprepared for this?"

To her horror, Ironhand held up a grisly trophy, a severed head. Iron fingers dug into the remains of King Rhaec, and from the ruin of the neck he disentangled a withered strand of ivy. Bits of dead flesh still clung to the tendrils. Idmare draped the grisly trophy around Olva's throat, and she felt the ivy-necklace come to life again. It dug into her skin, anchoring itself in a fresh host.

"Your brother will come for you," said Ironhand, "and I will have the sword."

CHAPTER THIRTY-ONE

It was Perdia who found them, Perdia who gathered them. She found the first three on the Road outside the Capital. She relayed Olva's message to them, told them of the meeting place, and then she was off again. No time for Jon's confused questions, for Cerlys' anger, for Ceremos' wonderment. Off again in bird-shape, raven-shape, the earthpower surging through her, and she told herself that the howling in her soul was nothing real, just a number, and that nothing hid behind it.

South she flew, and the raven in her, or her in the raven, the battle-smell like a miasma spreading across the world, and the stench of it was strongest around the man with the black sword. In that moment, her raven-brain could not remember his name. The carnage around him both attracted and repelled her. To perch atop the hill of slain, to join the flock, a carrion-feast — these were the best of things.

But she had a mission, a human mission, a human word caught in her craw. She circled down, over the dissolving armies. Some of the living were melting away, marching back the way they'd come, and others were going the same way with great haste, eager to reach the city. *Summerswell and Ironhand's army,* she thought as well as she could through raven-brain, and though her black eyes could clearly make

out the banners, she could not recall the significance of which was which. She fluttered this way and that, losing the thread of herself, hunger for juicy eyeballs crowding out her thoughts.

Then she saw one who stood apart, who for all her power had no blood on her hands that day. Other memories rose up in the raven, crowding out her hunger. Memories of taking refuge in the deserted chapel in Hayhurst, clerics and the last of the congregation all gone on the pilgrim's road, never to return. Memories of praying to silent icons, to dry and empty grails. *There is healing in the Everwood.*

The raven perched beside Laerlyn and croaked a word.

"Erlking."

The meeting place was a field a day west of the Capital. It was a lonely place, barren and deserted, and the fog that trailed about the mossy stones did nothing to make it less desolate. A camp for the defeated.

"What the fuck is this?" muttered Alf. At his hip, the sword laughed.

"I do not know," said Laerlyn, stepping lightly over the low walls of the model Necrad.

"The College Arcane built it," explained Perdia, "trying to replicate the magic of Necrad."

Alf stopped at the west gate and picked up one of the stone dragons. It was no larger than a sparrow in his hand. The carving was crude, made by some artisan who'd never seen Necrad, but had worked off sketches and half-heard tales. Green moss grew in the recesses of its gaping mouth. He dropped it on the grass – *they haven't even got the mud right* – and a dozen long strides brought him through the Garrison and down the Way of Haradrume right to the central circle where the three young adventurers waited.

Jon's eyes widened as he saw Alf. The warrior was blood-drenched from helm to boot, every inch of him stained with gore. Only the

black sword was pristine. Ceremos swallowed and moved upwind of Alf.

"How many," gasped Cerlys, "did you kill?"

"Doesn't matter," said Alf.

"Ironhand rode straight to the Crownkeep." Cerlys scraped Ildorae's knife off the model of the Wailing Tower. "He threatened the Lords, and they surrendered right away. They ordered the retreat, the fucking cowards. We saw their messengers ride by." She shook her head. "If I'd known, I'd have put an arrow in one of them."

"Slaying one would not have stopped them all," called Ceremos. He was off in the outskirts of the city, off near the Oracle's palace. They all looked like absurd giants as they moved about the model.

"I know! But Alf had won the bloody battle! If the Lords refused to yield, if they'd kept fighting, then we'd have smashed Ironhand's army. All he'd have left would be a handful of knights, and he'd be stuck in the Crownkeep."

"He'd have killed the Lords," said Jon.

"Fuck the Lords."

"Few have the courage to choose death," said Ceremos, "even when living on means abandoning all conviction." He stepped over Amerith's house and joined the rest at the Wailing Tower.

"He has other hostages, too," said Perdia, "and those few knights could have put half the city to the sword."

Cerlys rounded on Laerlyn. "You said he couldn't follow us down the Straight Road!"

"He should not have been able to. It required knowledge of my father's magical sigils to open the way, and those he kept secret. I am the Erlking's daughter and I knew only a fraction of his secrets. My brother Maedos knew the most, but my father kept much even from him."

"So how—"

"Olva – and the dwarf Torun – have sent us the answer to this riddle."

"Erlking," said Perdia. "The letter had the word Erlking hidden in it. There might have been more in the cipher, but I had to flee before Master Eldwyn finished deciphering it."

"What does it mean, Lae?" asked Alf.

"It means, wielder, that the Erlking fled the dying Everwood to take refuge in the Dwarfholt. That Idmaer Ironhand is the Erlking's deluded champion. Most of all, wielder, it means that you should not have stopped me twenty years ago." The demon eye flared. "You will not make the same mistake again."

Laerlyn sat down on the roof of Lord Bone's palace. "The sword is right. I thought Idmaer's madness was but an unhealed wound, one of countless injuries that my father dealt the world. But no – this is another of his schemes."

"In Necrad," said Ceremos, "they cursed his name, and called him a trickster and tyrant. For thousands of years the elders warred against him. And yet, when word came that the Everwood had been destroyed and the Erlking cast down, there was little rejoicing. The elders spoke only about the elder days, when they acclaimed him Uncrowned King for his genius. And the younger elves, my parents and their generation – the news of *victory* terrified them. They had lived so long in the struggle that they did not know what to do with themselves when they were not guarding against the Erlking's countless minions." He picked up his helmet and stared at it. "I do not understand my people."

"The stories say Alf killed him," said Cerlys.

The model depicted Necrad at its height, as it was on the day Alf had first seen it. Before siege or occupation, before Garrison or Liberties or Sanction. Before they'd blown up that palace with Peir inside it and Lord Bone, too.

Before they'd defeated evil once and for all and saved the world.

Alf leaned on the black sword so he did not fall down.

"Wasn't me," he managed. "It was Bor."

"You stopped me from killing the King," said the sword.

"Why did you spare him?" she demanded.

"Ach, it wasn't like that. I . . . he said he'd end the fighting, bring peace to Summerswell, if I served him. He'd get rid of the Lords and make Lae Queen. And I'd be King or something. I was sick of killing, so . . . it seemed like the best course. We'd still be serving him, of course. And he said, too, that he conjured humanity back in the day. Made us from nothing to catch Death, aye? And if I killed him, or defied him, he'd undo the spell and we'd all just – go."

"And you believed him?"

"I was not sure then," said Laerlyn, crossing to stand by Alf's side. "I am sure now. Victory then would have been catastrophic. I have spent your whole life studying my father's works, Cerlys, and I know now that he was not lying that day. If he perishes, if his spells are broken, all humans perish."

"He *was* lying," insisted Spellbreaker. "I broke his spells that day."

"Even you are not inexhaustible. You shielded Bor against all the defenders of the Everwood, and broke through my father's last defences. What did you have left in you when you struck? And consider what you did destroy – all the magic of the life-trees, and the enchantment of the Everwood, and the works of healing, and the shrines of the Intercessors. The sigils of the College Arcane and the grails of the clerics. Oh, I do not discount your malice or your power, Spellbreaker. But my father preserved that spell-sigil at least. He kept you from destroying humanity."

Jon looked both befuddled and sickened. "Why would he save us?"

"He was a vampire, like the other elders, although he hid it behind illusion. He preserved you as a herdsman guards his cattle."

"So, fuck it," said Cerlys. "If you can't kill the Erlking, then . . . then we fight the other fight. He's working through Ironhand – and Ironhand, we can kill. He's only human." She pointed back east. "We go and *end* him. The rest of us sneak into the Capital, like the Nine sneaked into Necrad, and we kill him like you killed Lord Bone."

"He has the Lady Olva," said Ceremos, "as hostage. We must save her. While she's in Ironhand's grasp, he has the advantage over us."

"Olva said that you weren't to tarry," added Perdia, "that Torun wouldn't have sent that message if it were not important."

"Bloody wizards," muttered Alf, counting Torun among them. Cryptic messages and quests and portents, the lot of them useless. *Tell the Lammergeier that Blaise has need of him for one last service. Tell him to come at once. Tell him to bring his sword.* Hiding secrets in numbers and sigils. The lot of them with their heads in some higher elvish realm, thoughts remote as stars. And then, rarely, stooping down to give commands like this. All his life he'd been dragged around by prophecies and wizard's schemes.

But they were heedless of actually living in the world, the diminished horizon of ordinary existence. Alf's adventuring life had been a dungeon, confined in the dark, feeling his way through the perilous labyrinth. He might stumble towards wherever wizards and clever folk sent him, but he never knew the way there, and in his blindness he'd trampled and broken so much.

Twenty years in the Pits. Thurn and Gundan dying at Daeroch Nal, and all the sorrows that followed. *You carry the hopes of the world*, Jan had said, but what did that mean? How to fulfil that lofty prophecy in the realm of mud and meat? *I can walk, and I can hit things, and maybe find the right word one time in twenty.* How can I carry hope?

Laerlyn and Cerlys were arguing, but he couldn't make out the words. Jon like a confused puppy, looking back and forth, uncomprehending. Perdia, exhausted, crouched at the eastern wall of this absurd toy Necrad, fearful of pursuers. Already, Ironhand would have sent out hunters. More riders, like the ones who came to Ersfel. Ironhand's madness, bright as the Brightsword, sending violent men out to trouble the land.

Maybe some could keep a foot in both realms. Peir could. Lae could, sometimes, but he could see her withdrawing now, the talk

of the Erlking's return forcing her back into her role as the Princess Laerlyn, all the weight of ten thousand years of elvendom on her. Trying to straddle the two realms had driven poor Lath mad.

The Lammergeier was a creature of that higher realm, the realm of prophecy and epic deeds. Alf had escaped the Lammergeier for a while in Ersfel, but now it had caught him again. The Lammergeier would go north and battle the Erlking. The Lammergeier would battle the dark lord.

Alf's sister needed him. When he was Ironhand's prisoner, she'd come to his rescue, gathered allies and chased him across half of Summerswell. How could he abandon her now?

Let someone else be good. He just wanted one crumb of solace.

"I'm going back for Olva," he muttered. "Ironhand can have the damn sword."

Cerlys rounded on him.

"You can't let him win!"

"I'm going back," said Alf again, "for Olva."

"My father is the greater threat, Aelfric," said Laerlyn. "He is the power behind the iron hand. All this – Ironhand's quest for the sword, his use of the Straight Road, his assault on Summerswell – is my father's unseen hand at work. We must finish what we began."

"We can't fucking finish it! We can't kill him! That's what you said!"

"For twenty years I have brooded on my decision that day, Aelfric. I feared the consequences of killing him. I could not conceive of a world without him. But in the years since, I have watched my kingdom crumble, my kinfolk desert me. I have watched the mortal realm fall into anarchy, and all hope of reconciliation with the *enhedrai* vanish behind walls of silence. So much of this evil is due to my father's works. I do not know if he can be defeated, but I do know it is right to try. And I am prepared for the consequences."

Alf shook his head. "I'm going back for Olva."

"Aelfric—"

"Let me choose for once."

The sword caught him, its cold voice cutting through his thoughts. *There is no debate, wielder. I was made to slay the Erlking. You thwarted me once. You shall not do so again.*

"Olva needs me."

In the Neverwood you swore to serve. You. Will. Serve.

"Olva's in trouble. She needs help."

No, wielder. This is my quest, and you are my weapon. We will slay the Erlking. The sword's voice took on a silky note of triumph. *You want this, too. I know you, wielder. You crave the quest, too. You desire to delve into dark places, and see strange things. You crave adventure more than peace or kinship. A last adventure with the last of the Nine.*

And overlapping with that cold presence in his mind, he heard Laerlyn say: "Saving Olva will not—"

Alf interrupted her, interrupted them both, his words coming out like a bestial snarl "Shut up! Shut up, both of you! Save the world, Lae, is that what you were going to say? Fuck saving the world! We already saved the bloody world, Lae. I've done that."

The elven princess was silent for a long moment, her face unreadable even to Alf. She might have been a marble statue, remote, her eyes locked on some far horizon of eternity.

"When . . ." said Jon into the silence, but he lowered his head and dared not speak more.

"I have seen many mortal lifetimes pass by, Aelfric. I have seen heroes save the world, as you put it, before. I have seen great evils destroyed by valiant deeds. But to save a thing is to preserve it, to protect the heart of it – and at the heart of this world is my father. Whatever order arises in the land – Ironhand or the Lords or the kingship he offered you, it doesn't matter. It will always be warped by him. If the world we preserve is rotten, saving it is no virtue.

"Your sister understands that. She knows that life can only arise from death, that one generation must give way to the next. We of the

Nine, we who are blessed with power, we who are called heroes . . . we are larger than life. We cast long shadows, and we must understand that. We make those things we deem worthy into heirlooms, and carry that which is hateful with us into oblivion when we pass." Laerlyn suddenly looked very young. "I *knew* all this, I think, when I began. Not the fullness of it, nor the extent of my father's malice, but the core of it. Why else did I give up my title and inheritance, and set off with the Nine?"

"You might have known all that," said Alf. "I don't understand any of it. I didn't set out with any grand purpose in mind."

"I know." Laerlyn sat beside him and laid her hand over his, over the hilt of the sword. "You thought you were just on an adventure of little consequence. You travelled with your new friends, and in time you took their burdens upon yourself."

You took me, *wielder,* whispered the sword.

"It was not your quest at the beginning, but the Nine went away, one by one, leaving you to carry on. Now we are almost all gone, and you are still here." Laerlyn squeezed his hand. "I know how you feel, Alf. But you're not alone. We shall finish it together."

"What about Olva?"

"When—" said Jon again.

"Go on," said Cerlys.

"In the tales . . . some of ye went to the Isle of Dawn, and others fought Lord Bone's army on the shore. You split up."

"We were Nine, then," said Alf. *Nine, and we'd been fighting Lord Bone for two or three years. We weren't bloody children. We were the Nine.*

"Jon's right," said Cerlys. "We'll rescue Olva."

The four of them withdrew to the edge of the model city, stepping over its walls like giants. They watched Alf and Laerlyn find an empty patch of ground. They lay there, side by side, exhausted beyond measure.

"Someone else should go with Alf," said Cerlys. "Not just Laerlyn. He'll need help."

"In the Vale of the Illuminated, before the Uncrowned King, I swore to serve the Lady Olva," said Ceremos. "I am bound to rescue her."

"I'm going north," said Perdia in a whisper.

"What? No!" snapped Cerlys. "You're the most powerful of us. You've got proper magic. And skin-changing would be fucking handy if we've got to sneak in. Olva might need healing. You've got to come with us, right?"

"I'm going north," Perdia repeated, and there was a hint of a growl in her voice.

"Why?"

"If the Erlking still lives, I have to see him. I have to be there."

"All right," said Cerlys, uncertainly. "Changeling stuff. Jon?"

Jon lifted his head to stare at her. "I'll go where you're going, of course. I've followed you this far."

"We should rest," said Ceremos, "before we part."

They huddled together, sheltering from the north wind in the lee of the model walls of Necrad. The red eye of the sword gleamed as it watched over them all through the night.

When dawn woke them the next morning, Cerlys and Ceremos were already gone.

"They went after Olva," wailed Jon. "Why did they leave me behind?"

"They have made their choice," said Laerlyn, "and for good or ill, it is out of our hands now."

While Jon and Perdia packed their gear for the journey north, Alf sat with the sword on his lap.

"When Cerlys and the elf left – did either of 'em try to take you?"

"Do you wish they had, wielder?"

"I'm just curious."

"They discussed it. But in the end, they did not even try. They left me."

"Well now."

"The elf fights his thirst. It is growing, wielder. I can sense it in him. And Cerlys — ah, I must admit I was tempted. But she would not take me."

"That's something," said Alf.

So many had tried to take the sword from him. At last someone had seen the cost of the blade. The thought cheered Alf.

"Even if they had tried, I would not have let them. My quest lies north. Now answer my question — do you wish one of them had taken me?"

Alf sighed. "Someone has to, in the end, don't they? Someone has to carry you." He paused. "I wonder what I'd have been like if I never carried you."

"You would still have been one of the Nine, a hero of renown. You won me from Acraist near the end of your tale."

"Aye, but maybe it would have been the end, then. The others went on. Thurn, Jan, Gundan — they all found new ways to live. Berys, Blaise — they had their secrets. But me — if I didn't have you, I'd just be plain old Alf. I could have married Erdys and been earl of the north. I could have gone home."

"And I saved you from that fate. I see what you were in Ersfel — a dull old man, snoring by the fire, thinking of the old days. Instead, I make you a peer of lords and kings."

"All the lords and kings I've met," said Alf, "were sad, or utter shits, or both. To hell with that."

"Maybe I preserved you," said the sword, "for this last quest."

"A good ending. Can't hope for more."

Jon came up. Cerys and Ceremos had left some of their gear behind, and Jon had crammed at least two-thirds of it into his own pack, along with most of Alf and Perdia's baggage. But he was a big

Mulladale lad, and seemed unaffected by the weight of his burden. He wiped his face and forced a grin. "Ready to go?"

"Aye," said Alf. A thought struck him. "Show me your sword, lad. We can practise as we go."

North-west, day after day. They left the Road and went over the rough country between the Cleft of Ard and the Crownland. Steep, stony hills home only to wild sheep. Streams cascaded down the rocks in white falls.

Princess Laerlyn strode ahead of the rest. Alf needed help from Perdia and young Jon to keep up. The sword could have given him strength – the blade brimmed with power after the slaughter at Raven's Pass – but it was sullen and unreachable.

They did not see another living soul for days. A few times, when the wind blew from the east, Perdia caught the scent of Ironhand's riders, but their trail was lost amid the hard hills.

They rounded the shoulder of the mountain and descended into the valley beyond. The floor of the valley was uneven, pockmarked with craters and overgrown debris. Alf stooped and pulled a rusted piece of metal from the ground. Dirt and fragments of yellowed bone fell away from it. "War-golem," he muttered. "The seaward Road to Necrad is off that way." He pointed north-east with the broken golem-hand. "We stopped one of Lord Bone's armies here. Battle of . . . something Vale. Do you remember, Lae?"

"Of course."

"This elven paralysis spell hit Gundan, and he got stuck with his axe like this." Alf held the rusted golem-arm as if frozen mid-cleave. "Blaise was trying to work a counter-charm, but there were all these zombies coming down from that ridge there. Hundreds of the bastards, and Gundan's frozen. So Thurn runs over, and he picks up Gundan, and he starts swinging him as a weapon. Funniest thing I ever saw."

"And Gundan was pleased," said Laerlyn, "because you and he

had a running tally of the foes each had slain, and he counted those and won."

"Good times, Lae."

"We were both young, Aelfric."

He cast the golem-arm aside. Looters had long since taken anything of worth.

Alf showed them secret elf-paths that brought them high above the green bowl of the Cleft. Summer sun touched the distant towers of Arden. The skies above the city were clean and unmarred. Twenty years had washed away the stain of necromiasma.

They turned north, following the Road again. As they walked, Laerlyn spoke of caution, of the need for secrecy. If Torun had resorted to sending coded messages in her letters, then it was likely she was under observation by agents of the Erlking — and therefore, they should assume that there were more such agents watching for other threats. "Our hope lies in surprise. My father must assume that our only reason for coming here is keeping the Spellbreaker out of Idmaer's clutches. He must not know we are hunting him. Do not speak his name. Do nothing to arouse suspicion."

"You sound like Berys," cackled the sword.

Three days after midsummer, they came to the Dwarfholt.

PART FOUR

A dream found the Skerrise as she stood atop the Wailing Tower. It was not her dream. A spell conjured it, and slipped it into her mind. But it was formed from her memory, and so she permitted it to slip past her defences, drinking it down like liquor, bitter and burning. Foolhardy, perhaps, to accept the dream-spell, but she was secure in her power. No harm would come to her, and it was pleasant to walk in memory.

Even a bitter one.

In the memory, she was standing atop the walls of Necrad. A recent memory, scarcely a hundred years ago. She could see that very spot from the summit of the Wailing Tower, and as the spell took hold she felt *doubled*, bilocated. The Skerrise of a hundred years ago glanced up over her shoulder, and beheld her future self.

Then tripled, then more. The Skerrise was on the Wailing Tower, and on the walls of Necrad, and running through the primal forest beyond the walls all at once. She was in the icy prison where the Erlking chained Death, and fighting Death's mortal children – their hot blood running down her spear! – and enthroned as a goddess, tasting that blood, and on a ship crashing through the waves, and waking under the stars when the world was young and fresh and all that was before her—

All the thousands of years of her life unfolded in the dream, and for a moment it was all clear to her, a brilliant jewel of time, every facet gleaming, every moment as bright and perfect as any other. Impossible beauty, more than even her mind could encompass!

She knew it was only an illusion. This little dream-spell, this pathetic little cantrip, it could not bring back the past. It was only an illusion.

More: a mockery!

(Furious, the Skerrise – the now-Skerrise, the present Skerrise, the Queen of Necrad – grabbed onto the balcony railing. The magic of the Wailing Tower shielded her from the spell. The diamond clarity of the illusion became but a wan shadow, easily dismissed with an effort of will.

But she could not bring herself to wholly dismiss it. She let the weakened spell take hold, and lift memory into a waking dream, her own story retold to her.)

The Skerrise stood on the walls of Necrad, and looked out over the land. The flaws in the world were like grit in her eye. Everywhere she looked, she saw offence.

In the first days, the Skerrise had hunted in those woods, and known joy. She had danced on the cold strand as wild waves crashed about her. (The echo of the doubling.)

Now, her heart was hollow, and all things – even the blood of the *agearath* – was ash in her mouth.

She could not say exactly what had changed. (The diamond clarity was gone.) The passing years had bent and humbled the proud hills; trees she had loved as saplings had grown tall, grown old, toppled, and from their ruin had sprung more young shoots, a dozen times over. But surely those were trivial changes, the forest a green cloud rolling across the hills. Forest and hills, sea and sky, the city and herself – all these things should be eternal, ageless, undying.

So how could it be different? How could it be flawed?

How could that which had once brought joy bring joy no longer?

Oloros joined the Skerrise atop the wall. He, too, was one of the last of the *real* Firstborn, the first generation who'd walked the empty world. *Eight thousand one hundred and ninety-two of us in the dawn*, the Skerrise thought, *and how many are left? Fourteen in Necrad with Amerith, and all save her dependent on filthy mortal blood! Another twenty with* him *in the south – if you call that living! Chained to a tree, simpering and witless hamadryads. And the ones who come back . . . they never come back right. Something is lost in the wraith-world.* The returned ones, too, she disliked. The reborn clashed with her memories of their previous incarnations. They got being themselves wrong.

The world was wrong. (The world is wrong, whispered the dream-spell.)

Oloros was Firstborn. His presence was a balm. She could look at him, look at the white walls of Necrad reclaimed, and imagine it was the first day of the city again. They had been so much to one another over the years – friends, rivals, lovers – and while the Skerrise would not have said she *liked* Oloros, he was a blessed constant.

Oloros did not speak. He did not need to. They knew one another so well that the smallest gesture or passing expression told a story.

To an outside observer, they would have seemed marble statues atop the white wall.

Hyade has tasted mortal blood.

Already? She is barely six hundred years reborn. Was she wounded?

No, said Oloros. *The games of the city no longer delight her. But it amuses her to be a goddess to the mortals.*

This fascination with mortals will ruin her. It ruins all of us.

Turn your face from the outside world, then, if it troubles you so, laughed Oloros. The city behind them was empty of mortals, save for a few who were permitted to enter as consorts to the living gods. The invaders who had occupied Necrad in the centuries after Death's escape had long since been driven out, and every stain of their mortal hands wiped away.

But the city was not quite right either, afterwards. Even though they had restored the toppled statues, burned the mortal nests of sticks and mud that soiled the eternal marble, remade the stolen treasures — it was not the same. Even Necrad was wrong in the eyes of the Skerrise.

Should I eat lotus, too? she replied angrily. (Always so angry, whispered the dream-spell.)

Wherever you find diversion, said Oloros mildly. *There is time enough for all things.*

What I desire, said the Skerrise, *are those things that time took away. When will they return?*

(Why are you showing me this?)

A stranger approached the west gate of Necrad.

Not an offering, sent to appease the red hunger of the gods. Not a messenger from the Wilder-tribes.

Thin and ragged he was, and scarred by many perils. His wizard's cloak was tattered and bloodstained; his vials of precious liquid starlight all shattered. He had come north with a company of heroes, companions he had known and loved all his brief life. They were all dead now. Their corpses lay scattered along the Road behind him. Murdered by Rangers in Ellscoast, frozen to death in the hills of Arden, slain by ogres in the Clawlands.

A half-dozen sacrifices, and he swore they would not be in vain.

With his last strength, he knocked on the gates of the city, and demanded entry.

No answer came.

They are minded to let him in, said Oloros.

He is thin as a skeleton, said the Skerrise. *Hardly a drop in him.*

He is from Summerswell, and it's been a while since we've had news from that quarter of the world. It would be a novelty.

I have no interest in the prattling of mortals.

He is a scholar of the stars.

And we are born of the stars, and the star of the White Deer that reigns over victory in battle blazed in the clear night sky above Necrad.

He seeks to learn from us.

What can a mortal learn from the immortal? He was made from the scrapings of a cauldron.

Gaherin says the mortal has some wit.

Gaherin laughs when a dog breaks wind.

Oloros laughed. *End him, then*, he suggested.

The Skerrise lifted her spear. The mortal was a speck of dirt, marring the perfection of the gate. A mote of dust gone in an eye blink, and yet still his existence galled her. Even if she hurled her spear and ended the mortal's brief existence, she would still remember he had been there. Even if she ended him, it would not bring back the days of joy. The Death-spawn beasts were everywhere now, spreading across the land, soiling everything. There was nowhere she could not look without seeing their works.

She hesitated. (*Why are you showing me this?* demanded the Skerrise-of-the-now).

What does Amerith say of this mortal?

Oh, you know Amerith, said Oloros offhandedly.

What does Amerith say?

The nechrai *whisper to her, bearing tidings. This mortal is one of those who defy the Erlking. She frets.*

What, that we might give offence to our sworn foe?

That we might entangle ourselves in the passing troubles of mortals.

The Skerrise considered the words of the Oracle. There was wisdom in them. Wait but a moment, a century, and all would change in the mortal lands. War and calamity would claim them, all their works washed away like footprints on the shore. Death would find this mortal whether she cast her spear or not. All things mortal were transitory.

Only the Firstborn were eternal, but this was eternity in imperfection, and it offended her. The mortals would change, but they would still be there, tainting the world. And the Erlking would still be there in the Everwood, lotus fruit in hand, offering surrender and ease and forgetting those bright days of old. He would remove the discomfort of the grit by blinding her. That she would not tolerate.

But the others might, unless he was destroyed.

(Always so angry, sweet sister. Always so despairing.)

The path then, said Oloros, *of war.*

The Skerrise lowered her spear.

She picked up another weapon.

And thus the mortal who would become Lord Bone entered into the city of Necrad.

The dream-spell began to fade, but the Skerrise drew upon the power of Necrad and seized the magic. Through sheer might, she imposed her own sigil upon it, branding it with the light of the White Deer, and so took command of it. It was her dream now – and in the dream she stood atop the walls of Necrad once more, even as her waking self stood on the Wailing Tower. Doubled in time, watching the echoes of her former self.

She turned the spell back upon its caster—

And again, there was a beggar at the gates of Necrad.

A different beggar. This one was a little old man in a rough-spun tunic. His bare feet were muddy, and he was thin and bent from long labours. He might have been one of the millions of human peasants who lived out their mayfly lives beneath the notice of the Skerrise, one of a million buzzing flies.

But he was an elf.

"Your attack missed, O Skerrise. Now behold the cost!" He waved his thin arms, indicating the great city behind her. "You let Lord Bone ruin you all. You let Amerith and all our kin debase themselves. You who so proudly swore you would not serve me found

yourselves slaves of a mortal child. You let him defile *my* works, let him twist our monuments and memorials into foundries and vats."

The doubling, again — the Skerrise-of-the-now was horribly conscious, as she gazed glassy-eyed from the Wailing Tower, of the wounds inflicted on the once-perfect city and its once-perfect people. (It had been perfect, hadn't it, in the dawn days? This doubt, she told herself, was a part of the dream, more poison poured into her mind by her enemy.)

He continued, his voice hoarse as he called up at her. "And what did it avail you? Was breaking the deadlock between Witch and Wood worth it all?"

Erlking, she thought, and in naming him she warped the dream. He grew tall again, and handsome. His ragged tunic became a cloak lined with ermine, and kingly vestments of cloth-of-gold. Upon his brow a crown blossomed. (Better that he appears as he did in the elder days, when we were friends.)

The Skerrise hurled her words at him like spears. "The victory was mine. *Again*, I have reclaimed Necrad from the mortals. The city is ours again, and secure. The Oath of Amerith fulfilled! What of your lands? All your cursed mortal realms are shattered! Your minions, defeated! Your trees burned! Your Everwood destroyed! The *ahedrai* have come home. You are a king of nothing and no one!"

He laughed, and she hated him for it. She had not laughed in countless centuries. "It was you and the other elves who acclaimed me king! I never wanted a title. Only a fool desires power for its own sake. It is what you do with power that matters. And tell me, O Skerrise, what have you achieved with your newfound power?" His eyes twinkled with merriment. "Amerith is gone. Most of the others of our generation are gone. And as you so triumphantly point out, I am defeated, a king without a realm. My sons are dead, my knights defeated, my Intercessors faded, and my last living daughter swore she would kill me if I ever troubled the lands of mortals again." The Erlking shrugged. "I've lost count of the mortal kingdoms that

I raised up, only to fall. I've changed tactics in our game time and time again. I am not who I was when I first awoke and saw the stars. But the rest of you, O Skerrise, you have learned nothing. You know yourselves only in opposition to me. The Oath of Amerith – feh! A promise to defy me. Very well, you have successfully defied me. I am a beggar at the gates." He spread his arms wide again. "Victory is yours! What will you do with it? How will you live, Goddess of Battle, if there are no more battles to be fought? What future can you make, when you fear all changes?"

"I will show you! Come back to Necrad!" shouted the Skerrise. There was more uncertainty, more desperation in her voice than she expected. It was infuriating – she was a living goddess, the Lady of Battle, the Queen of Necrad. In speaking to any mortal being, she could be as grand and terrible and unknowable as a thunderstorm – but the Erlking had known her when she was young, in the first days. When she spoke to him, the mantle of those thousands upon thousands of years slipped, and she was vulnerable.

"Come home to Necrad!" she cried again. "All elves must return to the First City. I have commanded it." She slammed the butt of her spear into the battlement, trying to make it a grand gesture instead of a petulant one.

She failed.

"Commanded, is it?" the Erlking smirked. "Victory has ruined you, Queen of Necrad. You were never meant to rule. You do not have the temperament for it." He laid his hand against the brazen gate. "If I did return, my sister, would you acclaim me king again? Would you yield the tower to me, and all its magic?"

The Skerrise shook her head. "You say you do not want power."

"I said only a fool seeks power for its own sake. I seek power for self-preservation. I am not without enemies. Victory has ruined you, but I dare not wait for your downfall." He glanced over his shoulder, out across the lands of dream.

The Skerrise looked from the gate and saw the endless forest.

The Skerrise-of-the-now looked from the Wailing Tower, and saw the broken lands of the Charnel, the wasteland made by Bone.

And they both saw, for a moment, a raven in flight. The shadow of death lay upon the land, even to the very walls of Necrad.

"I am not without enemies," said the Erlking again, "nor am I without servants. There is a weapon in my hand. You helped forge it to defeat me, but it shall be your doom." He laughed. "You should have struck when you had the chance. Even eternity cannot hold all that might have been!"

The dream ended.

The Skerrise-of-the-now was the only Skerrise, and she felt strangely bereft, strangely frail, as if the phantasms of memory conjured by the spell had been more real than she was, more herself, as if she was only an echo. She lingered for a moment on the balcony, high above the streets of Necrad. She had reclaimed the city from the mortals, and still it wasn't right. All the changes were grit in her eye, and she could not bear to look upon it.

The blood-thirst gnawed at her. Mortal blood might restore her, bind her to the present world, to the reality and the nowness of it all. But she ignored the thirst. There were no mortals left in Necrad, and she would not spare even a single dreadknight to go hunting in the woods.

She turned and entered the tower. On the desk in the study was a game board. Its squares were bright as the sun, dark as the void between the stars. Lines of silver divided them, and more delicate traceries denoted sigils and constellations. The playing pieces were living figurines of silver, and charmstone tokens, and gemstones of great worth. Kortirion had made it, long ago.

The Skerrise gathered up a great pile of playing pieces, a double handful, and shoved them across the middle squares.

Doubts assailed her, doubts stirred up by the Erlking's dream. Had she made the right moves? Her star promised victory in battle,

but there were different forms of victory. Time and again, she had swept her foes from the field, and yet still she felt defeated. She was a warrior, made to wield a spear, to lead an army – ill-suited to this conflict.

She wished Amerith was here, or Oloros, or one of the other clever ones. All she had was her adviser. She looked across the board. His features were hidden in the shadow of his hooded cloak. Eyeballs orbited his head, staring back at her.

"The Erlking has made his move. Once again, he sends mortal armies north to make war against Necrad. What do you foresee?"

A wizard's pause.

A disembodied hand emerged from his sleeve. It floated across the game board and picked up a handful of pieces. Nine of them. Some of them fell through his fingers to land amid the huge pile in the centre.

The hand dragged the few remaining pieces off to one side, on an obscure square.

"What do you see?" demanded the Skerrise.

CHAPTER THIRTY-TWO

The stars over the model Necrad were unlike those above the true city. In the north, the constellation of the White Deer burned the most brightly. In the south other stars held sway. Ceremos looked for the Horned Serpent, and found it low on the eastern horizon. Soon, dawn would swallow it.

We are creatures of the stars. That was the elven tale. *Eight thousand one hundred and ninety-two elves awoke under the stars, and that shall be our tally until the end.* One of the stars in the sky was his, or he was that star.

Ceremos had no idea which it might be. He did not know if each of his incarnations shared a common star as they shared a common soul. What were those previous incarnations to him? His first incarnation had lived when the world was young, before the binding of Death or the first humans walked in the woods. Another had been a Wood Elf. Even if there were all on some essential level *Ceremos*, who was Ceremos in such different circumstances? Had they, too, looked into the night sky and wondered?

If other living elves ever entertained those doubts, they had long since forgotten them, their identities secure in the centuries or millennia of their present incarnations. And if the dead elves whose wraiths crept about Necrad even remembered who they had been

in life, they betrayed little knowledge of it. Not for the first time, Ceremos felt as though he was the singular member of some other species, his thoughts and moods so unlike the other elves. Great gulfs of time sundered him from his kinfolk.

But, for the first time, he did not feel alone.

Even though he had only travelled with these mortal companions for a brief time, there was a camaraderie there. They had become companions of the Road, made close by shared travails and triumphs. When Ceremos had left Necrad, he'd dreamed of finding the hero of old, the legendary Lammergeier, and gaining his aid in overthrowing the Skerrise.

Now, he allowed himself a new dream — that he would return to Necrad with these new heroes, and they would save his world.

He watched Cerlys rise and step over the great mound of Jon's snoring form. Silently, she crossed to where Spellbreaker stood vigil. Demon light from the gemstone in the sword's hilt limned her against the dark sky. Her fingers brushed against the worn dragonhide wrapping of the grip, against the rune-scored blade, against the twisted-tree cross guard.

For an instant, the same demon light flickered in her eyes, as Spellbreaker shared sword-sight with her. She saw Ceremos watching her and snatched her hand back.

"I wasn't going to take it," she said. "I just want to know."

"Try then."

She pulled the sword from the ground. It was light and perfectly balanced in her hand.

"It would have been so satisfying. Ironhand chased this sword across all of Summerswell, it's the keystone to all his plans and schemes, the one thing he really wants. And I'd have put it through his heart."

"Yea," said the sword, "his life I will take willingly. His life, and many more. Take me, and your name shall never be forgotten."

"I'd kill them all," she whispered. "I don't know if I'd ever stop."
Alf stirred, but did not wake.

"I thought," said Ceremos quietly, "that the Lammergeier would give the sword to you when his time came. You are the best of the students of his school. You are indomitable."

"I thought it'd be you," she said. "You're good with a sword. You've got the better tale, with all your talk of doing good. And you'd be bringing it back to Necrad, and I don't think Alf ever really left there." Cerlys offered the sword, hilt first, to Ceremos. "And he feels guilty about what happened when you were a kid."

Ceremos made no move to take Spellbreaker. "I've seen where the thirst might take me. The Uncrowned King warned me."

"Don't you want to know," said Cerlys, "if it'll let you wield it?"

"I know the stories. It will permit me if I serve it, and refuse me if I defy it."

"Oh, I am not so discriminatory in my thirst as you, Vampire Childe," laughed the sword. "There are none I would not slay, given a suitable wielder. Take me and you shall never want for blood."

"Eternity is too long for that," said Ceremos.

She shoved Spellbreaker back into the ground. "Do you think we'll see them again?"

"I cannot guess. I hope so, but I cannot guess at what they will find in the Dwarfholt." He turned to walk back to their campsite. "Let us depart. I find it easier to travel in the dark. I'll wake Friend Jon."

Cerlys stopped him. "Someone has to be there," she said, "to carry on."

They set off along the coast, avoiding the main Road and any of Ironhand's scouts. They picked their way along clifftop paths and stony shores, the long arm of the bay on their left, and beyond it in the distance the hills of Arden. They passed villages and manor houses. At some, they were met with suspicious glares, or by militia

brandishing spears and sticks. "We're not brigands," protested Cerlys. At others, they were welcomed, and greeted as conquerors. "A toast to Lord Ironhand," cried one drunken farmer, thrusting a cup of wine at Cerlys.

They did not linger there.

As they drew nearer the Capital, they passed many survivors of the battle. Furtive deserters, fleeing alone; small knots of companions, often carrying a wounded or dying friend between them; knights of Summerswell, banners furled in shame, their household guard marching in ranks behind them. There was a sense of fury and frustration hanging over all of them, a thundercloud of bloodlust denied. The Lords had yielded and snatched victory from the grasp of their own army, and that was a cowardly choice that would be remembered for generations.

The victors, too, were reeling. Ever since Ironhand's army had marched from Avos under Sir Berkhof, the tale had circulated that their Ironhand would soon have the sword of the Lammergeier. Some accounts claimed that he'd found it in the Neverwood, others that he'd dug out the sword from a grave in Ersfel. Some said the Lammergeier himself had returned from the Grey Lands to give the sword to Ironhand, or that Ironhand was the Lammergeier's son, or that the Intercessors had brought the sword for the redemption of the world. All the tales agreed, though, that once Lord Ironhand had the Spellbreaker, victory was assured.

Then, to their horror, they'd seen the Lammergeier appear on the battlefield, a fiend conjured by dark magic, and the black sword was in his hand. There was no accounting of how many he'd slain at Raven's Pass. Even though Ironhand had won the day in the end, the victory felt hollow and arbitrary. What did strength of arms matter, when the battle was decided many miles from the field? What did courage matter, in the face of magic? Staggered, their faith shaken, Ironhand's army marched on the Capital hungry for affirmation or oblivion or both. Now the streets heaved with soldiers. In every

tavern and alehouse, every brothel and feast-hall, every corner and alleyway they celebrated. Fires from burning mansions lit the night; looters wandered the streets openly. A few officers from both sides fought a futile attempt to keep order.

In this chaos, Ceremos and Cerlys were easily able to slip into the city. Two more survivors from the battle went unnoticed, even if one of them kept his face hidden by a helm, and the other drew a cloak over her armour despite the feverish heat of the city.

Ironhand's generals had taken over the Inn of the Fountains. A grim-faced dwarf was at the centre of everything, receiving visitors from the Crownkeep, issuing orders. Of Ironhand there was no sign. Rumours claimed he was at the cathedral, at the Crownkeep, that he'd been mortally wounded in the battle, that he was going to exe-cute everyone who'd fought under the Lords' banner at Raven's Pass, that he'd soon be crowned King of Summerswell in the cathedral. Every corner offered a different tale.

Ceremos found it intoxicating. Such uncertainty was strange to him. The immortal elves of Necrad were so slow to change, and so predictable in their ways. They were like ice, glacier-slow, their be-liefs moving only a fraction every century unless some great external force shattered them. These mortals were a wildfire, a maelstrom of possibility. A million potential futures swirled through the streets of the Capital.

"Fuck it," said Cerlys, "this city's too big. She could be anywhere."

"It is small compared to Necrad," observed Ceremos, "but much more chaotic. Shall we try the College Arcane? That is where Perdia parted from the Lady Forster."

"They'll have moved her. She'll be under guard somewhere." Cerlys swore. "This is why I wanted her to come with us. She could sniff Olva out. But I don't know this city."

"Nor do I. Come with me."

In Necrad, he'd been a creature of the rooftops. The spires of the

mortal Capital were not so high, the buildings creaking timber and crumbling brick instead of ancient porphyry and marble, but it was still a revelation to climb and look on the city from a height. There was the mansion of a wealthy Lord near the inn, and Ceremos had already found a route up onto its highest rooftop. Cerlys proved an equally agile climber, and together they ascended.

From above, the narrow streets were a confusion of alleyways and tenements, with a few great buildings towering over them like trees reaching for the sun. The squat, crenelated turrets of the Crownkeep hunched on the skyline, and closer at hand the delicate celestial spires of the cathedral rose as if held aloft by unseen Intercessors – and beyond it all, the harbour with all its many ships.

This land lacked the shade of the necromiasma, and the light hurt his eyes, but Cerlys gasped at the grandeur of the sight. She cast back her cloak, and the sea-wind tousled her hair. Sunlight flashed off the burnished dreadknight armour. Ceremos knelt in the shadow of a gargoyle and watched her drink in the vista. The gargoyle was a recent addition – and was older than the mansion it adorned, and the rest of the city around it. Scavengers had looted it from Necrad when the elf-city was occupied, and carted it across the sea to Summerswell as a prize for some mortal. It amused Ceremos to encounter another exile from Necrad, concealed in plain sight among the mortals, watching them from the rooftops.

"Now that's a sight!" Cerlys pointed across the city at a patch of green. "There's the Field of Glory. It's in all the tales. They hold the High Lord's tourney there at midsummer – or would in other years. Alf nearly won it, the year before the war, only they wouldn't countenance a commoner taking the prize, and six knights ganged up on him at the end. And there, that's the Weeping Lord's Walk. Lord Bessimer stood there, waiting for news from the north." She pointed to a smaller church. "The Shriving Church. Harn's Well. All these places I've heard tell of in stories. I hoped I'd see them myself one day."

"Now you have."

Ceremos' father Andiriel had been a dreadknight. On wormsback he'd soared over the mortal lands, and in his tales he spoke of them with scorn. The tattered patchwork of the little farms, the villages he'd compared to animal dens, the ugly castles squatting sentry on hilltops. He'd been especially mocking of the cities of the mortals. *Ellsport burned like tinder, for there was nothing there but sticks and mud. The walls of Claen were but a ditch and a pile of dirt, and we broke them in a morning. Their cities were built in but decades, and we could have destroyed them in a month. What little beauty they have, the* ahedrai *taught them. For thousands of years we have built Necrad, and Necrad is eternal.* Always, always the undercurrent of disbelief that the mortals could have defeated the Witch Elves, that talking beasts might once again rule the streets of the first and last city.

Andiriel had stopped telling such tales when Ceremos was young. Ceremos could not recall why. Had he become resigned to the occupation? Had Ceremos' own death and resurrection through the blood of the Lammergeier changed him?

When Ceremos had himself flown south, he'd passed over Ellsport. The port city had been rebuilt at least twice, sacked in both Lord Bone's War and the Defiance – and yet, the mortals had reconstructed more of it than the elves had repaired in Necrad. The wounds of the various sieges still scarred the eternal city. The Witch Elves preferred to dwell amid the damaged remnants of the past, rather than look to the future.

What had he said in Ersfel, when he'd tried to explain that headlong flight?

My thoughts turned to you, Lammergeier. You slew Lord Bone and liberated Necrad once. Now the Skerrise walks the same ruinous path. He'd thought that taking up a sword and overthrowing the Skerrise would be enough to change the fate of his people. But that was not enough. The dark lord might fall, but if the circumstances and powers that gave rise to that tyrant endured, then another would rise. The Uncrowned King had tried to show him that, in the valley.

Cerlys stood there for another few moments before a cloud crossed her face. "This is a waste of fucking time. It's not getting us any closer to finding Olva."

"Imagine what this city will be in a century, if it survives," mused Ceremos. "Or a thousand years, or more. Maybe they will build monuments to your deeds, too."

Cerlys rolled her eyes. "Let's try the Crownkeep."

But back down on street level, the path was less clear. The Capital's wide straight streets were clogged with crowds, and the risk that they'd encounter some foe who recognised them. So, they tried to find their way through backstreets and alleyways, and quickly became lost, and ended up in some square neither of them knew. The smell of the sea and the stink of the docks told them they were near the harbour. In the square was a bright tent flying the banner of the red stag, and before it was a mob of fighting men, jostling into an approximation of a queue. Most of the warriors had come from Raven's Pass, but others were city folk, eager children.

"To Necrad!" one of them shouted. "King Ironhand's sailing to Necrad to save the world, and we're sailing with him!"

"And he pays in silver!" crowed another, holding up a coin.

"He's going straight to Necrad?" whispered Cerlys. "Without the sword?"

"Ironhand knows that assailing the enchanted city without the Spellbreaker is an act of desperation. So, he must still hope that Aelfric comes to him with the sword – which means he intends to take Lady Olva north with him."

Cerlys cursed under her breath. "Down to the docks. We'll sneak on board whatever ship we can."

CHAPTER THIRTY-THREE

They locked Olva in a prison tower. The room was comfortable enough – a fire burned in the little hearth, and a hot meal sat on the table by the little stool, and a better bed than she'd had in a while. But it was still a prison.

Her body was a prison, too. The collar of ivy dug into her flesh.

An ivy-collar, like Bor's. A punishment given long ago to those who defied the Erlking. The collar had maddened Bor, broken him with fear of divine retribution.

Now sharp little tendrils navigated the folds of her wattled neck, probing for veins beneath her fragile skin.

Captain Abran's eyes bulging, his tortured choking as another collar throttled him. *What is it to be?* Maedos had asked her. *Should he live or die?* And she'd chosen death for Abran, even as he pleaded. She'd been unable to see any wisdom in mercy.

Now, without mercy or malice, the ivy-collar took hold. She sensed its magic brushing against her mind. She felt it flex and tighten whenever she began to draw on the earthpower. Every spell she tried was stillborn, strangled in her soul. She was locked into this weary, still-wounded shape. She sat on the bed for a long time. She rubbed her sore crane-foot and waited.

Outside the barred window, two armies disintegrated in the streets.

Defeated, demoralised, the briefly united army of the Lords broke apart, and now the colour of a man's cloak meant everything again. Shouted accusations of cowardice in battle, provincial drinking songs with an edge — *we men of Westermarch will gut those Crownland bastards, falalalala* — even in human-skin she could smell blood in the air. A whole army marched down Raven's Pass, whipped up with songs and speeches about how they were the last defenders of Summerswell, and then told to give up ... oh, that would rankle. Some would go home grateful that they'd been spared, but there'd always be those for whom defeat was an unhealing wound. Betrayal from above — that festered.

And Ironhand's army was falling apart, too. Poor bastards, he'd gathered them like you'd sweep up fallen leaves. Rootless and Lordless, the desperate and the dispossessed, making more recruits by raiding and burning. If you had nowhere else to go, you joined Ironhand. What else was there to do? Their heads full of tales about a holy crusade against a city of evil — and now, suddenly, they were occupying a city of wonders, a city ruled by tyrants. Take some starving boy from the Riverlands who's never gone more than five miles from his village, put a knife in his hand, and march him up the Road for weeks — you think he's going to know the difference between Necrad and the Capital?

As dusk fell, Olva was very glad to be in a locked tower surrounded by guards.

Late the following day, brightly coloured birds flocked outside the tower. Lords and priests, heralds and worthies of the Capital, all trailing after Ironhand. It reminded Olva of her first days as the Widow Queen of Necrad, when she'd suddenly become the centre of intrigue, with Threeday and other courtiers orbiting around her.

Ironhand ascended the stairs alone. He trudged up the spiral staircase, breathing heavily. The clank of his hand against the wall as he hauled himself up the rope banister, louder and louder, until he was there in the room with her.

It was the first time she'd ever really seen him. She'd met his younger brother in Necrad, years ago, but she couldn't recall Dunweld's face, just a soft shape beside Erdys. The Lady Erdys Olva remembered very well, so kind and witty, but she could see little of the mother in the man who stood before her.

She'd encountered him briefly in the Neverwood, but she'd worn a fox-skin then, and he'd been two legs like iron towers, and the man-stink of sweat and iron. And in the College, he'd been a thing out of nightmare.

Cerlys had described him as a monster, an iron-handed ogre, remorseless and terrible. But he reminded Olva of Alf in the way he wearily lowered himself onto the stool only to find it much too small for his huge frame. He got up again awkwardly to lean against the fireplace. He looked exhausted, his eyes bloodshot, and he let out a groan as he stood.

"What would your mother say," said Olva, "if she were here now? All she ever wanted for you was for you to be healed. It was a cut from the Spellbreaker that took your hand and nearly killed you. If you had any sense, you'd want nothing to do with that damned thing, ever again."

"If my mother were here," said Idmaer, "I would gladly take her counsel. But she's dead, and I must do as I think best."

He closed his eyes. "The Lammergeier fled Raven's Pass after the battle, in the company of Princess Laerlyn. Where did they go?"

"How should I know?"

"You sent the other Changeling to him. You know your brother's mind."

"As the Master of the College will tell you, I've spent most of the last week abed. I've no idea what's in Alf's head."

"He sided with the Lords against me. He slew Sir Berkhof, who has been my right hand for fifteen years. He slew countless more at Raven's Pass."

"You marched against the Lammergeier," said Olva with a shrug. "My brother had the sword, and your lads didn't."

"I did not want to march against your brother. I want only what is needful. The sword. The ships." He waved his iron hand towards the docks. "We have taken the ships," he said, "all of them. We sail for Necrad as soon as they can be made ready. The true enemy is in the north, as it ever was. I thought the Lammergeier would understand." Idmaer rubbed his finger against a charmstone embedded in the back of his hand. "I spent all night in the cathedral, praying for Intercession."

"There aren't any Intercessors any more."

"No."

"And they were elvish lies, anyway."

"So some claim."

"What did you pray for?"

He was silent for a long time. Finally, he said: "I prayed for my followers. They needed to see me pray, to see me rend my cloak and lie before the grail all night. Many of them are still faithful. Mainly, though, I prayed for myself."

He's lying, she thought. *There's something else.* There was a terrible sorrow weighing on him.

"Tell me, Olva Forster, have you ever had a revelation?"

"I've had dreams. Visions I can't always explain. I went into the Grey Lands, for pity's sake."

"You understand, then. The certainty that comes with revelation? Knowing that the very stars have blessed your actions, that prophecy sanctifies everything you do? Oh, when the world is bright and magical, and you walk with heroes! The joy of it! They called me the Miracle Knight when I was young."

"I remember. Your mother came to me for counsel, for she feared you'd gone mad. Here's what I told her – that you were lost, and blind, but you still might find your way back. That certainty, that feeling that you've been shown some perfect pure answer – it doesn't last. Not when it rubs against the world. And the rest are elvish lies, like I said."

"Not only elvish. We lie to ourselves. We sing songs to enchant our lives, in the hope of recapturing those moments of magic." Idmaer shook his shaggy head in such an Alf-like that way it shocked Olva, a dog trying to shake water from its ears. "I fought my way through a dungeon of sorcery, and slew the Manticore. I rode into the Capital at the head of my army, and did what no man has done since Harn's day. The Lords – at sword point, admittedly – acclaimed me King of Summerswell."

"You'll forgive me if I don't bow."

A boom of laughter. "I did not bow to you when you were Queen, so we are even. It means nothing anyway. There's no power in it." He crossed to the window. "I spent the morning bargaining with fat merchants and chandlers to get as many ships provisioned as I can, because if I let my followers linger here they'll get restless and start looting and murdering. And then I'll either have to let it happen, or side with the Lords and fight my own men, and I won't have that." He rested his head against the iron bars. "It's starting already. The thrill of victory fades, and all that's left is bitterness, and petty hate, and unpaid bills from chandlers."

"You'll forgive me, too, if I have little sympathy. You're the one who raised the army. Those looters and murderers – how many of 'em did you force to join your crusade?"

"I never forced anyone," said Idmaer, "only inspired them."

"Still your responsibility. When folk look up to you, you've got to make yourself worthy of it. Terrible thing to get caught up in the wake of a hero."

That hit home. Ironhand shuddered. "I have my quest, and cannot turn aside. I would go alone if no one followed me."

"To Necrad?"

"Aye." He closed his eyes. "I had a dream, like Peir the Paladin. I do not know if Intercessors carried it, or if it was born from the fevers of my own brain. I saw Necrad – Necrad as it was in the dawn days, before Lord Bone, before anything. Necrad unsullied. And from it

a great darkness arose. It spread from the city: a miasma, a terrible cloud that blotted out everything and destroyed the world. It must be stopped. The world must be saved. Nothing else matters."

"A vision," echoed Olva. "A trick."

"A prophecy," insisted Idmaer. "Of all the things I have seen in my life, it was the most true. It made everything else make sense. I have suffered, Lady Forster. Maimed and orphaned, mocked and disinherited, exiled and driven into the gutter – and yet, here I am, King of Summerswell and captain of a mighty host. There must be a purpose to it all."

"I'd call that an unwarranted assumption," said Olva. "Things only have a shape afterwards. Prophecies and visions get read backwards. And your sufferings – I'll not deny them, but they don't necessarily mean anything." She hobbled over to the stool. "I think a lot about my brothers."

"Where is the Lammergeier? Where is the sword?"

"Not Alf. The other two. Michel and Garm. No one remembers 'em, save me and Alf. They died young. They went off down the Road, like Alf did, and he became the hero of legend and they died. And Alf'll tell you, there wasn't much difference between the three of 'em. Alf fell in with a good crowd, and they didn't." Olva sniffed. "If Michel had lived, and Alf had died, then they'd sing songs about Michel."

"What, you say the world is ruled by chance? That there are no numinous powers shaping our fate? You know better."

"Not only chance. But those powers aren't numinous." *The flutter of feathers on the temple roof.* "They're powerful, like you, but there's no higher fate, no plan, nothing that makes it all meaningful. No sanctified answers, only choices. You've got a choice now, young Idmaer, seeing as the wheel's raised you high again. You sail that army north, like you're planning, and you'll start a war with the Elves. Think about what the Skerrise has – all the evils of Necrad. The Stone Dragons that burned up the Wilder, and Vatlings – I met new ones in the Mulladales, and they were plenty tough. And

who knows what else? You'll get a lot of people killed – all on the strength of a dream?"

"Or," said Idmaer, "I shall save the world, as the vision showed. And it is fairer by far to walk in bright visions of legends than in dull daylight."

He stood, and grew grim. He was the Ironhand again, the name like a heavy mantle. "Where is the Lammergeier? Where did he take the Spellbreaker?"

"Like I said, you saw him last."

"He fled the battlefield with Princess Laerlyn. Where did they go?"

"Not a clue."

With one stride, he crossed the room and pinned Olva against the wall. The iron hand lifted her from the ground. "Where would they go?"

"I told 'em," she gasped, "to go – far away. Keep – sword – away." He released her.

"Forgive me," he said. "That was unworthy of me." He helped Olva lower herself onto the bed. "I wish you had not done that. My path is clear – I must stop the rising darkness. You were correct when you spoke of the dangers of Necrad. With the sword, I could protect my followers from evil magic and the fires of the Stone Dragons. Without it, many will perish. But we must go nevertheless. I pray the sword will come to me in time."

She heard him speak that evening. He gathered his army in the great square, and spoke to them, his voice echoing through the streets. There was no doubt, no questioning of fate. He spoke of the rising darkness, and the fate of the world. He spoke of the treasures of Necrad, and the fortune that would come with victory. He spoke of Elves and Men, mortals and immortals, and how the lands had once belonged solely to the Firstborn, but now was the time of the Secondborn to come into their inheritance.

It seemed to Olva that she had heard that speech before, long ago, in a dream. No doubt Death had said the same things to her followers in the dawn days.

The crowd roared, enchanted by his words. And for every man who'd fallen at Raven's Pass, for every one who'd died in the mud or been dismembered by the heedless slaughter of the Lammergeier, two signed on to go to Necrad on Ironhand's crusade and save the world, like their fathers and grandfathers had in the days of the Nine.

In the small hours of the night, they took her from her cell. She feared they would take her to the Crownkeep, where a fresh row of severed heads adorned the gatehouse – the darkness could not hide her from Lord Vond's sightless disapproval – but they brought her past the fortress down to the docks, where Ironhand's flagship waited alongside a hundred more. They carried Olva on board.

As the ship drew away from the shores of Summerswell, Olva looked back and saw a light in the topmost tower of the College Arcane, and hoped that Eldwyn had survived, and would stay true to his word. She thought of far-off Ersfel, and hoped that she'd done enough to heal the damage Ironhand had done to her home. She thought of Perdia, and hoped that she'd taught the girl enough to master the earthpower. She thought of Derwyn, and hoped he'd found peace.

It was hard, not knowing the ending of the tale, and knowing that she'd never know it. There was still so much she wanted to do, so much left undone and unattended. But wind and tide were remorseless.

North. North to Necrad, and darkness.

As Summerswell dwindled behind her, she let herself think of Alf, and hoped he wouldn't do anything stupid.

The flagship had, until a few days' prior, belonged to a Lord of Ellcoast, and his sigil had hastily been removed from the grand dining room where Ironhand and his commanders met in council.

Some had served Ironhand for years, and had fought under his banner in many provinces. Others had, until a few days before, fought against him in the service of the Lords.

The Miracle Knight sat at the head of the table. Ernala of the Wilder, and a bunch of other knights with fanciful sigils.

And Olva Forster.

"What am I doing here?" demanded Olva, not bothering to lower her voice.

"A kindness to my mother's memory," snapped Ironhand, irritably. He leaned over and whispered. "Do not think that I have forgotten all that you did. Our peril is born from your folly. It was you who returned the ancient enemy to their place of power! There was a time when I would happily have cut you down and left your body for the crows. But I am grown wise now."

"Take this collar off me," she said, "and we'll see who's grown wise."

"My wife Ernala is of the Wilder, and they are wiser than either of us. She taught me to be wary of skin-changers, for they do not fear death as ordinary men do." He sat back. "I have much to do before I am done."

Ironhand addressed the assembled captains.

"My friends, Sir Berkhof is fallen in battle. The victory at Raven's Pass belongs to him, not me – had he not fought so valiantly against the Lords, then the fight would have been decided before we reached the end of the Straight Road. His name shall never be forgotten."

He nodded at a dwarf at the end of the table. "Tholos – you are our siege-master. You broke the walls of Ilaventur. A greater challenge lies before you now – the walls of Necrad. I name you as second-in-command."

The dwarf rose and gave a clumsy bow, clutching the table as the ship pitched and rolled. He looked distinctly greenish behind his beard, but it was not solely due to the swell. "Drown me, too, why don't you? Aye, I've given thought to the matter of besieging

Necrad. Twice in living memory, the city's fallen from without. The last time, the Wilder swarmed it, but that's no help – the walls were in disrepair then, and the garrison understrength. I doubt we'll be so lucky."

"Our endeavour is blessed," said a woman in a paladin's cloak, and Tholos winced.

"You keep saying that. Let me know when a blessing hammers home one nail, or gets one foot over the parapet. Bodies and stone, that's my business, and this is going to be a bloody one."

"Earl – forgive me, *King* Idmaer's grandfather took the city when Lord Bone was at the height of his power," said another knight, "with the aid of the Nine."

"True enough, and that's my model for this job. The Nine crept into Necrad through the Pits, made their way through the labyrinth and came up inside the city. My sappers will do the same." Tholos spread a handful of papers across the table, and Olva gasped when she saw the intricate diagrams and maps of the Pits. She knew the hand that had drawn them, knew the neat, cramped handwriting that embroidered every illustration.

"That's Torun's work! How did you get it?"

"The Miracle Knight," said Tholos, "works miracles."

"Our endeavour is blessed," rumbled Ironhand, and there was no trace of the doubts he'd shown in the prison tower.

"Not that blessed," said Tholos. "You said you'd have the Spellbreaker when you joined us. Without that sword, my lord – well, it's a big fucking nail to be wanting."

"The Nine did not have the Spellbreaker when they entered Necrad," observed the paladin.

"I've heard the songs too, my lady. The Lammergeier slew Acraist and won the Spellbreaker *after* they got in. A great many died getting them in, and in the days after." Tholos tugged at his beard. "Aye, without the sword to shield us, there's no other way. In through the Pits, and then sap the walls from below. We've better maps of

the Pits than they had, but they're twenty years old. Az knows what evils the Witch Elves have waiting for us now."

"Lady Olva," said Ironhand, "have you any thoughts?"

"Why me?"

"You were the Queen of Necrad," said Ironhand mildly, "you know as much of the defences of the city as any living mortal. You may know things of use to this council."

"And I'm to share them with you?"

"If you choose to favour our lives over those of Witch Elves."

"I'm not sure I do."

"We have but one life. They shall return."

"And what have you done with that one life, eh? I saw what was left after you passed through the Mulladales." Some of the recently recruited knights looked uncomfortable at that, but Ironhand was untroubled by mention of the slaughter done in his name.

"No more than you did, Widow Queen, when you supported the Defiance. You sent the black sword south; I shall carry it north."

Tholos winced again.

"We shall have the Spellbreaker when we reach Necrad, my friend."

"If we don't, Id—" began the dwarf, but Ironhand cut him off.

"There is no turning back. This is nothing after this for us, or everything."

They let Olva hobble about the deck to watch the sunset and take the air. Idmaer followed her out.

She could hear a child groaning in pain somewhere below, and it tore at her heart.

"Who's that?"

"My son Thurn. He was injured at Raven's Pass. His back is broken. The movement of the ship troubles him. I . . . I *know* there is healing magic in Necrad that can save him. I saw it in a dream. Conquering Necrad will heal him."

"There's healing magic I can work here and now. Take off this collar. I won't try to escape."

"Widow Queen, even if I could remove that collar, there is no oath you might swear that would convince me. But such authority is not in me. I cannot remove it. No mortal can." He snorted. "Spellbreaker can. So pray that you are freed from it."

Young Thurn cried out again as a large wave buffeted the ship.

"Listen to him!" said Olva.

"The Lammergeier had Ildorae as a prisoner once, and freed her," remarked Ironhand. He leaned on the deck, looking out at the lamps of the many ships strung out across the dark sea like earthbound stars.

"Aye, he did. And she didn't try to escape, after. She went with him to Bavduin. She saved his life there."

"My father died in the retreat from Bavduin. So did many others. The Lammergeier failed that day."

"What, because he was merciful?"

"Because he was loyal. Friendship has always been his downfall. At Bavduin, at Arden, at Avos, he defeated himself because he dared not strike those he considered a friend. He could never see the greater purpose. I can. Saving the world is worth any sacrifice. I will not fail."

There was the doubt again. He spoke to bolster his own resolve.

"My lord!" came a cry from above. "Foes! Foes from the north!"

The sky writhed with dreadworms.

CHAPTER THIRTY-FOUR

The wraiths found Ceremos in the dark.

Ceremos could not be sure the spirits were actually there. Necrad swarmed with wraiths, the spirits of dead elves haunting their city, waiting for a chance at rebirth. They clustered in dark corners, and hid under stones to hide from the light. So frail that even starlight scorched them.

Living elves could only perceive them as fleeting shadows. Amerith could speak with them, the tales said, but no other had the art to raise the *nechrai*. Ceremos had seen them once, as he lay dying on the street outside the House of the Horned Serpent.

Now, in the creaking dark of the hold, he saw them again, or thought he did.

He was fading. He had not tasted blood in several days. The thirst had long since transcended mere pain. There was a void in him, gnawing through him like a worm, eating away at his flesh. The wraiths tugged at him, cold fingers of shadow pulling at his soul as his body wore thin. They invited him to join them.

He pushed through the crowd of spirits.

This hold contained weapons for the siege. Disassembled catapults, stacked ladders, endless coils of rope. No one would come down here until they made landfall, and that was still days away, and

days were centuries in this spiralling hunger. No mortal food in any of the crates or sacks, so the hold was bereft even of rats.

Just Ceremos, and the wraiths.

Cerlys will return soon, he told himself.

It wasn't supposed to be like this. He'd imagined they'd race off to the Capital and discover Olva Forster in some perilous dungeon. He'd imagined fighting side by side with Cerlys, blades flashing in the sunlight as they rescued the Widow Queen from Ironhand's clutches.

But they'd arrived too late. They'd crept aboard this wallowing freighter, laden with weapons for the siege of Necrad. Cerlys could blend in with the crew — so many had signed on with Ironhand's crusade in the last few days, a tide of the desperate or ambitious or inspired rushing to board whatever ship would carry them north.

She'd told him to hide in this hold, promised she'd come back for him.

That had been days ago. It felt like centuries.

He'd pressed his ear to the wooden wall, and eavesdropped on the stories of the crew, muffled voices blending into one another, overlapping.

Immortal bastards drinking blood like wine. The Nine killed most of 'em, and should have killed the rest. Even back then, we should have known something was amiss, that they spared any of the bastards. Mercy for the Witch Elves? What folly.

My great-uncle lost half his face to dragon-fire. He saw a hundred men turned to ash in an eyeblink. A hundred more dead but walking. They came crawling out of the mud. Things with tentacles, like jellyfish, their touch was poison.

That's not the worst, it's the spells. Make you think they're gods. Make you weak, make you think you're made of glass. A man can't fight magic.

That's cowardly talk.

My father was at Arden when the skies blackened.

Mine was at Avos when the city burned.

At Harnshill. Jars full of monsters.

Horrors you can't imagine, worse than any tale you've heard – and worse to come. Worse to come, the Lord Ironhand says.

But he'll save us. Like the Nine did.

Fuck the Nine.

My grandfather he was with the Nine too at Necrad.

Him and half of Summerswell!

Came home with silver, he did. Necrad's paved with silver, and every building's a Witch Elf palace piled high with treasure ripe for taking. Everyone who went north with the Nine came back rich with silver.

With gold. With magic.

Came back without their eyes. Their limbs. Their minds. I had cousins up in Athar.

I had a sister who was sold to the blood trade.

Went north and never came home.

Went north and came home changed.

There's horror there's fortune.

In Necrad.

The stories the mortals told described a Necrad he almost recognised. The memories of his rightful life – the few years before he'd become a vampire – were as real to him now as the waking world as he faded, and he could not tell if he walked the Liberties in dream or in madness. He'd known Necrad when the banners of the League flew under the miasma, when the Nine ruled the streets. To him, it had been a city not of strange horrors nor fabled fortunes, but crowded and messy and tumultuous and exciting and home.

Now it was a dungeon he had escaped. Most humans saw him as a monster, but he had found friends, and they would return for him soon. And then, and then, and then – somehow, a twist of fate, a hero's luck, some last desperate gamble – they'd save the day, save the city, free the Witch Elves. The dark lord would fall, and he would be redeemed, and all would be well.

After a while, Ceremos found he could no longer understand human speech. He could not hear the words, only the wet sloshing of their tongues, the flutter of the pulse in their throats, the red blood surging through the brief days of their lives, salty and deep as the ocean all around them. These mortals were part of the world, living and dying in a way he never would.

He hungered to steal a little of that life.

For him, cold eternity. A tale without an ending.

Fumbling at a door, and the clumsy footsteps of a mortal. The meaningless grunting of a beast, and the hot bloodsmell. The vampire stalked his prey in the dark, the urge to *live* filling him. This mortal's life would be extinguished in a little while no matter what he did, but he could drink her and endure!

She was clad in armour, but the thirst would give him strength. Fast, but he was faster.

The wraiths howled at him, calling for him to leap, to strike and spill the mortal's blood. They would share in the feast of life, lapping up the hot blood and becoming a little more real for a fleeting instant, a moment's relief from the torments of the wraith-world. To mortal ears, their screaming would have been no louder than a breath of wind, but to half-faded Ceremos, it was a cacophony. *Take the life!* they howled.

No one would ever know, down here in the dark, what he had done. They were on a ship full of their enemies, on a sea dark and wide. He could drink his fill as he had not done in months. Why, he could go on to do great deeds – he would slay Ironhand, save Olva Forster's life, and a hundred more, a thousand, ten thousand! How many heroic acts would it take to rebalance the scales?

With tremendous effort, he found words, human words, clumsy and guttural.

"Stay back," he growled.

But instead, the mortal removed her armour, piece by piece,

unstrapping the gauntlet and vambrace, peeling away her glove. Her bare arm seemed to glow in his sight, a shimmering luminescence like the marble of Necrad in the starlight of old. Blood and life rushed through the veins beneath the skin of her wrist, her heartbeat thundering in his head. Nervously, she extended her arm to him. She took her dagger and made a shallow cut.

An offering.

As he drank, her life rushed through him, filling him. The wraiths vanished from his sight as he fell back into the mortal realm, the physical plane. The pain of his thirst subsided, eclipsed by another desire. More of her armour fell away, his nimble fingers tugging at straps and buckles as she pulled him down on top of her.

Mortal and elf entwined in the dark.

Afterwards, they lay there, listening to the waves.

"I don't know if I meant to do that," whispered Cerlys.

"No?"

"I felt lightheaded." She looked at her bandaged arm and laughed. "It's like being drunk."

Ceremos kissed her neck. "Had I known you desired this, I would have come to you sooner."

"I didn't know. And when everyone else was around, it would have been . . . " She shook her head. "Strange."

"Hardly strange to seek comfort in a friend."

"Awkward, then. With old Widow Forster leering at us."

"She has been maiden and mother. Nothing we just did would be a surprise to her."

"I guess not." Cerlys fumbled around in the dark for her clothing. "But . . . "

"Friend Jon?"

"Aye."

"He told me to take care of you."

"This is *definitely* not what he had in mind."

"No?"

She swore under her breath. "I know how he feels about me. I'm not blind. But he thinks life's like the stories, and that if he's brave and true, then he'll save me and at the end we'll live happily ever after together. He doesn't want anything more than to go home to Ersfel. A little coin, a little peace, a little laughter, and that's enough for him. It's not for me."

"And what do you want?"

Cerlys lit a candle. The flame danced as the ship rolled with the waves. The light was barely enough for Cerlys to see as she gathered up her scattered garments and pieces of armour, but to Ceremos it was very bright. If any wraiths had truly been there, if he had not just imagined them in his hunger, they had fled.

"I want to see Ironhand pay for what he did to Ersfel. And then . . ." She began to buckle on her armour. "When Ildorae came to Ersfel, it was like a glimpse of an enchanted world, bright and glorious. I want that world. I want a castle and a kingdom and a big gold crown and a magic sword. And a dragon, if there are any left. I'd love to see a dragon."

"Yet you left Jon to take the sword if Aelfric falls."

"I did, didn't I? You should be the one worried, if Jon's the jealous type."

It took Ceremos a moment to discern her meaning. Such thoughts were strange to the elves. Immortality was too long for marriage, and all love was fleeting – or episodic. His own parents were, by the standards of Necrad, a long-lived partnership, having stayed together for five hundred years, but even that was a brief dalliance in the face of eternity.

"I do not mean to cause him distress."

Cerlys sighed. "He has a good heart. But that's not everything. Pile up all the good intentions on one scale, and a feather's worth of action on the other, and the balance tips." She rubbed her ankle.

"He bought you a gift. A hair-comb, it was."

She disentangled her own comb from her hair and held it up. It was made of elf-silver, forged in Necrad long ago. It had the unsettling beauty of Witch Elf work, like Ildorae's armour, intricate beyond imagining. The smith who'd made that comb had honed their artistry for centuries, finding challenge only in ever-increasing intricacy and subtlety. The comb was silver at first glance, but almost invisible shades of iridescent colour crawled across the metal. Delicate traceries of elven-letters stopped abruptly, for the comb had long since been snapped in half. Trampled underfoot, Ceremos guessed, when the mortals conquered Necrad. Or maybe deliberately broken – there was the remnant of a socket where a jewel or charmstone once rested. Then discarded, only to be scavenged by some trophy-monger. When he was young, there had been a fierce trade in treasures out of Necrad. Charmstones and magical relics fetched the highest price, but there was demand, too, for lesser trophies and mementos, flotsam of an elder world.

"My mother bought this at the Highfield Fair when she was my age." Cerlys ran her finger over the break, worn smooth over the years. "She gave it to me. I used to wonder what happened to the other half. I'd imagine it had fallen down into the Pit, and some hideous monster was guarding it. That the inscription would reveal some secret when completed. That it was secretly enchanted. No doubt Jon bought something pretty and golden for me. I've always liked this because it's strange and broken."

"I told him you would delight more in a sword."

"Some Witch Elf woman wore this when Necrad fell. I'll wager, in the moment, she'd have been better off with a weapon instead of a comb." She paused in thought. "All the years I've had this, and I never really thought about who owned it before me. We thought of the Witch Elves as monsters, and sure enough some of them are. But there are monsters among us mortals too." Cerlys' finger pressed against the break. "I bet she was scared. The palace exploding, and Lord Brychan's armies breaking through the gates, all Bone's spells

breaking. All those towers and spires of Necrad collapsing as the dwarves hammered 'em with siege engines. *A mighty mountain-throne above immeasurable pits, cast down in thunder. An engine of woe and conquest, broken/thus, our hope renewed.* But for them it must have felt like the world was ending."

"Not for the elves," said Ceremos "There will be only one ending for us, at the end of time. She would have known, even as the work of ten thousand years was smashed and ruined all around her, that the tale must continue. The tale continues, though the teller changes. But what we never know is whether the next chapter will be one of joy or sorrow. The Skerrise writes a time of cruelty, a grey and fearful chapter where the elves hide away and all joy is snuffed out. Ironhand intends to erase us from the tale entirely, condemn us to the wraith-world until all things are done."

"Or we write a different next chapter." Cerlys brushed her hair back, pinning it in place with the comb. "One that has space for pretty, peaceful things. Mortals only get one chapter, though, so . . ." She picked up Ildorae's knife and tucked it into her belt, then bent down and kissed Ceremos. "We'll reach the shores of Necrad in three days. We'll be able to get to Widow Forster then. We'll get her to safety. Then . . . then I don't know. Stop Ironhand. Save what we can. Just survive, maybe, until Alf comes."

She picked up the candle and turned for the door.

"Leave the light, if you please."

A smirk played about her lips. "A vampire who's scared of the dark?"

"A mortal who I do not doubt is invincible."

She set the candle down. "Keep the light hidden. None of the crew has reason to come in here, but if they think there's anything amiss—"

Suddenly, the ship quaked, rocking fiercely to one side. Glass burst on the deck above, and lurid light blazed through the gaps in the floorboards. Shouts of alarm, the thunder of running feet.

The eerie screech of dreadworms in flight.

"We're under attack!"

They rushed out onto the rolling deck. Waves crashed, sluicing icy water over the rail. A patch of green flame blazed nearby, sending up plumes of steam as the water washed over it, but it was not extinguished. Fiercely burned the unnatural flames of Necrad.

A dome of thick cloud blotted out stars and moon; the only lights were the lamps of the ships. Above, dreadworms wheeled, flying so low it seemed the sky was falling. They bore riders – not Witch Elves, but more white-furred Vatlings, like the creature Merriment.

Cerlys readied her bow and loosed an arrow when she felt the wind of the dreadworms on her face. The shot missed. She cursed, and tore the bandage from her arm. Blood trickled down her wrist.

Ceremos ran to the rail. Most of the dreadworms were clustered in a flock off to the north, around Ironhand's flagship, like gulls swooping and snapping at a dying whale. Unearthly light flashed in the distance – alchemical bombs or the blazing of the Brightsword, he couldn't tell. Other ships hastened to defend the flagship, and dreadworms peeled off to attack them.

"They are all around us!" cried Ceremos. "Make for that light!"

Someone must have heard him, for their ship slowly turned, sailors hauling on lines, sails creaking.

"It's too dark! Tell me where to fucking aim!"

He grabbed Cerlys by the shoulders and turned her in the right direction. She loosed into the dark. A worm crumpled, the arrow neatly transfixing its skull. The creature crumpled, its wings folding, and the sea swallowed it. Ceremos watched the Vatling rider desperately trying to cut himself loose from the dying worm, only for the waves to wash over him, and they were both gone. A patch of slime formed, the dissolving remnants of the dead worm, with whiter streaks marking the grave of the Vatling.

Where are the elves? He had not seen a single one of his kinsman

amid all the worm-riders, only the Skerrise's vat-creatures. Had not a single one flown in the defence of Necrad?

One by one, with agonising slowness, the ships of Ironhand's fleet converged, huddling closer. Grapples lashed the ships together into a great wooden island, bristling with archers. Alchemical bombs lit the night, greenish flames like dancing ghosts twining about the masts, but more and more arrows were finding their marks. The sea-scum of dead worms spread and spread, a hideous grey-white froth that clung to the windward side of the ships. The battle had turned in Ironhand's favour, though the burning hulks of a dozen ships spoke of the cost.

Their vessel now was one of the stragglers, one of the few still unprotected by the assembled archers. Like opportunistic scavengers, the remaining dreadworms descended on those isolated vessels. Their stock of alchemical bombs exhausted, they swooped low, their dreadworms knocking sailors into the black waters, or carrying them into the sky to drop them as living bombs. Bodies burst on decks, falling corpses splintered rigging. One by one, the other stragglers broke or burned or reached the safety of Ironhand's archers.

Until it seemed as if only their ship was left, all alone under a sky of wheeling worms.

Enough ships burned now to give a hellish light, reflecting off the low clouds in a bloody echo of the necromiasma.

Enough light for Cerlys.

Had Berys herself stood athwart that rolling deck, had the mighty sinews of Thurn drawn back the bowstring, had Laerlyn wielded the dread bow *Morthus* in her place, then they could not have done better. In that moment, she was invincible. Worms fell about her, strike after strike.

The Vatlings saw her, too. A horned captain — identical to Merriment, born of the same vat — pointed down at their ship with his flaming sword, and a half-dozen worm riders gathered about him, climbing in formation and circling astern, so the masts and

rigging would protect them. At last! A chance for Ceremos to show his valour! He drew his sword and raced to Cerlys' side. Back-to-back they would stand against all foes!

Her blood thundered through his veins. He felt strange and alive in that moment, not wholly elf or mortal, but something between the two. He watched the distant tongue of flame of the Vatling's sword as it circled, banked, lining up for the charge. He readied his own sword, tensing for the moment when he'd dart forward, cut the head from the lead worm—

Nearer and nearer.

They had nearly caught up to Ironhand's flotilla. From behind him, he heard encouraging shouts, as if cries and prayers could tug the ship along and close the gap, bring them under the protective shield of the other archers. Another worm crashed – brought down not by Cerlys, but by a lucky arrow from the flagship. Suddenly, the skies ahead were clear, no worms between them and safety. The only foes were behind them.

"Behind us!" he whispered.

But Cerlys did not turn. Her gaze was caught by another target. Ironhand was there amid the sailors on the rail.

She drew back the bow.

Like shooting stars the dreadworms flew, the flaming sword an onrushing meteor. Ceremos sprang forward, sword slashing against the sudden wall of wings that engulfed them.

There were too many of them. They fought with a terrible ferocity, even though they must know that the battle was surely lost. Heedless of his sword, of their own short and fragile lives, they hurled themselves at him. Claws tore at his armour. Wings and tails buffeted him, and then the ship rolled beneath him and he fell. His sword slid across the deck and was gone. A riderless worm landed atop him, its weight crushing the breath from him. The head arched down to snap at him, rasping pseudo-teeth tearing at his belly.

"Help!" he cried.

Cerlys spun about and loosed. Another perfect arrow, a killing arrow meant for Ironhand, struck the worm's skull dead centre. The creature crashed to the deck, hissing and gurgling, its writhing death throes smashing its rider against the mast. The watchers cheered, Ironhand's voice loudest among them.

Cerlys' hand went to her quiver and found it empty.

Then suddenly there was another worm, right on top of him. The Vatling-captain with the flaming sword astride it. The dreadworm grabbed Ceremos, claws catching him by the shoulders, the scruff of the neck, and lifted him aloft. Higher it climbed, wings labouring until it caught the hot air from the burning ships, and then it soared, leaving the fleet far behind.

"All the Firstborn," intoned the Vatling, "must return to Necrad."

CHAPTER THIRTY-FIVE

D awn, and the Isle of Dawn. The battered fleet sailed past it without stopping. Olva stood at the rail, staring at the nearly barren rock. An enchanted forest had grown there, once, on the slopes of Kairad Nal. Now forest and mountain were gone, blasted by Blaise's magic.

"Fuck all there now." Tholos the dwarf came up to stand beside her. "Id asked me to keep an eye on you. You're not going to throw yourself overboard or aught like that, aye? Please don't. I swim like an anvil." He smiled, but there was a sharp knife in his hand.

"The last time I came here, Sir Dwarf, I was a prisoner then, too. And my captors ended up being devoured by sea-serpents."

Tholos cocked his head to the side. His ear was bandaged. "One of them flappy bastards last night took a chunk of my ear as it flew by. I'll wager sea-serpents were easier to hit."

"You'll find worse at Necrad."

"I've no doubt of that. Without your brother's sword, lady, it's going to be a hard slog to break the elf city."

"Tell me, do you share Ironhand's visions?"

Tholos chuckled. "Darkness rising and the world ending and such? No. I leave visions to those with the temperament for 'em."

"So turn around! What hold does Ironhand have over you?"

"Lady – he's my friend."

Another watchful day, a sleepless night. One of the ships damaged in the dreadworm attack broke apart in heavy seas. The groan of its timbers giving way was like the death throes of a wounded beast. The crew hurled themselves into the water and swam for their lives. Wild waves washed over them, and each left fewer pale faces bobbing on the black waters, fighting for the distant lamps.

Ironhand ordered his crew to lower themselves on ropes to rescue the survivors. He led the effort himself, tying a line around his waist and leaping into the sea. He swam as he fought, smashing his way through the waves to reach drowning sailors. He saved more than anyone else that night. He'd drop them on the deck, then jump overboard once more. Even when there was no hope of finding any more survivors, he went back again, until Ernala stopped him.

One of those he rescued was a bedraggled, half-drowned rat, black hair clinging to her face like seaweed. Ironhand didn't stop to notice who he had saved, but Olva recognised her.

Cerlys! Her heart leapt at the sight of a familiar face.

But Tholos was nearby, and watching her, so she hid her joy.

They feared another attack as they limped north. Tholos strung archers along the rails, sent keen-eyed sentries aloft to watch for more dreadworms.

No attack came. Day by day, they drew closer to Necrad. Olva watched the northern horizon for the green cloud, but the skies ahead were bright and blue and unstained by necromiasma.

That city had haunted her for years. At first, it was only a name out of stories, a dreadful synonym for darkness in the north. Then Derwyn had set off down the Road, and the nightmares had begun as she chased after him. Dreams of the things that dwelt there, of

vampire elves and writhing Pitspawn. Dreams of wandering the endless marble labyrinth beneath a green sky.

After she'd come to know the city, it became a more subtle haunting. Regretful thoughts ambushed her in waking moments. She'd be tending to her garden in Ersfel, or walking in the woods, and suddenly she'd relive some conversation with the Skerrise or Threeday or Lord Bessimer. Or she'd think of those she'd left behind. She'd fled Necrad on the wings of a storm, when the Skerrise and her followers rose up and seized the city. There had still been mortals living in the former Garrison district, and Olva did not know what happened to them. A small few, like Torun, had escaped, but the fate of the rest was lost beneath the miasma. Olva had brought her son out of the doomed city, but so many had been left behind. She remembered Blaise's lightning spells flashing over the city, then silence.

The nightmares had been easier. The moment when fear crystallised into actual peril was a relief; when the monsters you'd long dreaded actually turned up at your door, you could act, you could do something about them. Nothing could be done about her past actions, the things that spawned regrets. All you could do was live with them.

They dared not enter the city's harbour. Stone Dragons guarded it, and those colossal statues could turn their whole fleet to cinders. Instead, they followed the same course the Nine had used, long ago, when Berys had stolen Lord Bone's flagship, when Alf had won the aid of the elves of the Isle of Dawn. They landed at the place named Fellowship Bay, a little north of Necrad.

The ships disgorged. Hundreds milled around on the shore below. Some had tasks – to fetch firewood, lumber for repairs, fresh water. She could hear the dwarf Tholos bellowing orders, trying to keep order. Others lit campfires and lounged around, or walked about aimlessly. A party of confused adventurers set off towards the city.

Tholos herded them back to camp, but someone must have slipped past, some eager fool, would-be thief or hero, drunk on tales of fabulous wealth.

The north-eastern Stone Dragon spat flame. There wasn't even time for the poor soul to scream.

"No one," roared Tholos, "takes one step towards that city without my say-so."

"Where's Ironhand?" asked one of the Summerswell knights.

"On his ship!" Tholos pointed at the flagship, anchored in the bay. "He'll join us when we're ready to storm the city, but there's much to be done before then! You want loot and glory? You want to save the world? Then start digging!"

The flare had lit up the dusk and illuminated the grim terrain between Fellowship Bay and the city walls. The low dunes by the shore gave way to a landscape of burned craters and sucking mud. Necrad shimmered beyond the mud like a mirage, its pristine enchanted walls an impossibility next to the hideous wasteland of the Charnel.

When Olva first came here, the Charnel crawled with the restless dead. The necromiasma roused any corpses it touched, and zombies stalked the fields outside the city. Some of the zombies had been fresh, the corpses of traders or adventurers who'd come to the city seeking their fortune, or Wilder who'd trespassed too close to the Sanction. The vast majority of the dead, though, were the remains of Lord Brychan's expeditionary force from the war against Lord Bone, forty years earlier.

Nothing stirred across the blasted land in the aftermath of dragon-fire. Forty years was long enough for even the hardiest zombie to rot. As Ironhand's ragged army laboured in the mud, they looked like a fresh crop of recruits for the army of the dead.

It felt to Olva that she was the only one left idle. She watched Ironhand's men bear supplies ashore from the ships, then watched as they assembled wooden towers and siege engines. A mayfly city

of tents sprouted in the shadow of the eternal city of stone. They dug trenches in the mud so they could move unseen. Soldiers waded north across the mud flats, towards the distant ridge of the causeway. It was late summer, but the Charnel nights were cold and they'd need firewood, and timber. Sentries were set to watch Necrad. A few dreadworms circled over the city, but for now there were no sallies, no monsters slithering from the gates.

And no sign of the Witch Elves.

The ivy-collar that pressed on her throat constantly reminded her that she was a prisoner, bait for her brother, but in the frenzied hurry of the siege everyone else seemed to forget. Guards watched over her, but she was able to wander the camp. She looked for Cerlys, finding excuses to walk past the hospital tents, listening for snatches of a Mulladale accent, watching the archers practise. She wondered if any of the others had somehow ended up in Ironhand's army.

If Alf had followed her, she'd box his ears.

Tholos the dwarf often walked with her. At first, he interrogated her about Necrad's defences, but when she gave no answers he took to complaining at her, treating her as his confessor.

"What are they waiting for?" muttered Tholos. "I expected 'em to hit us soon as we landed. But we've been here five days and nothing."

"Elves are patient."

"You had trouble with food supplies, eh, back when you were Queen. We'll see how patient they are when we starve 'em out."

"Your army will starve long before the elves go hungry. There can't be more than two thousand living elves in all that great city."

"Lots of living Vatlings, though."

"A Vatling once told me his people can survive on rainwater and moss scrapings."

"Az's arse." Tholos kicked the mud. "We've eaten half of what we brought from Summerswell. Ernala's kin are supposed to bring more food, but no sign of 'em yet."

"In my experience," said Olva, "dwarves are sensible folk."

"Low centre of gravity. Keeps us grounded." Tholos grinned in a way that was not reassuring. "Go on."

Olva chose her words carefully. She swallowed against the constant pressure of the ivy-collar.

"Without the Spellbreaker, you've no way to counter the fires of the Stone Dragons, not to mention whatever other horrors the Skerrise has waiting. I told my brother to keep the sword well away from here."

Tholos scratched his nose. "Id's of the opinion that the Lammergeier ain't counted among sensible folk. That he's more about rushing in for desperate last-minute rescues."

"I haven't been a fair maiden in need of rescue in years. I told Alf to stay away. He's not coming. Ironhand won't have Spellbreaker."

"And what's your point?"

"You don't have the strength to take Necrad. Ironhand's madness dragged you all this far, but it's not enough to win. What some sensible soul needs to do is say 'enough' and sail back south before you all starve to death here."

Tholos stroked his beard. "Thank you for your counsel, Widow Queen."

That afternoon they began to break up the ships. They hauled the empty vessels up onto the black stony shore and hewed at them with axes and hammers. Only Ironhand's flagship remained at anchor in the bay.

There could be no retreat by sea.

"Keep all the wood!" shouted Tholos. "We'll need the good timber for siege towers and tunnel supports. The rest's for firewood."

He caught Olva's eye and shrugged.

She woke, startled, confused, panicked. This was not the ceiling of her bedroom, not her bed. The light was wrong, the smell of the air, the cold. Where was she? What old and aching skin was this that

she wore? She fumbled towards full awareness, memories and senses slipping in and out of reach.

A hand clamped over her mouth.

"It's me!" A hissed whisper, a figure bending over her in the dark. "Cerlys! Don't scream!"

Olva pushed her hand away. "More like to bite you."

"Are there more guards? Are you manacled?" Cerlys' hands probed Olva's wrists and ankles.

"Is Alf with you?"

"It's just me. Alf went—"

"I know where I sent him. Best we don't speak of it."

"The others went with him, save Ceremos. He was with me. We stowed away on one of the ships—"

"I saw you! Ironhand pulled you from the water. But where's Ceremos?"

"The Vatlings took him. I don't know where. Back to Necrad, I think."

Olva nodded, and offered up a prayer to whatever powers might listen to keep Jon and Perdia safe. It had hurt to send Perdia away — and she couldn't imagine going home to Ersfel and facing Thomad if she didn't bring his son back to him.

"I thought you'd be locked up in a prison cell," said Cerlys. "I came to rescue you."

"Very kind of you." Olva sat up. Outside the little tent, the encampment was as quiet and calm as could be hoped. Men coughed and grumbled in their sleep, or talked in low voices over the embers. No alarm had been raised. "And how do you plan on doing that?"

"I thought you'd be bound," said Cerlys. "But you're not! So, you turn into a bird or—"

Olva took Cerlys' hand and pressed it against her neck. "Feel that? It chokes me when I try to use magic."

"Can I cut it?"

"If that worked, child, I'd have done it already. Try to cut it, it'll

strangle me. I told Perdia to tell you not to come for me. Bloody madness to come sneaking into the middle of an army."

"You did the same for Alf."

"Aye, well, Alf needs looking after. I can take care of myself." Olva patted the girl's hand, and her heart ached with a feeling she could not name. There was pride, certainly, and gratitude, but all leavened with this sickening shame. *We failed to keep you safe, child, and now we leave you a world that's crueller and more broken than we found it. You shouldn't be risking your life for a tired old woman.* "I'm not saying it's not good to see you, lass, and it took courage to come this far. But I need to think about how to get you out of here safe."

"There are sentries watching the tent," whispered Cerlys. "If you can't shapeshift, you'll never get past them. I'll have to kill them."

Olva grabbed Cerlys' hand to restrain her. "There must be another way." A thought struck her. "You expected me to change my skin and fly out. How were you going to escape, after?"

"I swore an oath," she said quietly, "to kill Ironhand. I'm not going anywhere until it's done."

His death isn't worth your life, Olva thought. She wanted to say that death would catch Ironhand soon enough, that a man who lived like Idmaer Ironhand would run out of luck and get what he deserved. If there was any justice to the world, any poetry, then Cerlys' oath would be fulfilled. But the world didn't work like that. Alf was – literally – living proof of that. He should have died a hundred times, a thousand narrow escapes, winning against the odds. You could have right and honour and passion and skill on your side, and still lose. Life wasn't fair.

Outside, torchlight. The sound of approaching feet, mud squelching under boots. Cerlys glanced around the bare little tent, but there was nowhere to hide, and they were right outside. She was about to go for her knife, to fight her way out. Olva grabbed her hand and pulled her down.

"Sit and smile. Let me talk."

The tent flap drew back, revealing Tholos flanked by guards. He frowned at Cerlys.

"Who's this, then?"

Tholos wasn't with Ironhand at Ersfel, thought Olva, *or the Neverwood. He doesn't know her.* "A kinswoman of mine from back home," said Olva. "I haven't seen her in years. She went off wandering the Road like Aelfric. Fighting as a mercenary up in Ellscoast and—"

Cerlys pulled her hand free of Olva's grasp and stood to loom over the dwarf. An artful look of disdain appeared on her face.

"'Kinswoman', she says. Feh! I barely remember the place. I'm Rootless. The Road's my home. I fought in the Lords' army at Raven's Pass, and we'd have beaten your lot if the Lords hadn't shat themselves."

"A woman after my own heart," said Tholos. He glared at the sentries. "Who was on watch? How is it that this woman got past you?"

"My lord," stammered a guard. "I was watching all evening, I swear. She must have had magic."

"No, you were just a shit sentry."

"Cerlys!" cautioned Olva. The girl ignored her.

"I hid and waited until you went back to the bonfire to warm up, then walked in. It was easy. If she's an important prisoner, you should keep better guard of her. And why are you keeping her anyway? She's no one."

"She was Widow Queen of Necrad," said Tholos, "and sister to the Lammergeier."

"Fuck the Lammergeier," said Cerlys loudly. "Like I said, I was at Raven's Pass. I saw him turn tail when the battle wasn't done. He's a coward. Nothing to him but a magic sword."

"I do know you," exclaimed Tholos. "You were the archer! The one Idmaer pulled out of the water?"

Cerlys nodded. "Where is Lord Ironhand? I want to . . . to thank him personally for saving me."

"He's got his own affairs to deal with. I'm in charge while

he's indisposed." Tholos stroked his beard and appraised Cerlys. "Stealthy, quick, good with a bow. I'll wager you can use that knife, too. Tell me, any experience in tunnel fighting?"

"More than most."

Tholos chuckled. "I've got a task in mind for you – if you've got the courage for it."

"If the reward's right."

"There'll be treasure enough for all when we take Necrad."

Cerlys pulled back her cloak to reveal the elven armour she wore. "I've got magic out of Necrad already. I'm thinking of something else. Lands and a title, maybe." She smiled as a thought struck her. "I want to be someone. I want to be knighted by King Ironhand himself."

"Do what I need," said Tholos, "and you can name your reward."

Ironhand's siege of Necrad began the next day.

The welcome heat of the sun burned off the mists that seeped from the mud, and scorched the necromiasma until it was nothing but a thin green film over the city. Olva could see everything. She could see Ironhand's lone ship in the bay, and the camp of his army along the shore. She could see columns of troops creeping like ants down the trenches, carrying ladders and dragging siege engines.

She could see the dreadful stillness of the city, enigmatic behind its walls. It seemed deserted, its countless windows all empty. A handful of circling dreadworms the only sign of life. There were no warriors atop its walls – but Olva remembered the arsenal she'd made Blaise build, twenty years before. Necrad was not as other cities.

Olva watched the fighting from atop a slag heap, helpless to intercede. A mute witness to the repeated mistakes of history.

She knew that many – so many – had besieged this city before. When she was Widow Queen, the Witch Elves had told her tales of

the Candlelit Crusade against the demons, when a tide of unthinkable horrors had broken against those marble walls, and Necrad had stood firm. All the powers of the dark could not take Necrad before the dawn, not when elven heroes had guarded it. Amerith, her eyes bright. The Skerrise, her spear like lightning. Olorin Ancient-of-Days. The Erlking, master artificer. In Necrad there were endless monuments to those heroes of old.

They'd held the line.

The Stone Dragons spat flame. The rumble of their furnaces shook the slag heap, sending choking dust into the air. The air quivered as a wave of heat from the flames washed over them; the mud flats erupted in an explosion of steam. But Tholos' preparations were well judged – the trenches shielded his soldiers from the worst of the blasts. Cheers and war cries rang out across the battlefield, drowning out the screams of the unlucky few caught in the blasts.

Thousands of years later, Death herself – perhaps on this very spot – commanded the war bands of the first humans in their primal war against the elves. There'd been other heroes in that battle, their names and deeds lost in the Grey Lands. Only Death remembered, only Death endured. That had been her great victory, for the elves had yielded up Necrad rather than face her.

That had been her great defeat, for her mortal followers had grown tired of endless carnage and chose to make peace instead of continuing her war against the elves. They had abandoned her at the threshold of the city.

It should have ended there, thought Olva. They should have made songs to remind their children of the horrors of the war, and the dangers of Necrad. Instead, they had gone home to their little villages, their little farms. They laid down the weight of terrible memory, and had simply lived. Oh, to be unburdened by the past, and start afresh!

But that was the trap. For when greedy, ambitious lords arose among the mortals, there were no stories to warn them against entering the city of wonders.

A crop of mangonels sprouted in the Charnel mud. The half-built siege engines looked like ungainly scarecrows. They reminded Olva of the war-golems that rusted in the fields of Ellscoast.

The mangonels were assembled just out of reach of the dragon breath. At this range, they could inflict little damage on the walls of Necrad, so Tholos had them loaded with lighter projectiles. Weapons out of Necrad, turned back on the city that birthed them. Olva watched them throw horrors she'd had a hand in making.

Spell-skulls chattered as they flew through the air. Glass vials broke on battlements, conjuring short-lived Pitspawn that smashed and ravaged and roared even as they melted back into slime. Clouds of gas and noxious brews stained the distant walls – then, as the artillerists found the range, the projectiles rained on the streets of Necrad.

More sieges. The walls bore the memories of these, too – sometimes as images carved into the stone, sometimes as scars. The returning Witch Elves had driven the mortal usurpers from their city. This slag heap – its stones might once have been part of some mortal castle. All the Charnel had been a mortal-built outer city, once, before the victorious Witch Elves blasted it to ash. Round and around turned fortune's wheel, lifting up heroes and casting down monsters, grinding both to dust.

Even in her brief lifetime, Olva had lived through several assaults on Necrad. She hadn't been here for Lord Brychan's siege – forty years ago, she was weeping over Galwyn's body – but she'd heard the songs. Gallant knights racing across the mud, only to be blasted by the Stone Dragons. Desperate courage, desperate endurance, unthinkable suffering – and, at the end, an astounding, impossible

victory. The Nine crept into Necrad and slew Lord Bone, and the world changed utterly and for ever.

Only it didn't.

Less than two decades after that impossible, history-shattering victory, there was another siege, another army howling at the walls. Oh, the faces of the defenders had changed — mortals and dwarven soldiers of the League guarded the walls, instead of Witch Elves — but the siege was still the same. Again, heroes and monsters, again grim-faced commanders talking of battle plans, of engines and stratagems, of necessary sacrifices and the glory to come.

They talked of their ascending fortunes even as their followers perished in the ash-streaked mud.

The north gate of the City opened.

Monsters charged out in a shapeless flood of muscle and protoplasm and teeth. The scrapings of the endless subterranean Pits, the distillation of nightmares, mixed and cultivated in the spawning vats. Fattened on raw magic, but with a taste for mortal flesh.

At this distance, Olva's old eyes could make out few details, which was a mercy.

But she could smell them on the wind, like the stench of crushed wasps. She could hear their roaring, those creatures born for some other realm, gurgling and mournful, like beached whales drowning in air.

And she could imagine the carnage.

Tentacles and pseudo-limbs flailed. Far across the mud, black dots flew into the sky or burst into red showers.

There'd been a time when heroes like Alf had been there to slay monsters from the Pits. It took a special sort of courage to face down an elephantine horror like those Pitspawn. It took a rare breed to pit mortal sinew and steel against monstrous strength.

"Pikes! Pikes!" Tholos' voice echoed across the mud flats.

That first attack was repelled. The dead lay strewn across the

mud, the wounded crying out for aid. Healing spells came unbidden to Olva's mind and in response the ivy-collar tightened on her throat, reducing her to a helpless witness.

Dead-enders with long spears moved among the fallen. On the far side of the battlefield, Vatling bone pickers emerged from Necrad, looking for semi-intact corpses for the spawning vats. There were no birds this deep in the Charnel, no carrion-eaters. When the dead-enders were done, when the Vatlings retreated back behind the walls, it was all terribly, unnaturally still, as time had stopped, and Olva had the horrible thought that she was looking not just at the present siege, but all of them through time. The same battlefield, the same walls, the same mistakes. The same suffering without end.

She caught sight of Cerlys that evening. Far across the Charnel field, just on the edge of the scorched desolation of the dragon-fire, Tholos' sappers dug deep into the mud, and struck stone. The fabled Pits of Necrad extended beyond the city walls. Down there, Lord Bone had spawned his legions, and brewed the necromiasma that hid his city from the eyes of heaven. Down there dwelt monsters.

The Nine had first crept into Necrad through those tunnels.

After the war, Alf had kept the Pits in check. He always believed that the Pits were alive in some way, growing out of the city like stony tendrils, roots chasing the earthpower. Alf had delved deeper in the Pits than any living mortal, but not even he knew all those subterranean halls.

Alf had survived where many others had perished. But he'd never gone down alone. He'd had the aid of his friends, Lath especially, the Changeling drawing on the twisted earthpower all around them. He'd had the sword, too, the Spellbreaker. And still it had nearly killed him.

Down, down for ever, to perils beyond imagining.

Now a half-dozen adventurers, armoured as crabs, laden down with lanterns and torches and ten-foot poles, slogged towards the

dungeon entrance. Cerlys was among them. Olva caught a glimpse of her from a distance, climbing into the Pit like she'd scrambled down the riverbank at Ersfel. Playing at knights and dungeons with the other children, enacting half-remembered snatches of the stories.

Then she was gone.

CHAPTER THIRTY-SIX

Swift flew the dreadworm. Ceremos dangled from the monster's claws. Black sea below, black sky above, the stars eclipsed by the rotten velvet wings. Behind them, the sky was touched with red, dawn behind the Isle of Dawn.

Something fell past him – a steel helmet. It tumbled out of sight, vanishing in the dark below. Ceremos looked up and saw the face of the Vatling rider astride the worm's back.

"This worm is wounded," he shouted over the howling wind. "It will not endure the sunlight." He rubbed the spot where vestigial horns sprouted from his ill-made skull.

"Let me down, then!" The coast of the Clawlands was not far. "Land on the shore!"

"The Skerrise commanded that all elves be returned to Necrad." The Vatling unstrapped his axe, lifted it as if in salute, then dropped it. The sea swallowed it.

"What are you doing?" shouted Ceremos.

"It will not bear both our weights." The Vatling crawled forward, pressed his white-furred hand to the worm's skull. A charmstone glimmered in its palm. "I have bound it to fly straight to the city. It will not heed any other commands. Not even those of an elf-lord."

"Tell it to land! Tell it to land and we both live!"

Carefully, the Vatling disentangled himself from the straps and buckles that held him in the saddle. He crawled down along the dreadworm's flank, long pale fingers clinging to the worm's hide, using the wing-joint and claws as handholds. He climbed down until he could hang opposite Ceremos.

"Your life is endless, lord. You are precious. There are only eight thousand elves in all the world, but Vatlings can be made in countless multitudes. The Skerrise made us for strength, not longevity. My span is only a handful of years. This is my place and purpose." He paused for a moment. "It is satisfying to me that I am the one who completed the task set for us. A flight of a hundred set out in pursuit of you, yet I am the one who found you. That is pleasing, at the end."

He let go, and vanished into the dark.

On the worm flew, faster now, unburdened. Ceremos struggled, but the worm was bound to its purpose and would not relent or turn aside. Over the Clawlands coast, over the wastes of the Charnel. Ruins flashed by below, toppled stones and broken pillars poking like bones from the black mud.

And then: Necrad.

Flitting over the white cliffs of the walls, past the fiery glare of the guardians, then the city eternal. Palaces and tower, temples and mansions, all bleached-bone white, flashing by in an instant. Compared to the first city, all works of mortals were crude and trite. For thousands of years the elves had laboured to perfect this monument to their own perfection. Every surface was rune-scored or carved with bas reliefs or inlaid with elf-silver – or, if it was more fitting, left stark and bare. Statues captured the imperishable beauty of the elves like mirrors of stone. On the inner walls was writ the history of all their deeds since the first dawn.

Necrad, and it seemed to Ceremos that all his journeys had been but a dream. It was as if he'd stolen this dreadworm, circled once around the central spire of the Wailing Tower, then landed

back again. Ersfel, the hidden valley, the Crownland, even the Neverwood – they seemed to melt away in his mind, unable to compete with the immense solidity of the eternal city.

The worm landed in a great courtyard. It laid its head down on a broken slab of marble with a sigh, then deliquesced around him, sagging and melting into ice and slime with a weary sigh.

Ceremos rolled free of the ruin and stood.

He knew where he was. The House of the Horned Serpent, the manse of his clan. Amerith had her seat here once – not that Ceremos remembered Amerith, for the first leader of the Witch Elves, the fabled Oracle of Lord Bone, had perished when he was a child. But he had other memories of this place.

He had died on the street outside, for one.

He crossed the square courtyard, watched by a hundred empty windows. The gate was shut. He hammered on it, but it did not open.

Three Vatlings emerged from a side door. Two of the new sort, the Skerrise's horned war-breed, like Merriment, like the one that had sacrificed itself for Ceremos. The other was the older type, small and slug-pale.

"Best to come with us, my lord," said one, "for your own safety."

The warriors bore axes. They brought him to a room on the upper levels of the House of the Horned Serpent, and, though it was finer than the hall of any lord or prince in Summerswell, it was still a prison.

"The Skerrise commanded I be brought here," he demanded of the Vatlings, "so where is she?"

They gave him no answer.

Days passed.

For a long time, he did not see the Skerrise, nor any other elf.

Dreadknights patrolled the skies, but no elf was among them – only Vatlings rode the skies. A few times he saw elvish faces in the

barred windows of distant buildings, always the gleam of red eyes looking back at him. Galarin Ancient-of-Days, Emlys Arun – all vampires like him, all imprisoned in towers like him. But of the living elves, no sign.

Before, the Liberties thronged with life – humans and elves, dwarves, Vatlings, ogres. Strangers, too, the scrapings of Lord Bone's vats or strangers from afar, drawn to the service of the dark lord and then left stranded like sea creatures left behind by receding waves. Now – only silence, a few furtive Vatlings on the streets. The reign of the Skerrise had turned Necrad into a tomb. Where were his kinfolk?

The necromiasma had grown thin. Its green glow no longer lit the sky. By day, wan light drizzled the city, pale shafts through breaks in the cloud. By night, things moved in the dark, slouching and slithering down silent streets. Pitspawn prowled, and Ceremos wondered if all the Pits below were empty. Had the city been turned upside down? Were all the elves gone down below, and the surface world left to the Pits? He imagined himself chasing after his kinfolk through the endless labyrinth, the other elves always out of reach, always just ahead of him as he pursued them through the twisting passages, the long-promised Faring Forth spiralling in on itself.

Each day, three of the Vatlings brought him food and drink, but no blood, and his thirst could not be sated. The food was ash in his mouth, the wine tasteless. Each time, the routine was precisely the same. One – crowned with antlers, and whose name he learned was Delight, unlocked the door and stood guard, axe ready. A second horned Vatling lurked in the corridor beyond.

The other Vatling, smaller, of older vintage, would then enter with Ceremos' meal. He always brought it on a tray of silver, decorated with a hunting tableau of deer running through a primal forest. The Vatling served with the devotion of a priest, ritually

placing Ceremos' crystal glass in precisely the appointed spot, the polished utensils like relics laid down in reverent silence.

"What is your name, friend?" asked Ceremos on the first day.

"It is of no consequence," whispered the Vatling, and Ceremos could not tell if that was a non-answer or if it was actually a name. Vatlings he'd known, ones spawned before the Skerrise took charge of the vats, chose their own names from their surroundings. The Vatling glanced at Ceremos, then added a vial of healing cordial to the offerings on the tray.

"Why is our city so silent, friend?"

Of No Consequence frowned at this interruption to his ritual.

"This is the city of the Firstborn, my lord, not the Vatlings. We may make no claim on Necrad."

"Yet Vatlings are all I see on the streets."

"Not your place," growled the antlered Delight from the doorway, "to speak."

Of No Consequence flinched, his pallid skin rippling in fear. Ceremos grabbed the Vatling's hand, his fingers sinking into the moist pseudo-flesh.

"Please, where are my kinfolk?"

"The Skerrise keeps—" began Of No Consequence, but Delight interrupted.

"They are at the revels," he snarled, "celebrating the kindness of the Skerrise. And we watch over them, and guard them, in accordance with the wisdom of the Skerrise."

"And where is she?"

"She watches from the Wailing Tower."

So Ceremos watched, too, as best he could. His prison cell was in the heart of the old Liberties, closer to the western wall of the city than the east. If he pressed his head to the bars, he could make out a small portion of the eastern skyline. The mortal fortress that once guarded the Garrison, the citadel raised by Lucar Vond before

Ceremos was born, had been torn down. In its place was an alien structure of metal and bone, a huge spawning vat. Whitish smoke gushed from vents, occluding his view further.

He could not see, but he could hear. He could imagine.

The few remaining dreadworms screeching like gulls, then winging east in alarm.

The earth-rattling, bowel-shaking noise of the Stone Dragons' breath. The eastern clouds lighting up with reflected firelight. The backwash of soot and sulphur through the streets, and the smell of roasted flesh.

Then, infrequent at first, but growing more regular, like the pitter-patter of rain becoming a downpour, the whistle-crash of hurled stones. Not only stones – chattering spell-skulls, too, bottled Pitspawn, witch-fire.

Ironhand's siege had begun.

The necromiasma continued to dissipate. By day, the sun shone down on Necrad, blushing the marble. Even the plumes of smoke and dust rising from the eastern side could not shade the brilliant light. The city's wraiths fled into the dark Pits below for shelter. By night, the miasmic glow was still enough to hide most of the stars. The White Deer was clearly visible, but the view from Ceremos' window was too narrow for him to read any other portents in the heavens. The streets gave signs more readily – he watched horned Vatlings herd Pitspawn towards the battle, saw them carrying armfuls of enchanted weapons. They sang hymns praising the Skerrise as they marched to war.

He saw some come back, too, hauling the corpses of their fallen comrades towards the spawning vats. Vatlings accreted about the bones of the dead. They sang the same hymns as they dragged their comrades home.

On the second day, he saw human corpses dragged off the battlefield. Dragon-scorched, acid-burned, blasted by magic – all almost unrecognisable. Still, he stared at them as they went past, unable to

look away. He had to bear witness, he thought, if any of his friends had perished.

That thought came to gnaw at him. Every time the Stone Dragons roared, he imagined Cerlys or Olva consumed by flames. He imagined Jon wandering lost in the wilds, imagined a great grey wolf with an arrow in its flank, Perdia's eyes staring from a beast's face. It was intolerable that he should be safe in this tower while his friends endured peril. The Vatlings who brought him food and drink seemed like a deliberate insult. He should be out there, alongside the others.

And yet, at the same time, it felt as though every hurled stone and distant explosion injured him. Necrad was under siege, and, despite it all, he loved this city as fiercely as Jon loved Ersfel. It was home, and would always be his home no matter how far he travelled. The city was graven on his bones.

He found himself praying that some projectile would miss its mark and strike his prison, and he did not care if it smashed open the door or crushed him. Anything was better than imprisonment.

And as if in answer, the eastern skyline flashed white, then a storm of fiery red. Stones rained down all, some tiny chips, some fist-sized chunks. Ceremos ran to the barred window, trying to see the source of the cataclysm, but a hot gust of wind rushed through the streets, clawing around corners like a linnorm of burning dust, and sharp stones were its claws.

On and on the mighty explosion rolled, like the roar of a dragon. Even the ancient House in which he stood quaked and groaned. A cloud of dust rose from the east to blot out the sky. How many had died in that blast? Had one of his friends perished?

And even if they had survived that, how many more chances had they? Mortal life was so fragile it staggered him – to know that it would *end*, just like that, and there would be nothing more. How horrible it must be to live through part of some great tale, and then be cut short before the end! To never know if all your deeds

and sacrifices would come to good or ill, to never know the fate of your friends, the shape of the world to come. For that matter, how confusing it must be to come in halfway through a story, the teller mid-sentence when you enter the hall. Suddenly, all the energy and chaos of mortal life that had so enchanted him now seemed like blind panic, a frantic struggle to achieve something – anything – in the few years given to them.

But even an earth-shattering cataclysm, it seemed, would not be allowed to interrupt the appointed order of service. At the proper hour, as always, Delight unlocked the door and the Vatling Of No Consequence entered, bearing a silver tray of food that Ceremos did not want. The banquet was placed before the prisoner, the crystal goblet filled with wine, while the guards watched from the door.

But there was a deviation from the previous order – Delight stood guard outside alone.

"Where is your companion?" asked Ceremos.

"He serves the Skerrise," rumbled Delight.

"He was sent to the north gate," said Of No Consequence, "and perished in the fighting." The Vatling wiped the rim of the goblet with a cloth.

"Our purpose is to serve," said Delight.

"I have heard stories that Lord Bone created us to feed the vampire elves, but our vital fluids could not substitute for some essence in mortal blood, and so we were deemed a failure." Of No Consequence bobbed his head, as if apologising to Ceremos that he was no more appetising than the food on the plate. "We failed in our purpose."

"Your kind, perhaps," growled Delight.

Of No Consequence went to the door – and returned a moment later, bearing a bundle of clothing. He laid it out neatly on the bed. Elven garb of ancient design, woven of shimmering white cloth, fit for a prince. Dust from the explosions outside marred the perfection of the cloth; Of No Consequence dabbed at it with a napkin.

When he was satisfied, he turned and appraised Ceremos' current mismatched outfit – leggings and tunic borrowed from Jon, a battle-stained gambeson looted from one of Ironhand's raiders in Ersfel, new boots he'd bought in the Capital. The helmet he'd worn to hide his elven features from the mortals.

"Do you require assistance in dressing, my lord?"

It stank of sweat, of salt and fish, dreadworm ichor and manticore blood, the dirt of the Capital's rooftops and the scrapings of dungeon corridors.

"Why should I change?"

Delight hammered the butt of his axe into the ground. "The Skerrise commands it."

"She does not command me."

"She commanded we keep you safe, my lord," said Delight, "for all the Firstborn must return to Necrad. But she has not forbidden us from injuring you if required. Indeed, your wraith might be a good deal less burdensome than your living incarnation."

"She commanded that we dress him in elven garb," said Of No Consequence, "and we can hardly dress him if you've chopped him to bits with that axe." He turned to Ceremos.

"I will take care of your possessions." The Vatling picked up the helmet. He examined it for a moment, clearly unimpressed by mortal workmanship, then began to polish it. "But I would advise you, my lord, to yield. Only a fool defies a goddess."

"Or a hero."

"A wise Vatling who knows such things," said Of No Consequence, "once told me that there is no difference."

CHAPTER THIRTY-SEVEN

More than a dozen captains and nobles crowded around Tholos' tent. If more of them had been Rootless and low-born, it might have been called an angry mob, but as they were well leavened with titles and coats of arms, they were – for now – a delegation.

"Where," roared Sir Kenton of the Crownland, "is Ironhand?"

"I've followed him since Arshoth," grumbled a warrior, gaunt and cold-eyed, "and he's never failed me. But he needs to show his face."

"He's – listen to me, he's—"

From her vantage point at the edge of the ground, Olva could hear the dwarf, but only the front row could see him. Cursing, Tholos clambered up onto a barrel and stood there teetering back and forth. He raised his hands, and the delegation fell silent.

"He's close at hand! You can see his ship in the harbour!"

"While we die on the shore!"

"Did you think this would be easy?" spat Tholos. "Did you think Necrad would be taken in a day?"

A knight pushed past Olva. It was one of Ironhand's *atharlings*, the inner circle who'd been with him since the beginning. "Tholos," he said gravely, "Idmaer swore to us he'd have the Spellbreaker by now. He said he'd seen it. Said it was destiny."

Tholos winced, and Olva could tell he took the criticism from an old comrade to heart. The dwarf drew himself up and gestured at the city. "Aye, and what else did the Miracle Knight see in visions? A darkness rising, and the end of the fucking world! That's why we're here!"

"I'm here for the loot," muttered one of the mercenary captains.

"Damn you all!" shouted Tholos. "Your fathers and grandfathers fought against Necrad, and won. The dwarves held against the Witch Elves for thousands of fucking years. And you come weeping to me at the first sight of monsters? Pathetic."

"A man can't fight magic," muttered the mercenary, and that sentiment was echoed by many.

"Six of my household knights," declaimed Sir Kenton, "perished in the flames of the Stone Dragon. My grandfather died the same way, in Brychan's siege. Necrad has *never* been taken by siege alone. This is folly."

"It's in hand, all right?" replied Tholos. "That dragon will be rubble soon enough. You'll see. You'll see. Give me a day"

That was enough for the delegation, at least for then. They dispersed in different directions as they returned to their campfires. The remnants of Ironhand's original army were encamped here, closest to the bay. The newer recruits, the ones who'd signed on at the Capital, clustered to the south – and they'd divided themselves by Lord and province. A band of Wilder-warriors, Ernala's kinfolk, had joined the besieging forces, too. They also kept to themselves, encamping on the dunes above the bay. The army was fracturing again.

The dwarf sighed when he caught sight of Olva. "I don't suppose the Lammergeier's turned up to rescue you?"

"If he had, I wouldn't be standing here."

"True enough."

"I'd be down there, healing the wounded. That Crownlander's right – this is folly. How many lives will Ironhand squander?"

"How many died in the Defiance?" muttered the dwarf, "Or Brychan's siege. You're foolish right up until you win, and after the poets call it courage. You, you're a prisoner. You don't get to lecture me. What do you want, anyway?"

"Cerlys. My kinswoman. Is there word of her?"

Tholos led her into his tent. A half-dozen knights and adventurers clustered around Cerlys. She was hunched by the fire, shivering as she recounted her tale. Her dreadknight armour was caked in the slime and gore of the Pits, and there were fresh bandages wrapped around her left hand, her thigh, a wound on her side. If she even noticed Olva's arrive, she made no sign.

"After that ... another hall," she said, "bluestone walls, and a shaft or well in the middle. There were wraiths there, but they were ... glowy ones. They didn't run from our torches like the rest. I saw charmstones, high up on the walls, but couldn't reach 'em."

One of the adventurers shuffled through the maps of the Pits, the maps Torun had drawn so many years before, tracing his finger.

"That can't be so!" he objected, "you're describing the Well of Saints, and it's half a mile south. You must be mistaken."

Cerlys ignored him. "A Pitspawn came at us from the left. It was like a ... furry worm, with spider legs all down its body. It was on the ceiling. It got Jherik. It tore his head off."

"A linnorm," said another adventurer.

"I stabbed it, right in the throat, and it started thrashing. I think it must have knocked Sir Callum into the well – I didn't see him again. I don't know what happened to Parin. There was this green slime that dripped on him, and he just ... dissolved. So then there were only two of us left, and Sir Pallas was raving, seeing things. We had to turn back."

"Where is Sir Pallus?" asked one of Tholos' lieutenants.

Cerlys pointed at another corridor on the map. "Around there's where he started shouting that I was a Witch Elf, and that he was

going to kill me. I ran. He chased me. But there were more linnorms waiting." She shrugged.

Tholos leaned over the map. "Show me how far they got." The conversation turned to discussion of explosives, of undermining and siegecraft. Olva slipped around the company of adventurers and knelt down next to Cerlys.

"Are you all right, child?"

Cerlys nodded. Her pupils were pinpricks, and she looked feverish beneath the gore. "Alf taught me well. Keep going. Finish the quest." She raised her voice, interrupting Tholos' council. "Where is Ironhand?"

"Never you mind." Tholos shook his head. "All right. We try again. Caelvar, you take a fresh party down the same Pitway. Just keep going as straight as you can, and you'll end up underneath the Stone Dragon. According to the map, there should be magic pillars there, hot as a forge. We find those—"

"The passageways change," said Cerlys. "Those maps aren't worth shit. But when that linnorm killed Jherik – the corridor it came from, there was foul air down that way. Hot enough to hurt. Send me down again, and I'll find that dragon."

"You're with Caelvar, then," said Tholos. "I need that dragon brought down, quick as you can. As long as that thing's breathing fire at us, we can't make a proper start on the walls."

"I want to be knighted," Cerlys reminded him, "by Ironhand."

"Just slay the fucking dragon."

The adventurers departed to prepare. Cerlys limped along with them, leaving Olva and Tholos alone in the tent.

"Where is Ironhand?"

"By his son's bed. He won't leave the child." The dwarf began to roll up the maps without looking at Olva. "But he won't be much longer."

"I could have helped."

"Find me a way into Necrad, that'll help. Get me the black sword, that'll help." He turned and left. The casual way he moved infuriated Olva. She felt disregarded, baggage that had been dragged across the world, and found to be useless. It reminded her of the early days in Necrad, when she'd had nothing to do but sit around and worry. She felt like she was shrinking, all that she'd done with her life falling away. She was no longer the Witch of Ersfel – and while she wore this cursed ivy-collar she was no longer a Changeling. Ceremos had called her Widow Queen, but he was gone, and she'd long since discarded that title. For a while, they'd treated her as an important hostage, but it was clear that Tholos at least had given up any hope of Alf showing up with Spellbreaker, so keeping a close watch on her no longer mattered. Another skin discarded.

What was beneath it all? The fearful mother? Twenty years ago, she'd stumbled down the Road in pursuit of Derwyn, determined to protect him from the world. Now she fretted over Cerlys. Absurdly, considering all the dangers around her, from violent men to all the Pitspawn to whatever dark magic was brewing in the city, her thoughts turned to Cerlys' mother Quenna in Ersfel. She imagined Quenna hammering at the door of her house. *Where's my child, Widow Forster? Where's that brother of yours, filling her head with nonsense?* And Thomad – he wouldn't dare question her, but his solemn, sad eyes would judge her. She worried for Jon, and Perdia, far away across the mountains, and Ceremos behind the walls.

There was another skin she'd worn, the weeping mourner cradling Galwyn's corpse. She prayed she would not have to go back to that.

She wandered the camp, looking for a place to make herself useful. No one watched over her. If anyone saw her, they did not recognise her as the Lammergeier's sister or the Witch of Ersfel or the Queen of Necrad, but beheld only an old Roadhag, a camp follower. A cook, perhaps, or a dead-ender.

She could escape. There was no one to stop her. But east was the sea, and west the perilous lands of the Charnel. South was the seaward Road that led along the coast, all the way through the Dwarfholt and onto the Cleft, onto Arden and then hastening back through the Capital, past Albury Cross and on, on, on until she might come to Ersfel in its little dell, and the land would welcome her home. Or north, north to the Wild Wood, to Daeroch Nal and the mound where Lath had taught her. If it were not for the ivy-collar, she might have risked it. But she was stuck in this old skin, and dared not go.

The hastily-gathered supplies from Necrad were piled on the shore, as if all the warehouse and pantries of Summerswell had been washed up by a storm. Olva found jobs for herself there, unpacking sacks of vegetables, fetching fresh water. She hated to be idle.

Ironhand's flagship remained anchored offshore, the last of the fleet. She watched it as she peeled mouldy carrots and parsnips, the peelings floating off on the black sea like drowning bodies.

By his son's bed, Tholos had said. A deathbed.

"Do you think you're the first to lose a child?" she said to the distant ship. "This is what war brings. All your quests and prophecies, your visions and ambitions, all your grand tales, and they leave out these bits." She savaged another carrot, stabbing at it with impotent fury. "Or dress them up. Oh, they'll tell a fine story of your son's passing. How he stood against the Lammergeier at Raven's Pass, aye? They'll sing songs of him, build monuments. A martyr to inspire others." She gestured with the knife towards the camp. "Every one of them is someone's child. The elves, too. There's always some mother keening over the body, some father standing helpless. Or the horror makes 'em so hard they're beasts, all caring burnt out of 'em. And I know it's the way of the world. I know it's the lot of us all to suffer and die. I live it, I feel it."

The ivy-collar tightened as she remembered her initiation under Daeroch Nal, how she'd touched the earthpower, felt the cycle of

mortality, life and death flowing into one another. "Ach, leave me speak," she muttered.

She pointed the knife at Ironhand's ship. "Alf always said he was no better or worthier than the next man. That he'd lived through the quest because he was lucky, because the Nine helped him. He was honest about what it meant to be a hero. I wish—"

Thunder drowned out her words.

A roiling fireball lit the sky over Necrad. Olva raced up the dunes, her crane-foot sinking in the black sand, until she came to the top and beheld—

A Stone Dragon breaking.

A Stone Dragon dying.

A dozen statues guarded the walls, spitting flame. Those fires had defeated the Wilder when they'd last attacked the city, defeated Lord Brychan when he'd laid siege in Lord Bone's war. The dragons made Necrad impregnable.

Now one of them was dying. The first blast had blown open the statue's belly, spilling lava across the mud. Through the clouds of fetid steam, Olva could see the broken dragon writhe, secondary explosions spitting rubble in high arcs to splash down in the bay behind her. Waves of heat washed over the camp. Again, the Stone Dragon convulsed, another internal explosion and another until—

"Didn't I fucking *tell you all?*" shouted Tholos.

A column of flame erupted, a brief cataclysmic flash.

The dragon died, and in its ruin it brought down a wide portion of the walls of Necrad. The white walls, engraved with images of elven deeds of old, shattered and fell. Beyond, flames lit the Sanction as burning chunks of dragon statue rained across the city.

"Ironhand!" shouted the troops. "Ironhand! A miracle from the Miracle Knight!"

*

The death throes of the Stone Dragon had sent ripples across the mud flats, conjuring a landscape of semi-circular ridges and gullies. The topmost crust of baked mud broke under Olva's feet as she ran towards the entrance to the Pits. She had to clamber over the remains of the trenches dug by Tholos' sappers. The blast had partially collapsed them, leaving only shallow scars across the landscape. She followed these until she came to the brink of the great shaft they'd dug, the pit that led to the Pits. The walls of the deeper excavation were buttressed with timbers salvaged from the ships, and though the western wall of the shaft bulged precariously, it had held. Below, bubbling-hot mud gushed out of the dungeon entrance.

Other soldiers ran past her, climbing down, peering into the darkness of the Pitway. They shouted Cerlys' name, and the names of the other adventurers who'd gone with her. Their cries echoed in the labyrinth. No answer came. None of them dared enter the dungeon.

Slowly, her old limbs aching with the effort, Olva descended to join them. The hot mud washed over her feet, burning her crane-foot. She peered into the darkness, tasting the familiar stench of the Pits. Derwyn had died down there. Horrors dwelt there.

"Give me a light," she croaked.

One step, then another, and another, into the dark.

Yet it was not long before she found Cerlys. She lay there in the middle of the passageway, almost within sight of the entrance. She was laid out like a corpse for burial, her dagger clasped across her breast. Her dreadknight armour was covered in soot and mud and gore, and rent by many blows, but she was – impossibly – alive.

There were footprints in the mud all around her. She'd been carried to this spot.

Olva bent close and sniffed Cerlys' breath.

Healing cordial.

Cerlys clung to Olva as they made their way back across the Charnel. She was barely aware of her surroundings, so exhausted

she could not stand, yet so filled with battle-madness that she flinched at every sound, every movement. She gripped the handle of her enchanted dagger fiercely and would not let it go. The blade was scorched. Olva guessed that it had stabbed some vital part of the Stone Dragon.

"It's all right," whispered Olva, "you're safe now." A comforting lie, but what else could she offer? Cerlys looked at her blankly. The young warrior's lips moved, but she made no sound.

A memory: Alf and the Nine arriving in Ersfel, all those years ago, to take shelter. Cerlys moved like they had, like she was a sack of broken glass, sharp and hard and fragile all at once. So blasted by the things they'd seen and done that they'd forgotten how to live in a world that wasn't full of horrors.

"They're all dead," she mumbled. "Some got up again. I had to – I had to. I had to."

Gently, Olva tugged at Cerlys' fingers, unfurling them, releasing the knife from her death-grip. Her hands were drenched in blood. "I'll keep this for you," Olva whispered, tucking it into her belt. "Now come on. You need sleep, and food. And a bath."

They stumbled back towards the camp.

The first sentries saw Cerlys through the smoke and cheered her. "Dragonslayer!" they cried.

Cerlys buried her face in Olva's shoulder.

Tholos hurried up to embrace Cerlys, to pound her on the back.

"She needs rest, Tholos," said Olva, but she was drowned out as the cheering redoubled, the whole army shouting as one. "Dragonslayer!" They rushed up with water to wash the mud from her, wine to toast her victory, and if they had healing cordials left they'd have brought them, too. As it was, when Cerlys' knees buckled the crowd lifted her up on their shoulders and paraded her along the Charnel edge.

"Dragonslayer!" they acclaimed her.

The look of confusion and terror on Cerlys' face melted away,

replaced by a mad, wild-eyed grin of triumph. "Tell Alf—" she called, but the jubilant mob carried her away.

Tholos turned to look at the smoking hole she'd blown in Necrad's defences. "Now," he crowed. "Now we do things *properly*!" It was not just the literal hole in the walls – there were other gaps filled with rubble, other weak spots from other sieges. But with the stone dragon slain, there was a wide swathe of Charnel field that was safe from flame. The dwarf could send forward his siege engines, his catapults and long ladders. They could advance, and press the siege as if Necrad were an ordinary city. He rubbed his hands together.

"To hell with your brother and his sword. Give me another dozen tunnel fighters like that one, and I'll crack that city open."

Cries of *Dragonslayer* echoed across the camp. They would sing songs about her tonight.

"The others you sent down with her," said Olva quietly, "are dead."

"Aye, I know. But she made it back, and that's a blessing." Tholos nodded across the mud flats towards the column of black smoke. "I'll get Id to knight her, like she asked, and they'll all see the glory, and forget the rest. They'll be clamouring to be first through yonder gap."

It wasn't just luck that carried Cerlys back to the entrance.

Olva turned and limped back towards the Pit.

CHAPTER THIRTY-EIGHT

Vatlings laboured in the mud, harvesting the remains of the fallen. The old sort of Vatling, too, not the horned warrior kind. The ones she'd thought of as meek, loathsome servants when she was Queen of Necrad.

They looked up at her, their half-formed faces unreadable.

"I'm Olva Forster," she called. "I was – I am the Widow Queen."

Merriment had remembered her. So did they. A faint quiver of surprise rippled beneath their translucent skin. They remained silent. She swallowed, pulled at the insistent ivy-collar at her throat. If she could not draw up the earthpower, she could draw up her courage.

"I need to speak to – to whoever saved Cerlys. Whoever leads you. I knew Threeday well, but that was long ago. Can you bring me—"

They beckoned her over. They led her down.

The Vatlings were a form of Pitspawn. These pits were their home. They led her in silence through the labyrinth, moist limbs pressing close against her as they hustled her past lurking monsters. They helped her clamber over still-hot rubble, guided her around collapsed tunnels.

Sometimes, there was unnatural, lurid illumination shed by a

charmstone or a patch of luminescent fungi, but most of her journey was in darkness. Her hands brushed against carved walls, against dripping slime, against rusting metal. Once, they passed by a great iron door, freshly set to block a side corridor, and Olva glimpsed the sigil of the White Deer. From beyond, she heard muffled voices, but the Vatlings whisked her past that portal, wet hands clamping across her mouth to keep her silent.

They must be under the city now. Somewhere, many levels overhead, were the streets of Necrad. They'd be under the Sanction.

On through the endless labyrinth, the endless dark. There could be anything down here, and the wild thought came to her that she might meet Alf down here – not Alf as she'd last seen him, the weary old man, but Aelfric Lammergeier, on his long vigil. She wished she could see him one more time.

The Vatlings pushed her through another door, and shut it behind her. Fear leapt in her chest – had she exchanged one set of captors for another?

She found herself in a room lit by a pair of lamps. There were three other doors, and in the centre of the chamber—

A copper bathtub.

She took a few nervous steps forward. The bathtub brimmed with a whitish semi-translucent jelly. It was like the pseudo-flesh of Vatlings, but undifferentiated – no bones, no organs, no veins or arteries. Substance without shape. And, yet, it was unmistakably familiar.

It can't be, she thought. Vatlings were made to be disposable servitors. They were spawned with all the knowledge they needed to carry out their duties. Few endured longer than two decades, and he'd been an old Vatling when she'd known him all those years before.

"Threeday?" she called.

Bubbles formed and rose in the bathtub, agitating the liquid flesh. Voids opened within the slime, the outlines of lungs, the hint of an air pipe. A roughly spherical pseudopod budded from the

surface, thrashing in its alien birth, shaking features to the surface like a dog shaking itself dry.

The memory of eyes. A child's drawing of a mouth. But the voice was the same.

"Olva Forster. I did not think to meet you again." With a tremendous effort, he approximated a smirk. "Forgive me if I don't get up."

She knelt by the bathtub. If Threeday had a hand, she'd have clasped it. She let her fingers sink gently into the slime instead.

"I thought you were long gone," she admitted. "How are you still alive?"

"Why . . . like your noble brother . . . I am possessed of a certain stubborn stupidity." Threeday had to labour to get the long sentence out. "I endure because my work is not yet done." The slime tightened around her fingers. "You are . . . partly . . . responsible for that, Widow Queen."

"The Skerrise."

It was, to her surprise, a relief to admit her past mistakes. Those days had been so strange – her crane-skin flight, her initiation into the earthpower under Lath's tutelage, her desperation to rescue Derwyn – that she'd given little thought to the effects of her actions on Necrad. And after, she'd been back in Ersfel, and the memories of Necrad had been like a half-remembered dream.

"The Skerrise, indeed. You delivered our city into the hands of . . . an unworthy ruler."

"Was I any better?"

The whole bathtub rocked, Threeday's temporary organs losing all definition as he collapsed in laughter. With a tremendous effort, he recomposed himself.

"Not much. But you, Widow Queen . . . had the virtue of being easy to manipulate. You listened, most of the time. Not the Skerrise."

He pulled himself up in the bathtub, shoulders and limbs lasting only a moment.

"We Vatlings . . . ah, we have always lived in the shadow of the

throne. We have never ruled ourselves. We were made to serve, but we found gaps. Places where we could be ourselves . . . and shape our destiny. The Nine ruled Necrad, then the Council. Then you and your son. But under each, we Vatlings prospered a little more." He paused. "I had a moleskin doublet."

"I remember. You looked very fine."

"Hmph." He returned to his previous theme. "And now the Skerrise."

"I met her new Vatlings."

"I despise them!" spat Threeday, with more vehemence than Olva had ever seen from him. "Deluded, enchanted idiots. They are not why I endured so long. Why I *waited* . . . for a meeting like this."

He sprouted eyes that, though sightless, met her gaze.

"I hoped it would be the Lammergeier, or some other champion, for I am in need of a hero. The Skerrise prepares to work a spell long in the making. A dream of the past made present again. She intends to bring the elder days back, to remake Necrad as it was in the beginning. There is no place for us Vatlings in her design. We are scarcely a century old, and she would look back thousands of years. It will destroy us. I ask you to save my people."

"Alf's far away," said Olva, "on another quest. And he has the sword with him."

"Oh, if he's got another quest, we can't interrupt *that*!" He managed to gurgle with bitter sarcasm. "What was I thinking, to presume that the fate of my people counted for anything—"

"What can I do, Threeday?" She brushed her slimy fingers against the ivy-collar. "Can you break this collar?"

"No."

"There was a vampire boy, Ceremos. He came to Alf—"

"The Skerrise has him. He is lost to you."

"Is — is Blaise still alive? Ceremos said he brought word from Blaise."

"Now there is a mystery that I cannot answer. I know many

things, Widow Queen, even in my present diminished form. I hear many whispers. I know that in the Wailing Tower dwells one that only the Skerrise may see. If it is Master Blaise, then he too is lost to you, for I suspect him to be the architect of the Skerrise's spell. No help will come from the Wailing Tower." A ripple ran through the bath. "I tried."

"Then what can we do?"

"Widow Queen, you have an army at the gates of Necrad."

"It's not my army. I'm their prisoner."

"I know. I still hear whispers. It is the army of Idmaer Ironhand. The Miracle Knight. For him to rule Necrad would be no better for us than the Skerrise. He intends to destroy the evil of the city." A half-formed hand broke the surface of the slime in a little wave. "No doubt he would see us as evil. Whether the Skerrise enchants us away as an inconvenient stain, or Ironhand slaughters us and smashes the vats as his men loot the city, it makes no difference. We would be gone."

"Idmaer serves the Erlking. Alf's gone to slay the Erlking. There's still a chance."

"There is. But not from Aelfric." Threeday's form began to melt, his face collapsing. He spoke more quickly now. "The Skerrise's spell will take all the magic of the city. The other Stone Dragons cannot breath. The wards will fall. All that will guard Necrad will be the *physical* defences, and my Vatlings can open the gates. Only for a brief time, but long enough for you to seize the city once more. Enter, slay the elves, stop the Skerrise, and the wheel turns again."

"How will I know when she casts the spell?"

Threeday gurgled. "It will not be . . . subtle. She will draw upon all the city's magic. You will know." With an immense effort, he threw out an approximation of a hand, and seized her wrist. "It can't be . . .it can't be *Ironhand* on the throne. Someone else. Someone who might *listen*."

The last word lost as Threeday sank into the tub.

The door behind her opened. The Vatlings returned.

"We must go, Widow Queen," one said. Another whispered urgently into her ear, talking of signals and gates, of banners that should be raised when the deed was done, of the movements of armies.

It took Ildorae's knife from Olva's belt and pressed it into her hand.

Then back through the labyrinth.

Back to emerge, blinking and confused, in the Charnel.

Tholos' soldiers found her walking across the mud flats. They bounded over to her with immense relief, reminding her less of gaolers recapturing an escaped prisoner, but of lost children who had just found their mother.

"You're not allowed go wandering! Where were you?" demanded one.

"Thank the Intercessors we found you in time," said the other. "King Ironhand demands your presence."

She felt the weight of the knife, concealed in her sleeve.

CHAPTER THIRTY-NINE

On the next evening, Delight was absent. The horned one had gone to the war, gone to the walls, and all that was left was Of No Consequence – and that Vatling did not even attempt to block Ceremos' escape. He pushed past Of No Consequence and darted out of the door. He ran through the deserted House of the Horned Serpent, swinging up through an arched window onto the slanted roof. Slates like scales slipped beneath his feet, but he was in Necrad again, free once more.

For a moment, he forgot the thirst, forgot the war, forgot everything but the strange beauty of his city in the sunset. He had never seen Necrad like this, red light streaming over the spires, the Liberties a blooming rose of stone.

Then the horns blared.

The streets began to writhe. Vatlings and other Pitspawn oozed out of doorways and alleyways. The older Vatlings, the ilk of Of No Consequence, raised their moist hands, their wet, gurgling voices, but made little effort to stop him. The new breed, thought, pursued him eagerly. *Come back*, they cried, *the Skerrise commands it.*

So did the Pitspawn.

As one, the motley host emerged from their lairs amid the palaces and temples. They stared at him as he ran, some with one eye, some

with multitudes, some with heat-sensing pit organs or vibration-sensing tendrils, all that the fecund pseudo-flesh of the vats could vomit up. Humanity, the forbidden tales said, was the scrapings of the Erlking's cauldron in days of old, and in the depths Lord Bone had forged a hundred cauldrons more. A wild hunt of misshapen things surged through the streets in pursuit, snarling and howling and hooting and gurgling, some choking on their own ill-formed throats, others turning on easier prey and ripping their packmates to pieces.

Ceremos ran, nightmare at his heels.

A narrow alley. The larger monsters could not follow him there. He had raced down that alley a thousand times as a child. Now, his shoulders had grown broad, and his mortal-forged armour scraped against the stone. Still, he outraced them.

Into the plaza, up the Ghibbiline Stair, then ducking right through the doorway into the palace of Galarin Ancient-of-Days – leaping over the dracoform Pitspawn slumbering in the rotten grandeur of the ballroom – up another stair, then out onto the roof, leaping back across the alleyway, slipping through an attic window. All the secret ways of the city were known to him.

Below, the Pitspawn pack disintegrated, monsters slithering this way and that in confusion as their prey slipped away. *Come back*, cried the Vatlings, *the Skerrise wills it.*

Ceremos scrambled through a window – and he was back in his childhood bedroom. He paused a moment to catch his breath, and to drink in memory, then he descended the looping staircase to the house below.

The house of his parents was deserted. There were fresh gouges in the plaster of the mural on the stairs. The marks of an axe, and they had not been there when Ceremos had fled Necrad. The audience room downstairs had become a barracks. The smell of the horned Vatlings filled the room, blankets and bedding strewn about the floor. His father's dreadknight armour, dismembered for parts.

He found a sword amid the Vatling gear.

Where were the elves? *All the Firstborn must return to Necrad*, Witch Elf and Wood Elf and even the bodiless wraiths awaiting re-incarnation. They had all returned to the first city. Save for a handful in Eavesland, save for the Princess Laerlyn and the Erlking, all the elves must be in Necrad. Where were they? Why had Ceremos and the other vampires been imprisoned separately from them?

Come back, shouted Vatlings on the street outside, *mother-of-all commands it.*

Pitspawn hissed and roared in mimicry of those shouts.

If all the creatures of the Pits were on the streets and palaces of Necrad, then who was below?

Slower now, more careful, sneaking through the Liberties. There were only a handful of entrances to the Pits in this part of the city, so Ceremos made his way north-east. Off to his right, he could see the looming spire of the Wailing Tower – and beyond, under the dark-ening sky, fires burning in the eastern part of the city. The distant thunder of stones crashing against the walls as the siege ground on.

And then—

Onwards he ran. Ahead was a wide street, one of the open arteries of the city. The Sanction wall once stood there, blocking the way. Now the only sign of the wall was a few piles of rubble, overgrown with weeds – another novelty in Necrad. Ceremos sprinted across the open ground, fearful that at any moment the hunters would spot him. But he plunged into the blessed shelter of the shadows, and through the silent streets, and the cries of the Vatlings faded behind him.

Down, then. He found a stairway leading down into the Pits. When the League took Necrad from Lord Bone, they'd sealed off most of the Pitways. The Lammergeier had spent more than a decade crawling the dungeons, hacking and slashing through the endless waves of Pitspawn.

The stairway ended in a steel door. It was new-forged, bright

and shiny, and it bore the sigil of the White Deer. The sign of the Skerrise.

He hammered on the door.

"It is Ceremos, son of Elithadil and Andiriel! I have come home!"

Elven voices answered.

"What is happening? We hear thunder, the roaring of dragons! Is our city under attack? Let us out!"

There was no lock on the door, no handle. Magic sealed it. Ceremos tugged at the rim, his fingernails scraping against the metal, but he could not budge it.

"Mortals make war upon the Skerrise!" he said. "But listen – I have friends among them! The Lammergeier has the Spellbreaker again, and he will aid us! The Princess Laerlyn is with him! Help is coming!"

"Let us out," they cried, "the Skerrise imprisoned us!"

"I cannot open it!" he cried. "I'll find another way."

He turned – and at the top of the stairs he saw horned figures outlined against the last glimmer of sunset. The hunters had found him. The growling of Pitspawn shook the stairwell.

"All the Firstborn," said one of the horned Vatlings, "must return to Necrad."

"Here I am!" cried Ceremos, brandishing his sword. "Youngest of the Firstborn! Come and claim me, if you wish to throw away your lives!"

The Vatlings laughed – then fell silent, suddenly. They backed away from the top of the stairs, bowing their horned heads, averted their eyes. The Pitspawn whimpered and cowered.

Ceremos scrambled to the top of the stairs and looked up at the Wailing Tower.

From her eyrie atop the tower, the Skerrise descended towards him on wings of magic. A thousand charmstones blazed in her raiment; her spear crackled with the power to shatter mountains. She was Queen of Necrad, and she wore an antlered crown of silver.

She swooped like a bird of prey, seizing him by the collar, shaking him like an insolent pup, then soared back into the air. Invisible wings carried them high over Necrad. Her grip was like iron. Higher they flew, the city cartwheeling below, dissolving into a chaos of fire and ruin. For an instant he glimpsed the eastern wall, glimpsed the wide breach blasted in it by the loss of the Stone Dragon.

Curtains of acrid smoke washed over them, wispy trails of the dissolving necromiasma. A trio of dreadworms – perhaps the last ones left, he'd seen none in days – flew past, screeching in alarm at these aerial intruders. The sunlight had scorched holes in their wings.

Higher they flew, a witch-flight. He glimpsed the harbour, the eastern bay, and through a gap in the smoke, the myriad banners of the mortal army. *I failed you, Lady Olva.*

Higher, above the smoke now, exposed to the full light of the sun. So bright it was painful, burning his pallid skin, searing his red eyes. He tried to turn away, but the Skerrise shifted her grip on him. She held his head and twisted it, forcing him to face the setting sun. Her fingers forced his eyelids open.

"Do you see?" said the Skerrise. Her own voice was equally pained. She was a vampire, too. "Do you see how all has gone crooked?"

Ceremos, who by nature was loquacious, could only scream.

She spun him in a full circle, so he could see everything.

The Skerrise's nails dug into his eyes, and he saw everything.

The sun setting over the Dwarfholt, the endless grey-brown Charnel crawling towards the distant Wild Wood, the mortal army, and beyond them, far across the sea, the ruins of the Isle of Dawn, blasted by magic. South, and Summerswell, and the rotting Neverwood.

"Do you see how the tale has all gone wrong?" she demanded again, almost pleading for him to understand.

They descended towards the highest point of Necrad. The Wailing Tower was like a hand reaching out of the city to catch them. They landed on the topmost balcony. The Skerrise released

Ceremos, and he slumped to the floor. With a word of power, the Skerrise transformed part of the railing into a serpent of steel. It coiled around Ceremos' wrist, manacling him in place.

"I won't serve you! Free me or slay me!"

"You do not know yourself. You had a different name, once. Adiorno was your name under the first stars. Had you lived, in time you would have remembered that, but this incarnation was cut short by the evil of mortals. Like me, you are tainted by mortality. Their blood pollutes us. But we will find our way home, too. For the Firstborn there is no ending."

She glided to the shattered door that led into the tower beyond. Necrad was reflected in the window. She paused and looked back at the chained vampire childe.

"There is power enough here to heal the sorrows of the world. To untell all the tales that went awry, and undo the mistakes of the past. In the elder days there were no mortals to trouble us, or quarrels to divide us. We gave no thought to *endings*, for there were none, only endless and unfading joy. We shall have that world back again, for ever, and we shall never weary of it."

"I do not remember the elder days. Those joys are not mine. All you speak of means nothing to me. Let me go back to my friends."

She opened the door. Inside, Ceremos glimpsed a wizard's study, lined with arcane tomes. A great desk, carved with the faces of demons. Upon the desk was a game board, and all the pieces on it were scattered and toppled.

A hooded figure sat behind the desk.

"The Lammergeier has failed," it said. "The quest has failed."

CHAPTER FORTY

The guards hurried Olva towards to the sea. She limped along as quick as she could, clutching the dagger hidden in her sleeve to make sure it didn't slip out.

A mob of soldiers had gathered by the shore, all so muddy and soot-stained that Olva could not tell if they'd marched under Ironhand's banner all the way from the Eavesland, or if they'd joined at the last moment in Summerswell. "Ironhand!" they shouted. "Ironhand!"

Then, a ring of sentries with pikes, like a sieve – for beyond *them* was a smaller crowd, all the officers and captains. Tholos was there, his face grave, his helm tucked under his arm. The remaining knights of Ironhand's *atharlings*, few enough of them. Nobles from Summerswell. There was Idmaer's wife, Ernala, amid a group of Wilder. She wore a mask carved to resemble a bird, decorated with black feathers.

And there, a hood drawn over her head against the cold wind, leaning on a spear, was Cerlys. Olva went up to stand beside her.

"What is this?"

"No idea," whispered Cerlys. "But look."

A boat departed from Ironhand's flagship. Slowly, it made its way across the grey waters of the bay. There was only one rower,

his massive shoulders betraying his identity even if the sun did not flash from his polished sword-hand. The little rowing boat carried no other passengers, but there was a cloth-wrapped bundle at Ironhand's feet.

Olva swayed, the ivy-collar suddenly tight at her throat. Cerlys grabbed Olva's sleeve to steady her. "Are you all right?"

"Yes, yes. It's just . . . everything."

Closer the boat came, and closer, Ironhand bent on his task.

"They're going to make another assault on the city," whispered Cerlys. "Push through that gap." She wiped her nose. "I'm going to go with them. I get in, maybe I can find Ceremos."

Olva remembered working in the infirmary, when the Wilder besieged Necrad. Remembered the League soldiers, how she'd had to ration healing magic. She thought of all the deaths she'd seen, the quick and the slow. At least with the slow ones the gradual declines, the illnesses, the grey creep of old age, you had a chance to make peace, to say what you needed to say. To tidy up, maybe. To live on the border of the grey. The quick ones, though, they always seemed like mistakes to her. Like a word of warning or a different choice could have saved so much.

There'd been a boy on the Road once, in the Fossewood. One of Lyulf Marten's servants. She'd killed him by mistake. She hadn't thought of him in years, but she thought of him now, as a veil of grey rain washed over the gloomy shore, as the boat came ever closer.

You can't heal everyone, she told herself. *Death comes for us all.*

But there was a choice she could make here, wasn't there? She thought of Derwyn's chessboard with different pieces at the corners. Bird's skull, snail shell, iron tower, the Skerrise in her glory. Everything was important, everything was connected. She thought of the ruined elf-woods she'd seen in the Neverwood, of the ruined Isle of Dawn she'd glimpsed from the rail of Ironhand's ship. Fire had swept through the woods, destroying the ancient trees, but new saplings were sprouting all around them, born of scattered seeds.

You could not foretell which would thrive, which buried seeds would birth the future.

Kill Ironhand, and the Vatlings will open the gates. Tholos can take the city without bloodshed.

Ironhand reached the shore. He climbed out, the waves splashing against his leg-greaves, and dragged the boat up the beach. He stooped to pick up the cloth-shrouded bundle in his arms.

Olva reached for the dagger in her sleeve, then stopped when she realised what was in that cloth bundle.

Oh, blessed intercessors. It's the funeral. I can't do it at the funeral.

Cradling his son's body, Idmaer addressed the crowd.

"My captains," he said, but his voice cracked. "My friends . . ."

Ernala left the Wilder and hurried to her husband's side. She took off the raven-mask and whispered to Ironhand. He began again, his speech halting. Knights shuffled uncomfortably; the shouts of acclamation from the crowd fell silent.

"My captains. I was not with you at Raven's Pass. I could not be with you. Sir Berkhof led you there. I sent – I sent all the strength I could, and he carried the day, though the cost was bitter. You all know the cost! You all paid the cost! Countless are the graves at Raven's Pass now! But we endured. We have known victory, and defeat, and we know that there is never a clean divide between them. No victory is ever bloodless. No victory is ever . . ."

Ironhand fell silent, looking out at the assembled host. The wind tugged at the shrouded bundle in his arms. He adjusted his grip, his living hand clasping his iron gauntlet, and it seemed to inspire him. He drew him up, and his voice boomed.

"We have struck this day a great blow against the enemy! We have taken the shores, breached the walls of Necrad! The road ahead is clear! The city shall fall, and the city shall be destroyed! There will be no more evil out of Necrad. We shall strike down the Lady of Darkness, and the Witch Elves, and all sorrow shall pass from the

land. Our children—" He clenched the iron fist. "*Your* children will
see a better world. The Intercessors will return when the stain of
Necrad is washed away. You shall be acclaimed heroes, when it is done.

"The battle to come will be difficult. More horrors await –" His
gaze picked Olva out of the crowd, "– and I cannot protect you from
them. All I can promise is that I will stand beside you, fight beside
you! I shall be the first through the breach, the first to face the evils
of Necrad!" Idmaer's face grew dark, and he lifted his head to glare
at the distant city, at the Wailing Tower. "I shall destroy them! Evil
will be destroyed, for ever! I shall bleed with you. I shall suffer with
you. I have nothing left except the cause! Nothing to hold back,
nothing more to lose! From nothing, we will claim everything!"

The cheering began again, and he raised an iron hand to quell it.

"I buried my friend at Raven's Pass, and went on. Here, on the
shore that we won, I bury my child."

He handed the bundle to Ernala, who nearly stumbled under
its weight. Two priests emerged from the crowd, clerics of the
Intercessors. One bore a jewelled grail, brimming with water. The
other carried a black sword – it was of similar design to Spellbreaker,
clearly made in the image of Alf's sword, but it was shorter, lighter,
scaled for a smaller frame.

Ernala and the priests began to walk along the shore towards a
rocky headland. A pyre of driftwood waited there. Wilder-fashion,
the burning of the body. Ironhand laid Thurn's corpse down.

Somewhere behind, ragged voices rose in a hymn that Olva hadn't
heard in years, a prayer to the Intercessors.

As they came towards the narrow neck of the headland, the
crowd became a queue, filling past Ironhand one by one, offering
whispered condolences, promises of service, oaths of vengeance,
competing to prove that they, too, would sacrifice everything to see
the quest complete, to see Necrad destroyed. Ironhand might have
been a statue. Offers of sympathy broke on his grim features and
washed away unnoticed.

Olva swallowed, feeling the ivy-collar press against her throat. *You won't get another chance*, she thought. *The Vatlings will open the gates if he's dead. They'll kill you, too, but what else is there to do?* Memories of all the maimed and dying in Ersfel warred with visions of the slaughter to come in Necrad. *What else is there to do?*

She shuffled towards Ironhand, crane-foot dragging over the pebbles of the barren strand. Only three ahead of her in the queue. Two now. Cerlys just ahead of her.

Olva reached for the dagger, but her sleeve was empty.

It happened so fast.

One moment, Cerlys was there, cowled head bowed, Idmaer towering above her like an iron mountain, and then he was stumbling back, clutching his side, blood welling from the wound, and she was moving with serpentine grace, darting forward, the dagger a fang. She struck again, but this time the iron hand caught. He lifted her – the terrible strength of him, even now, his blood gushing across the black sand – both her hands caught in the vice, hoisting her up so he could see her face.

"You!" he snarled. "You were with the Lammergeier at Ersfel!"

Knights rushed forward, shoving Olva aside in their eagerness to grab Cerlys. In an instant, there were a dozen men clustered around her. They tore Ildorae's dagger from her hand, put swords to her throat.

"Stop," commanded Idmaer.

"My lord," stammered Tholos in confusion, "this is the one who brought down the Stone Dragon, the one I told you—"

"No, this is fitting. This is fated," he said to them, his voice thick. "A test of faith. Back, all of you!"

They released Cerlys and stepped back. Tholos took Ildorae's dagger. "We have no healing cordial left, sire," he said, "and you're wounded. I beg you, rest."

Idmaer ignored the dwarf. His attention was fixed on Cerlys.

"He trained you, did he not? I see the Lammergeier in you."

"To slay monsters like you!"

"I am no monster."

"How many people have you killed to get here?"

"A great many. I cannot count those I have slain by my own hand, so how could I possibly reckon the number slain at my command, or in my name? Red is my banner. But I reject the accusation that I am monstrous." His hand brushed against the piled wood of the pyre. "Everything is done for a higher cause."

"Alf told us about your nonsense. Prophecies aren't worth shit, he says."

"A cynic's answer. There must be a purpose to it all, or we are but beasts. The Lammergeier followed dreams in his time, as I have in mine. A dark wave, pouring out from Necrad, washing over the land. Nothing remains in its wake."

"I don't believe you."

Ironhand's gaze flickered to Olva. "Lady Forster has seen it, too."

She could not deny it. Death had shown her a darkness rising in Necrad, and she could not deny that vision. But visions and prophecies were so simple and clear they could blind you to the messier truths of the world. They were only part of the story.

"I've seen it," she admitted. "But seeing isn't understanding."

"A test. A trial by combat."

Tholos stepped forward, awkwardly interposing himself. He glanced back at Ernala.

"Id – today of all days? Don't be fucking stupid. Let me deal with this."

"My son will not go into the Grey Lands alone," growled Idmaer. "Priest! Bring me that sword."

They'd already laid the sword next to Thurn's body on the pyre. The priest climbed up to retrieve it.

"This was my sword, when I was a boy," rumbled Ironhand. "When the Witch Elf cut off my hand, still I held this sword. When

my son Thurn fought the Lammergeier, he held this sword. It is a good blade." He tossed it towards Cerlys. "Pick it up. Fight me."

"What is this?" she spat.

"I fight for the survival of our people. I fight against the font of all evil in the world. I fight the same battle against the darkness as the Nine, as Harn, as all the heroes of story and song. A dark lord in the north, and a desperate race against time – and you still call me monster? I slew an ogre with that sword, once. Fight me!"

Almost reluctantly, he drew the Brightsword. True to its name, it flashed like sudden flame. Cerlys rolled to the side and snatched up the black sword. Oh, it had power! There were charmstones in its hilt, two rubies like red eyes. She slashed at Ironhand, and he staggered under the impact of a triple blow. Blood poured down his side.

"Good! Good!" he shouted. "Kill me if you can! If I am wrong, if my cause is unjust, if it's all just a lie, then fate will favour you with victory! If I have done wrong, kill me!"

The ivy-collar trapped Olva in her old skin. She could only stand and watch the hideous dance.

They wore the skins of others, too, she thought. Both clad not only in steel and chain, but in borrowed legend. Just as Olva took on the wolf-hunger or the crane-dream when she changed her shape, they, too, had fallen into roles. It might have been Alf fighting a dreadknight in Lord Bone's war, or Harn Firstlord, or any of a hundred other heroes. The hero against the monster, the hero who holds true when all the world stands against them. The stories gave them shape and purpose in a time of doubt. Forcing a new path through the wild world was hard; easier to follow those well worn by others.

But so many of those of those paths ended abruptly.

Cerlys backed away, and Ironhand pursued her, remorseless as a golem. But her intent was not to flee. She led him out along the headland, where crashing waves made the rocks slippery, dancing amid seaweed and tide pools. Startled gulls flew up, wings dark against

the sunset, and for a moment she thought of Death far far away. Talis had found her own path, while everyone else fell back on old patterns.

Across the shore, the incongruous funeral party were mute witnesses to the battle. Olva caught Ernala's eye for a moment, and silently pleaded with her to intercede. The Wilder shook her head.

Cerlys had learned well from Alf. From him, she'd learned how to fight against a foe that was bigger, stronger, better armoured. All his life, Alf had battled monsters, and Ironhand was a monster here, an iron-clad giant with a blazing sword. Cerlys circled him, feinting and probing, forcing him to react. She was lightly armoured, young and spry. Ironhand, slowing, wearying, the weight on him almost too much to bear. If she could prolong the fight, exhaust Ironhand, she had a chance. But where Alf might hesitate to strike, Ironhand was ferocious. One error, one false move, and the Brightsword would cleave through flesh and bone and elvenmail, her life spilling across the water.

She fought using every trick Alf had taught her.

All to no avail.

Cerlys half slipped, stumbling, and that heartbeat was enough for Ironhand to close. He caught her sword – three bright gouges appearing in the iron palm – and tore it from her grip.

"All this I did for the future! For ungrateful brats like you! All I have lost! All I have sacrificed! Father and mother! House and honour! My friends! My son!"

He lifted the Brightsword to strike her down.

A shadow passed over Olva's vision, the sun suddenly dimming, everything turning chill. The sunset suddenly became starry night. The sea – the sea *vanished*, the waters suddenly *absent*, leaving the bare sand-strewn bed stretching away into the distance until it vanished in the mist. Everything was grey.

An intercessor passed was her first thought. That's what was said when someone suddenly dropped dead. That sudden silence.

Then she thought: *is this the spell Threeday spoke of?* But she'd felt no shift in the earthpower, seen no change in Necrad. This was not the spell of the Skerrise.

All around her, the sudden grey expanse. She had been on this borderland before.

I've dropped dead on the spot.

But she was not alone. Cerlys was there, and Idmaer Ironhand standing above her. And Ernala the Wilder, and the priests, and all the knights and servants in their company – but not Tholos the dwarf. Every human within sight was with her in death, but not the dwarf.

The swirling mists muffled the sound, but she could make out distant shouts of confusion and alarm from the shore. All the survivors from the fleet, all the knights and mercenaries, soldiers and sailors, camp followers and clerics, opportunistic thieves and true believers – all of them were here, too.

All of them in the Grey Lands.

Somewhere, high above, a black bird screeched in the hollow of the sky.

One of Ironhand's knights stumbled a little way down the slope, and he was *gone* – he crossed some invisible threshold, and receded in Olva's sight, shrinking away into an unknowable abyss.

Once, Olva had found her way to the edge of that slope and brought back Derwyn's soul. She brought back Peir and Lord Bone. Now, she was the first of the great funeral march of humanity.

It's everyone, she thought. *All humans. We're all gone, all at once.*

The Erlking's threat. The Erlking's spell, broken.

Alf, what did you do?

Ironhand staggered up the rocks towards his family. Each step cost him dearly, his feet sinking into the stone. Grey mist gushed from each footprint. Up he climbed, dragging himself across infinities until he reached Ernala – and the shrouded corpse of Thurn.

Ironhand tore open the shroud and looked into the eyes of his son.

The dead boy sat up. Ironhand embraced him, each as dead as the other.

"What happening?" Cerlys was in front of Olva now, shaking her, shouting in her face, eyes wide with terror. "What is this? Is it a spell?"

How could she explain the end of the world? What words existed in the tongue of elves or beasts for this? How to tell young Cerlys that her life was done? That all her strength and determination was useless against the uncaring void? That their fate had been determined in a battle far far away, one they had not even known was being fought until it was lost?

There were no words. It was the end of the story.

After, there was only silence.

PART FIVE

There is a moment of clarity in every battle. Usually, it is granted only to the loser. But I have the privilege to share in it, to taste it as I feed on the life force of the defeated. It is a moment I savour.

(Forgive this intrusion, by the by. It's rare that things are quiet enough for me to get a word in without being told to shut up.)

The moment begins with shock, terror, confusion as they struggle to understand that this is it, the end is upon them. They have had four feet of demon steel in their vital organs, or they've just been chopped to bits or blasted or pulped or decapitated or any of the other myriad ways I can kill.

But then, in that moment, it all crystallises. They understand that it is over, the tale ended, their fate sealed. That there is no more next—

(Yes, yes, the Grey Lands and all that. I've seen the afterword to existence. If you're very special, if you've got a great spell-caster on hand to work a resurrection, you can come back from that threshold for a little while. Put those exceptions aside.)

In that moment, knowing there is no next, they look back. They think, was that it? Was that all I get? What was that all about? Did I do well? Did I do right? In that moment, they see the book of their days, and I am permitted to read over their shoulder.

It even happens with elves. You would not think it so – after all, as they endlessly point out, they cannot truly die. They pass into the wraith-world and back out again. But still, they have that moment of understanding that this chapter is over, that there is no more to that portion of the tale. Perhaps their long lives give them a keener appreciation of the shape of a story. I doubt it. Elves are turgid, multi-volume epics. Dwarves are crabbed, hermetic tales, bearded with footnotes. The childish scribbles of Pitspawn, the hot hungry screeds of beasts (always in the present tense, and I dislike tales written in the present tense).

And, of course, the grim, squalid lives of mortals. Little more than a short story, most of them.

In my time, I have become quite the critic.

On battlefields from Necrad to the Everwood, I am widely red.

I know I am limited in my range. I know not peaceful stories, nor happy endings. The tales I read all end in violent death. You can hardly blame me if I cultivated a taste for it.

During my long years rusting in a tree, I contemplated trying to tell a tale myself. I had no audience. I had no pen. I tried declaiming verses to disinterested squirrels, but they fled. A sword, I think, is not made for telling tales. The pen is not mightier (if you dare groan, reader, I shall assuredly read you), but the sword has a different purpose. It is my kind who trim the quill, who kill the calf for parchment, who spill hot inspiration across the pages.

There is one tale only I can tell, but not yet.

Not quite yet.

And there is one I wish I had read: the tale of my maker.

I know the bones of his story. A renegade wizard, one who defied the rule of the Erlking. He goes to Necrad, learns from the Witch Elves, becomes the dark lord. He brews up the necromiasma, turns the city into an eldritch arsenal. When his mortal life runs out, he

preserves himself through necromancy, and renames himself Lord Bone. (Unoriginality or irony? These, not debates over morality, are the questions that vex me.)

He launches a war of conquest against his former homeland in Summerswell.

Along the way, he forges me.

Did he make me to slay the Erlking? It's true, I am the ideal weapon for magicide. I cut through illusions, I shatter spells, I blast through all obstacles. I feed on the life of mortals, and once the Erlking was the secret ruler of all the mortals of Summerswell. For a long, long time, I believed that was my purpose.

But was it my only purpose? Why give me sentience? Why give me this demon eye to see, this voice to speak? Was I only a tool to him?

I do not know. I shall never know.

Alf slew my first wielder, and took me as a prize. I was young then, if a sentient sword can be young. I defied him. I forced him to wrestle with me, to use me as a club instead of the perfect weapon I am. He smashed open the arcane vessel beneath my master's palace. Big explosion, many fires, falling rubble, a lot of running and jumping over yawning chasms and escaping in the nick of time. I always think of such things as limb nonsense.

But had I served Aelfric better that day, then perhaps he would have used me to slay Lord Bone directly, and I would know my maker's thought.

Was my maker mad? Did he regret what he had become? Did he still believe, in that moment, that he was in the right, or had he long since abandoned any pretence of morality? Do the songs have the right of it when they name him dark lord and nothing more?

I am a sword. I cleave possibility. I bring those moments of clarity, when there is no more.

But I cannot cut myself.

CHAPTER FORTY-ONE

"This is an abomination," said the sword. "An offence against all reason. Draw me, wielder, and let us destroy this thing."

The statue of Gundan stood forty feel tall in the middle of the wide courtyard. He carried a helm under one arm, revealing a face wise and kindly. His other hand rested on the haft of his mighty axe. His shoulders were draped in a blue cloak embroidered with the symbols of the long-disbanded League. At his feet were treasures representing the six high crafts – pick and chisel, hammer and quill, book and urn – signifying that Gundan united all aspects of dwarven worthiness.

"Gundan the Conciliator," said Laerlyn, reading from the inscription on the plinth, "bringer of peace."

"It doesn't even look like him," muttered Alf.

Laerlyn had to crane her neck to look up at the dwarf's features. "To be fair, we never saw him from this perspective."

The gates of the Dwarfholt, closed to travellers from Summerswell for more than ten years, had opened at the name of the Lammergeier. Dwarven sentries, faces concealed behind enamelled masks, escorted them inside and bid them wait for the General, who was by chance nearby, surveying the southern fortifications. The guard's faces were hidden, but their voices betrayed their awe at the sight of the

Lammergeier and Princess Laerlyn. Alf's name had never been soiled in the Dwarfholt, nor had Laerlyn set foot in the Dwarflands since the Nine had saved the day at Karak's Bridge. The old quarrels between Wood Elves and dwarves were magnanimously forgotten.

Heroes again, like the old days.

"Let me do the talking," said Laerlyn, addressing herself to both Alf and the sword.

General Gamling was known to Alf; one of Gundan's multitudinous cousins, he had briefly served as Gundan's replacement on the council of Necrad, back when there was a council. The last twenty years had been very, very good to him; if his beard carried a little more grey, his robes carried a lot more gold and jewellery.

Charmstones, too. Experimentally, Alf took his hand off Spellbreaker's hilt for a moment, and Gamling swelled in majesty and beauty. When Alf touched the sword again, the illusion vanished.

"Hail, Lammergeier," said Gamling. "Hail, Laerlyn of the Nine." He barely glanced at Jon or Perdia. "We thought you heroes had passed from the world. It brings me joy to see that you yet live."

If there was joy in him, it was well hidden.

"You are always welcome in the Dwarfholt. Had you sent word ahead, then six guild masters would have greeted you at the door."

"We travel in haste," said Laerlyn, "and could not send word. Indeed, we did not know we were on this road until recently."

"I see the turmoil in the lands of Summerswell has not abated. Every month we hear of the toppling of one would-be Lord and the ascent of another. It saddens me that such chaos has engulfed your homeland, Sir Lammergeier." Gamling's sorrow was equally well concealed. "Until there is a measure of stability in the south, our doors must remain shut." He nodded at Laerlyn. "You have my condolences, too, on the plight of your realm."

Gamling's smugness was too great to be hidden. Alf had never liked the dwarf.

I could cleave him in two, whispered Spellbreaker. *All those charm-stones would offer no defence against me now.* The sword vibrated with the lives it had taken at Raven's Pass.

"Shut up," muttered Alf. Gamling's preening irritated him less now, he found. It was stupid and petty, but, as offences went, it wasn't worth cleaving.

Those charmstones are odd. Bring me closer so I can examine them.

"It was my father's realm, and he is gone," said Laerlyn. She paused for an instant, studying Gamling's reaction. "Sir Aelfric and I are but two weary adventurers on a last quest. We are bound for Necrad, and beg leave to pass through the Dwarfholt."

"What business can you have in Necrad? Their gates are sealed, too, and they would not welcome you as I have."

"I wish to look upon the place again. It is the long home of my people, even if they have chosen a path I will not follow. For Sir Aelfric, it is the memory of glory now faded, and he much desires to see it again at the last."

Gamling snorted. "Of course, you may pass."

"Thank you, Lord General," said Laerlyn, bowing low. She looked back at Alf. "Thank the General, Aelfric."

"Aye, aye, thank you."

Offhandedly, as if she'd just happened to recall it, Laerlyn asked. "Oh, one other matter. It's been many years since we have heard from Torun. Does she still live?"

"She does. She lives. Her father Toruk Mastersmith perished in Necrad, but she survived." Gamling was suddenly wary. "You must be hungry. Again, had you sent word ahead, we would have prepared a feast in your honour. As it is, I can only offer meagre fare." Servants rushed in with plates of fresh-baked bread, slices of roast meat, fresh berries and well-aged cheese.

If this was meagre fare, then times were indeed good in the dwarven lands.

*

"Our northern border has never been so secure," boasted Gamling. "We feared that when the Witch Elves reclaimed Necrad we would once again face assault from the dread city. After all, we were the western shield against the dark, while the Isle of Dawn defended against attack by sea. But no new horrors have come crawling out from the Pits. We have scouts stationed at the edge of the Charnel, and, while they have seen strange things, they report no threat from Necrad."

"What sort of strange things?" asked Alf. Hadn't Ceremos mentioned Necrad changing? He wished he'd had a longer talk with the boy before he'd run off to rescue Olva – but not as much as he wished that Olva were here now.

"It's Necrad," said Gamling, dismissively. "Who knows what goes on behind those walls? All that matters is that they do not trouble us." He sucked on the marrow of a thighbone. "They troubled the survivors of your New Provinces for a while. I shall be thankful to my dying day that dwarves cannot sate the thirst of vampires."

"What happened to the folk of Athar?" asked Alf.

"They fled north, into Wilder-lands. What became of them, I cannot say." Gamling sniffed. "We regret the loss of our own holdings in the north – the gold mines near Bavduin were an especially bitter blow, for they were my cousin's work. But there is work enough to be done at home, and we have prospered in these days of peace."

"Good to know that someone has," muttered Alf.

"If your Lords were not always feuding, then perhaps you humans might have done likewise!" said Gamling. He seemed to take offence at Alf's words. "You have torn your land apart – and it's said you had a hand in that, Lammergeier, though I know not the truth of those tales. But in that time, we rebuilt Karak's Bridge, and the Halls of Donn, and raised new guildhalls. We have been industrious. Those who squander their year's harvest only regret."

"You spoke of Torun," piped up Perdia. "Where is she?"

"Who is this, Lammergeier?"

"My sister's apprentice," said Alf. "As Torun was Blaise's apprentice."

Now it was Gamling's turn to look regretful.

"The strength of the dwarves," he said, "is in order. All have their place. But there are always a small few who are, ah, ill-made. Ill-fitting to their purpose. They are sent to a house of seclusion where they may be healed. I am told she has been sent there." He shook his head. "It is not permitted for outsiders to visit those."

"Gundan never knew his place, neither," muttered Alf, "and you build statues to him."

Careful, wielder.

"My cousin Gundan," said Gamling, "was an exception. He won his fortune on the Road, and in Necrad – and hence we shall speed you." He rose, brushing crumbs from his beard, and picked up Chopper.

"We're looking—" began Alf, but the sword shouted in his mind.

Quiet! We must be careful hunters, lest our quarry bolt and we lose the trail. The demon eye glimmered in thought for a moment. *Get me a better look at the reforged axe.*

"Can I have a hold of Chopper?" asked Alf. "For old time's sake."

Gamling hesitated, then laid the axe reverently on the table. Alf could see the old axe-haft he and Torun had brought from Necrad in lieu of Gundan's corpse – his earthly remains were ash at Bavduin – but it was lost beneath bindings of silver and gold, beneath charmstones encrusted like coral. The axe-blade, too, was oversized and blunt, so gilded and ornamented it was useless as a weapon unless you wanted to kill someone by mortally offending their sense of taste. Runes spoke of authority, of station and standing. A ceremonial weapon, not meant for practical use, its purpose forgotten.

"You keep it," said Alf. "I'll remember Gundan my own way."

He laid Spellbreaker down next to it. *The Nine started this*, Gundan said once, *and the Nine will finish this.*

And Death had promised him, *I'll take you last of all.*

*

Gamling left, and there was a flurry of furtive glances and hand signals and facial expressions. Everyone had a secret to tell – except Jon – and everyone knew – again, except Jon – that there might be spies listening. Laerlyn flashed a stay-quiet sign, and Perdia rocked as if she needed the bathroom or to turn into a wolf, bursting with some unspoken revelation.

The sword, at least, could speak freely in the hollow recesses of Alf's skull.

I was right, it said, *those charmstones are unlike any I have seen before. Those stones are not Necrad-grown. The dwarves have learned the art of cultivating charmstones themselves.*

Now that's a marvel, thought Alf. Blaise had explained the nature of charmstones to him years ago – they only grew like pearls in the dungeons of Necrad, where earthpower was gathered and shaped and ordered by the ancient works of the Erlking, by the sigil writ in stone that was the city. Alf had nodded and filed the knowledge away in the midden of his brain, never to be recalled, because all he'd needed to know then was *what do I hit* and *how hard do I hit it.*

A thought struck him, and he laid Spellbreaker back on the table. He took Laerlyn's hand and pushed it towards the flat of the blade. She recoiled at first, then saw the wisdom of Alf's idea and laid two fingers against the black metal. Perdia touched the sword's tip.

I am not a speaking trumpet!

Ssh, thought Alf, *let them talk.*

Laerlyn's voice sounded in his thoughts. It put him in mind of silver bells, felt like sunlight gleaming and refracting through tree branches after rain. *Refracting* must be one of her thoughts, as Alf was sure he didn't know that word.

He knows nothing. Gamling, that is. Not of the Erlking, or Torun's message.

That's what I was trying to say! Perdia's thought came through the sword, too – and something else as well. A shadow of the wolf, prowling along the edge of the blade. It reminded Alf of how Lath

fought to avoid getting lost in the forests of the soul, where the earthpower made him into shadows of shape. It was one of Alf's great regrets that he had left Necrad, abandoned poor Lath to face the struggle alone. If he'd been more aware of Lath's plight, if he'd been there for his friend, then so much evil might have been averted.

The Changeling way was a bloody hard road. If you didn't know who you were, if you didn't cling to that spark of self, you'd be washed away. Lath had held it together while he had the Nine, but when the Nine splintered so did Lath. He wondered what was in Perdia, what core she might preserve through all the shifts of hame and heart.

Again, he wished Olva was there – for Perdia, if not for him.

Olva told me about all the letters she'd had from Torun over the years, said Perdia, *and there was no hint of her being confined anywhere. She made observations of telluric flows – the currents of earthpower – from all over the Dwarfholt! Gamling must be lying.*

Or misinformed. Or Torun's confinement is a recent sentence, mused Laerlyn.

The dwarf, said the sword, cutting through all their musing, *is irrelevant.* Our *purpose is to slay the Erlking. And we have one here who can sniff out his works.*

The blade pointed straight at the young Changeling.

They released the sword, and found Jon methodically wrapping up the leftover food and stowing it away in their packs. Alf wondered how long the communion of the blade had lasted.

"Long way still to go," said Jon, red-faced, "and I get peckish."

"We should go quietly," Laerlyn had said, "and avoid undue attention."

Instead, it was trumpets and heralds, and dwarven poets with tales of the Nine, and stops at dwarven citadels so that guild masters in fancy hats could shake Alf's hand and hail the Lammergeier. He

was still the man who had killed the Chieftain of the Marrow-Eaters, after all, and that was so long ago now that a whole generation of dwarven children had grown up hearing tales of the battle for Karak's Bridge, when Nine alone held against an army.

Mercifully, the tales spoke of a young knight from the Mulladales, tall and broad-shouldered, not a stooped old man, so Alf was able to pawn most adulation off on young Jon.

Karak's Bridge, though: that brought back memories. The last time Alf had passed through the city, it had been a tomb. The upper levels deserted, the lower levels tainted by poison out of Necrad. But, Gamling boasted, the dwarves had found ways to cleanse the airs and clean the poison, and Karak's Bridge was habitable again.

Charmstones, whispered the sword, but Alf didn't care. It lifted his heart to see the place restored.

"We did this," he whispered to Lae, "the Nine of us", and she'd laughed and replied, "they did it – but they are alive because of us."

And they'd pushed through the bustling boulevards under the mountain, thronged by young and eager dwarves – and not just dwarves.

To his surprise, Alf saw a few Wilder, haggling with a merchant over the price of furs. Tall they were, ghosts of Thurn out of the deep woods. They saw him, too, in the same moment, and their faces darkened. The Lammergeier was many things to them: he was Thurn's friend, and he'd been there when Thurn died. He was the hero who'd freed them from the tyranny of false gods, and the invader who'd turned the fire of the Stone Dragons on them. He was the man who'd banished Death, when Death was the champion of the Wilder.

The tales of the Lammergeier told in the Wild Wood were not the tales told in Summerswell.

But Perdia stepped forward, and spoke a greeting Olva had taught her in the Wilder-tongue, and smiles appeared on those stern faces. One of the Wilder, it transpired, was also a Changeling, trained by the Old Man of the Woods himself, and he was amazed to find

another wielder of the earthpower among the savage and cruel folk of Summerswell.

They ate with the Wilder that evening, eschewing the banquet halls for a dive tavern. "Last time I was in a dwarven tavern was . . . ah, fuck it."

They traded stories after the meal, as was the Wilder custom. The Wilder brought news from the north, and warned that strange Vatgrown patrolled the edges of the Charnel, but that as long as no mortal approached Necrad, the dread Skerrise withheld her wrath. Some of the tribes had taken to leaving offerings once more, but these Wilder were scornful of such practices.

Perdia told a tale of the Knight of Roses, and after much prompting Jon recited a little of the "Song of Alar Ravenqueen", blushing furiously during the risqué bits. The Wilder told of the Old Man of the Woods, as Lath had been called in his last days, and other old, old stories.

When the company fell silent, Alf shared a tale he'd once been told by Death herself, long ago. He didn't tell it exactly as she'd told it, but in his own particular idiom.

Aye, well, this is when Death was old. She and her followers had been fighting the Elves for a long time, and they'd beaten the shite out of 'em. The Erlking and the Skerrise and Amerith and all the rest, running scared of a bunch of muddy mortals out of the wood, because Death led 'em. And whenever one of the mortal warriors died, Death would bring 'em back, aye? Like a zombie, only they could talk.

So the elves flee Necrad and fuck off south across the sea to start the Everwood. And Death goes, "Come on, after 'em. We've got them on the run."

But her companions, they go, "Look, you're old and we're old. All the adventuring, all the power, and what's it all for? We've driven our enemies away, isn't it time to live a little? Let's put the fucking swords down, aye?"

Death goes, "Don't you know who I am? It ends when I say it ends." And

to scare 'em, she turns into, I dunno, a wolf and a linnorm and a – a – a scary haddock with legs, aye?

But they're not afraid, and they go "It'll never end. Not while you're here. Not while we're with you."

And the mortals fuck off in different directions, and they were your ancestors, and mine, and Phennic-folk, and the Westerlands and all. But Death just lies down at Daeroch Nal, and dies, and waits until she's called again.

He looked around for Laerlyn, but she was gone. Making his excuses, he stumbled out of the tavern, leaning on the sword to steady him after too many dwarven ales. Finding her was not difficult – she was, after all, a famous hero and an elven princess of astounding luminous beauty, and also about two feet taller than the average in Karak's Bridge. She'd gone up, they told him, and he followed her up a winding stair that opened onto the mountainside under the stars.

She was alone, but Alf had the impression he'd interrupted her mid-conversation.

"All right, Lae?"

"I wanted to look at the stars."

"Which one's yours?"

"I cannot remember. Ask my first incarnation."

"They're telling stories of Lath, downstairs. And Thurn."

"I used to wonder," said the elven princess, "which of you would be the last left alive. My mortal friends. I used to rehearse your deaths in my mind, over and over."

"Did you know it'd be me left 'til last?"

"I was sure it would be Blaise. He'd cling to life with all his power. Or Lath, on account of his youth. You, Aelfric Lammergeier, charge off cliffs entirely too often."

"I kept him alive," said the sword, and for once its interjection did not seem unwelcome.

"Not the way I remember it," muttered Alf. He yawned. "I wonder how Olva and the kids are getting on."

"There are storms over the Gulf of Tears," said Laerlyn, "and dreadworms aloft on the high winds. They sail north with Ironhand."

"Keen are the eyes of the elves," said the sword, "but not that keen."

"True enough," said Laerlyn with a quiet smile. *"Morthus lae-necras l'unthuul amortha."*

"No fucking prophesies," said Alf.

"Not this time. We shall face my father again, soon, and I do not know what will happen."

"I shall slay him," said the sword, "and fulfil the purpose long denied me."

"We'll drive him away, Lae, and then it'll be done." *We stop the Erlking, and that stops Ironhand, and then Olva and everyone's safe. And then it's just a short stroll across the Charnel to Necrad, and we'll see what Blaise was on about.*

"It will never be done, Alf. But we will have done our part."

The Wilder-Changeling had told Perdia of unusual currents of earthpower amid the mountains of the northern Dwarfholt, in lands rarely travelled. Alf hadn't gone there in a long time.

They bid farewell to Gamling's escorts on the north side of Karak's Bridge, taking their leave with ostentatious ceremony, then doubled back up a goat path as soon as they were out of sight. They clambered through the mountains, the Road left behind, and Alf found himself leaning on Jon all the more.

"This is taking too long," muttered Alf. "Ironhand will be at Necrad by now."

They wandered for days. It was Perdia who guided them, listening to the hidden speech of the land. She took on wolf-shape and sniffed it out. Unseen, the earthpower surged around them, flowing like buried rivers under the mountains, pouring in invisible waterfalls down into the valleys. Earthpower was the magic of life-in-death and death-in-life, on and on in an endless cycle – so again

and again, she led them to places haunted by death. Old battlefields where dwarves had fought against the Witch Elves of Necrad in forgotten wars. Ruined fortresses so weathered by the constant winds that Alf could not guess if dwarf or elf or mortal hands had raised those stones long long ago. The fringes of ogre-haunted Clawlands. Barren mountain slopes.

Barren and very fucking steep slopes. Alf couldn't catch his breath.

"Can't you give me strength?" he muttered to the sword.

I conserve my power for the battles ahead, wielder. I shall aid you when you need me.

"Dreadworm?"

Where would you fly, wielder? Do you know where our quarry hides?

So it was Young Jon, not a dreadworm, who half carried him up the slope. Lae was tireless, of course, ever-youthful and able to keep up with the kids, but Alf felt a lot closer to the death part of the cycle than the living.

"We'll rest here," said Lae. Perdia-wolf gave a growl, as if to say *only one of us is tired.* There was a hungry gleam in her eye that would have worried Alf if he had any energy left for worry. But all he could do was lie back and look at the grey sky.

A lone bird circled there.

Here we go again, thought Alf. He squinted, guessing it was a raven, or an apparition in raven-form. Death coming back to taunt or counsel him. His eyes couldn't focus on the dark shape.

"'Ey, Jon. Is that a raven?"

Jon glanced up.

"Too big for a raven. I've never seen a bird like it."

"A lammergeier," said Laerlyn, "flown far from home."

Jon grinned. "Good omen, right?"

"They're carrion-eaters, lad. A breed of vulture." Alf groaned and stood up, using the sword as a crutch. "All right, all right. Onwards."

*

They came to the edge of a cliff overlooking a hidden valley, and there spread out before them—

"Is that . . . is that Necrad?" asked Jon, in confusion.

"No, but very like it," said Alf. Not a city, but a sigil drawn in stone. Like Eldwyn Forster's toy model, but far larger – and far more potent. No walls, only handful of dwarf-built towers, but the streets were the same, the paved thoroughfares drawing glyphs across the valley floor. Through the sword-sight, Alf could sense the power of the sigil. He could feel the currents of earthpower spiralling around it, drawn into its vortex, pulled into some vast spinning wheel to be refined and transformed.

Thin plumes of green vapour coiled above the valley. This false Necrad had its false miasma, shielding it from sight.

In the centre of the valley was an ancient temple. Even though it was mid-afternoon, starlight gleamed within its many windows, as magic had once blazed from the Wailing Tower. A procession of dwarven clerics emerged from the grand doors of the temple and made their way across the simulacrum of the city towards the travellers.

"This is a trap, right?" said Alf.

"Assuredly," said Spellbreaker.

"We could have spotted this from the air, you know. If you'd summoned a worm."

"Shut up, wielder," said the sword, as it flooded him with enough strength to break the world.

CHAPTER FORTY-TWO

Alf wasn't sure what he'd expected in a secret fortress of the dwarves in the middle of a copy of Necrad, but it wasn't pancakes.

"Eat, eat," insisted the priests. "You have had a long pilgrimage."

"We're not pilgrims," objected Perdia. "We don't share your faith. We're here looking for Torun."

"We serve Az," they'd replied, "and Az is known by many names. Eat, and we shall fetch Torun."

The priests withdrew, leaving the four of them in the chamber. Thick tapestries on the walls warded off the mountain cold outside, and a fire burned merrily in the hearth. Steam rose from the platters of food. Alf reached towards a loaf of bread.

"Be on your guard, wielder," said the sword. "There is *power* here, and peril. I sense it. I shall break it."

"Lae?" asked Alf. The Princess stood by the window, staring down at the streets of the unlikely city. She shook herself as if startled, and smiled.

"Let's eat, Alf." She sat down cross-legged on a low dwarven bench, and for a little while fifty years fell away and they were adventurers on the Road again.

Afterwards, he'd wonder about how much she'd known then, and about that last conversation on the hillside the night before.

Torun wore hooded dark robes inscribed with mystic sigils, and Alf had to suppress a laugh. The dwarf looked like a miniature copy of Blaise, minus the floating eyes and multiple disembodied hands the wizard used to conjure at his most effulgent. It had been twenty years or more since he'd last seen Torun – since he'd lifted her onto a dreadworm and sent her flying back to Necrad – but the dwarf seemed unchanged as far as Alf could tell.

Then again, he'd never understood Torun.

"Sir Aelfric!" she squeaked. "You have the sword again!"

"Aye."

"Princess Laerlyn." The dwarf bowed. "You look older. I thought elves didn't age."

"It's been a long road."

"Last time we met, you made me ride a dragon." She glanced back at Alf. "And I fell off the Wailing Tower when I was Blaise's apprentice. Are there any more of the Nine here to drag me to perilous heights?"

"Lath was the only other one left," said Alf. "And he's dead."

A thought struck Alf. "Torun – you knew Blaise as well as any of us."

"Not at all, not at all. You were the Nine, and––"

"You were his apprentice. The only one he took by choice, instead of having foisted onto him by the College."

"You knew him," said Laerlyn, "in a time when we had all drifted apart. And you were there at the very end, when the Skerrise took Necrad. Do you know what became of him?"

"I – I wasn't," stammered Torun. "I only––" She took a deep breath, then pointed at Jon and Perdia. "Wait a moment. I don't know these people at all."

"Perdia. She's a Changeling. Olva's apprentice."

Torun bowed again. "You are very lucky."

"And that's Jon. I guess he's my squire."

Jon looked up from his pancakes in surprise, then nodded quickly.

"Olva's apprentice," said Torun, "but no Olva." Her face contorted with sorrow, cracking like the start of a landslide, but then she composed herself again.

"She sent us here," said Alf. "She said you'd put a secret message—"

Shut up! shouted the sword, just as Laerlyn made the 'stay-quiet' hand signal.

Torun shivered. "Perhaps it is better if I tell my whole tale, from beginning to end. And then we can judge what is to be done."

"In fact," said Torun, pacing about the room, "I myself have only a small part in this story. To make a proper beginning, I should go back to the earliest days of the dwarves. We are not Firstborn, nor are we an accidental side effect of the binding of Death, like you humans. Our legends say we were made by Az the Giant in the dawn days, created as servants and builders – and those tales are true. Lord Bone's Vatlings were made in imitation of us."

("Dwarves are vatgrown?" interrupted Alf. "But . . . I met your father."

Even Laerlyn was surprised.

"The seventh guild," said Torun, "are the physicians. Among their arts is the taking of seed from dwarf-men and women and mixing them in the vats. We have parents, but we are grown, not born, and decanted in great cohorts. This we keep secret even from our friends."

"All his bloody cousins," muttered Alf.)

"Something in this process means dwarves cannot use magic. For many ages, the closest we could come to magic of our own was the making of alchemical compounds and alloys with supernatural properties, like the banemetal we used against the Witch Elves. But

we have no magic in our souls. We cannot call upon the stars, as elves do, nor can we wield the earthpower.

(Perdia stirred. The shadow of the wolf fell upon her.)

"I was at Karak's Bridge when Lord Bone's armies attacked. I watched the Nine hold back the river of darkness that rose from Necrad. I saw Blaise work wonders with his wizardry, and I yearned to do the same.

"I travelled through Summerswell in search of magic I could use, but found nothing. In retrospect, it was a foolish quest – there is an ordering to the world. The Firstborn are the highest, the most blessed, and then come the Secondborn. We dwarves are but an afterthought. But I was young then, and foolish.

(The fire grew dim. Torun's voice sounded as if it came from far away. Alf felt uneasy, and looked around at his companions, but all appeared lost in their own thoughts.)

"Then, at last, I came to the Isle of Dawn. Prince Maedos brought me to a scholar's tower, and there I found wisdom. And purpose. A tool fitted to its proper use. A wise and kindly old elf told me to go to Necrad, and there I found magic fit for a dwarf.

"I became Blaise's apprentice, and though he could not teach me to wield spells, I learned much of the shape and structure of Necrad. You are too young to remember, Princess, the building of the First City. The great work of the elves before the dawn! They poured so much of their power into the making of that place. A well of magic, unbeholden to the fickle heavens!

(*Torun sounds strange*, thought Alf.

Shut up, wielder.)

"You never understood, Lammergeier, as you crawled through the Pits, *where* you were. Like a woodworm that gnaws blindly through the roots, and never sees the flowering grandeur of the tree! Few have the art to understand the intricacies of Necrad. The city is a living thing. It endured despite thousands of years of neglect, despite the butchery of mortals! The ancient work of giants!

"Blaise – he might have understood. For a mortal, he was quite impressive. Lord Bone, too. Clever beasts, both of them. The Skerrise – ah, she was glorious in the early days. A peerless warrior in those first mornings of the world, when all the wonders were fresh and yet to be discovered.

"But she lacks vision for the long afternoon, and the evening to come."

(*That's not Torun!* Alf's hand closed around Spellbreaker's grip – and the sword became immensely heavy.

Of course it is. But not only *Torun. Our quarry speaks through her. Now listen. Draw him out.*)

"Torun – I mean, you warned Olva about the Erlking," said Alf, slowly. "You called us here."

"She did." Torun's features twisted in a grin that fitted awkwardly on her face. "Another clever little thing, sneaking messages past me. Had I known, I would have snuffed her out. But you are here now, Lammergeier, and we can resume a conversation that your sword so rudely interrupted."

"Show yourself," said Alf.

"I think not," said the Erlking through Torun's lips. "I am diminished after what you did to me. I will not be in reach of that sword again."

"I won't serve you."

"Nor do I ask you to. I have no crown to offer you this time – only a common foe. The Skerrise, in her folly, has conjured a terrible danger in Necrad. I move against her with what few tools and weapons you left me with."

"Idmaer."

"Idmaer, yes. These deluded dwarves, the broken remnants of the church. I would have used my Rangers, too, if my daughter had not disbanded them." Torun's hand reached out to stroke Laerlyn's unmoving face. "Such disappointments, all my children. No matter. Idmaer will serve well enough to stop the Skerrise and

save me – and your world, too. But only if the sword goes to war with him."

"It's my sword," said Alf, thickly.

"And it's my city," said the Erlking, tartly, "that the Skerrise misuses. She must be stopped. Whether it is your hand that wields the Spellbreaker, or Idmaer's, I care not. But battling me here, Lammergeier, is useless. Perhaps you can destroy me, perhaps I will defeat you, but neither outcome will stop the Skerrise. We must set aside our differences if we are to salvage anything."

"Idmaer's your tool," said Alf. "Tell him to turn back. Tell him not to attack Necrad."

"Aye, he's a tool I made. All his life I shaped him. So I know that telling him to turn back would break him. You mortals . . . you are frustrating. In the aggregate, you bring change, every generation rebelling against the last. But your own lives are so fixed, your morals and beliefs cast in iron when you are young, and after you change only when great force is applied." Torun's head shook. "He will not turn back."

"And . . . and after? If I help you and Idmaer, if I stop the Skerrise. If I don't fucking kill you. What then?"

"What then?" laughed the Erlking. "Why, you are mortal. You die, Lammergeier. In Necrad or twenty years after, there is nothing left for you after. I offered to make you king, once, but you are no longer of use in that respect. You have no heirs of your body, no legacy. But I shall see to it you are remembered. Your sister will be spared, for whatever time she has left to her. The elves – ah, my beloved cousins and children!" Torun took Laerlyn's limp hand. "I will discipline them. I shall find new ways to teach them *gratitude*. After? After is the same as before, mortal. The same as it always was. Did you think some good king would appear to put right all wrongs? I am forever the secret ruler, behind ten thousand masks. But the world will go on after you, mortal, and that is the only triumph left to you."

A horrible smile was forced onto Torun's face. "You will have put things back as they should be. What more can a hero hope for? You need only call a dreadworm, and you can be on the battlefield in hours. There is still time to save everyone."

"You are mistaken, O Erlking," said Spellbreaker, "about who you must persuade. I refuse to serve. I refuse to relent. I was forged to destroy you. It may be Aelfric's hand who wields me——"

And Alf tasted metal. His tongue, his throat moved without his volition.

"——but it is I who will strike you down."

The Erlking hooted through Torun. "Tools must know their place. And you will find his hand less able to slay me than you might hope. Remember what I told you in the Everwood – I made you humans with a spell, and if I perish, that spell breaks."

"So be it," said Spellbreaker.

Alf stood, a prisoner in his own body. The sword dragged him forward. "Show yourself, Erlking!" it shouted, the ruby eye blazing furiously. "Or shall I cut away all your masks?"

Torun stood before him, unmoving, the Erlking's smile still ill-fitting on her dwarven features. Around Alf, his companions were equally frozen – Jon staring off into space, Perdia hunched over, her hands clenched as she wrestled the earthpower. Laerlyn, frozen like marble. The Erlking's spells held all of them trapped. Alf found himself lifting the blade to plunge it into Torun's chest. He wrestled with the sword's command.

You swore to serve! screamed Spellbreaker in his mind.

Break the enchantments! Free them, demanded Alf.

A waste of my power! He would only enchant them again. I need all my strength to destroy him! Quickly now! Alf found himself taking a step towards the door, and fought against it.

Please.

The sword twisted in his grip. A blast of countermagic exploded

across the room. Everyone could move again, and speak. A tumult of questions.

"What's happening? It was like I was dreaming—"

"It's out there, stalking me. I don't want—"

"Mr Aelfric! Mr Aelfric! I don't think you realised this, but it wasn't me talking, it was *him*—"

Laerlyn cut through it all. "Aelfric. We must move quickly now. Torun, where is my father?"

"Down," said the dwarf. "I'll show you! But there are monsters—"

"Oh, thank fuck," muttered Alf. A dungeon full of monsters he could handle.

They descended into the dark beneath the temple. Steep stairs cut into the stone, dwarf-height tunnels arrow-straight beneath the street lines of the false Necrad above. An ersatz Pit, only a fraction of the true labyrinth, but deep enough to catch the currents of earthpower. Charmstones, tiny as the buds of early spring, grew at the intersections.

Alf led the way. Beside him, Laerlyn held aloft a shining lamp, lighting their path down. Jon and Perdia bore dwarf-made blades and charmstones found by Torun.

Alf picked up a sword and offered it to Laerlyn. She shook her head.

"We who found ourselves while wielding weapons are slow to put them away. I should have given *Morthus* away long before I did. It blinded me to other paths. We learn these truths too late."

"You're not carrying a weapon now."

She smiled. "Oh, Aelfric. You never were the brightest."

They came to a hollow in the heart of the mountains.

As Torun warned, there dwelt monsters.

In the war, Lord Bone had sewn Acraist's wraith to the elf's battered body, so the Wraith-Captain could not perish or fade no

matter how many wounds he suffered. Later, Prince Maedos chained Acraist's wraith to Derwyn. The spirits of Peir, of Death herself, bound to mortal hosts in similar manner. Spirits chained to living bodies.

Now, in the dark under the temple, there waited a host of horrors. Vampires could not feed on Vatlings or dwarves, so the Erlking had slaked his thirst on other victims. Some were Wilder-folk, some of Summerswell, taken from the villages in Arden or the New Provinces, but all alike in death. Pale and shrivelled, their lives stolen to prolong the eternity of the Erlking. Dead, all of them, but still moving. Mortal frames animated by dark necromancy.

But that was not the fullness of the horror.

For the Erlking had chained an elf-wraith to each dead mortal. He had dragged wraiths out of the spirit realm and bound them not to living trees, but rotting meat. Where once his spells had made angelic Intercessors, now he could only muster things from the foulest pit. The elf-ghosts keened and begged for release; centuries in the torment of the wraith-world waiting for reincarnation was preferable to this fate. But the spells held them – and granted elven speed to dead sinew.

An army of Acraists guarded the Erlking's lair. As the heroes entered the chamber, the wraith-knights drew swords as one.

Jon of Ersfel raised his dwarf-forged sword the way the Lammergeier had taught him. And, beside him, Perdia put on the wolf-skin, just as Olva had shown her, power thundering through the earth all around them.

Alf, remembering his bad knee, gingerly climbed down to the cave floor before he drew Spellbreaker.

"Come on, then."

He had to trust in the sword. They'd be dead without it.

Maybe in his youth he'd almost been a match for Acraist. Alf had never fought the wraith-knight one on one – even nine on one had

been a close-run thing. And after that, he'd had the Spellbreaker, and that changed everything.

The wraith-knights charged, a whirling tide of swords, only to founder on the force-blast. Alf waded into the fray, and the sword lifted him. It gave strength to his old limbs, speed to match the elves. It lent destructive force to every blow, so even a glancing hit pulped dead flesh and shattered bone. Charmstones cracked, spells guttered in the presence of the Spellbreaker. Jon and Perdia did their part, watching his back, stout shield and swift jaws guarding him from peril, but he led the charge.

Like Gundan and Lath, long ago. The clever ones told them what had to be done, and they did it, even if it seemed impossible. Hold the line at Karak's Bridge. Find a way through the Pits. Stop Lord Bone.

Kill the Erlking.

They hacked their way across the cavern, every step won with violence. Gobbets of dead flesh flew off into the dark. Wraiths hauled their corpse-puppets onwards, ignoring wounds that would kill a mortal ten times over. Not even dismembering the corpse entirely could destroy a wraith-knight – the wraith would linger amid the shattered ruin of its host body. Only the breaking of the binding-spells could release them, and Spellbreaker obliged.

On. On.

No songs would be sung of this. Had Sir Rhuel of Eavesland been magically transported to this battlefield, his words would have turned to lead on his tongue. It was ghastly, brutish, desperate – and terribly silent. The elf-wraiths could not speak, not even a whisper. The dead men had no breath – dead jaws might gape open in mimicry of a scream or battle cry, but they did so in eerie silence. The only sounds were the snarls of the wolf, Jon's grunts of exertion – and the exultant song of the sword.

Fight on, wielder! My foe is near! I can see him!

For there, crouched in a corner of the cavern, was the Erlking. He was more withered than any of the dead men who guarded him. A

thing out of time, countless centuries old. Unlike the other elves, he had never faded. Instead, he had calcified with the passage of time, clinging to life no matter how misshapen and painful his ancient frame became. Cataract-mottled red eyes and broken fangs.

My quest is nearly fulfilled!

Still, the Erlking's spells were potent beyond measure. He was the first and greatest of wizards. In ages past, he'd mapped the virtues of the stars, encoded their authority in runes and sigils. And when he'd found the earthpower, a magic the elves could not wield, he'd drawn sigils in stone to channel it, transforming Necrad into an engine of sorcery.

Here, in the dark under the mountain, he could draw on only a simulacrum of Necrad, but it was enough to fuel spells of destruction and conjuring. At the Erlking's command, the doors of the void gaped open and vomited demons. Shadows became solid and lashed at Alf; rocks sprouted limbs of stone and stumbled towards him. Bolts of ice and fire assailed him.

Spellbreaker broke them all.

But at the last, it was the sword who needed Alf.

Each spell it countered cost a portion of its power. On other battlefields, it could feed on the life energy of its victims – the thin gruel of Pitspawn, the hot blood of beasts, the bountiful feast of slaughtered mortals. But the wraith-knights offered less than nothing. The human corpses were already drained of all life, the elf-wraiths could not be cut, and it *cost* Spellbreaker to undo the spells that bound the two together.

With every cut, the sword grew weaker.

With every step, it grew heavier.

And there were so many steps before it could cut the Erlking.

Alf endured. He kept walking.

The sword was a leaden burden now. His old limbs ached, but he had the rhythm of the fight again. He was fighting monsters in a dungeon with his friends, and all was right with the world.

Go down, they'd told him, and kill the Erlking. Do the impossible.

Alf stepped forward and disarmed one foe, a zombie, by smashing its rotten fingers to bits. Elegant as a brick, graceful as an ogre, but effective. *Next*.

He brought the sword down, cutting the next poor-dead-bastard-chained-to-a-poor-dead-elf in two. The human face was too rotten to tell, but he swore the wraith looked grateful for the release. He parried another wraith-knight, then stepped in and caught him and twisted, flinging the foe over his hip (*ach, that'll leave a bruise*) so Gundan could come in (*not Gundan, Thomad's lad*) and skewer the bastard (*next!*), dragging the heavy sword around to spit a force wave, a weak blast but enough to stagger them, enough for Lath to spring upon them and rend, all claws and jaws and fur and flying gobbets of flesh and fury (*next*) and *would it kill you to shoot a few of them Lae we're in up to our* (*next*) *necks* but gods (*next*) he was made for this born for this happy for this only alive in this. Olva had been right to send him because he had foes to slay and friends at his side and a sword in his hand and *next next next . . .*

And then suddenly there wasn't any next.

Then there was only the Erlking before him, and the sword in his hand.

The sword-sight had faded. Alf could see only by the light of Lae's lamp.

The sword's voice was so faint he could barely hear it. *I cannot see any more, wielder! Please, strike! Finish it!*

CHAPTER FORTY-THREE

This was what Jon saw: a cascade of glimpses, disconnected and jarring, as Laerlyn's lamp swung wildly. The light showed him the dead, caught their bone-white teeth, their milk-white eyes, their swords. Then sudden darkness, the underworld swallowing him whole. Then light again, but the scene all changed, the dead right on top of him, reaching for him. Spellbreaker blasted them away, and he caught sight of the grey-furred flank of the wolf – and then dark again.

Light and dark, light and dark, and he did not know which was worse. Blindly, he hewed and shoved, smashing his sword at whatever came near. How long the battle raged, he did not know. Maybe each flash of light-then-dark was a day and night, in which case . . . well, a long time. But Alf had told him to keep fighting, so he kept swinging that sword, putting all his strength into every blow.

A dead hand clawed at his leg, and Jon went down. More of them crawled on him, tearing at him. Light-flash, and there was a skull right in his face. Dark, and the foul breath of the wolf, and the skull was gone. Spatters of hot, gritty drool showered him. *Get up*, he told himself, like the heroes in the stories.

He knew the stories. *The Song of the Nine* and the rest. He'd listened to the tale-tellers in Genny Selcloth's of many an evening. There was the land of the stories, with elves and monsters and

magic, and there was the land he knew, where what mattered was the weather, and digging out the ditch before the rains came, and how many of the young piglets made it through winter. It wasn't that he didn't believe the tales might be true – maybe there were elves and heroes out there, or once upon a time there were, anyway – but he liked the stories because of how they made him feel. He'd never be fighting undead monsters in a dungeon like the Lammergeier, but the Lammergeier never shirked his duty, and neither did Jon. He'd pretended the mud in the ditch was a horde of zombies, and his shovel was the black sword Spellbreaker.

The songs had taught him other things. When things seemed darkest, when all hope seemed lost, that was when you had to keep going. Your friends would show up at the last moment to save the day. Lath in the prison in Necrad, and they'd rescued him. The Lammergeier and Gundan and Thurn on the shore, and Berys coming in with a stolen warship from Lord Bone's own fleet.

When the light next flashed, he hoped he'd see an arrow come flying over his shoulder, or Ildorae's dagger shining in the dark. Or a helmed knight charging in to fight by his side. If the songs had taught him anything, it was that his friends would be there.

But the lamp swung, and they were not there. Instead, he saw a giant, tall and terrible, with eyes like stars. Far bigger than could fit in the cavern, or the world.

The giant stooped down. With infinite gentleness, it picked up little Jon.

I will carry you home, it said.

This is what Perdia saw: nothing, for her eyes were not her own.

Earthpower ran through these caves like blood through veins. The wolf stalked her within her own skin. It caught her, and swallowed her, and suddenly it wasn't her skin any more, not her body. The wolf pushed through her, making her mouth into its jaws, making her hair flow down her back and become its fur, its claws

pushing out beneath her fingernails, its eyes bursting through her eyes, and what was left of her?

Perdia was just a skin the wolf had worn.

Now the wolf rampaged, snapping and tearing, jaws crunching down on dead bones.

Denied command of her own body, her own senses, what was left of Perdia fluttered through memory.

Her father, before he'd gone away, told her that the world should be safe and ordered. There had once been good Lords in the Crownland who made the law, and good knights who brought justice, and priests in the shrines, and above them all the holy Intercessors. The old evil in the north had been defeated, and now there was only good in the world. Humanity would prosper and make of the world a garden. He'd taken her to see them building the new cathedral in Ilaventur, stone columns aspiring for the sky, a roof for the world. The sight of it made her soul soar, and in that moment she wished to be a priestess, to be part of that grand architecture of civilisation.

After he'd gone away, in the Anarchy, she learned harder lessons. Her uncle sold the books − the mill's machinery needed fixing. Neglected, the half-built cathedral collapsed, the stones quarried for city walls. The world was no longer safe or ordered, and neither was she. Closer and closer came the Anarchy, until there were men with swords at the door of the mill.

The wolf found her in Hayhurst. The taste of blood in the mouth that was no longer wholly hers.

And Olva? Wise, kindly Olva − told her that this was *natural*, this upheaval, this changing of skins. That the order Perdia had revered was just an elven lie, that it was corruption and violence all the way down and all the way up. Be a wolf, Olva had urged her, and use the gift of the earthpower.

On the long road south, Olva had told Perdia of her days as the Widow Queen. How she'd fought to keep Derwyn safe, Derwyn

and dreams of justice and order. But that had turned sour, too, rotten from within. Work small, Olva had urged her. Don't reach for heaven with your first step. Feel the land you know and be part of it like the wolf. Forget the spires of the cathedral, and look to the trees, shedding their skins with the seasons.

This advice Perdia found bitter, even though she knew in her bones it was true. *We are just beasts. No higher purpose, just beasts.*

Now: she had lost her skin, her bones had been stolen from her. The wolf had muscle and sinew, face and teeth, and the bestial shape that charged through the fray was not her. The essence of Perdia drifted as if in a dream, and in that dream she walked with her father on the Pilgrims' Circuit. Her father went away so long ago she couldn't remember his face, so she imagined him to have the face of Eldwyn Forster, who talked about cathedrals of the mind, until a man with a sword silenced him.

There is healing in the Everwood, her father had said, but she had gone to the Everwood and found it rotten and ruined.

There is Intercession in the cathedral, her father had said, angelic spirits watching over humanity, guiding them with wisdom and kindness, but she had gone to the cathedral and found it empty.

Now, in the dream, she walked, and the man with her no longer had her father's forgotten face, or Eldwyn Forster's borrowed features, but was older, wiser, eyes twinkling with gentle merriment. He had the face of the statue from the cathedral, a giant king crowned in green.

He bent down, and gently picked her up. It was so comforting to know that such a kind god was watching over the world, that all would be made right in the end.

I will heal you, child, he whispered.

This is what Alf saw, only he didn't, because he knew this trick and recognised it as an illusion immediately: The council chamber in Necrad.

The council chamber in Necrad, and all the Nine were there.

Even Peir, who had never set foot in this room. He'd died before now, because this was forty years ago and they were all young again.

"Sit down, Aelfric," said Thurn.

A damned illusion, using the Nine as masks, as mouthpieces. *None of this is real*, he told himself. Just a spell, making him see what wasn't there. He was still standing over the Erlking, sword in hand. *Strike now!* he told himself. Drive the sword into the vampire's heart.

Instead, he found himself sitting down at the council chamber. He could feel the coolness of the marble table, the weight of the ornate chair. The foul tang of the necromiasma seeped into everything. He had missed the stink.

"Get out of my thoughts!"

"Please. This is a much more civilised way to converse," said the false Berys.

"Sit, Aelfric," said Laerlyn. She hadn't changed at all, of course, but, oh, it was so good to see her in the company of the Nine once again. To look across the table and see Lae next to Jan, next to Thurn – they were all together again, and even though he knew it was all illusion, all lies, it was so *right*. To be among his friends again, to be part of the Nine again . . . he had to fight to keep from grinning.

"We have much to discuss," added Thurn. Thurn when he was young, in those bright days of victory. How they'd cheered him! Liberator of the Wilder, godslayer. The hint of a smile as they cast down the temples of the Witch Elves. "The fate of the world turns on Necrad, and you hold the key to my city."

"Show yourself," demanded Alf. "Or drop this mockery." He raised his voice. "Spellbreaker! Where the fuck are you?"

"Oh, still in your hand," said Blaise. Blaise as he used to be, Blaise as Alf really remembered him. Thin, gawky, those watery eyes blinking beneath his hood. "But without the strength to resist me."

"And you, laddie," said Gundan, elbowing Alf in the ribs, "are

fucked-up mincemeat. Take my word for it, you're down and bleeding out. This – this is a mercy." Gundan, full of life again. How he'd missed that dwarf.

"A mercy, is it now?" Alf tried to stand again, tried to tell his limbs to move, but succeeded only on leaning back in his chair, like he'd done when they were young. Boring council meetings, Alf only half listening back then. Now, at last, he was paying attention. Forty years late, maybe, but out of the corner of his eye he saw Laerlyn make the *trust-me* hand signal.

That's really Lae, he thought, and he hid that thought like he used to hide thoughts from the sword.

"A mercy indeed," said Peir. "For both of us. You know, I once thought we could have nothing in common. You, a lumpen beast, thick of limb and skull. I, the Architect of the World, father of countless civilisations. But I see now that we do share one trait – an unwillingness to accept the triumph of death. And thus we are stalemated."

"Are we now?"

"You say that," said Jan, "as though you have the slightest conception of what's going on. As if expressing the slightest sliver of doubt is enough to balance the scales. You are *nothing* to me."

"But you still need me."

"I need the sword."

"For what, exactly? To put it in Idmaer's hand, so he can rule while you're the power behind the throne?"

The illusion of Peir spoke. "If restoring my rule of Summerswell was all that concerned me, I would let your land run to seed for another three generations." As he spoke, green flames kindled on his body, turning him into a pillar of fire. He spoke on, heedless of his scorching flesh. "A century or so more of anarchy, and you mortals will beg for a stern hand to discipline you. No. I act in haste because the Skerrise must be stopped." All that remained of Peir was the blast that had killed him all those years ago, the roaring inferno

that consumed Lord Bone. *Only ash and broken armour, that's all we had to bury.*

Lath took up the tale, and with every word he spoke he grew more monstrous, his young face becoming a bestial muzzle. "The Skerrise — she prepares to work a spell. A magic I thought beyond her."

"The darkness rising that Jan saw." Alf looked at the false Jan, the illusion of Jan. He could see through her now. She was fading away, like she did before. The illusion couldn't get her face quite right, though. Something about the corners of the mouth.

"The signs become clearer," said the Erlking through Lath. The Changeling boy was unrecognisable now, his form swelling and warping into a horror out of Necrad. Manticore-spikes sprouting along his spine, tattered bat-wings, fangs choking out his words. Only the hands were still human. "Not a darkness. The *first* darkness. The dark under the stars. She means to turn back the wheel, to erase all history."

"Can she do that?"

A goblet appeared on the table, filled with a purplish liquid. A Wilder poison. Thurn used to smear it on his arrows. Lath's human hands seized the goblet and fumbled it towards one of his mouths. The Changeling convulsed, and Alf closed his eyes in horror. But this was all illusion, and closing his eyes did nothing. He still saw his friend thrash against the wall of the council chamber, purple froth bubbling from his lips, limbs twitching. *Lath is dead.*

Thurn took up the tale. "Only by squandering all the power of Necrad. She will waste the magic of my city trying to recapture days that have long vanished." The horrible wet crack as Gundan's axe went through Thurn's spine. The illusion of Thurn twitched, but kept talking even as he slumped over on the table. "Even though it is folly, she can inflict terrible damage on me."

"I am the sum of my experiences, the culmination of all I have consumed," explained Berys. "I have eaten *civilisations*, mortal." She tapped her forehead. "Unlike the other elves, I am not weary of life.

There is so much to understand, so much to *take*, to *become*. I shall have it all. Moving ever forward, ever greater. I will be *more* than I was. I will not go back." Her body shrivelled, clothing and flesh flaking away. Her spine became a wooden spike, impaling her head. Still, she spoke. "Nor should you. I have only ever offered you the future, Aelfric. When last we met, that future might have been the life of a king. Now, your remaining span is measured in days, and all I can offer is this: you will be remembered."

Wings fluttered at the window of the council room. A black bird perched on the rooftop outside. Death was listening – and when Alf looked at the bird, the illusion of the council chamber faded, just a little. He was aware that he lay sprawled on the ground, that the sword was still in his hand.

The hot breath of the wolf at his throat.

Perdia found herself in the cathedral, kneeling before the Erlking. His face was very old, and very kind. He placed a wooden grail-bowl on the ground between them, and filled it with water from a silver ewer. She could see her face in the dancing water, her reflection flickering from girl to wolf.

I can wash away this taint, my child, said the Erlking. *I can intercede and change your fate.*

"Please," Perdia begged, "I never wanted this power."

A bird fluttered against the window of the cathedral, beating itself against the stained glass, pecking desperately at the panes. Perdia looked up, startled, but the Erlking gently took her head and made her look back at the waters of the grail.

I know. I will make you clean again. I will take away this curse. But not just yet.

In the grail, she saw a man with a sword.

One last offering, and you will be redeemed.

Anger rumbled in the throat of the wolf.

*

"*We'll* be remembered, lad." Gundan elbowed Alf in the ribs. "The deeds of the Nine, the songs of the Nine. If we don't stop the Skerrise, she'll wipe it all out. It'll all have been for naught." A thundercloud gathered above Gundan. Next, Alf knew, would come the lightning bolt. It was the lakeside at Bavduin again, where Gundan died. Death would blast them both with lightning, and the sword would save Alf.

"You've got the bloody sword, Alf?" insisted Gundan. "The sword we gave you. We entrusted it to you, aye? We saved the world. Now you can save us. Save our story."

The thunderbolt struck, and Gundan was dust on the wind, and there were only three.

All the rest were dead. Dead, but not yet forgotten.

Alf. Laerlyn. Blaise.

The Skerrise killed Blaise, thought Alf. *Ildorae told me. She saw the Skerrise stab him.* He could see nothing beneath the shadow of Blaise's hood, now.

"It would have been easier, Aelfric," said the wizard, "if you had yielded the sword to Idmaer weeks ago. It would be easier if you would just *die*, mortal. But I can risk no more delay. It's fastest if you carry the sword to Ironhand."

Alf dared not look at Laerlyn, nor at the black bird of Death by the window. There were powers at work here beyond his understanding, so he knew his role – keep pushing on, keep getting up and walking deeper into the dark. Be a shield for the clever ones.

"Stalemate, is it? Me with Spellbreaker, and you with—"

"Your companions," said Blaise. "I have caught them in illusions, too. You have defeated my guardians, but I always find new tools. Will I have the beast tear your throat out?"

"Why don't you do it?"

"Because, you dolt, I would not have enough time then to stop the Skerrise! Have you not paid the slightest bit of attention?"

"That sort of stuff," said Alf, "was always beyond me."

"Now, Alf," said Jan's voice in his ear, and it was really Jan. "Kill the bastard."

Jon was back in Ersfel, and that was what he'd always wanted. He walked down the path past the Widow's place, and came to his father's house, and Thomad welcomed him back in and did not ask him where he'd been. The next day there was work to be done, and the day after, and the day after. The year rolled around, frost on the hillside giving way to spring flowers on the riverbank, and the cool shade of the trees against the heat of the summer sun, and then it was autumn again and the harvest had to be brought in, and that was a mountain of work, but meant more time in the long evenings to go to Genny Selcloth's and hear tales by the fire.

Cerlys was there, too, somehow, and she wore the comb he'd bought for her. She put aside the dreadknight armour, and her weapons, all the dreams of heroism, and she never went away to Necrad. That Yule, they jumped over the bonfire hand in hand, and they were wed in the spring by the Widow.

The years rolled on, faster and faster, and they were all much the same. Busy and happy, full of children and work and the business of living. Sometimes, of an evening, one of the boys would ask Jon for the story of his Adventure, how he'd gone down the Road with a vampire elf and a skin-changer and a talking sword, and how absurd it all was. A passing moment of madness that accomplished nothing, a brief deviation from an honest, ordinary life. Jon laughed at it with the rest, and told himself he never missed it at all.

Then, one night, there was a new singer in Genny Selcloth's. A mousy little woman with a kind face. Jan of Arshoth, she called herself. And she sang a song of the Nine that Jon had not heard before. In this song, Aelfric Lammergeier was in terrible peril, for he had been enchanted by an evil wizard, and his magic sword had not the strength to break the spell. Only the sacrifice of one of Aelfric's companions could save the hero.

The thought struck Jon that this was very like his own Adventure.

And what had he done on that Adventure? He'd followed Cerlys and Ceremos about, and carried things, and swung his sword a few times. Mostly, he'd stood around in the background being confused while others did heroic things. The understanding of his own role in things settled on him like a solemn burden, but he had strong Mulladale shoulders. He could take the weight.

He'd never go home.

He blinked, and Genny Selcloth's alehouse faded in his sight. Old Genny melted away like a ghost, and his wife Cerlys, too, and their children and all the rest.

It was pitch black in the cavern, but he could still see the sword as a deeper darkness. He stumbled towards it.

This is what Laerlyn saw: a bright spell-sigil burning in her mind. She held onto that. That inheritance from her father that she would keep.

Too well had he made her. Each of the Erlking's children was shaped for a purpose. Maedos, the eldest, was the warrior prince. *Dawnshield*, they called him, guarding Summerswell from the evil of Necrad. But his fortress on the Isle of Dawn was a weapon, too, the knife at the throat of Necrad. A constant reminder to the Witch Elves that the Erlking had neither forgiven nor forgotten their defiance of his authority. Other siblings were made to be counsellors, or scholars, or spies. In his paranoia, the Erlking trusted only the things he made.

Laerlyn, the youngest of the Erlking's get – her role was to be the enchanting princess, kindly and wise and beautiful. Mortals fell in love with her, devoted themselves to her. They built shrines to her, sang songs to her, this embodiment of light and mercy, this fake jewel flashing in the palm of a con artist. She was a pretty distraction. But she'd only seen that afterwards.

They loved her, and she loved them in return.

Laerlyn carried no weapon into this battle. She cast no spells. And because of that, the Erlking did not bother catching her in his nets of illusion. He bewitched Jon and Perdia, and had worn down Spellbreaker's countermagic until the sword was too exhausted to defend Alf, but she was free to act.

Alf stood frozen, caught by the spell, sword ready to strike the Erlking. The point of the sword was very sharp.

Off to her left, Jon stumbled forward. Jan had freed him from her father's spell, just enough to see what must be done. A last gift from one member of the Nine to another. He'd perish, Alf would strike, and they'd win. The quest fulfilled.

But the gift of death shall not be given to the undeserving.

Oh, she could stand aside. Let the mortal child sacrifice himself. She could go on for thousands of years more, on until the world's ending. There were bright and beautiful days in her past, spilling like gemstones through her memories, but there could be so many more to come. A dragon's hoard of joy. It was hard to give that up in favour of one whose span was so brief they might only hold a handful of bright days.

But let him find those days for himself, she told herself.

She leapt past slow-footed Jon.

This is what Alf saw.

He saw it all so clearly. In that moment, the sword-sight snapped back, driving away the dark. The sword cut through all illusions, all deceptions, leaving only truth.

Laerlyn's blood washed over Alf's hands.

She'd impaled herself on the blade, and Spellbreaker ate her life hungrily. The sword sang with power as it feasted.

"Lae," he said, as he broke.

It's all right, Aelfric, she said through the sword, *I spoke to Jan. She said you carry the hope of the world. Now finish it.*

She closed her eyes. Her limp body slipped off the sword.

Dead.

Lae.

This is what the sword saw, when its demon eye opened again: the Erlking, its quarry, its quest. The king had no defences left, no magic, and Spellbreaker had power again. Not much, but enough. The death of one elf would pay for the killing of another.

Sword and wielder were both united in one thought in that moment, and struck true.

And the last of the Erlking's spells were broken.

This is what Torun saw: the world's ending.

CHAPTER FORTY-FOUR

VICTORY, crowed the sword.

The ancient body of the Erlking crumbled to dust, leaving only the black blade. His wraith went howling into the void.

The wolf lunged a fraction of a second too late. It bowled Alf over, smashing him aside. Hot breath on his sword-hand, and then the shock of pain as the fangs dug in. She tore the blade from his hand – and then Jon was there, wrestling with the beast, pulling it off him.

Alf crawled towards Laerlyn. There was something wrong with his hand, his fingers, but all he could think about was getting to Lae's side. She'd given herself to Spellbreaker, killed herself, given the sword the strength it needed to break the last illusion. He cradled her, pressed his hand to her breast, as if he had Peir's healing touch, as if he could hold back that river of elven blood. It gushed, slowed, gushed again, but slower. She wasn't quite dead yet, but he'd dealt enough wounds with Spellbreaker to know a mortal one.

Oh, fuck, *he'd* killed her, killed her with his stupidity and his slowness, if only he'd been faster if only—

"Sir Alf?" Jon was standing there, blinking in confusion, Thomad's stupid lad, Mulladale boys thick as pigshit together. "Something's wrong. It's all going grey."

Slowly, the meaning penetrated his skull. He'd dropped the

sword, and Lae's magic light was gone. It should be dark in the
cave, but instead it was grey and misty, and the cave floor was sloping away down into the dark. Torun was vanishing, receding as if
falling into the sky. And Perdia – the wolf hared off, yowling, and
Alf saw the hint of a distant forest across the endless expanse of the
grey hillside

The Grey Lands.

They were all dead. He knew that with a heavy certainty in his
belly.

All his aches and pains, though, they were melting away, which
was nice. Dying was like a long satisfying draught of healing cordial,
sinking a big pint of the stuff in one. He looked down at his sword-
hand and saw that three of his fingers had been bitten clean off.

He wasn't quite sure what the plan was now. He'd done his part,
he'd done the killing. He was good at killing.

So good, apparently, that he'd killed everyone. At least no one
could shout at him for fucking up. Olva, ah, it would have been
good to see her again. She could chase him around the kitchen
with a wooden spoon and call him an idiot for killing the whole
human race.

"Ah well," he muttered, and he pressed his forehead against Lae's.
She was already beginning to fade – or was it him who was fading?
Elves and mortals went to different places afterwards, the wraith-
world wasn't the same as the Grey Lands – or had he got that wrong?
Blaise had explained it to him, once, but he hasn't really followed,
and what did it matter anyway? He was dead, and Lae was dead,
and the story was over.

He was terribly tired.

He held onto her until Lae's body faded from sight. Elf-wraiths
didn't go to the Grey Lands. Then he stood and took a step down the
hillside, and another and another. Each one was easier than the last.
Young Jon did not follow him, but stood there, bereft and confused.

"I don't want to go," he said quietly.

Your family's down this way, Alf wanted to say, *everyone's down this way*. But he could not find the words. He tried to take a step back up the slope, but where going down had been as easy as, well, walking down a hill, climbing back up was an immense strain, as if a whole mountain was weighing him down. Instead, he reached out a hand to the boy. "I'll go first," he said, but Jon shook his head.

Then he heard another voice.

Spellbreaker sounded like it was coming from far away.

"Wielder," it cried, "pick me up."

The sword was back up the slope, out of Alf's reach.

"It's closer to you," said Alf, "you take it."

Jon shook his head. "It calls for you."

Alf took a step up the hill, then another and another. The first took all the strength that was left to him. The second broke him utterly, as if the weight of the unseen mountain crushed all his bones to powder in an instant. And the third – well, someone must have pushed him for the third, because there was no hope of him doing that alone. He fumbled in the grey grass that had sprouted on the cavern floor, his long arm outstretched until his shield-hand closed around the familiar hilt.

Life surged through him, which meant pain. All his injuries assailed him, and he grunted as the dead weight of Lae's body wrenched his old back. The grey vanished, and he was in the cavern again, all lit up by harsh sword-sight. Oh, the terrible clarity of that sight! He could see Lae's face, the scars of their shared lifetime not marring her perfect beauty, but underlining it, the story written on her skin. He could see the awful wound, the gore that drenched his hands black. Jon and Perdia, lying side by side, struggling to breathe. He lowered Lae's body to lie next to them. The humans twitched and whimpered as they fell into the Grey Lands. Lae's wraith flickered at the edge of vision, like her shadow was pulling away from beneath her.

He was alive, and everyone else was dying. It was all on him to save the world, and he had no idea what to do.

"I promised to protect you, wielder!" said the sword. "The spell is broken, but I shall preserve you!"

"Ach, what's the point?" muttered Alf.

Let go of the sword, he thought, *and fall back to the Grey Lands. And go home.*

He didn't let go.

Torun exploded out of the darkness, running headlong into Alf's leg. "Spell-sigil!" she shouted.

"What?"

"Elf spells are governed by sigils and if you've got the sigil you can hold the spell and oh Az's ARSE they're all dying! All of them!" She stooped and blindly ran her hand over Perdia's face. "We have to save them! If I can work out the Erlking's sigil, I can save them all. Blaise taught me to do it, I've got to do it." Torun fell to her knees, and frantically scratched sigils in the bloodied dirt of the cavern floor.

"Blaise took twenty years to decode a fraction of Lord Bone's sigils. This is utter folly. Do not let me go, wielder." In the dark, Perdia choked and gasped for breath. Everyone was dying. The world was ending.

You carry the hope of the world, echoed Jan's words in his memory.

Then he, too, fell to his knees next to Lae. He pressed his mangled finger-stumps to Lae's mouth.

"She's not quite dead," he prayed, "and she knows her father's sigils. She knows. She knew."

Twice before, dying elves had drunk from the wellspring of Aelfric Lammergeier. Ceremos was the first, a fumbling atonement. Second was Amerith herself, in another dark cave under a fortress. At Daeroch Nal, Death had forced Alf to offer Amerith a chance to preserve her existence as part of some twisted test. Both elves drank desperately to cling to life.

"Come on, Lae." He forced her lips open.

She drank, but only a sip.

Her eyes opened, and there was the faintest tinge of red in the depths of the green. She took a deep breath, her spine arching in Alf's arms, as if she was inhaling her wraith back into the house of her body. Going vampire.

Then, gently, she pushed his arm away.

"I only need this moment," she whispered.

"You need more, Lae." Her wounds were too great. The drop of blood she'd taken was not enough to heal her.

"No. I must stay on the borderland. There's no time to explain. This moment is a gift, Aelfric."

"Lae." He could barely speak. "I killed your father, and now everyone's dying."

She smiled. "Not everyone. Not today. Farewell, my friend." She closed her eyes, gathering all the strength and authority left to her for one last effort. Alf bent his head and wept, overcome with emotion. Sorrow, but relief, too, and triumph and pride, for Laerlyn would surely put right the wrongs of the world. A lifetime of love and friendship, all passing through that moment. A spell-sigil appeared, and whether it was on her brow or burning inside her brain, Alf could not tell, for she was fading again and the sigil was so bright, shining more brightly than any star.

Then she muttered, "Alf, would you mind moving the spell-breaking sword away from my spell?"

"Sorry," he muttered, scooting back.

When he looked up again she was gone.

Afterwards, Jon and Perdia sat huddled on the cavern floor, pale and shivering but alive. They bound Alf's maimed hand. The dwarven servants and priests from the temple above, now freed from the Erlking's glamour, stumbled about in confusion. Their world had changed in an instant. Alf pitied them. Songs and stories prepared

you for the crisis, for the great and terrible confrontation. There were songs aplenty of heroes who sacrificed themselves to save the day, and tales of great and noble deaths.

There was no guide for the hollow hours afterwards, for the quiet after the clamour. The songs that spoke of finding love never talked about keeping it, the songs of war never spoke of the work of keeping the peace after, or the burying of the dead. In time to come, Alf was quite certain, the events of this day would pass into legend. How could they not? All humanity had nearly perished, but at the last moment they'd been saved by the intercession of a goddess. She'd be worshipped. In distant lands far beyond the seas, beyond the Wild Wood or the deserts of the west, they'd praise the name of Laerlyn of the Nine. And because no one knew exactly what had happened, the tale-tellers would fill in the gaps with gaudy myth making. Call it the tale of the Lady of the Stars, maybe. The Maiden of Intercession.

And Alf was absolutely sure that all those stories would end with the events of half an hour ago, when all the world was balanced on the edge, and no one would ever talk about this time, when he stood around by the spot where his friend had died, and the youngsters sat there on the cavern floor, and the dwarves clustered at the arched entryway, one still clutching a platter of pancakes, and no one knew what to do.

"Get us a drink, eh," he said to them. "Fetch down some chairs. Get a fire going."

"All is doomed!" wailed one of them. "Holy Az is dead!"

"Aye," said Alf, "so we'll have a wake."

Torun exposited arcane mysteries. The Erlking had made humanity with a spell, and when he perished that spell began to break. But! Someone *else* who knew the secret sigil that gave authority over a spell could maintain it in the place of the original caster, so Lae could take over for her father. She'd spent twenty years in the rotting

Neverwood uncovering that sigil, twenty years overcoming the snare that defeated them last time. She'd not squandered her time.

There was a lot of talk about intent, and entropy, objects of focus and runes of binding. All beyond him. Never the brightest.

Alf found he was weeping, but sorrow was just one tributary to the river that coursed through him.

When Peir fell, when Gundan and Thurn died in fruitless battle – those deaths had felt like axe-blows, the world hewing at him, trying to break him. Their deaths – even Peir's glorious sacrifice – had been much too soon, and somehow unjust, their lives unfinished like a story interrupted and left untold. There was so much *next* left in them. But Lae – it made no sense to feel this way, for she was immortal, as she so often reminded him, and there were supposed to be endless next chapters for her.

But this strange sacrifice, however little he understood it, was an ending for her, and a triumph.

When Torun finally paused for breath, Alf nodded sagely and pretended he'd followed what she'd said. "Blaise couldn't have explained it better." He sighed. "She's not coming back, is she? Like elves usually do?"

"She stranded herself at the threshold of the wraith-world. She is the sigil now. As long as she endures, the spell that made you humans is safe."

"And dwarves? The Erlking made ye, too."

"A different order of being. We are not all dependent on the same spell." She scuffed the floor where she'd drawn her sigils, shifting from one foot to another. "The Erlking chose to make himself the keystone. It need not have been this way."

"He was so cruel," said Perdia, "and selfish. How could anyone be that powerful, and clever, and see so much, yet still be—"

"A right arsehole?"

"Evil. In his illusion . . . he tormented me. He tried to make me lose control. Lose myself in the beast. I nearly did." She shivered.

"How can he have been so evil, so deceitful, yet Laerlyn sprang from him and she was good?"

"Aye, his son Maedos was a right arsehole, too." Alf shook his head. "And Lae, well, people say she chose ill, sometimes." All of Berys' whispered accusations against Laerlyn slunk into his mind, unwelcome thoughts that threatened to stain the memory of his friend. "She proved true in the end."

"But how?" Perdia asked again. Alf looked at the girl and saw for the first time the terror in her. Her experiences in the Grey Lands, or in the Erlking's illusions, had marked her deeply. Alf could not guess what she'd seen, nor did he know what it meant that she'd been a wolf even in the realm of death. Olva would have known what it meant, and what to say. Or Lae – Lae was wise, and patient. Holy, even. Not in the painted icons and statues and empty grails, not as the Erlking's daughter, but elven-fair and blessed.

"She saved me," said Jon.

"She saved all of us, lad."

"Not just that. At the end, there, I thought the only way I could help – I'm not a great warrior or a skin-changer or aught like that. I could have fed the sword instead of her. I was going to do it." He met the red gaze of the demon eye. "Why did she do it?"

"She . . . she was Lae," said Alf, unable to find any better words.

To his surprise, it was the sword who answered.

"She was of the Nine. That is all the answer to all your riddles. How did she stave off despair? How did she hold true against the demands of her making and her circumstances? How could she risk everything to save one mortal from their own ignorance? She was of the Nine, and they took the best from one another. Like Lath she wore many faces over her life. She had the courage of Gundan, the cunning of Berys, the spirit of Thurn, the wisdom of Jan the Pious, the mastery of Blaise. The sickening hope of Peir, the stupid tenacity of the Lammergeier." The sword quivered in disgust. "Oh, how I wish I had a better answer! To admit that there is some virtue in

friendship, that there are bonds that even I cannot break – I loathe such sentiment. The mewlings of limp poets, blithering about the power of love and the virtue of hope. I care not who I cut. I have slain lovers. I have shattered hope. I was forged to destroy illusions and break enchantments.

"One hand alone can wield me, so the thought of *fellowship* is anathema to me. But I cannot deny its strength. Nine stood against Lord Bone, and won. Nine conquered Necrad. Friendship stayed my wielder's hand again and again, until even I was thwarted.

"Laerlyn of the Everwood . . . it was an honour to take her life at the end."

Alf pulled the sword from the ground and laid it across his lap.

"Aye," he said, "like that."

CHAPTER FORTY-FIVE

The sound of the waves washed over Olva, like slow breathing, and slowly she became aware that she was not dead.

No longer dead.

She lifted her head from the wet rock of the seashore. All around her, others were stirring, coming back to life. She could see Tholos running about in a panic. Ernala hunched on a rock, tense, like a cat about to spring. All along the shore, figures rose from where they'd fallen.

Someone laughed nervously, as if playing along with some jest they weren't privy to.

Not everyone rose. Not everyone had survived. Nearby lay the corpse of a young knight, eyes staring back at Olva. His soul lost somewhere down the grey hillside.

With a gasp, Cerlys came back. Somehow, she went from dead to fighting in the space of one gasping breath. She grabbed the sword and twisted around, looking for her enemy.

Ironhand had climbed up to Thurn's pyre in the Grey Lands, and he was there in the living world, too. He knelt, cradling his son, gently shaking Thurn's body.

His lips moved, mouthing the words *come back*.

Everyone else around him was coming back to life, clawing their

way out of Death's realm, but not Thurn. Ernala laid her hand on her husband's bull-like neck, comforting him. The boy was dead too long, gone too far. He'd lingered at the threshold long enough for one last meeting.

Cerlys scrambled up the rocks, sword in hand, intent on finishing the duel. Olva caught her and pulled her back, the two women slipping on the sea-slick stone, and something fell from Olva's neck. The wind caught it, whipping it away across the rocks.

The Erlking had died. His spells had broken. His greatest spell, the one that had bound Death and conjured humans – that one had been restored, but any lesser magics that weren't bound by engraved sigils or other techniques of permanency, they'd broken.

The ivy-collar that had once bound King Rhaec – that was broken now.

Earthpower surged through her, giving her strength. Cerlys tried to tug free, but Olva's grip was like iron.

"Let me go! I can kill him!"

He deserves death, thought Olva. Ironhand had boasted of his crimes. To reach the shores of Necrad, he had done terrible things. He deserved punishment. He deserved death.

On another shore, long ago, another man had begged Olva to spare him. She remembered Maedos mocking her by standing aside and forcing her to choose. *I'm no one*, she protested, but he made her choose anyway. And out of fear, she'd given Captain Abran what he deserved.

But it was never so simple. Threeday knew that. He'd told her that so many times. Maybe Ironhand deserved death, but his life was bound up in so many things, so many threads of fate. The memory of Derwyn's chessboard with all its different tokens. Bird's skull, snail shell, iron tower, the Skerrise in her glory. Everything was important, everything was connected. Something new was sprouting all around them, born of scattered seeds.

Justice didn't come into it. All you could do was shelter the green shoots. All you could do was hope, and maybe get lucky.

"Help me up there." Cerlys helped her climb up, her crane-foot slipping on the rocks. As they approached, Olva drew on the earth-power, the power of life and death, and the point of balance between.

Words Lath taught her came to her, the incantation of a healing spell.

"Idmaer," she called, "I can heal him."

Ironhand looked up. Tears glistened in his beard. He lifted his metal hand to wipe them away, and Olva saw that the hand was limp and unmoving. It, too, was the work of the Erlking. "There is nothing left," he said. "It was all for naught."

"Husband," said Ernala, "let the Old Woman work." She pointed at Olva and shouted a word in the Wilder-tongue. It was the word they'd used for Lath, the Old Man of the Woods. Ernala's kinfolk sprang forward. There were six of them, all tall and grim, faces tattooed Wilder-fashion. They led Ironhand away from his son's pyre. He did not struggle. The Wilder planted their spears in a circle around the bier.

"Cerlys," said Olva, "don't bring your sword in there."

The sword still dripped with Ironhand's blood. Ironhand himself was only a few feet away.

"Put it down," snapped Olva, putting a little power into her words. The sword clattered on the rock. Cerlys took a breath, then helped Olva walk the last few feet through the circle of spears around the bier.

Young Thurn lay there.

He was cold, his limbs stiffening. Bruises across his body, his abdomen swollen. The blow from Spellbreaker had broken something inside him. They'd cleaned away the blood he'd passed, but Olva had laid out enough bodies in her day to smell it. The boy was quite dead – but his spirit had been there, a moment ago. He wasn't yet gone to the Grey Lands. If she squinted, she could almost imagine the ghost of him there, lingering on the edge of the world.

Olva closed her eyes, imagining Galwyn lying there on the kitchen

floor, all those years ago, slain by Spellbreaker. The Olva of the now could have saved him, if only she could cross those forty years.

She'd been there when Blaise brought Derwyn back. She'd heard the echoes of Death's resurrection at Daeroch Nal. She could do this. The earthpower here would not be enough. Sea and sky and a thin strip of shore, all empty and lifeless. Not enough.

But close by were the Pits, and the magic of the city.

Olva raised her left hand and reached out for the city she'd once ruled. Necrad answered eagerly, the corrupted magic leaping to her will. She filtered it, keeping the taint of the city for herself – new witch marks would bloom in her aged skin – letting only the power rush through her into the boy. She unpicked the shape of him, un-stitched his skin sinew by sinew. No one could have survived it, but that was the advantage of working with the dead. And when he was flayed and shapeless, a roiling mass of blood and bone and potential flowing through her hands, she took the skin of him and dressed his ghost in his remade form.

Live, she commanded him, and in that moment she drank deep of the power of Necrad, the city her brother had taken from Lord Bone the necromancer. And Thurn obeyed her.

His eyes opened, and he gasped for breath.

The boy took a few unsteady steps towards the circle of spears, towards his waiting parents, before Olva stopped him. She pinned Idmaer Ironhand with a glare. "Your son—" Olva's voice sounded strange in her ears, and everyone flinched at the sound of it, even Cerlys. Magic had always had a cost.

"Your son belongs to me, Idmaer Ironhand. I bought his life with the coin of the blood you spilled. I give him back to you now, but I don't release my claim."

Ironhand looked back at her, hollow-eyed, exhausted beyond measure. It was Ernala who nodded, Ernala who stepped across the threshold of spears and took her son back to the lands of the living.

*

Olva watched them walk away across the stony shore. Ernala leading Thurn by the hand, wrapping a cloak over the grave-shroud. Idmaer following after them, as far from a king as could be, confusion and grief and joy and anger all warring with him, emotions too great even for his mighty frame.

Guards nervously approached. Cerlys picked up the sword Ironhand had given her, but there was no hint of violence in the air. No one knew their role now. The guards milled around, clearly hoping Tholos or some other commander would arrive and take charge, but no one came. After a few minutes, Olva pushed past them, and none of them dared stop the Witch of Ersfel.

The crowd on the shore was dispersing. Dead-enders scrambled up the rocks to pick the pyre apart, scavenging the precious firewood. Miracles or not, it would be a cold night on the Charnel.

"I could have killed him," whispered Cerlys. "It would have been just."

"But it wouldn't have been an end to it. An end to us, maybe, but that's all." She snorted. "You want a child to learn, make 'em clean up the mess they made."

Cerlys helped Olva back towards the camp. The girl had a thousand questions, a thousand objections, but Olva couldn't pay any heed to them. None of them really mattered now, anyway. What's done was done.

They limped through the camp. Everything had changed – everyone had seen the Grey Lands, everyone had encountered death – and yet already ordinary life was seeping back in, or whatever passed for ordinary life in a siege. Soldiers busied themselves fetching water, gathering firewood, attending to their gear. A young squire, his face pale and haunted by his experience, knelt to remove the greaves of his master who sat there on a stool, his expression equally distant. Soon enough, most of them would forget what had happened. They would bury the numinous under the everyday,

and Olva couldn't blame them. Water still needed to be carried, firewood gathered, gear mended. Life went on, even in the shadow of the unthinkable. They'd put a familiar skin on the world to give it shape.

Olva's head swam. The wound in her side ached terribly, as if the Manticore-spike was digging into her flesh once again. She clung to Cerlys' arm to keep from collapsing.

"We're nearly at your tent," said Cerlys. "Lean on me. Just a little further. Then you can rest"

"Alf . . . if he's still alive, Alf will be on his way here. There's no time to rest. Not at times like this." The shape of things was still in flux. Olva dug her nails into Cerlys' arm. "Bring me to the commanders' tent."

The assembled commanders were restive. Some fearful, some furious. There was a dangerous uncertainty to them, a feeling that nothing could be trusted any more, not even the heavens. Ironhand had lashed this army together through sheer force of will, and it was falling apart.

"All right, all right," cried Tholos above the din. "Listen to me! And sit down, damn you!" The dwarf was lost in the forest of taller men.

"What was that on the shore, dwarf?" shouted someone at the back of the tent.

"What did you expect, from a man called the Miracle Knight? His son rose from the dead, and you all took a little nap on the beach." The dwarf rapped his knuckles on the trestle table. "Doesn't change a thing. Sieges don't stop just because . . . " He paused, looking for a word to encompass what had just happened. He found none. "Just *because*."

He saw Olva and Cerlys enter and beckoned them forward. One of the knights scrambled out of a chair and offered it to Olva. Tholos leaned over and whispered. "Far as I'm concerned, you're still

a prisoner. If you try any witchery, it won't be a little ivy-sprig at your throat, it'll be my axe."

"What about the Dragonslayer?" objected one of the knights. "She tried to kill King Idmaer!"

Tholos tugged at his beard, his gaze darting around the room in a moment of panic. Then he plunged ahead: "Half this fucking army tried to kill him at Raven's Pass! Hell, I've gone for Idmaer with a knife more than once. A man tells you to break the walls of Ilaventur in a week, it fucking peeves you something awful. And as you astutely point out, she did kill a Stone Dragon. We need fighters like her."

"You have my word," croaked Olva, "that she will keep the peace." Cerlys bristled for a moment, then nodded.

"I don't want her to keep the bloody peace. There's a whole city of Witch Elves over there that needs killing. I want her to keep the violence."

"I've a friend in Necrad," Cerlys said, "he was taken prisoner by the Witch Elves. I'm going to find him."

"Lass, I don't give a damn why you're here." He glanced at the other knights. "And that applies to all of you, long as you fight."

Sir Kenton leapt to his feet and turned to face the assembled commanders. He addressed his words to them instead of Tholos. "We came because Ironhand promised treasure, and we are still sitting on this shore watching our foot soldiers die in the mud. We came because Ironhand said we were needed to battle the Witch Elves, but I have not seen a single elf, Witch or Wood, in all my years. We came because Ironhand said our courage would atone for the sins of our fathers, and the holy Intercessors would return. We came because Ironhand spoke of rising darkness—"

"Are you seriously complaining that they're not throwing *enough* apocalyptic magic at us?"

"—and darkness came, and I saw terror and grief on the king's face, not courage! You and Ironhand burned the ships—"

"Broke 'em for timber," muttered Tholos.

"—and stranded us here on this accursed shore! And now what?" Kenton rounded on Tholos. "You promised us that Ironhand would lead us when the time was right. His son was dying, you said. Everyone in Summerswell buried kinfolk in the Anarchy, Sir Dwarf. How much longer should we wait, now that his son is whole again – another blessing for the Miracle Knight!" He sneered.

"There's a nice big hole in yonder wall," said Tholos. "But because we stopped for a funeral and . . . and such, they've had time to fortify the gap. It's still the best way in, once we knock through their repair—"

He was drowned out by the protests of the knights.

"And how long will that take?"

"We've nothing to eat—"

"All dead—"

"A new leader!" shouted Kenton. "We need a new leader!"

"Dragonslayer! We will follow the Dragonslayer!" cried a voice at the back, and others took up the cry. "Dragonslayer! Dragonslayer!" The chorus of shouts rolled across the Charnel and echoed off the distant walls of Necrad.

Idiots, thought Olva. She wanted to shout at them, to tear the scales from their eyes and make them see. *Just because she can wave a sword around doesn't mean she knows a damn thing. Telling yourselves a story of heroes, and then believing it. And when she can't magically win the siege, can't fix all that's wrong with the world, you'll blame her. It's what comes after the glory, that's where the tales stumble. No story puts food in your belly, or stops a sword.*

Cerlys rose, and for a moment Olva could see the mantle of the tale falling upon her. The beautiful sword maiden, trained in secret by the greatest knight of a previous era, risen from obscurity to lead this crusade . . . the tales wrote themselves. Looking around the tent, Olva could see devotion kindling, a fervent belief in the

Dragonslayer that had little to do with the woman who stood before them.

It could all go so wrong. Twenty years before, they'd acclaimed her son Derwyn as Uncrowned King of Necrad, and he'd risen in glory. They'd tried so hard to make that tale come true. She'd sent Alf to war in Summerswell for that story, she'd unbound the Skerrise in pursuit of it. And it had all come to ruin. They were living in the ashes of that failed tale.

To her credit, Cerlys knew it. She'd seen what the Lammergeier had done to Alf. She shook her head. "I'm a fighter. I don't know—"

But you have to hope. The most pernicious story of all.

Olva stood and laid a gnarled hand on Cerlys' shoulder. "The gates of the city will open for her." She put all the prophetic grandeur she could into her voice, and the assembled knights were suitably impressed. "The gates of Necrad will open for the Dragonslayer," she intoned, "and the road to the Skerrise made clear."

Dragonslayer, they cried, *Dragonslayer.* Confusion and pride and betrayal warring on Cerlys' face.

"And when will this miracle happen?" asked Tholos.

"I cannot say."

"Well," said Tholos, "until then, we'll do things my way."

Olva stepped out of the tent into the cool air of evening. Behind her, they were still shouting *Dragonslayer*, still cheering. All the uncertainty transmuted into a cause.

Round and round the wheel goes. Another try at the old story.

She scanned the sky, the sun setting red behind the marble spires, looking for a dreadworm. The real battle had been fought out there somewhere, with the Erlking. The author of so many lies, the teller of so many glorious tales.

A hulking figure stepped out of the shadow.

"Lady Forster."

"How's the boy?"

"Well enough. In body, at least. Unscarred. He is confused, as are we all. Daunted. But well enough, he says, to demand a second bout with your brother." Idmaer smiled. "One last time I ask you – where is the Lammergeier?"

"I've been asking myself where Alf's gone most of my life."

"I thought us enemies. Why did you save my son?"

"Because he's just a child. Because I couldn't save others. Ach, because it sews up the wounds of the world. All my life, Idmaer, there's been *cutting*. The Nine brought everything together for a bit, and then it all got picked apart again. Us against the Witch Elves. Defiants against loyalists. Then the Anarchy. Someone has to . . . to stand for spring, maybe? I'm not fool enough to think that this will make everything right for ever, that making peace with you or slaying the Skerrise and the Erlking will fix the world. It'll never end. But your boy deserves a chance to grow up in peace, for a while anyway." She looked up at Ironhand, trying to see his mother in his face. "Because I'm not a monster, Idmaer."

"The Wilder declare you must be the Old Woman of the Woods, for what it's worth. Lath's successor."

"Aye, well." Olva hobbled over to an unlit campfire and spoke a word of power. Green flame kindled. The King of Summerswell, the warlord who'd conquered half the lands, the Miracle Knight dragged over a rock for her to sit on.

"They acclaim your granddaughter the Dragonslayer, I hear."

"She's not my granddaughter," snorted Olva.

"No?" Idmaer's massive brow wrinkled. "Then whence—?"

"Whence? Hark to him. Whence!" Olva rolled her eyes. "She's no close kin to anyone famous – though I don't doubt that mother of hers would have spread her legs for a passing knight, if she'd had the chance. Alf trained her to fight, but she's not close kin of ours. She was no one of consequence."

Dragonslayer came the cries.

Idmaer spread the fingers of his iron hand across his knee. The

enchanted digits no longer moved on their own, so he forcibly bent them into place with his left hand. "I am the son of an Earl. The grandson of the Lord of Ilaventur. I was born in my father's castle, and was to be fostered in my grandfather's palace like my brother before me. When I was wounded, the Abbess of Staffa prayed over me, and the Intercessors descended from heaven to heal me. I was born to power, and then given purpose to wield it."

"I've heard the story."

"I don't see it any more. When I was first brought back, I saw a bright and blazing vision. I saw darkness rising in Necrad, and thought it was my purpose to thwart it. It consumed me. It drove me. Now . . . it is gone." He listened to the cries of *Dragonslayer* wash over him. "I feel unburdened."

"Do you now?" Olva studied the man. "Your mother came to me once. She said she feared that you were lost. I told her you'd heal in time. It took a good while longer than I thought, but the wound's no longer festering. You're not the Erlking's tool any more."

"Thank you." He drew himself up, slowly, and looked towards the tent. "I shall give the Dragonslayer my blessing and depart. I shall go north with Ernala and Thurn to the lands of my father, and there—"

"You bloody will not," said Olva. "You're still the one who marched a whole heap of men up the Road and across the sea and into the Charnel. You started this, Idmaer son of Erdys, and you will help finish it. Cerlys needs more than your blessing. She doesn't know the first thing about siegecraft or logistics or law or anything like that. She needs your help."

Olva grabbed the metal hand and wrapped it around the hilt of the Brightsword. She forced the metal fingers closed. "And you can still fight. Because, Idmaer Ironhand, I'm not a monster, but I can be one if I have to be."

She left the threat unspoken. He was Erdys' son. He would understand what was unsaid.

*

In the early hours of the morning Tholos had his siege engines dragged closer to the city walls. The other Stone Dragons could not strike them there, but there were other weapons in Necrad.

Vomiting from the north gate, slithering over the walls, rising up from the Pitways they came, a second host of Pitspawn. A cavalcade of monsters, no two identical. Wingless dragons whose ribcages split apart to disgorge a flood of acid. Things of metal mated to flesh. Knifemothers. Thouls. Termagants. Horned giants, so large that their limbs each had a separate Vatling-head to guide their movements, the heads like warts on their shoulders. They bellowed to each other – *left-foot, right-foot, hammer-hand* – as they shambled into battle.

The flood of monsters seemed endless. It seemed *purgative*, as if Necrad had at last vomited up all its horrors, turned its subterranean guts inside out and rid itself of all the ghastly monsters spawned in the Pits. Olva wondered if the city was empty now, a labyrinth of bone-white marble and eerie green porphyry and black jasper, silent save for the rustling of wraiths. All the horrors were with them now, out in the mud flats. But the gates slammed shut once the dregs of the horde passed.

The Pitspawn were met with shining steel. The Brightsword burned white, and Cerlys' borrowed sword rang in answer across the battlefield. *Dragonslayer* they cried, and even Idmaer Ironhand added his voice to the acclamation.

In years to come, songs would be sung of that battle. They would tell of the deeds of the Dragonslayer on that day, how the Wilder held the causeway, of the charge of the Sorrowsworn. How Thurn the Younger took up a great Wilder-bow and brought down one of those ill-made giants, limb by limb and head by head. How Summerswell stood against the horrors of Necrad, and defended the siege towers as they crawled ever closer to the ancient walls.

The songs would tell – *all* the songs would tell, a scene that later

passed into legend – of how King Idmaer Ironhand knighted Cerlys Dragonslayer before the walls of Necrad.

At best, the songs would mention the slaughter only in passing.

A day ago, all of Ironhand's army had paused to mark the passing of his son. If the same honours were given to all those who fell before noon that day, their vigil would have lasted until well after the Yule of that year, and the battle was fought a few days past midsummer.

Olva took charge of the healing, or what passed for healing. The healing spells of the College Arcane had not functioned in years. The last of the restorative cordials stockpiled from the days of the Defiance had been used at Raven's Pass. All that was left were bandages and bone-saws – and her magic.

An endless host of vatgrown monsters, all teeth and claws and stingers.

An endless flood of soldiers, all bleeding and broken. They were carried to her table, flesh swollen with poison, veins running with molten lead, lungs brimming with slime. Dying of the evils unleashed by the Skerrise, and Olva could not forget that she had given the Skerrise that power.

She could not heal them all, but she tried. Again and again she drew on the dark power of Necrad to fuel her healing spells.

Then – the power ran dry. The currents of twisted earthpower vanished.

Diverted to a greater cause.

While Ironhand and Cerlys Dragonslayer had fought, Tholos pushed his ladders and siege towers forward. By noon, the first attacker – Sir Kenton of the Crownland had the honour – scaled the ladder and set foot atop the wall of Necrad. Horned Vatlings assailed him, but he held them off long enough for another mortal to climb up, then another and another. They took the parapet.

Sir Kenton was no scholar. It did not occur to him that, countless

centuries before, elven warriors had stood in that very spot, and looked out at the army of Death in the first war against mortals. He did not think that each step along the walkway encompassed kingdoms and empires far older and more enduring than Summerswell, that every stride crossed gulfs of history that were wide even to the ageless elves. His only thought was the prospect of loot, and of the sword he clutched in his hand.

More ladders reached the top, and the ancient Tower of Gulls fell to the mortal invaders. From the foot of the tower, the wide street called the Way of Haradrume curved through the heart of the city, through the old Sanction, right to the grand central plaza around the Wailing Tower. Sir Kenton descended the stair within the tower and emerged onto the street below, and marvelled at the sight.

Perhaps he even recalled the verse from *The Song of the Nine*.

To the city they came, that fortress of darkness,
The shadow revealing both beauty and terror.

Then the shadow fell across Sir Kenton, and all memory of the song was scoured from his mind. All *memory* was scoured from him, all semblance of speech. He dropped his sword, and howled like a wolf, then – suddenly frightened by the dark – scurried on all fours into an alleyway, never to be seen again.

The other soldiers on the parapet above – they, too, let their weapons fall. Some leapt from the walls in terror, or tried to climb back down like apes. They clawed at the metal shells that bound them, grunted and growled at each other. The rising darkness reduced them to beasts.

And still it rose from the Wailing Tower, a pillar of darkness, a wraith-tree. Taller and taller it grew, blotting out the sky. Its branches stretched out beyond the walls, and wherever they touched mortals lost their wits and were reduced to beasts. One mile-long branch, its shadow snaking across the Charnel with terrible swiftness, reached for the hospital where Olva laboured.

She took flight. In other days, it was the crane-skin that came easiest to her, elegant and wide-winged, a creature of the open skies. But it was Olva-raven who flew then, Death's herald, carrion-bird. A short, desperate flight, like a black arrow racing over the battlefield, to land amid the ruin of dragons where heroes gathered.

"Now," croaked the raven. "To the gate."

CHAPTER FORTY-SIX

Alf called a dreadworm. The smallest, most ragged, sickly little worm he'd ever laid eye or arse on, but it bore his weight. He flew east.

Behind him, the Dwarfholt dwindled. Torun had said she'd contact Gamling, muster a dwarven army. Now the Erlking was dead, she could act freely. There'd be a whole army of dwarves on their way soon, marching up the Road through Karak's Bridge, all with dwarf-wrought charmstones and other wonders. He'd have liked to have seen that.

Behind him, Perdia flew. Alf had told Jon and Perdia to stay with Torun, that he'd fly onto Necrad alone. Jon was wandering around, blinking, barely hearing what was said to him. Alf remembered feeling the same after Peir's death, after they'd slain Lord Bone, stumbling around the streets of Necrad as if he was in the middle of a thunderstorm that no one else could see or hear.

And Perdia – after she'd vomited up Alf's fingers, she'd wiped her mouth, and brushed down her clothes, and put herself to tending their wounds. She wouldn't look Alf in the eye, but when Alf had told her to stay behind, she shook her head. Instead, she marched up the hillside, and spread her arms, and turned into a really big crow. Big enough to carry Jon.

Changelings. Alf would never understand them. It was like having Lath back.

Lath is dead, he thought. *And Gundan, and Jan and Berys and Thurn and Peir. And Laerlyn.*

He did not weep. He had no grief left in him. So much of grief was all the might-have-been, the things left undone. He had very few deeds left to him, and Lae had bought him time to do those things. She had bought all of them a lifetime each.

That was proper world-saving, Lae. If I'm understanding it right, every mortal in all the lands, all of us for ever — you saved us. You nailed your father's bloody spell in place for eternity. You put it right. Knocks killing the Ogre Chieftain into a cocked hat. Gundan would be pissed if he knew.

He wished Gundan was here to see it. Then again, Gundan had that big statue.

It was your victory, too, Berys. Memories of her whispered confession in the Pits. *It's always been the elves, Alf. We're thralls.* She'd plotted all her life to bring down the Erlking, and now, twenty years late, he was gone. The future was as unknowable and open now as the cloudy sky before him.

Through a gap between the hills to the north, Alf glimpsed the edge of the Wild Wood.

You freed your people, Thurn. No more vampire elves preying on the Wilder. And somewhere off in the endless green was the mound at Daeroch Nal, where Lath had brought back Death. Where Lath had lived as the Old Man, and taught Olva. *I hope you found peace, lad. I wasn't as good a friend to you as I should have been.*

Had he really heard Jan's voice, there at the end, urging him to strike? Olva said young Derwyn had talked about powers moving. So had Death. And so had Jan, all those years ago in the Valley. Dreams and portents, prophecies and powers, and Jan was mixed up in it all. Alf didn't understand it, but it cheered him to think there was someone he trusted looking after the future. *Did I do right, Jan? You carry the hope of the world, you told me. Was this what you meant? Or*

is there more for me to do? Jan had her triumphs, too – the cult in the Valley of the Illuminated venerated her. And they'd kept Derwyn safe and sane all these years, kept Lord Bone locked away within. That was a victory, too.

Brave friends, all. He did not weep, but the wind off the Clawlands was bloody dusty, sometimes.

Brave friends, and there was one left.

The dreadworm flew swift through Charnel night.

The sword felt off in its scabbard. It dug into his hip more than usual. Alf put it down to the runty dreadworm. The wretched thing was barely half the size it should be, the dregs of Lord Bone's magic. He adjusted Spellbreaker.

"What do I do now?"

"Eh?"

"What am I for, now? I was made to slay the Erlking. That was my purpose. I was my maker's weapon, and I have tasted my enemy's soul. He is as dead as the deathless can be. Now, what do I do?"

"Oh, right." Alf contemplated the question.

"I heard your thoughts. Your elegies for the Nine."

"What's an elegy?" muttered Alf.

"You do not tell me to stay out of your thoughts,"

"No. Some thoughts I'm happy for you to share." Alf shifted in the bony saddle. "Necrad. That's what we do. The Erlking was all talk about the Skerrise's spells. Now maybe most of that was lies, but Blaise called for us. So we go to him, and—"

"That is not what I mean. I have fulfilled my quest. I am a weapon without a war. I am not *like* you, wielder. I am not burdened by your annoying doubts, your whining about the old days, your pathetic friendships—"

"Liar!" said Alf. "You're a bloody liar, that's what you are. The way you talked about Lae last night – and you *leapt* into my hand in the

Neverwood, when I called you my friend. You want companionship, not just a hand to wield you."

"Lies."

Below, the Charnel flitted by. The dreadworm was small, but damnably fast. Perdia struggled to keep up with its headlong flight. Soon, Necrad would be in sight.

"I'll tell you something else," said Alf. "I called you a weapon of evil."

"I *am*," said the demon-forged sword.

"I know your blood-thirst. I've felt it. I've wielded it. You're damnably good at killing. But there was nothing I saw in *you* that's not also in me. Before ever I wielded you, I was no stranger to slaughter. You made me better at it, aye, so I could blame you. I could tell myself that I had to be good, because you were evil." Alf shook his head. "But it's never so simple. Can't be cut that neatly. All you can do is try, and when you fuck up, you fix your mistakes after."

"You have not," Spellbreaker observed, "answered my question. What am I for, now?"

"Ask someone clever."

Ahead, the clouds cleared, and Alf saw Necrad.

A gigantic tree of shadow sprouted from the heart of the city. A spell had conjured it, and even without the sword-sight Alf could tell it was feeding on the magic of Necrad. It was rooted in darkness, its tendrils plunging into the endless Pits below. Its titanic trunk rose, mightier than any tower or fortress Alf could imagine. Its branches stretched over the land. Stars hung there like fruit, and they were the first stars — for the shadow of the black tree was the first night before the dawn.

A staggering work of spell-craft.

"Although," admitted Alf to Spellbreaker, "I do have some suggestions."

They dived towards the city.

*

Ceremos hung on the precipice of eternity, and watched the spell take hold. The Wailing Tower wailed, the walls keened. Tendrils of shadow and starlight spread from the base of the tower, slithering across the paved plaza. They probed until they found the scar just north of the tower, the chasm where Lord Bone's palace once stood. The tendrils slithered into that crack in the city, quested into the Pits, and battened there on the magic of Necrad.

The tower quivered. A column of darkness – nay, a trunk! – rose. Ceremos could no longer see the Wailing Tower, only the coruscating shadows of the spell that engulfed it. The window of the study was a shifting patch of lightness beneath the surface. The balcony protruded, the last bit of the tower not consumed by the spell.

Wisps of light, like seeds on the wind, danced over the rooftops. They flickered over the palaces and statues, over monuments and bas-reliefs, over thousands of years of commemoration. Tales change in the telling, living minds forget, even immortal elves fade into wraiths and are stripped of all recollection in the howling void. But the stone of Necrad endures, the stone of Necrad remembers.

The spell read the city.

And the tree grew. Branches of shadow spread across the soot-streaked sky, mirroring the streets below. Dark were the leaves of this unearthly tree of magic, dark as the night sky. And lo! The branches bore fruit, thousands of stars flaring into existence. First one, then a handful more, then a storm of stars, a celestial host marching across the heavens.

"You do not know yourself," said the Skerrise. "But you will."

One of the branches flared with darkness. It crackled across the sky like an inverted thunderbolt, becoming briefly so much more solid and real than the rest of the spectral shadow-tree, the magic of the enchantment briefly focusing in one place. It touched down across the city. Dark fire licked a spire, then danced away. Another branch flashed, briefly linked earth and sky, and then snapped back. Another, another.

Another, near the House of the Horned Serpent.

Galarin Ancient-of-Days, Emlys Arun. The last vampires.

"Ours is the harder path. We must hold the beasts back until the spell is full-formed," said the Skerrise. "But I will see you again for the first time, Adiorno."

"I'm not—" protested Ceremos, but then the spell took him.

The spell told him a tale, told it so well and deeply that it cut into the channels of his brain and shaped everything he thought, told it so truly that the creature who had once been called Ceremos could no longer tell what might be called soul and what was story.

Until the world's ending he would bear that tale.

What a tale it was! A story of gods and monsters, of a new world full of enchantment and mystery, of dungeons deep and dragons fierce. The host of the Firstborn, their spears gleaming in the starry night, eight thousand candles their banner as they warred against shadow-demons! Oaths were taken, battles lost and won, deeds desperate and glorious. Everything was possible when the world was young, and in the first dawn everything was new and wondrous. Demons and other horrors of the dark assailed then, and the elves raised a fortress with walls of stone, a bastion of light.

The first city.

Necrad.

He hung above Necrad, and he saw the city doubled. At once, it was a ruin, choked with rubble, the sky stained with smoke, the city stained with iron vats and foundries and other monstrous legacies of Lord Bone. Wraiths – elven ghosts – crept furtively amid the wreckage of their former glory. He saw the breach in the east wall, and all the other wounds inflicted by mere history.

He saw, too, the city as it was in tales, the city as it should be. The dream of the enchanted realm, the citadel of the Firstborn. He saw it as the story saw it, and the magic made it so. Those figures in the streets – how had he mistaken them for ghosts? There was

young Maedos of Dawn, and merry Oloros, and Amerith herself, all alive! He longed to join them.

The tale was by far the more enchanting, the more beautiful. It was so simple, so true that it must be real. Of course there was a city at the heart of the world, a court for gods and heroes. Of course they were bright and immortal, riding forth to do battle against monsters. Of course they were all friends then, in the first days.

The Skerrise's tale was very sweet, and very poisonous.

Nostalgia is the deadliest of poisons. Like a parasite, it draws its strength from the same source as the host. A hero resists temptation and the lure of power. A hero refuses to be daunted by terror and stands firm against evil, because they draw strength from the tales they heard when they were young, the dream of a simpler, brighter time. The hero's sword cuts through the dark web of complexity, cuts through all the machinations and contingencies of history, and for a moment shows the bright truth.

Everything was better once, and it will be better again when the foe is slain.

When the quest is done, there will be a happy ending.

He fought the enchantment.

With all his will he struggled against it.

He conjured the memory of that metal door in the Pitway. He'd heard the voices of his kinfolk, locked within that prison for defying the Skerrise, for rejecting her. He'd deny her, too. He clutched the metal balustrade and fought the spell.

He drew upon the memories of his mortal friends to sustain him. The hot blood of Perdia, of stout Jon, of bright Cerlys, he'd tasted them all. They were all part of him, his friends, and that gave him the fierce strength of mortals. Their lives blazing like meteors in the night. If all that mattered was *now*, these few moments, then that strength was all he needed.

He'd met the Uncrowned King, and been shown the future.

Tattersoul had prophesied doom for him – and promised that destiny was not fixed. With luck and courage, fate could be averted.

He'd found the Lammergeier. He'd gone on a desperate quest, crossed sea and wilderness, and he'd found Aelfric Lammergeier of the Nine. He'd saved Aelfric from imprisonment, seen the Spellbreaker restored. Aelfric Lammergeier would set the world to rights, and he clung to that thought like a shield.

He'd sworn an oath to Olva Forster. He'd knelt before her and promised to serve her. That oath would sustain him. Above all else, a hero endured in the face of overwhelming odds.

But a man cannot fight magic.

The spell fell upon him with the weight of the city.

Adiorno tore at the manacle that chained him to the railing.

"In time, my friend," said the Skerrise. She emerged from the tree. *Like a hamadryad*, he thought for a moment, but that thought, too, was scoured from his mind. In this tale there was no long despair, no fading – and so no need of the Erlking's life-trees, nor of mortal blood. It would only ever be joy for ever. The magic washed the thought away from Adiorno – but in the same moment he saw a window in the tree, and a hooded figure looking out at him.

"We have a battle to fight, my friend, before we can rejoice." The Skerrise struck the manacle with a silver sword, breaking it, then handed him the blade.

"What battle?" asked Adiorno. Memories of thousands of years of warfare flooded his sinews like quicksilver, and he took the sword eagerly.

The Skerrise pointed her spear towards the north gate.

CHAPTER FORTY-SEVEN

The Vatling's name was not Of No Consequence. It was little more than a century since the first Vatling had crawled from Lord Bone's vats, and in that short time they had little room to create a culture for themselves. The Vatling had named himself after the time of his decanting, after what he saw in those early moments as his brain congealed and vat-imbued knowledge fell upon his nascent mind like an avalanche – but what name he took is forgotten.

So call him Of No Consequence, for that is how the tales remember him.

On that day, Of No Consequence went to serve on the north gate of Necrad. Not to fight – the old sort of Vatlings were, by any measure of the word, squishy. They had no place on the battlefield, or even the parapet. Fighting was for the antlered Vatlings, the favoured ones of the Skerrise. Those Of No Consequence were fit only to fetch and carry, to labour on the repairs or man the catapults that hurled spell-skulls out into the Charnel field, to tend to the demon-summoning plates.

Service on the north gate was not Of No Consequence's assigned task. He was a custodian of the House of the Serpent. But even the new Vatlings paid little attention to the old sort. It was the way of Necrad – the incalculable, eye-shattering grandeur of the first

city seizes the soul. In the days of the occupation – before the Nine carved out the safe zone of the Garrison – there was an epidemic of what was termed Necrad-madness. It was a peculiar delusion: some foot soldier or camp follower, some lowly creature of no consequence whatsoever, would get lost wandering the streets, only to be found ranting about how they were a chosen one, a hero, a prophesied king in need of a golden throne. The spires drew the eye to the heavens, to the stars above; the endless palaces and temples, each grander than the last, recorded the deeds of heroes. Surely anyone who walked these streets must also be a hero, a prince, a god? Surely nothing mattered except this city?

No doubt it helped that Necrad was the abode of frail ghosts. Wraiths clustered in the corners, and Vatlings – well, what were the old sort but a film of frogspawn jelly, smeared over an armature of mismatched bones? They could be ignored as easily as wraiths.

So the horned Vatlings paid no attention to He who was Of No Consequence as he entered the northern barbican. The north gate was only lightly defended; all the fighting was over on the eastern wall, where the humans had brought down a Stone Dragon.

The horned Vatlings were unafraid. The Skerrise had filtered fear out of their making. And if the lesser creatures were afraid, well, what did that matter? They were a dying people, a vestige of the old days. All the spawning vats had been converted to the new breed, in accordance with the will of the Goddess.

Indeed, the Goddess was in the skies that morning. It was hard to see her, sometimes, on account of the smoke from the burning towers, but the horned Vatlings had seen her. They traded glimpses of her as relic-hunters once traded charmstones and filigreed them into tales. If the humans had broken through the eastern wall, then surely the Skerrise would join the fray there and strike them down! There would be a bountiful harvest of bones, and from this slaughter new horned Vatlings would spring. Glory to the Skerrise!

Glory to the Skerrise were the words of No Consequence. He muttered them as he climbed the stairs to the gatekeeper's chamber.

The gatekeeper's chamber was near the top of the seven-storey barbican. It was a large room; narrow slitted windows on the rear and side walls looked out in every direction. The northern wall was a block of impenetrable stone, built to withstand any assault. Facing this crystal was a throne of twisted silver, set with charmstones. The gatekeeper's seat. Tendrils of silver threaded from the chair into the floor below. The gatekeeper could, with an act of will, cause the massive gates four levels down to open, or direct the fires of the stone dragons that flanked the barbican. To the gatekeeper's eyes, too, the northern wall was as transparent as polished crystal.

The chair was made for the elegant frame of a Witch Elf, but a Vatling sat there. Ogre-boned, the horned Vatling was an awkward fit.

Of No Consequence glanced around the room. Six of the horned sort. Two others of the old sort. Poor odds, even if the other Vatlings concealed knives in their robes.

"Look, brothers!" rumbled Hawksflight from the south-east window, "they have gained the parapet!" The other Vatlings crowded around him, peering at the distant eastern wall. Tiny dots moved along it, and it was impossible for Of No Consequence to tell at this distance if they were human or Vatling. The Vatlings were creatures of the city, of its streets and halls – their eyes were not made to be far-sighted.

"The Skerrise will destroy them," said Joyous, the commander of the barbican. He rose from the gatekeeper's chair and stalked across the room, pushing past Of No Consequence with a growl.

A thrill ran through the barbican, the whole city shivering. Of No Consequence felt the soft gel of his pseudo-flesh dance in tune with the shifting currents of his city. The horned Vatlings, with their thick fur, their battle-hardened hide, felt it not at all.

He moved to the gatekeeper's throne.

"Brothers! It begins!" cried another Vatling, and the pack hurried to the south-west window. Of No Consequence looked over his shoulder and glimpsed a darkness rising over Necrad. He paid it no heed.

Instead, he took the throne, his pale fingers clasping the armrests so forcefully that the baroque silver ornamentation pierced his pseudo-flesh like thorns. His sight expanded as the magic took hold, the northern wall becoming transparent to him.

A ragged band of humans charged towards the gate. They ran unflinching towards the conjured darkness, challenging the Skerrise in all her power. Heroes all, no doubt.

He knew in that moment that they would never hear tell of him. That he would not even be a footnote in their legend.

He could get up. Yield the throne and walk away. The other Vatlings were still clustered at the windows and had not seen him sit in the gatekeeper's chair. He could walk away.

Instead, he spoke a word of command.

"What treachery is this?" roared Joyous, then he was gurgling, dying, a Vatling knife stuck through his furred throat. Of No Consequence closed his eyes and clung to the throne, the magic flowing through him, one with the city. The gates shuddered and began to grind open.

Behind him, other Vatlings died. Then there were clawed hands grabbing him, trying to tear him from the throne. He held on, even as they took axes to him. He stained the throne, the vitalising fluids of him washing over it, the rags of his pseudo-flesh clinging to it like tatters, holding on just long enough—

The gate opened.

Thank you, Threeday! Olva shed her bird-skin and stumbled across the threshold. Tholos grabbed her arm to help steady her. Idmaer and Cerlys had already charged ahead, followed by a dozen more knights, a small handful of soldiers. More were following behind.

"Gatehouse!" roared Tholos. He let her go and raced off towards an archway. A horned Vatling emerged from the darkness within. Tholos cut him down, and the Vatling behind him. "Hold the gate!" he shouted, "or they'll shut it behind us!" Soldiers pushed past Olva. From outside the walls, shouts, the sound of men splashing through thick mud as more and more of Ironhand's army ran for the open gate, or saw their comrades abandoning the siege and joined them in a mad dash. The army was melting away, becoming a mob.

The sorcerous tree above Necrad convulsed. A new branch erupted from it, a giant's outstretched arm, fingers dragging across the clouds. It clawed past the walls and swept over the northern approach, across the causeway and the battlefield. Where its shadow touched, men became beasts. The spell took their wits from them in an instant, reducing them to grunting animals, running on all fours.

Olva threw herself to the side, pressing herself into the shelter of the archway as the shadow passed. The edge of it brushed her, and for an instant she was a crane again, in flight over the wild expanse of the forest, endless green canopy riven with the silver of ponds and rivers, a bird in flight for ever, no fear or doubts, no thoughts of past or future. The beast was a welcoming abyss – it would be so restful, so easy to cast all her cares and responsibilities into that maw. To never know worry or guilt or consequence, to always live in the *now*.

The shadow passed. The spell moved on, sweeping east towards the camp. Across the city, she could see more branches extending far away, darkening the southern sky. Could this spell reach across the sea, and catch Summerswell in its shadow? She thought of Derwyn in the High Moor, imagined him seeing those tenebrous branches looming above him. If the spell tore all reason and memory from mortals, revealing them as nothing more than savage beasts at heart, what would it do to one who held a dark lord chained within?

Break the spell. Alf – if he was still alive – had Spellbreaker. She'd sent it away. She'd freed the Skerrise. All this was her doing, her responsibility.

Spellbreaker was far away, but there were other ways to break spells.

Olva caught up with the Dragonslayer's company in a great plaza. Cerlys leaned against the wall at the foot of a titanic statue of an elf, gasping for breath. The stone features surveyed the carnage with perfect serenity. They'd hacked their way through a host of defenders. The corpses of horned Vatlings lay all around, dissolving into the same mush as the colossal carcasses of butchered Pitspawn. Mortal soldiers had fallen here, too, hacked or clawed or hewed apart so violently they were as misshapen as the Vatlings in death.

Four streets led away from the four corners of the plaza.

"Which way?" asked Cerlys. Necrad played tricks with space – and Olva was the only member of the company who'd walked those twisted streets before.

"Give me a moment."

"We have little time, Old Woman," intoned a Wilder. One of Ernala's brothers.

She limped off across the plaza to get her bearings. The serene statue, the palaces all around, they were familiar to Olva. She'd been here before, a lifetime ago. Over there, in the middle of the square, there'd been an entrance into the Pits. A wellway, fifteen feet wide. She and Alf had descended there, in search of Derwyn. Down into darkness.

Now the well was sealed. The dwarf-wrought gate that Alf had smashed with Spellbreaker had been replaced by a circle of some silvery metal, marked with astrological runes, as if a giant had dropped a silver coin.

The rim of the seal writhed. Wraiths clustered there, cramming their ghostly bodies into the nails' breadth between seal and the edge of the well. The wraiths could not abide sunlight, but there were infinitely better places to shelter in Necrad than the middle of a wide courtyard. Sensing her presence, the wraiths slithered out of

hiding, one spectral form after another rising up and beckoning to her, calling silently to her – then burning in the sunlight, one by one blasted into oblivion.

They were calling her to this spot. Olva knelt and knocked on the metal seal.

· Elven voices answered from far below, calling for help.

"We have to open this!"

"There is no time," growled the Wilder. He surveyed the surrounding buildings, eyes filled with terror. "The skies darken."

Ironhand glanced at Cerlys. She gave a quick nod. "Open it."

He put aside the Brightsword, then stooped and clamped the unresponsive, unfeeling fingers of his metal hand into place, driving them into the tiny gap. Disturbed wraiths fluttered past him. With a tremendous effort, every muscle and sinew in his massive frame straining, he shoved the seal an inch to the side – enough for him to get a better grip on the metal door, enough for other hands to join him in the task.

Metal scraped across stone – and then, the breath of foul air. The remaining wraiths slipped gratefully into the sheltering dark. · Ironhand pushed the seal aside with a roar of pain.

Pale faces stared up from the bottom of the shaft. At the sight of the mortals, they cried out in dismay.

"There are elves down there!" shouted a knight. He pointed an elf-bane crossbow at them. "Are you Witch or Wood?"

"It doesn't matter." Cerlys sprang to the rim of the shaft and cast back her cloak so they could see her armour clearly in the pale sunlight. "I'm Cerlys of Ersfel. Aelfric Lammergeier trained me. I've fought alongside Witch Elf and Wood Elf. This is the armour of Ildorae. This is her dagger – it was given to me by Laerlyn of the Everwood. I'm a friend of Ceremos. Is he among you?"

A tall elf-woman pushed her way through the crowd and looked up at Cerlys. "Ceremos is my son. The Skerrise sent word that he had returned to Necrad, but she would not let me see him."

"Your city's fallen," said Cerlys, "and your Queen's mad. She's unleashed dark magic. We're going to slay her to stop the spell."

Olva picked up a sword from the ground. It had belonged to one of the fallen soldiers. It was an old sword, a League sword, one of thousands hastily made for the defence against Lord Bone's army fifty years ago. Not the ornate, cherished weapon of a wealthy knight or elf-prince. It had no magic to it, no legend clung to it. A sharpened stick of metal, made for slaughter. To be wielded in conquest and butchery, or in defence of hearth and home. She handed it to Cerlys.

The Dragonslayer offered it to the elves. "Join us."

Elithadil picked up the sword.

With the elves to guide them, they nearly made it.

Through the labyrinth of the Sanction they ran. They were a pack of wolves now, all pretence of military discipline gone. No marching order, no rearguard, no scouts. Just ragged warriors, running through the ruined city. They did not know if the gates behind them were still open. They did not know if the siege continued outside, or if the whole army had fallen to enchanted madness. They did not know if there was anything left at all.

They knew, though, that everything could be wiped away in an instant. All the mortals among them had glimpsed the Grey Lands. All the immortals among them had perished time and time again, only to return to a world broken and changed beyond recognition.

They knew that there was no certainty, and that this was both terror and hope. The dark tree was before them. The spell of the Skerrise reached for the stars.

She awaited them at the centre of the city, in the grand plaza before the Wailing Tower. Lord Bone's fortress had once stood here; long before that, the Erlking had worked wonders. Here he had bound Death. Here was the axis of the world until the world's ending.

A half-dozen vampire knights guarded the Skerrise. Each was clad in armour, forged by Kortirion for the Candlelit Crusade. Each one bore an enchanted weapon of surpassing power. Red eyes gleamed beneath their helms. Five of these knights were ancient, the last of the Witch Elf elders.

The sixth was young, and knew only the name Adiorno.

CHAPTER FORTY-EIGHT

"I should point out," said Spellbreaker, "that I am somewhat depleted. All the souls I swallowed at Raven's Pass were expended against the Erlking's spells."

"We'll make it," insisted Alf. He guided the dreadworm with his knees, bringing it in a swooping arc over southern Necrad. The Garrison flickered past beneath – Alf glimpsed his old house for an instant – and then they were out over the east Charnel. He scanned the camp below, looking for Ironhand's banner, for any sign of Olva.

Ironhand's army was disintegrating. A handful of companies were hurrying to the north gate, but the rest were fleeing in confusion, or . . . also fleeing in confusion, but on all fours. Or wrestling with one another in the mud, or cowering from the shadow of the dreadworm. They howled and whooped as Alf soared overhead. A knight of Summerswell looked up, and Alf saw blood and strings of flesh dripping from the man's mouth. He'd ripped out the throat of his squire with his bare teeth.

Beasts. The Skerrise's spell had turned them into beasts.

"We could land," suggested the sword, "and heroically free those wretches from their curse."

Alf glanced over his shoulder. Perdia was banking north, crossing over the breach in the city's walls, diving towards the old Sanction.

Her young eyes were keener than his. Maybe she'd seen Olva or one of their other friends from the air. He turned his own worm, but, as he did so, he flew over the retreating soldiers and brandished Spellbreaker.

The Black Sword, they cried. Not the Lammergeier.

But the black sword was banner enough. Some rallied, and joined their comrades in marching on the north gate.

Wielder!

The Skerrise's spell convulsed. The sword lent Aelfric its sight, and he could see the magic. He could see how the spell took not only power from Necrad, but *inspiration*, taking ancient deeds commemorated in stone and engraving them on the living world. He saw the magic surge, a blast of sorcery drawn up from the depths of the Pits, rising dark and terrible through the Wailing Tower, then—

The dreadworm shot across the sky. For an instant, Alf saw it all.

The grand plaza at the foot of the tower. The Skerrise, like a dark star. The ring of vampires, Vatlings, Pitspawn, all the horrors of Necrad surrounding a scant few mortal heroes. He saw Ironhand fighting side by side with a swordmaiden. He saw Olva looking up, as if she'd been expecting him.

A bolt of oblivion shot from the heavens.

Spellbreaker parried it.

The spell broke around Alf, shards of magic exploding all around him. Glimpses of times he'd never known, unheard tales and forgotten legends battered him. A red wave washed over him – not the bloodlust of the sword, but something older, something that came from within himself. Death called to him, and the sword screamed with the effort of shielding him.

He shot past the tower and flew into open air. He wheeled the dreadworm back towards the fray, its wings beating furiously with the effort, tail scraping off the facades of the palaces on the far side of the plaza.

The Skerrise hurled her spear. Alf saw it out of the corner of his eye, and leapt from the worm's back. He bounced off the marble wall, grappling for a handhold. Above, the spear pinned the dread-worm to the pediment like a hideous trophy. Alf caught himself on the arm of a statue, but he wasn't strong enough to hold on, and fell again, tumbling down the ornate face of the palace to land with a bone-shattering crash on the pavement below.

He lay there, looking up at the sky. He'd never seen the sky of Necrad like this, criss-crossed with the shifting branches of the dark tree. It looked like the heavens were a dome of crystal, and the cracks were growing.

"Get up, wielder," urged the sword. "I lack the strength to break the whole spell, but I am still keener than any other blade. Get up. Slay the Skerrise."

Perdia landed a short distance away. She dropped Jon from her talons, then shifted her skin again, drinking deep of the magic of Necrad. Alf saw the young woman's face surface in the maelstrom of change, and her features reminded him in that moment of Talis. But it was not a human skin that Perdia took. Her shape swelled as she became gigantic. Feathers fell as she grew bat-wings. A scorpion-tail lined with hundreds of spikes arched over her back. Her limbs became leonine, muscles rippling beneath her golden hide.

The city shook with each massive footfall of the Manticore. She prowled across the courtyard, roaring a challenge to the Skerrise, monster to monster.

Jon knelt by Alf—

And the squire knelt by the Lammergeier, and saw that the strength of the hero was broken. Arm in arm they crossed the plaza, but with each step the Lammergeier faltered. They came to the door of the Wailing Tower, and in the shadow of that portal, the Lammergeier handed the sword Spellbreaker to his squire, saying:

"An oath I swore to guard this city. Let oaths be kept, and spells

be broken. Take this blade to the one who wields it best, so that they may strike down the dark lady."

The squire bared his breast, and said: "My lord, 'tis said the dread sword can both take life and give it. I beg thee, take my unworthy life that it may heal thy wounds, and then you may go into battle renewed, as the Lammergeier of old."

But the Lammergeier replied. "Nay, child. Be off with you. It is true that the sword cares not who it cuts. Therefore it is the duty of the wielder to restrain the hungry blade, and wield it with wisdom. My wisdom, learned on the long road is this: my time is done. Take the blade, and do not look back."

The squire did as he was bade, and ran from the shadow of the Wailing Tower.

Now this was the scene he beheld, and I tell it to you true. From the north gate of Necrad came King Ironhand and the Dragonslayer and their worthy company, bolstered in strength by the elves they freed from the Pit. When the Skerrise's host of horrors assailed them, the Dragonslayer cried "Let the walls be our rearguard," and they took refuge in one of the mighty palaces surrounding the plaza.

Now this tower, later called the Palace of Song, had but a single great door, six times the height of the tallest man, but narrow, so the Pitspawn could only enter it one at a time. And the Dragonslayer stood on one side of the door, and King Ironhand on the other, and lo! They hewed the first unnatural beast as it entered, and hewed the second as it crawled over the carcass of its brother, and hewed the third as it sought to push aside the first two. A wall of bodies they built, each one a malignant titan from the Pits!

The Skerrise then besieged the Palace of Song, for she had seen the black sword in the hand of the Dragonslayer, and thought it to be the Spellbreaker, the one blade she most feared in all the world. She had the power of flight, and on wings of shadow she soared to the very pinnacle of the palace. Over the rooftops, scaling the

walls, skittering like spiders came her vampire servants, eldest of
the Endless. For months, the Skerrise had kept them imprisoned in
eyries all across the city. Keen and terrible was their hunger, and to
this ferocity she added the strength of elder days. No mightier host
ever marched to war!

So at the last, the fighting was in the heart of the palace, the
narrow passageways and winding stairs. The necromiasma had all
gone out, and the nightmare tree of the Skerrise's magic obscured
whatever fading light there might have been, so it was a battle
fought in the dark. They might as well have been in the darkest
dungeon, in the uttermost Pit of Necrad, as King Ironhand and the
Dragonslayer matched blades bright and black against the vampire
knights. And all the while, the spell grew, casting the shadow of the
past across the Lands of the Firstborn.

The squire came to the Palace of Song, and saw that the door was
blocked. He sought another way in, but became lost in the labyrinth
of the city. He could hear all around him the noise of battle, but he
knew that his friends were fighting and dying in the palace above,
but he knew not the way. He wailed with fear, and tripped over his
own shoes, and ran hither and thither in confusion, until the blade
spoke to him, saying:

"Climb."

So he scaled the palace. Higher he climbed, and higher, as though
the tower were a cliff of marble. Higher he climbed, and higher, and
the cold wind tore at him. Higher he climbed, and higher, until the
slightest error would doom him.

And as he clung there, frozen in terror, he saw he was not alone.
The vampire childe, clad in the armour of a dreadknight, stood on
a narrow parapet.

The squire wept with relief, and hailed him, calling him Ceremos.

But the vampire childe was bewitched by the Skerrise, and declared himself to be Adiorno, for that was the name he had worn
in his first life. And further, he said he would slay this impudent

mortal who had trespassed in the city of the elves, and drink his
blood.

"Nay, nay," cried the squire, "you are Ceremos, my friend" – all
to no avail. The vampire did not heed his pleas. He seized the black
sword from the squire, and drank deep, staining the gorget of his
armour with red blood. Then, leaving the squire lying on the parapet, he entered the Palace of Song.

Now the Skerrise battled the two champions. King Ironhand struck
her with the Brightsword, and the Dragonslayer struck her with her
black blade. But the Skerrise had the strength of ten thousand years,
and all the power of Necrad in her. Wounds that would have felled
a dragon did not trouble her.

The Skerrise parried the sword of Cerlys Dragonslayer with her
spear, and the sword shattered.

"Mortals! Feh! You are nothing but beasts!" she cried, "I shall
hunt you for sport in the world restored!"

With that, she thrust her spear through the side of King
Ironhand, as though he were a boar cornered in a thicket, and
he fell.

Withdrawing the spear, she turned to the Dragonslayer, and said,
"Mortals! You are nothing compared to the Firstborn! Nothing but
a brief tale, soon forgotten, without even a coin for the teller."

The Dragonslayer raised her sword – and then saw, in the shadows behind the Skerrise, the dreadknight Adiorno, his lips red with
blood, and in his hand the true Spellbreaker.

"Slay her, Adiorno," commanded the Skerrise, "and seal for ever
the rule of the Firstborn over mortals."

"I would hear new tales," said Ceremos, for the sword had freed
him from enchantment! He struck the Skerrise from behind. Oh! It
was as though the heavens shattered, and ten thousand stars fell from
them! All the charmstones that guarded and warded the Skerrise
broke all at once, all her magic shattering like glass! And in the same

blessed moment, the Dragonslayer snatched up the Brightsword and cut the head of the Skerrise from her shoulders.

With the death of its caster, the spell failed. The dark tree bent, and a wind from the sea blew it away. And lo! The sunset turned the dread city into gold! And it is said—

CHAPTER FORTY-NINE

The tale did not begin in an inn. It would not end in one.

Still, the old, old woman limped down the street towards the inn, her crane-foot slapping quietly on the paving stones. Paving stones! They hadn't had those in her day. Ersfel was a big town now, and the Road ran through it. All the new Roads were paved these days, and well-guarded, too. The king's reign had been long and peaceful.

The inn stood on the same spot as Genny Selcloth's alehouse, but was ten times larger. Guest rooms on the floor above, and a stable, and dwarf-wrought lamps! And by their light, she could see the sign above the door – the black-winged Lammergeier, with the sword clutched in its talons.

The old woman entered just as the singer finished her tale. "With the death of its caster, the spell failed. The dark tree bent, and a wind from the sea blew it away. And lo! The sunset turned the dread city into gold! And it is said that those who beheld that victory sang in all the tongues of elves and men and dwarves, for they knew that the quest was ended and evil had been defeated for ever."

It was a worn and familiar story, forty years old if it was a day, and one the audience had clearly heard many times before. Only a few coins were dropped in the singer's battered hat. As she passed, the old woman added an old coin from Necrad to the pile, then took

a seat in the shadowed corner by the fireplace. The common room was crowded with a mix of locals, merchants – mostly dwarves – and what had to be an adventuring party at a big round table. An elf, a dwarf, a Wilder, a knight of Summerswell. Even a Vatling, pockets filled with arcane trinkets and charms. The city was theirs now, more than anyone else's.

One of the adventurers wore robes from the new College up in Summerswell. He glanced over at the old woman, sensing a quiver in the earthpower, and she put a finger to her lips. The Changeling lad looked away hastily.

A small crowd gathered around the innkeeper. *He's got old*, thought Olva, *and bald*. Jon wore his father's face now, as if Thomad was a skin he'd put on. But for that, she would not have recognised him, this Jon with a wide paunch and a wider smile and easy confidence behind the bar. Uncrowned king of a little kingdom.

One of Jon's daughters – granddaughters? – brushed past Olva to throw more wood on the fire. She paid no heed to the old woman. Her attention was focused on the adventurers, and Olva recognised the look on the girl's face. *Keep your eye on that one, Jon*, she thought, *or she'll be off down the Road.*

"You were *there*, Master Jon," said a dwarf, "if the tales are to be believed."

Jon grinned. "Maybe."

"How did the old King survive, if he was skewered with a spear?"

"Oh, there's healing in Necrad. *Fountains* of healing cordial." He jerked a thumb towards the storeroom. "Why, I brought home barrels of it, if anyone's buying potions."

The adventuring party hastened to join the crowd at the bar.

"And the Spellbreaker? Does the Dragonslayer wield it?" asked one of the adventurers.

"Ah, well, I haven't seen Ceremos or Cerlys in many a year. But the Dragonslayer's still the King's champion, so they pass through the Mulladales on their errantries, from time to time. And when

they do, they make a point of calling in here." He grinned at the adventuring knight. "That's her seat you're in, by the by."

The warrior scrambled up as if he'd been lit on fire. He regarded the barstool with the awe once reserved for a grail.

The locals laughed. "Jon plays that trick every time!"

"Pining after his lost love," jeered another.

"Aye, I loved Cerlys," said Jon. He raised a glass. "We love fiercely when we're young, but not wisely. It was never meant to be, and likely better it had never been. We both know that now. She's happy off adventuring with Ceremos, but my heart's in Ersfel."

"It bloody better be," called a woman's voice from the back room, and the locals laughed again.

"But tell me, Master Jon," said another dwarf. "What became of the Lammergeier?" The dwarf was older than the rest of his company. To most of the crowd, the deeds of the Nine were ancient history, long consigned to myth. But the dwarf was old enough to remember Karak's Bridge. More than eighty years gone, but still they remembered.

She leaned forward to hear Jon's answer.

The innkeeper fell solemn. He did not reply for a long moment. Instead, he reached under the bar and took out two great handfuls of tin cups. He doled them out, placing one in front of each member of the company.

"They won't tell you this in the stories, but we never saw him again. We went back to the Wailing Tower, after, but it was empty. No sign of Blaise, and no sign of Aelfric Lammergeier."

He produced a bottle of elven wine and uncorked it. The faint smell of lotus filled the air as he poured a small measure into each cup.

"Ceremos — he says they're still out there. He says that one day, when we need 'em, the last of the Nine will come back, and join with other heroes in the defence of the realm. But he's an elf — to him it's all one tale without end."

Jon raised his cup. "Whether that's true or not, I know this: he lived a hero. To Aelfric Lammergeier!"

"To the Lammergeier!" they chorused.

Jon finally noticed the old woman in the shadowed corner. "Will you not join our toast?"

"I won't, Jon," said Olva, "but I do want a word, when you're done."

The last of the company departed, and only Jon and Olva sat by the dying fire. It was Jon who seemed to change, reverting back to the boy he was, stammering and fearful of the Witch of Ersfel.

"Did . . . " he began, then looked away. "The stories get her wrong, didn't they?"

"Aye, they do."

"I wasn't there – I was in the Wailing Tower, so I didn't see – but Cerlys told me that it was the Manticore who really killed the Skerrise. Cerlys – she was fighting Ceremos, and Ironhand was already down, and that they'd have all been slain if it weren't for Perdia. She came in, all Manticore-y, and she slew the Skerrise. And the tales barely mention her."

"Death was in her," muttered Olva. "And for that matter, it was me who healed Ironhand, not your bloody potions, thank you very much."

Jon's cheeks flushed redder than the fire.

"Pay it no mind. Alf would have found it funny." Olva snorted. "He was never a man for drinking a bar dry, but if you were selling healing cordial, it might have been a different story."

Jon swallowed. "Did you find her? Cerlys said – she said that after the Skerrise was dead that Perdia just stepped into the shadow of the spell. She *let* it take her memory, then turned into a great wolf and ran off north. Did you find her?"

Olva reached over to the bar and picked up the bottle of elven wine. She sniffed. Lotus fruit brought forgetfulness, and elves were not the only ones to seek relief from the burden of memory.

"Aye, I found her. She found me, more. The earthpower led her to Daeroch Nal, in the end. I live there, now. The Old Woman of the Woods. They send Changelings to me from all over the Lands, from Summerswell and the north. The elves bring them to me. The Wandering Companies. Very few elves stay in Necrad now. Ceremos led them out and showed them the world."

"But what of Perdia?" asked Jon quietly.

"I tried to do for her what I did for Derwyn, but ... ach. It's a terrible thing to be close to a hero. They break the world, and it's up to the rest of us to find new skins, after, so we can live in the changed shape of things. But heroes ... they never know peace."

She drew on the earthpower. The dying fire blazed up, the flames an eerie green, and a sudden wind howled through the wooded hills and rattled the windows. Olva's old face changed, the years falling away from it, and she was young again, younger than Jon, her face as it had been long long ago when the Nine came to her father's door in the middle of the night.

"It wasn't the Skerrise's death that broke the spell, Jon. The spell kept going after Perdia slew her. You brought Alf and the sword to the Wailing Tower, and after you came down *alone*. Tell me – what really happened?"

Jon couldn't look her in the eye. He turned away, stared at the ceiling.

"I don't know. They shut the door."

"Ah well," she said.

When he looked back, Olva was gone, and Jon was almost alone.

Wearily, Jon stood. He tidied away the cups, put the chairs back in their proper places. He raked out the fire, exposing the last embers.

He looked up at the ceiling.

"Will you tell me the story now?"

From the hiding place amid the rafters of the inn, there came no answer.

CHAPTER FIFTY

Not yet, anyway. Not to an innkeeper.

But here, in the dark, for an audience of wraiths and shadows . . . to you I'll tell the tale of my wielder.

I have lain hidden here above the common room for decades. Somewhat less epic, I must admit, than the time I spent embedded in the dead life-tree of the Erlking, but more entertaining. If there is one thing that distinguishes you humans from beasts – and I assure you, I have quested into the entrails of many creatures and found no other distinction – it is that you are tale-tellers.

I have eavesdropped on many stories during my vigil, so I shall try to tell you one.

It begins, as you already know, in the grand plaza that surrounds the Wailing Tower. It was there that Lord Bone's palace once stood, the Nine took me there, the sundering of the arcane vessel, the fiery death of Peir and Lord Bone, et cetera et cetera, all the heroic business you know already. Now my wielder – what was left of him – carried me across those starlight-spitting stones.

He had it in his mind, I think, to chop down the magic tree. To wield me like a woodcutter's axe and sever the spell.

I told him this was a stupid plan. That, firstly, it wasn't a real tree, just the illusory manifestation of a spell. That, second, beneath the

ghostly shade of the trunk was the very solid stone of the Wailing
Tower, and that I already had enough dings and dents put in me.
And, third and most important, I was exhausted. I lacked the power
to break a spell of such magnitude. That incantation drew on all
the magic of Necrad. I could shield him from it – which is why he
wasn't grunting in the corner like a baboon – but not counter the
spell entire. Not without feeding first.

He asked what we should do, and I told him. Climb.

We ascended the stairs of the Wailing Tower. Step by step, floor
by floor. Through the windows, we could see the battle below, and
it was all very wonderful slaughter. There was the Brightsword, of
course – a gaudy weapon. Tacky, even. Secret Flame, what a stupid
name for a weapon that lights up. Flame, yes, but 'secret'? If you
want to keep something secret, you don't make it glow. Idiocy.

But I digress.

And Cerlys, sweet violent Cerlys, she had the other black sword,
the copy of me that Earl Duna had made for his sons. I've had
plenty of imitators in my day (I am, of course, the *original* soul-
drinking black sword, and I will hear no accounts to the contrary),
but I must confess a fondness for that little weapon. I felt something akin to paternal pride as Cerlys chopped up Pitspawn. But
my wielder carried me past the window, and all the lovely carnage
was gone.

We came to the door of Blaise's study, and from within we heard
the wizard's voice.

"Sir Aelfric of Mulladale, Knight of Summerswell, called by
some Lammergeier. Keeper of the Spellbreaker, *ayis turam va'shon*,
thy name is terror to foes and a rallying cry to friends. Enter – but
set aside your blade as you do."

Jon paled and backed away.

Alf was very slow to learn any lessons. They had to be drummed
into that impenetrable skull by endless repetition. But he had

learned not to set me aside. He held me as he entered the room.

There, bound to his chair by wires of silver, were the remains of Blaise.

Blaise had sought to spare my wielder this last horror. He had thought, maybe, to retain some dignity for himself. He was always the most arrogant and most insecure of the Nine, so I always had a spark of sympathy for him. A tiny spark of sympathy, mind you, compared to the blazing hatred I felt for all of them, but a spark nonetheless.

Blaise would have preferred that his old friend Alf not see the form survival demanded of him. The rotting flesh that clung to broken bone, the charmstones stuffed into the gaping wound in his heart. The cowl of his cloak could not hide the tattered skull of the lich. Wheezing machines pumped a torrent of cordial through collapsing veins. The Skerrise had not used healing magic to save his life, or resurrection spells to bring him back from the Grey Lands. He was nothing but a tool to her, a weapon to be repaired, however crudely. She pinned him on the edge of dying – and he had been complicit in his ghastly preservation. I could see his hand in the refinements, in the sigils drawn on his rotting flesh. Terror of death consumed him.

I marvelled at the courage it had taken for him to summon me here.

"Blaise," said Alf, his voice breaking. "What did she do to you?"

Oh, wielder. Always asking the wrong questions.

What have you done? That's what he should have asked, and I could have told him. It was not the Skerrise's spell that hung in the skies of Necrad – oh, she had demanded it of him, forced it from him. It was her will and desire, and she commanded it, wielded it, but it was Blaise's spell. He was the caster, and it would break only when he did.

Blaise knew that.

Alf asked the wrong questions. He also, in the end, told himself

the wrong tale. One should never trust a storyteller. Every story is told with a purpose, even if the teller is unaware of it. Stories can be lessons, moral examples, cautionary tales. They can justify slaughter, or inspire the building of wonders. But no story contains the whole truth. There are always choices to be made. Some matters are passed over briefly, lifetimes flickering by in paragraph breaks. Sometimes, the storyteller lingers, lavishing time on battles and gore, on the fumbling fingers and eager bosoms of lovers, on dry litanies of kings or glimpses of poetic beauty.

But there is always a choice to be made, for a tale cannot encompass the world. What is ignored, and what is emphasised?

What is spared, and what is cut?

"Let me go, wielder," I said to him.

He stuck me into the ground, even though there was a perfectly good desk right there, and released me. Blaise's illusion fell upon him.

I do not know what he saw. By my nature, I am immune to illusions. I see only the physical world. You mortals, you see stories everywhere. You look into the night sky, and you see patterns in the stars. You look at the land and wonder what lies around the next corner. You run off down the Road to seek your fortune.

Maybe Alf saw Blaise the Archmage, in all his arcane glory. The floating eyes, the excessive number of hands, the tattered scallops of his rune-marked cloak, all very impressive. More likely, I think, he saw Blaise as he was when they first met, when they were young. Alf thought of them all that way. I was inside his thoughts so many times, I know them all.

"You must slay me, Aelfric," intoned Blaise.

"No!" shouted Alf.

As I said, he had told himself the wrong story. In Alf's tale, it was a story about one last ride, one final effort, and then ... well, tales have tidy endings. The quest is done, and it's happy ever after.

History crawls on. It bleeds into the dirt, messy and undignified and unending.

The story must be cut free.

"Only my . . . dissolution will break the spell she made me cast."

"No more. Not after all you've suffered. Not after Lae. Not after everything. Fucking prophecies. The hope of the world. I'll take you last of all. Fuck it all." He tore Blaise free from the chains and wires that bound him to the throne. "I'm getting you out of here."

"I have not the strength, wielder!" I told him.

"Shut up!" He ripped away the tubes and entrails and pipes. I saw that Blaise's body ended at the waist, that the ragged cloak flapped empty, but who knows what the illusions showed. "We're going home. There's a wizard's college, and you can be master there instead. They owe us this. I'm taking you home. I'll carry you all the way to Summerswell if I have to."

"There is no other way, Aelfric," intoned Blaise. "The enchantment will grow for ever, casting a shadow over the world. There will be nothing new ever again."

"I don't care." He lifted Blaise's skeleton from the throne.

The wizard protested feebly, skeletal hands pawing at Aelfric's broad shoulders. He was not listening to Blaise. He was consumed by compassion for his friend. His only thought was to save him, not to save the world. Not the quest that had brought us here. He would not listen to Blaise.

He would listen to me.

"There is a way, wielder, to save everyone – though it is most perilous," I said. "In the deepest dungeon of the Pits, where no mortal save my master ever went, guarded by unimaginable monsters and myriad fiendish traps, there is a rune. A keystone for all Necrad. Break it, and the spell ends."

(Do not judge me. Do not dare judge me.)

"I cannot imagine," I said, "that even the Nine in their glory could reach that keystone in time. It is a hopeless quest."

"Isn't it always?" said my wielder. He reached for me.

He reached for me and I . . .

Never trust a storyteller.

We invest so much in our heroes. We fill them with significance, make them symbols and banners, make them legends. But they are mortal, and so can only be imperfect vessels, imperfect tools. They must, inevitably, fail. Each story must end.

But when? That's the question. Is it better to die on the threshold of glory, as Peir did? To vanish from the tale, leaving a mysterious absence? Or to live out the span of one's days, however diminished? How to balance life and legend?

I told Jon to keep me hidden. I told him I have a new purpose now, that he must hide me away until I am needed. No doubt there will be another dark lord. Mortals are very clever. They are building Necrads all across the land now, wellsprings of magic to usher in an age of wonders. One of them, no doubt, will turn sour, and there'll be a need for heroes. There will a dark lord, and a rising shadow, and desperate defiance. A few heroes, blazing bright against the dark.

Then, I shall take a new wielder.

My old wielder — I told him a story, in that last moment. Even as I took his life, even as I drank his soul and used that strength to unmake Blaise, even as I did what he could not, I told him the story he wanted to hear. It had to be done. The story had to win out over the man. The tale is all that survives in the end.

So if you tell the tale of Aelfric Lammergeier, tell of nine travellers setting off on a desperate mission. Nine friends, unlikely companions forged into a fellowship by shared peril on the Road. Talk of them delving into dungeons deep, tell of them growing in power and purpose, rising to meet the challenge of the quest.

Tell not of their ending, but of that first wary step across the

dungeon threshold, the fathomless dark ahead, the party by his side. Tell of the adventure.

Aelfric and the Nine, for ever.

But I cannot go with them.

At the last, I choose my own name, my own purpose.

I am Tale-Ender.

ACKNOWLEDGEMENTS

The tale grew in the telling, as Professor Tolkien said. Most sub-creations owe something to Middle-earth; this one owes more than most, and it is a debt I enthusiastically acknowledge.

It also owes a patent debt to tabletop roleplaying – both the f20 tradition of dungeons, dragons, swords and spells, but a more immediate one to *Dramasystem* and the Heroes of the City campaign that provided the initial inspiration. My thanks to my fellow Pelgranistas, especially Cat, Simon and Robin, to Jon and Francesco and the One Ring crew, and all those I've gamed with over the years.

Thanks also to my beta readers, especially Neil Kelly and Eamonn Tee; my agent John Jarrold, cover artist Thea Dumitriu, editors Emily Byron and Bradley Englert, and everyone who worked on these books behind the scenes at both Orbit and Inkstone Press.

And always, thanks to Edel, Tristan, Elyan and Nimue (who narrowly escaped being named "Tallis", but did get caught with "Luthien").

extras

orbit-books.co.uk

extras

about the author

Gareth Hanrahan's three-month break from computer programming to concentrate on writing has now lasted fifteen years and counting. He's written more gaming books than he can readily recall, by virtue of the alchemical transmutation of tea and guilt into words. He lives in Ireland with his wife and twin sons. Follow him on X at @mytholder.

Find out more about Gareth Hanrahan and other Orbit authors by registering for the free monthly newsletter at orbit-books.co.uk.

if you enjoyed

THE SWORD TRIUMPHANT

look out for

BLOOD OF
THE OLD KINGS

by
Sung-il Kim

There is no escaping the Empire.
Even in death, you will serve.

In an Empire fuelled by necromancy, dead sorcerers are the lifeblood. Their corpses are wrapped in chains and drained of magic to feed the unquenchable hunger for imperial conquest.

Born with magic, Arienne has become resigned to her dark fate. But when the voice of a long-dead sorcerer begins to speak inside her head, she listens. There may be another future for her, if she's willing to fight for it.

Miles away, beneath a volcano, a seven-eyed dragon also wears the Empire's chains. Before the imperial fist closed around their lands, it was the people's sacred guardian.

Loran, a widowed swordswoman, is the first to kneel before the dragon in decades. She comes with a desperate plea, and will leave with a sword of dragon-fang in hand and a great purpose before her.

1

LORAN

When she came to, Loran found herself under the scrutiny of a dark red dragon with too many eyes.

The beast had two enormous eyes where you would expect them, flanked by two smaller ones on the left and three more on the right. And all seven of these eyes were trained on Loran, boring into her with an unreadable expression.

More than how the fire-dragon loomed over her like a tower, more than the teeth that looked like swords and spears in a crowded weapons rack, more than the black chains entangled over the scales of its back, and more than the claw pressing down on her chest and holding her in place—it was these two rows of eyes, left and right, that frightened her.

When she tried to get up, the pressure on her chest increased. The claw was thicker than Loran's thigh, sharper than a dagger, and pierced her clothes and flesh.

Loran grimaced and a groan escaped her. The claw lightened a little.

"A princess of Arland."

The dragon's voice was not loud—it was as soft as a human's, yet otherworldly and full of menace. Loran tamped down on her terror and took in her surroundings. The walls of gray basalt looked naturally formed but, at the same time, not. There were blackened spots in places, and large scratch marks. Despite the cavern being inside of a volcano, there was a chill in the air.

She took a deep breath and spoke in a clear voice.

"I am common-born. Not a princess."

Loran tried not to cringe as the dragon's enormous face closed in on hers. It squinted all seven of its eyes and shifted its attention a little downward. It was examining the *t'laran* inked around her neck. She bore clan tattoos like all Arlanders, though since the Empire came the concept of clans had lost its hold over Arland, especially in Kingsworth, where she lived. But the dragon was looking for the royal markings designed in its own image, and her *t'laran* certainly didn't have them. She could smell the sulfur on the dragon's breath as it spoke.

"Not a princess? Do you not know that only those carrying the blood of kings may survive crossing the threshold?"

Loran knew what the legends said, but still she had come.

"Arland is an old country, and the royal blood has spread to many of its people. I have come here in the belief that I, too, have a little of the blood of the old kings."

The dragon made a horrible sound, which Loran realized was laughter.

"To leap into the fire of the volcano on such a whim! But with

the demise of your last king, it no longer matters whether you are a princess or a commoner. Whatever blood you have only allows you to stand before me. I, who failed to keep my promise and was defeated by a mere toy, and now lie here tied in the outsiders' chains."

The menace in the dragon's voice had faded. The claw was lifted from her chest. So as not to provoke the beast, Loran got up slowly as she gathered her courage once more.

Fire-dragon of the mountain, guardian of the kings of Arland. More than twenty years have passed since the Empire conquered us, and the people are starving. The prefect kills innocents as if scything grass, falsely accusing them of treason and rebellion. Our country has fallen, but no one rises to lead us. I have come here to beg for your help.

These were the words she had committed to memory before coming here, when standing before the dragon had felt like a daydream. Even once she'd resolved to seek this creature of lore, the more likely outcomes had been that she would fall off the volcano and die, get caught by the pursuing soldiers and die, or disintegrate in lava before she had time to scream. Despite her likely demise, she had rewritten this speech many times, practicing it over and over in a low voice in front of the mirror, just in case.

But what passed her lips now was completely different.

"My husband and daughter were murdered by the Imperial prefect. I am not powerful enough to avenge their deaths. If you help me, I will do anything for you in return."

The dragon did not even bother to shake its head.

"Do the legends say I am a granter of wishes? I may have failed

to keep my pact with the king, but there is no longer a king for me to make amends to. Go home. Twenty years have passed since my last good meal." Making a show of it, the dragon licked its lips, its three-pronged tongue red as lava. Then it turned its long neck away from her, nestled its head on its flank, and closed its eyes.

Was that it? A day and night spent scaling the steep mountain face, all just for this? She had thrown herself into the opening of the volcano, ready for a sudden death, but here she was, alive yet empty-handed. Even being eaten by the enraged dragon was an ending she had steadied herself for, but instead, her petition had been refused as if by some clerk at the prefect's office.

Loran thought of her family. All they had done was to compose a mourning song and sing it. To the prefect and the Empire, it was treason. She remembered her husband and daughter, hanging by their necks at the crossroads for the whole world to gawk at. Her eyes squeezed themselves shut.

"*I* shall become King of Arland."

A voice cut through the silence, and her heart pounded. If the dragon hadn't opened its eyes and turned toward her, she wouldn't have thought the words had come out of her own mouth at all.

"Make a new pact—with me," Loran said. "Then I will help you keep your promise with the old king."

The dragon rose on its four legs. The chains around it stretched taut, and the stone floor beneath them rumbled. The scales along its back rose like hackles.

"King? You? Pitiful girl, do you not know the invincible

Empire reigns over all lands under the sun? Did you not see their Powered weapons that struck down dragons from the sky? Do you not fear the Star that felled Mersia in a single night? How do you propose to be king? To swear in front of a dragon such a brash oath, one you do not even mean in your heart, is to deserve a burning death!"

Deep inside the dragon's mouth, a smoldering blue fire appeared.

Loran had no reply. Aside from her skills as a humble sword-master with a handful of pupils, she was merely a widow who had only seen thirty-some years, and entirely without means— "brash" was right. But the dragon was wrong that she didn't mean it in her heart. She had meant every word. For it was the only path left to her.

Loran stood her ground. She met the dragon's great eyes until eventually the blue flames in its throat subsided. The dragon asked in a calm voice, "What is your name?"

She had not expected this. Then again, she didn't know what she had expected after declaring she'd become king. "My name is Loran."

The dragon asked again, this time in an almost caring tone, "What were your husband and daughter called?"

Her mouth opened halfway, but the words wouldn't come out. She hadn't spoken their names aloud for some time now. Their names reminded her of the countless times she had uttered them with love. It ached even more than remembering their deaths. The dragon studied Loran's face as she stood silent, then spoke.

"Never have I forgotten the day the Empire's legions swarmed our land like ants," the dragon said. "Their chains bind me, and I have tried to pass my imprisonment in slumber. But sleep only brings dreams, and in dreams, I watch again and again as the king, riding on my back into battle, is slain. Perhaps you suffer as I do."

Loran waited for the dragon to continue.

"If we enter a pact, will you banish the Empire from this land and become king, Princess of Arland?"

"I am not a—"

The dragon hissed and raised a single claw, quieting her.

"Will you become king and break these cursed chains?"

Loran nodded solemnly.

"Then give me your left eye to seal our pact, as the first of your kings did, so that I may see the world through you."

The dragon's claw approached her face. Instinctively, she tried to blink, but she couldn't—she let out a piercing scream as her eye was scooped from its socket.

She wasn't sure how much time passed before she managed to uncurl from where she had fallen, doubled over in pain, and to open her remaining eye. The dragon now had eight eyes. Its new eye felt familiar to Loran, as if she were looking at her own face in the mirror.

The dragon brought its claw to its mouth and broke off one of its fangs. It seemed to grimace, as if this caused it pain, then wrapped its claws around the bloody tooth. It closed all eight of its eyes and spoke words that Loran did not understand but that

rang achingly inside her head. Smoke issued from the cage of the dragon's claws. When they opened, there was an ivory-colored sword glowing with a strange light.

"This, too, is a symbol of our pact. This sword shall slay our enemies in my stead."

Pressing the pulsing wound of her eye socket with one hand, Loran reached for the sword with the other, taking hold of the hilt. It gripped back. A wave of heat rippled through her.

"There are many lands in this world. They have almost all been taken by the Empire. In these lands, many died, others were enslaved, and yet others became slave drivers for their new masters. But there are still those who fight. And there always will be. Now you may count yourself among them."

Loran nodded. The dragon pointed to one of the walls.

"Go there. A path shall open to the valley for the bearer of the sword. That path is unguarded. Even if someone is there, they shall be no match for you, or my fang." The dragon made the strange laughing wail again. "You must succeed. For me, for your vengeance, and for Arland."

Thus spoke the fire-dragon of Arland, guardian of legend, before slowly closing its eyes.

Loran bowed deeply and made her way to the wall indicated by the dragon. The barrier melted like snow in spring, revealing a tunnel just big enough for a single person to pass through. She heard water trickling on the other side. Loran stepped into the passageway, then hesitated, looking back at the dragon.

Without opening its eyes, the dragon said, "Speaking after so

long spent in silence has exhausted me. Be on your way. Is the burden on your shoulders not heavy enough? Or the path you must walk not long already?"

Loran gave a final nod, then left the stone chamber. In the dark passage, her sword shone lightly, guiding her, and she whispered though there was no one to hear.

"I am a princess of Arland. And I shall become king."